a BLEEDING STARS *novel*

A.L. JACKSON

First Edition

A.L. Jackson
www.aljacksonauthor.com
Cover Design by RBA Designs
Photo by Wander Aguiar Photography
Editing by AW Editing and Story Girl Editing
Formatting by Mesquite Business Services

Print ISBN: 978-1-946420-02-2
eBook ISBN: 978-1-938404-99-3

stand

MORE FROM A.L. JACKSON

Bleeding Stars

A Stone in the Sea
Drowning to Breathe
Where Lightning Strikes
Wait
Stay

The Regret Series
Lost to You
Take This Regret
If Forever Comes

The Closer to You Series
Come to Me Quietly
Come to Me Softly
Come to Me Recklessly

Stand-Alone Novels
Pulled
When We Collide

Coming Soon from A.L. Jackson
SHOW ME THE WAY
The first sexy, heart-warming romance in the new Fight For Me series, coming mid-2017

HOLLYWOOD CHRONICLES
A collaboration with USA Today Bestselling Author, Rebecca Shea

prologue

ZEE

SEVEN YEARS EARLIER

A smoky dimness cloaked the night sky. City lights glowed against the fog that sagged so low and thick, I could almost reach out and touch it. It cast my entire world in an ominous haze, everything I'd ever known vapors and mist.

I sucked in a desperate breath. Guilt ate me alive as I pressed my cell harder to my ear. "I'm sorry. I'm so goddamned sorry," I begged.

Grief clogged his voice as it traveled across the miles. "You're sorry? You were my best friend. My brother. I *trusted* you. Would have trusted you with my life."

I blinked hard, trying to see through the torment. "It was a mistake."

But simply labeling it a *mistake* felt like committing treason. Another dose added to the mounting disloyalty.

His words trembled with anger. "A mistake? You betrayed me."

My hand fisted in my hair, and I began to pace. With each desperate step, loneliness closed in. My chest felt too tight and too empty, like I could feel the connection that had always bound us together loosen.

Because I couldn't ever take back what I'd done.

I could feel the world splintering around me, my foundation crumbling beneath my feet.

Opening to reveal my wrong.

It tossed me headfirst into a bottomless chasm.

Endless.

Purgatory.

"I'm sorry, man. I'll do anything. Anything. Come back to LA. We'll work it out. Just…tell me you forgive me. Tell me you're okay…that this won't cause you to slip."

His laughter was hollow. "What's the point of staying clean…the point in working hard for what is right…when it's just taken away from you anyway?"

I gulped around the agony. "Mark—"

"I have to go."

He ended the call, and I choked over a strike of fear that hit me like a bolt of lightning.

Searching for an answer, for courage, I turned my face to the heavens that glowed like I was at the brink of day without the promise of a sunrise.

The stars were obscured.

Hidden.

Stars I knew shined and glimmered so damned bright when you stepped out of the limelight and depravity of this sordid city. Somehow, I'd always thought those twinkling stars the guardians of the wishes I'd cast upon their fallen as a child.

As if they held them protectively where they forever danced until the day those wishes were released and that dream became a reality.

In that moment, I swore I heard a silent curse uttered that left them permanently dimmed.

As a kid, I had breathed a million of those wishes.

Countless.

Infinite.

Now I could feel them falling all around me. Burning and bleeding out.

Disintegrating into nothing.

That had been the last time I talked to my brother. I knew I deserved it. I could never ask for anything more. I never questioned it. Never dreamed it could be any other way.

Not until the day I met *her*.

one

ZEE

It was late when I took the walkway toward the modest house in the quiet suburban neighborhood. My flight from Savannah had been delayed, and I was fucking wiped.

Ash and Willow had arrived a week ago. The rest of the band and their families would be there within the next few days so we could finalize plans for the next tour, which was kicking off next month.

Over the last couple of years, things had skyrocketed for Sunder, the band gaining more fame and prominence than we ever could have dreamed. We'd been working our asses off in Savannah, putting the final touches on the album we'd recorded while there over the last couple months.

Now we were shifting gears and turning our focus to the promotion, which meant playing live and getting in front of our fans.

Thank God we got to take a breather for a bit, because I was exhausted.

Still, I shouldn't have been surprised this was where my feet carried me the second we'd landed.

I rapped on the door.

Four months had passed since I'd been back in LA, a sin in and of itself, and my chest tightened with a shot of anticipation that always came with a healthy dose of regret as I lifted my hand to knock at the wood.

Waiting in the shadows of night, I sucked in a deep breath, wondering again how the fuck I'd gotten this deep. Torn between two worlds. Pretending one didn't exist.

I guess none of us really knew what direction our lives were gonna go. As kids, we imagined and dreamed. Most of the time, those dreams were bigger than life.

Outrageous and bold.

Unattainable and impractical.

Sometimes we got real close to reaching them, and other times we landed in an entirely different stratosphere.

What seemed ridiculous was I was the one who'd landed here. Living the life so many kids considered the wildest kind of dream.

The rock star life.

Endless roads and boundless fans.

Money, fame, and fortune.

Crazy, because I never really felt I was living it. Just a stranger who glided along the periphery. Close but never quite stepping over the line.

I hadn't wanted it. Had never pictured myself in this position. The things I'd wanted had been similar but distinct. Different but the same.

Truth of the matter? That'd been me and my brother Mark all along.

Polar opposites but entirely in sync.

Contradictory but identical.

He'd been my hero, and I'd been his rock.

Maybe that'd been our demise.

A light flipped on somewhere in the house, and anticipation flooded me. How could I regret any of that now? Maybe I'd done everything so incredibly wrong, but it's true what they say—sometimes miraculous, beautiful things come out of your greatest tragedy.

I'd be lying if I said the situation wasn't shitty, but that didn't mean it wasn't the best thing I had. What got me through the lonely nights.

A silhouette passed by the opaque drape that hung across the side window and movement rustled on the other side of the door. I swallowed around the nerves that gathered fast at the base of my throat.

This was the part I hated—dealing with her.

Metal scraped as the lock disengaged, and those nerves shivered and spiked with warning when the door barely cracked open two inches.

Guarded, a woman I'd never seen before peeked out at me, confusion in her sleepy gaze. "Can I help you?"

I did my best to ignore the dread that climbed into my chest.

"Is Veronica here?" The question came out harder than I intended.

Something registered on the woman's face. "Veronica? The girl who used to own this house?"

That dread took a sharp turn south and blazed into anger. "Used to?"

Warily, she blinked, stammered as if she was the one who needed to explain herself. "W-we bought this house almost three months ago."

I nodded, though it was entirely in disbelief. Of course, I wasn't really surprised now, was I?

Not at all.

I was fucking pissed.

I took a step back, trying to hold it together. "Sorry to bother you so late at night. I haven't been in town for a while."

She looked at me almost apologetically. "I hope you can touch base with her."

"Thanks," I said before I spun on my heel and yanked my phone from my pocket, thumbs banging out her number as I stalked back down the walkway.

It rang four times before her sickly sweet voice came on the line, recorded and just as fake as the rest of her. I listened to her message before I was growling the words right after the beep.

"You better have a good explanation. Because I'm fucking done."

two

ALEXIS

No fear. Just life.

No fear. Just life.

No fear. Just life.

I chanted it over and over beneath my breath and tried to make it true. To pretend terror didn't saturate my skin with a sickly sweat and that my breaths didn't come both labored and shallow as I tried not to inhale the vile stench of the darkened alleyway.

I could smell him everywhere, this nauseating odor that reeked of something wicked and corrupt.

I tried to stand my ground. I was there for my sister, and I wasn't leaving without her. But fear had me fumbling back another step. My back hit the pitted exterior wall, and I gasped when I realized I'd walked myself straight into a corner.

He sneered when he took a step closer.

My gaze darted to my right, my words dripping with a plea. With a promise. "Avril…please…come with me."

"Go." He didn't even glance at her when he issued his

command. He just glared down at me with a twisted grin that sent a shiver of fear down my spine.

Maybe it was worse that he was somehow attractive. Had he used that against her? Had he dragged her deeper into this disgusting world with some kind of depraved charm?

I begged my sister with my eyes.

Remember. Remember us. I'll help you. You don't have to be afraid.

"Go!" he shouted again. The single word struck in the air like a gavel blow.

Her entire body bowed, curling inward, her expression a pitiful, useless apology as she backed away.

Grief struck me from all sides when she turned and disappeared into the shadows like thin, transparent mist. Frail and weak.

She left me.

I wanted to chase her. To grab her. Shake her. Tell her she didn't have to live this life. How many times did I have to do it before she'd believe me?

But I couldn't move. I was pinned to the grimy wall by his salacious stare. He edged closer, and I kept my head to the side and squeezed my eyes closed as if it might hide me.

He pressed his body against mine.

Tears streaked free and revulsion rolled through my being. I inhaled a jagged breath that broke on a sob. "Please."

It was the wrong thing to say.

I already knew I'd stumbled into a world without compassion. A place void of grace.

I shouldn't have been surprised that instead of sympathy, he laughed and jammed a knee between my thighs, forcing my legs apart.

I gasped a cry as he fumbled to get under my shirt, his words menacing as he breathed them at my ear. "Told you the next time I saw you, you were gonna regret it, stupid bitch. Did you think I was joking? Think it's time I teach you a lesson. Girls that keep coming around here, they don't ever get to leave."

"No." I didn't want to beg, but it was there as panic surged through my veins. *Fight.* I bit and flailed and fought.

He growled and gripped both my wrists in one hand, and pinned them over my head, as his free hand tore at my shirt. I kicked, but he just pressed me harder against the wall. Coarse, ragged concrete cut into my back.

"Oh my God. No. Stop. Please."

"Shut the fuck up." Dark blond stubble lined his sharply angled jaw. It scraped across my face as he spat the words. "Don't say a goddamned word. Do you understand me? One sound and I end you."

No fear. Just life.

I screamed.

three

ZEE

With the back of my fist, I pounded on the metal door. Took me six different calls before I finally figured out where she was. Guess I should've realized she wouldn't be all that hard to find because there she was, in the same goddamned place.

Anger and frustration boiled in my blood, inciting a rage that felt impossible to contain. I shifted on my feet and counted to ten before I was hammering the door again.

It jerked open, the pissed-off, "What," spouted into the air before she caught sight of me standing there. She stumbled back a step, surprise all over her face. "Zee. What are you doing here? I thought you weren't going to be back for another week."

I laughed. But there wasn't anything friendly about it. "You're really gonna stand there and ask me what I'm doing here?"

My gaze moved over her shoulder, to the trashed out apartment behind her. Anxiety clutched at my chest. I couldn't fucking believe she'd bring him to this fucking hellhole.

Not after everything I'd done to make sure they were safe. "Pretty sure you need to start telling me what it is you're doing here, considering I just dropped by your house. Imagine my surprise when I found out that house isn't yours anymore."

The words all flooded out between gritted teeth.

She rolled her eyes. "It was my house. I was free to do with it as I pleased."

My voice dropped, harsh and hard. "That *I bought* you."

She shrugged a shoulder and the strap of the satiny camisole she was wearing slid off. I knew her well enough to know it wasn't an accident. "I needed the money."

"You have plenty of money."

"I spent it."

I angled my head so I could get in her face. "Are you fucking kidding me? You're telling me it's gone? You don't just spend that kind of money, Veronica. What the hell did you do with it?"

She gave me one of those looks she'd mastered, big brown eyes set against a dazzling face, all mixed up with the innocent quiver of her chin. It was the same damned expression that always managed to mold any situation in her favor.

It wasn't so hard to see the cunning behind it.

"You don't know what it's like being here alone while you're off doing whatever it is you do. It's not fair. *You promised me.*"

It's not fair?

I was about two seconds from shouting every reason this bullshit really wasn't fair in her face.

"And it's not like you don't have the money," she added like her actions didn't matter in the least.

"This has nothing to do with the money, Veronica. It's about the responsibility. About the fact you do things you promised me you wouldn't do. The fact that you should be thinking about *him* rather than yourself. Now tell me what you did with it."

A sinking feeling wrung me tight. Wasn't sure I wanted the answer.

She crossed her arms over her chest. "It's none of your business what I did with it."

"Yes, it is my business what you do with it. Do you think this bullshit doesn't affect him? I'm warning you, Veronica..."

She scoffed. "And what do you think you're going to do about it? I think we've already established the answer to that is *nothing*."

My fists clenched. I was two seconds from coming unglued. From blowing this flimsy understanding between us, every detail in her benefit, twisted in her favor.

Except for one—the one that mattered most.

"You took it too far this time, Veronica." The words grated, rough in my throat with the threat.

Defiantly, she took a step forward, lifting on her toes to get in my face. "You did this to me." She drove her index finger into my chest. Tiny daggers of guilt speared me with every jab. "Now you get to play by my rules."

"He's not a *game*. He's my life." God, she had me tied. Backed in a corner I didn't know if I'd ever escape.

"Then you know what you need to do to keep him that way." Her words rang with a threat, the bitch tightening that noose a little tighter, constricting air and life and the reason for my being.

The words were grit. "Where's Liam?"

She lifted a defiant chin. "Not here."

I could feel this insanity wanting to crawl out, this protectiveness that would send me right over the edge. "Where?"

"A friend's." Her answer was flippant. Inconsequential.

She had to be kidding me.

Fury stormed through my veins. Darkness. Hate. My laughter was bitter. "I'm finished letting you get away with this shit. I bought that house so he'd be safe. So you'd be safe."

She snaked her hand out, gripping my shirt, her body pressed to mine. "Then maybe you should come inside and remind me just how much you want me safe. Remind me how much you care about me. I know you miss me. Tell me I'm still your favorite secret."

I curled my hand around her wrist and pried her fingers free. "Not ever again."

She laughed a mocking sound and then yanked her arm out of my hold. "We'll see."

I stepped back before I did something I couldn't take back. "Next time I come by, he'd better be here."

I started backing down the grungy hall. Shouted voices echoed from behind doors in the middle of the night, this shitty side of town alive and well with its sleazy, debased offerings.

Anger struck every nerve, my muscles going rigid and tight.

Looking like sex and trash, Veronica slouched back against the middle of the doorframe, wearing nothing but a camisole and underwear, a smirk on her face. "Don't pretend like I don't know why you really come around."

I pointed at her, hating the way my voice shook. "Next time, Veronica. Next time."

four

ZEE

A streetlamp flickered above just as I froze when I heard the scream echo through the dense night air.

A plea for mercy.

A call for help.

Adrenaline thundered through my veins, mixing like poison where it gathered with the rage still simmering from the confrontation with Veronica.

It was an overwhelming feeling that gripped me everywhere, spurring me forward. It didn't matter that I was supposed to lay low. That I was supposed to do my best to remain unseen so the paps wouldn't go digging through my life.

I should make a call and walk on, mind my own business, but there was no fucking way I could ignore the desperate cry that rang from the alley and poured into the street.

There was no caution in my steps when I started running between two run-down apartment buildings, cutting behind a dumpster as I rushed for the alley.

My heart roared in my ears, and I swore I felt myself trip over some invisible line when I saw the fucker who had a woman tacked against a graffitied wall. Cries tumbled incoherently from her mouth, the girl begging and flailing helplessly.

The bastard had her wrists pinned above her head with one hand while he fought to get the other up her shirt.

Anger propelled me, and I rushed their direction without a single consideration of the consequences except for setting her free. I lunged. The asshole was so wrapped up in defiling her that he didn't even notice me until my shoulder rammed into his side.

He flew through the air.

The girl screamed a sound that landed somewhere in the realm of shock and relief while the piece of shit cursed when he slammed into the pitted, cracked asphalt, pooled with dirty drain water and littered with debris.

I dove for him again, straddling the pussy at the waist, pinning him down. "You piece of shit," I gritted as the rage I'd held back on Veronica came unleashed.

"Asshole…you're gonna wish you hadn't done that." He spat in my face, struggling to break free.

He was wrong.

Because I felt zero regret when I rammed my fist into his face. He returned the blow, pain shattering through the right side of my jaw, but I shook it off as I felt something inside me come unhinged.

I retaliated. Not for me. For her. Fist after fist. Crack after crack. Again and again.

Flesh against flesh and bone against bone.

He moaned, his fight weakening with each hit. I didn't stop until his head fully slumped back to the ground and his body went limp.

Struggling for a breath, I pushed myself off him, my eyes wide as I looked at him lying there. My lungs were so goddamned tight, nearly bursting with rage.

Adrenaline pumped too hard and too fast.

Blinding.

I looked at the piece of shit tossed out like a nasty, wasted pile on the ground.

Fury urged the twisted part of me to go back and finish the job. End him. The other part of me was drawn to the girl weeping where she'd slid to the filthy ground and curled into a ball.

My heart stampeded, a thunder that pounded at my ribs and incited chaos inside me I was sure I'd never felt before.

Carefully, I stood, my nerve-endings frayed, spikes of electricity prickling across the surface of my skin like tiny, powerful prods. I edged her direction, both terrified and compelled, somehow knowing this girl needed me.

Blonde hair was stuck to her tear-stained face and blood streaked from the corner of her mouth. She was rocking, and whimpers, which she tried to subdue, were sliding from her lips. When she peeked over at me, she had these eyes that lit up like the whitest flame against the darkness that threatened to consume her.

My chest tightened. I took another step.

My hand was shaking like a bitch when I reached out. She flinched when I set it on her arm.

"It's okay," I whispered. "It's okay. He's not going to hurt you. Not ever again. I won't let him hurt you."

She cried harder at my promise. The gut-wrenching sound somehow ached with relief. I dropped to the ground, and she let me pull her onto my lap. A relieved breath escaped me, because there was no avoiding the impulse I had to wrap her up. Hold her. Protect her.

Because this girl?

She felt light.

Too light.

Too soft and too good and too pure.

Out of place in this pit of misery.

Cautiously, I curled my arms around her.

She sobbed, and I did my best to hide her face in my chest, holding the back of her head in the splay of my hand, like with the action I could protect her from the evils that haunted these streets.

With my other hand, I dug in my pocket and pulled out my phone so I could call for help.

Her hands fisted in my shirt. "He was going to…" She trailed off, no doubt unable to form the words because the girl couldn't tolerate the thought.

Neither could I, because a fresh bout of rage went sailing through my senses.

I held her a little tighter. "I know…I've got you. I won't let anything happen to you."

I kept my eyes on the bastard on the ground while I impatiently waited for someone to pick up. Finally an operator answered.

"We need an ambulance and the police." It came out harsh as I rattled off the intersecting street and told them to hurry. For once, I was grateful I was no stranger to this side of town.

Felt like an hour passed while I sat there holding her, my guts in knots, terrified by the way I felt desperate to erase her pain.

When sirens screamed in the distance and that anxiety ebbed a fraction, I knew at least this girl was safe.

That was right before I sensed the cocksucker stirring. But he didn't groan.

He growled.

I was slammed with a rogue wave of that same protectiveness that threatened to drive me out of my mind. I surged to standing, taking the girl with me.

I set her on unsteady feet and shifted her behind me when he climbed to stand.

If he thought he was going to get to her, he was going to have to get through me first.

He looked like a demon, a web of blood streaking his face, eyes red in the darkness, evil radiating from his stance. He raked the back of his hand over the sneer plastered to his mouth. "Bitch…I warned you."

A terrified cry, barely audible, rasped into my back. Fingers curled into my shirt.

"I've got you. Trust me," I said so quietly I could only hope she heard.

Sirens grew closer, and I began to edge us back and to the side when the bastard took a step forward.

"Would think twice about that, asshole," I warned, voice going deathly low.

He laughed.

Dread shivered through my entire being when I saw him reach into the back of his pants. A flash of metal struck in the haze of night.

The prick had a gun.

The girl whimpered. No doubt she'd seen it, too.

My mind was frantic, fumbling for the best way to get out of this, calculating the best move to keep her safe.

"Yeah?" he challenged. "Would say the same to you."

At least the asshole had that on me. It had been fucking stupid coming down here unprepared. But it wasn't like I'd ever imagined where I'd land once I climbed off that plane tonight.

I never would have thought I'd end up staring down the barrel of a gun.

"Go… Run." It was the quietest plea uttered from the girl in her attempt to protect me. Stark terror ricocheted from her to me and back again. Her panicked, strained breaths glided through the thin material of my shirt, heat at my spine and chills across my skin.

Fuel for the adrenaline.

I didn't know if this moment was chance or fate or fluke. It didn't matter. No way would I leave this girl behind.

My hands went up, palms out.

Figured my best bet was to placate the fucker.

Buy some time.

"No need for any of that."

I took another cautious step back, edging her toward the street, my hands pushed out in front of us like they could somehow act as a shield. I prayed the whole time I was making the right choice and not inciting a madman.

My attention dipped to his gun and back to the hostile arrogance blazing from his eyes. "I'd think that would be a bad idea, now wouldn't you, considering the cops are about five seconds out?"

Seemed like it was just then he realized the sirens blaring down the road were meant for him, the whirl of reds and blues cutting into the night like a dizzying Tilt-A-Whirl.

He hesitated, rocking forward then back.

A cruiser skidded to a stop at the head of the alleyway.

Asshole turned his gaze to the girl, who was peering out from behind me, like maybe she'd been contemplating stepping out in front, like I'd ever let her take that fall.

He smirked at her. "Until next time."

Then he turned and ran. Two seconds later, the piece of shit was swallowed by the darkness at the opposite end of the alleyway.

My muscles bunched and ticked, my insides heavy with the need to chase him down. To take him out. Ensure that there would never be a next time.

But an officer was yelling *freeze*, and the only thing I could do was grip the girl's hands, which were suddenly clinging to the front of my shirt as she again started to sob into my back, the overflow of anxiety and fear pouring out in a rush of tears. "I'm so sorry. I'm so sorry." She kept saying it, again and again, like any of this could be her fault.

"Shh. He's gone. He's gone," I told her.

Slowly, I twisted around, hands in the air, voice gruff as I spoke to the approaching officer. "I was the one who made the call."

My eyes fell toward the girl I could feel staring up at my face.

Seemed like every emotion I'd ever felt was lodged like a jagged rock in my throat when I looked down at the tormented eyes blinking up at me. Eyes so intense. Too dark to be blue. Too distinct to be anything else.

Standing there, I felt staggered.

Maybe it was the confrontation.

Facing down death and willing to accept it if it meant saving a stranger from a fate I couldn't begin to fathom.

My fists ached with the foreign feeling left behind by my rage.

I didn't exactly have the reputation of a fighter. Call me a pussy or a pacifist. Truth was, I wasn't either of those things. I'd just always been clear about what I was living for.

For the last seven years, all my efforts had been carefully doled out on the two things that were important to me, because I couldn't afford to put that energy anywhere else.

Standing there, I knew this would cost me.

Everything important in our lives did. Nothing was free and every action came with a consequence.

No. I'd never been known as a fighter.

But looking down at this girl looking up at me?

I knew I'd never regret fighting for her.

five

ALEXIS

"What were you thinking?" Chelsey's entire face pinched with worry when she looked over at me. She was pacing the tiny curtained-off area where they had me in the emergency room.

She seemed so much like our mother right then, the corners of her blue eyes creased with worry, lines of maturity accentuating the soft curve of her face.

A cold chill rocked through my being. Three hours had passed, and I was still shaking. It was this uncontrollable fear that licked and tore at my insides.

I tugged the blanket tighter around my body. Maybe if I managed to squeeze it close enough, I'd wake up and this would be nothing but a terrible, horrible bad dream. Maybe if I prayed hard enough, I could go all the way back to the beginning. Change it. Do it all over again.

"She needed me." The words were a rasp. A scrape across my raw, aching throat. My own plea. God knew I was looking for a voice of reason in a world that made no sense.

That voice dropped to a whisper. "She's our sister."

My *twin* sister. My best friend. My other half.

Chelsey spun around and crossed to me in a flash. Her hands shot out, gripping me by the face and forcing me to meet her eyes, her expression anguished as she grated her appeal.

"She's our sister who's going to get you killed. Don't you see it yet, Alexis? You've been trying for years, and there's nothing left to do. Nothing you can change because she won't *change*. The only thing that's going to happen is I'm going to lose you, too, and I'm not willing to stand aside and let that happen."

Agony cut through me. A dull, bitter blade.

The desperation to save someone who didn't want to be saved.

All of it warred against a physical fear so deep I could feel it infiltrating my soul.

Vile, vile hands. Malicious threats in my ear. Sickening stench in my nose.

I didn't know if I could ever scrape him from my skin.

I felt…dirty. Sick.

Memories flashed from tonight, flickers and blips of black-and-white images—my sister's call, the evil I'd faced, my deliverer. That mysterious, intoxicating man that'd come to my rescue.

I'd almost thought I'd been hallucinating. My mind so desperate to remove myself from the situation, I'd been deluded into believing I was being saved. As if I'd been lost to a fantasy that there was someone brave and selfless enough to actually risk himself for me.

I'd crumbled with gratitude when I'd realized he wasn't a figment of my imagination.

I didn't think I'd ever, ever forget the expression on his face when they'd loaded me into the ambulance. The way he'd looked at me both soft and hard, as if him seeing me there caused him physical pain.

Chelsey gripped me tighter. "Promise me you won't ever go down there again. I don't care what she says, Alexis. Don't let her ruin you, too. I know you'd give up anything for her, but what about me?" Desperate, her fingertips curled into my cheeks. "Promise me."

My older sister loved me. Cared for me. But she didn't know what she was asking me to do.

I nodded, whispering, "Okay. I promise."

Even when I knew it wasn't true.

six

ZEE

"Any other information you can give will be appreciated."

I paused at the door. The glass was a hazy texture for privacy, the investigator's name stamped on the front. I looked back at him where his hand was still poised over the notepad on his desk that he'd been scrawling notes on for the last half hour.

"Believe me, I have anything to give? I'll bring it."

His head cocked and his eyes narrowed like he was searching me for truth. "And you're certain you've never seen the guy before?"

The investigator had been asking it again and again, looking for any detail I might've left out or tried to keep hidden. So maybe he was having a hard time believing it had been a chance encounter.

I was struck with another flash of that familiarity. It was so goddamned vague I shook it off. I gave him a harsh shake of my head. "No. And if I did? I wouldn't hesitate to hand it over. I want the bastard off the street just as much as you do."

Probably more.

The horror on that girl's face came unbidden into my mind. The way she'd felt in my arms. The need to protect her.

My entire body clenched. Adrenaline was still a wild hammer inciting a war in my veins. Every cell riding this twisted, savage high.

Maybe it was just exhaustion. I hadn't managed to catch even a wink of sleep last night. Not that it could have been considered night since I'd finally stumbled through my door when the sun was breaking the horizon.

I'd stayed to talk with the officers on the scene until well after the ambulance had carried the girl away.

They'd asked me to show up here at ten to answer more questions.

Thing was, I couldn't shake the feeling that everything was off. The unsettled sense that time had continued to spin on while I felt stuck in that dark hour.

Would *time* have ended for her had I not been there? Which led me to wondering what would have happened if things had ended up going down in a blaze of bullets and maybe time would have ended for me, too.

What then?

What about *him*?

Was it wrong I'd been willing to take the risk? Couldn't have stopped myself if I'd tried, anyway.

Hell, what kind of influence would I be for Liam if I hadn't stood up for what was right?

But since the smoke had cleared, my head was spinning with my responsibilities. With duty and obligation. Guilt rose, like it could take hold of all the emotions clotted in my chest, and tried to eclipse the nagging, almost frantic urge to seek her out.

I knew her full name.

It wouldn't be all that hard to find her.

I just wanted to make sure she was okay. To see her face and know this girl, who clearly was good and pure, wouldn't be held back by the scars that bastard had every intention of inflicting.

Maybe I wanted to see if this foreign feeling simmering in my gut was real. This overwhelming need to brush my fingers against her skin and let her know my touch would never hurt her.

It was a feeling I hadn't felt in a long, long time. Not since I lost *her*. Not since my life had quite literally been twisted in two.

And that feeling right there was the very reason I had to make sure I stayed away.

I couldn't afford it. Not when it would cost me everything.

"If I remember anything else, I'll call you," I told the investigator.

He gave me a nod. "I appreciate that."

I dipped my head once before I headed out into the hall and toward the waiting room out front. Guess I shouldn't have been surprised when I found Ash and Anthony sitting in the hard, plastic chairs lined against the wall.

The second they saw me, both of them shot to their feet.

Ash's entire being sagged with relief. "Zee... Thank God. Took you long enough in there. I came as soon as Anthony told me what was going down. I was out here about to lose my mind."

Ash Evans was Sunder's bassist. He was just about as cool as they came. Always quick with a grin and at the ready with a taunt or a tease, but none of it was done with spite or malice.

When I'd stepped up and taken my brother's place as drummer in the band seven years ago, Ash had been there, taking me under his wing. For years, he'd lived this over-the-top lifestyle, the guy a poster child for the old sex, drugs, and rock 'n' roll cliché.

And when the guy did it, he did it to the extreme.

That was until the day he'd found his wife, Willow, and realized there were better things to be living for.

Ash pulled me in for a hug, clapping me on the back. "Fuck, man, you scared the shit out of me."

I clapped him back. "All's good, man."

From over his shoulder, Anthony, Sunder's manager, caught my eye. Worry was written across every line of his face, the guy brimming with questions and concern.

Because when something happened to one of us? It affected all of us.

Protecting us was Anthony's job. The crazy thing was he didn't do it out of obligation or for a paycheck. He did it because he cared. He was no less a member of this mismatched family than any one of us.

Back before Sunder had made it, when the band was only beginning and was still made up of Mark, Sebastian who everyone called Baz, Lyrik, and Ash, Anthony had been at a show and seen the raw talent they possessed.

He'd taken them on as their manager, and stood by them through thick and thin.

Through all the bullshit trouble Lyrik and Baz had gotten themselves into during the early days of the band.

Through the tragedy of the band finding my brother, Mark, OD'ed on their tour bus and me stepping in to take his place.

He'd been there when the brutal truth of Mark's death had come out.

My guts clenched in regret and the gratitude I would always, always have for Anthony. Because Anthony was the only one who knew. He knew what I'd done. He knew what I had destroyed. He knew I was responsible.

Of course he'd tried to convince me everyone made mistakes. That everything was forgivable if you were truly sorry you committed the sin.

I knew better.

In the end, when I was adamant I was going through with it, he'd been the one who had facilitated the paperwork and the agreements so I could get away with my lies and live these two lives. Each of them flimsy and hinging on my ability to keep one from spilling into the other. Otherwise that dam would overflow and everything would go crashing down.

Which was why I did my best to lay low in a world where I'd always be in the limelight. Keeping quiet and behind the scenes. Keeping my actions on the straight and narrow so there'd be nothing to get the paps talking and digging.

Wasn't all that hard for a drummer, anyway.

Ash stepped back, still hanging on to me by the outside of my shoulders and looking me up and down. Like he was making sure I was still in one piece.

Like I said, I didn't exactly have the reputation of a fighter. Didn't mean I couldn't hold my own.

Ash looked me square. "What the fuck happened, man?"

I flexed my fists, stretching out my knuckles that were beat to hell. Scabs were beginning to form on the torn up skin. "I went to go visit an old friend. Was walking home and heard a girl calling for help. Just did what I had to do."

Incredulous, his brow rose. "You went to visit an old friend…in the middle of the night…on the shittiest side of town? That's some stupid shit, dude. You know better than that. And what friend was so important?"

This was the part I hated—misleading the guys. Making them believe I was someone I was not.

I kept my answers as vague and boring as possible. "Just someone I knew back in high school. It wasn't a big deal until I walked up on the shit that was definitely a big deal."

"So you jumped in." Ash said it like he was proud.

"Yeah." Like I'd do anything else.

A smirk kicked up on his mouth, the one the dude just loved to wear. "Look at that, our little Zee Kennedy, stepping into the ring. Never thought I'd see the day."

There was nothing little about me, but it sure as hell was the stigma I'd always worn. Mark's younger brother who'd stepped into his big brother's shoes that never quite fit.

It was easier that way, pretending I didn't want anything else.

Needing to get the attention off myself, I turned it on him and shot him a wry smile. "Watch yourself, asshole. At least it wasn't me getting my ass kicked."

Enough time had passed that I could tease him about the pack of assholes who'd attacked him and left him for dead more than a year ago back in Savannah.

"Ouch," he inflected with about as much feigned offense as he could find. "That's a low blow, man. A low, downright, dirty blow. That shit was five against one. Pussies. Every last one of them. But hey, what's that they say? You've gotta wade through the shit to get to the good waiting on the other side? And I'd gladly wade through shit every day of my life if it brought me to my Willow."

I lifted a brow. "I'm pretty sure no one said that except for you."

He lifted his hulking, tattooed arms out to the side in that over-the-top, cocky way. "What can I say? I'm wise beyond my years. Quote that shit."

My laughter was incredulous. "What you are is ridiculous."

His phone rang from his pocket and he dug it out. "Speaking of Willow, I'd better take this. If you thought I was freaked out over this, wait until you see her. Just warning you, man, you're in so much trouble. Prepare yourself to be mom'ed right after I convince her you are, in fact, okay."

"Oh, shit," I muttered, roughing a hand through my hair as a flash of affection pulsed at my chest.

All the girls were the best. Doting on us, covering us in all their love and support. Especially me, considering I was the only one not paired up, the permanent bachelor in this family that'd grown with each passing year.

Every single one of the guys had gotten damned lucky, that was for sure.

Ash grinned. "Tell me you don't love my woman taking care of you."

I widened my eyes. "I wouldn't dream of it."

Truth was, I loved Willow to pieces.

He was chuckling under his breath when he accepted her call and paced away to talk to her.

As soon as he did, Anthony closed the space between us, his head angled and his voice lowered to keep the conversation between us.

"What happened out there, Zee? This isn't good. Paps are

talking about it. Of course because they love to twist it to fit into whatever they want to see, they're pegging it as some sort of brawl over a girl, claiming you have some secret lover."

"Shit," I hissed beneath my breath. I shook my head and fought against another rush of that rage that flooded my nerves.

I eyed Anthony seriously, gritting my teeth. "She sold the house, man. I went over there last night and found the new owner there instead of her. Now she's living a half mile down the street from where we'd gotten her out of in the first place."

He reared back an inch, anger tightening his jaw. "Goddamn it. And the money?"

I shrugged through the resentment. "Gone."

He raked a frustrated hand over his face, words grit. "She's unbelievable."

I glanced over at Ash, who still had his back to us, then I turned my attention back on Anthony. "I don't know what the hell to do. Veronica might be a bitch, but the one thing I could always do was trust her to take good care of him."

Anthony tensed. "What you need to do is get him out of there."

"You think I don't want that?" Fear pounded at my chest. "But you know if I push for it, she's gonna run. You were the one who told me all along I don't have any rights."

Anthony threaded his fingers through his hair. "If you could prove she's neglecting him, you might have a chance, but I'm not sure moving him into an area you don't approve of is going to qualify as that."

A frustrated sigh filtered out. "Never should have put that house in her name."

I could feel him struggling not to give me a look that screamed *I told you so.* "She's a pro at manipulating you, Zee. She's been from the beginning."

Emotion throbbed in my throat. "I just can't take the chance of her running. Losing him would kill me."

His tongue darted across his lips as he processed. "You're in town for a while. Keep tabs on her while you're here. Find out what's going on with her. Document it. That way, we have evidence if you decide to make a move."

"I'd do it in a second, Anthony….but this life? Traveling? On the road? I don't want that for him. Besides for that, he loves his mom. Wouldn't think about taking him away from her unless he was in danger."

"I understand that." He set a hand on my shoulder. "You're a good man, Zee. I know you don't think it, but you've sacrificed yourself for everyone else. Last night, you did it again, as stupid as it was." He sent me a half grin.

"You know that's not true. But what happened last night…I'd do it all over again. Wouldn't even think twice about it."

"If I were in your place, I would've done the same damn thing." He squeezed my shoulder tighter. "There's no shame in helping someone, but you've got to know with being in the spotlight the way you are, people are going to talk. You've got to be prepared for that and what it might mean. How Veronica is going to react to it."

"I can't be ashamed about what I chose to do."

Ash was suddenly there, picking up on the last bit of the conversation. He slung his arm around my neck and started hauling me toward the door, smirking over at me as he did.

"So, now that we've got all the heavy shit out of the way, why don't you tell me just who it was you were visiting in the middle of the night. Time to fess it up, man. Tell me my boy here is finally getting some action, because that shit's just not normal. All the lovely ladies throwing themselves at you at every turn, and you shooting down every advance? I've been thinking it's about time to stage an intervention. Hell…last time I saw you with a girl you were just a kid…bet you didn't even shave."

I tried not to flinch.

I'd been deflecting this same thing for years. The constant razzing from the guys. All of them assumed I was some kind of freak since I didn't hook up. I'd always just let it slide right off my back, because in the end, it didn't matter. They didn't know any better because they had no clue what I'd lost.

"Not like that," I told him.

"That's a shame, man. A damn shame. The whole fighting thing? No shame. The no getting laid thing? Shame. Kick ass? No shame. No ass? Shame. Are you sensing a pattern here?" Ash's eyes were wide with the ribbing.

I chuckled under my breath. Only Ash. "Always such an asshole," I muttered.

Ash squeezed my neck tighter. "But you know you love me."

His voice dropped. "Seriously, though. I'm glad you're okay, man. Don't know what I'd do if something happened to you. You need to be careful."

"I know, I will."

Anthony held the door open for us and we stepped out into the day. Sunlight held fast to the sky, the air warm and thick.

I froze as a fresh pulse of that protectiveness I couldn't shake slid through my senses, twisting my guts and tightening my chest.

Ash stopped at my side, and Anthony finally slowed and turned when he realized neither of us were moving. I could feel their questions swirling through the air while I stood there staring like some kind of fool.

Because I knew that was exactly what this made me.

But I couldn't focus on anything but the girl who was walking my way. Couldn't feel anything but that tremor of energy that had flamed at my insides and spurred me forward last night.

In the light of day, it was just as strong, but somehow different. Muted to a slow burn that churned in my spirit as my gaze roamed her body. Desperate to find her whole and unbroken.

Felt like the ground shook below me when her head jerked up and she found me standing there.

My breaths came harder and harsher with every timid step that brought her in my direction. Her bottom lip was held captive between her teeth, and lines pinched between her brow as she watched me like I might be a figment of her imagination.

She came to a stop two feet away.

The space between us was alive, rippling and shivering and searching. Like maybe our souls recognized the gravity of what'd gone down last night.

Paths had been shifted. Fate deflected.

I knew I was a bastard for even letting myself think it after what had happened.

But fuck.

She was pretty.

So goddamned pretty with her red cupid mouth and her little crinkled nose. Her hair was long and almost white, piled in a messy knot high on her head. Wild pieces fell out like they refused to be contained.

My eyes traced every inch of that heart-shaped face, and something shocked through my senses when I let my gaze slowly glide down her body.

The girl was tight and tiny and sweet.

Delicate and strong.

Curved and soft and brave.

My fingers twitched and those knots in my stomach twisted in an entirely different way—attraction, lust, and curiosity.

Shit.

I couldn't feel any of those things, but there they were, thriving in that space between us.

But it was the bruise marring the hollow beneath one of those smoky eyes that sent a crackle of anger pulsing through the frenzy already lighting up my veins. The tiny cut on her lip that nearly sent me into a tailspin.

I ground my teeth, hit with the overpowering need to track the bastard down.

Awareness spun, and her teeth released her lip, both of them parting on a breath as she stared up at me.

And there was absolutely not a goddamned thing in the world I could do but let my fingers flutter out, not quite touching as they drummed over the spot where he'd hurt her.

I wanted to erase it.

But this girl—this girl who hadn't left my mind for even a second since they'd closed those ambulance doors and they'd taken her away—she smiled.

She smiled at me in some kind of wonder that ripped through me like a raging storm.

With a trembling hand, she reached up and took hold of my fingers that flitted close to her face, never looking away when she brought them to her mouth and pressed the gentlest kiss against my skin.

That simple gesture burned through me like a wildfire.

There was no sound, but I felt the whisper of her words as they moved against my fingers. "Thank you."

Two of the easiest words. I wasn't sure I'd ever heard them ring with such magnitude.

I stood there feeling my world coming apart around me.

I could feel it. The goodness and grace. I wanted to lean in and inhale it. Suck it down and take it inside. Make it a part of me.

I blinked, the words so thick it was difficult to form them. "I'd do it all over. A million times."

Her mouth trembled and her eyes glistened, her gaze sweeping me for the flash of a second before she turned back to stare at my face. Her voice shook with emotion. "I don't doubt that for a second."

"Come on, Alexis. We need to get inside. They're expecting us."

My attention shifted to the woman who spoke with some kind of quiet understanding. She was maybe a handful of years older than the girl standing in front of me. They resembled each other enough that I came to the quick conclusion they had to be sisters.

Alexis looked at her with a slow nod before she turned back to me, her expression so sincere and overwhelming. That single glance conveyed so much without her ever saying a thing.

Finally, she broke the connection that seemed to bind us

and let her sister take her by the arm. Her head dropped toward the ground, and her sister glanced over her shoulder at me as she led her toward the station door.

"Thank you," she mouthed, her own gratitude sliding out.

I shook my head at her. Saving her was something anyone would do. But something about my involvement felt like more. Like in one of those fateful moments last night, it'd become something different.

Something I couldn't ever allow it to be.

I watched until they disappeared inside, and I heaved out a strained breath, the connection severed.

"Well, hot damn." Ash's voice suddenly cut through the dense air, the guy acting the fool the way he always did. "Look at that. I do believe there's hope for our boy here, after all."

Uneasy, Anthony shifted on his feet.

I tossed a glare at Ash, probably harder than it needed to be. "Don't even go there. Not today."

I knew he was only messing with me. That he was just pushing me in a direction he thought I should go. But I couldn't stand for him to rub it in, to taunt me with what I might want.

Didn't matter how badly I wanted her. She was something I could never have.

seven

ALEXIS

"He's out there, Avril, and I have no idea what he might do to you." My voice dropped to a pained whisper as I spoke into the phone, clutching it as if it might be a lifeline. "I have no idea what he *has* done to you. Call me. Please. I need to know you're okay."

I ended the voice mail and my gaze automatically moved to the bay window that overlooked the tiny garden on the side of my even tinier house. My chest ached, swamped in sadness and worry, this overwhelming grief that gripped me and refused to let me go. I wasn't sure I'd ever felt a hopelessness like this.

She left me.

Chelsey had warned me for years Avril was only using me. Using guilt to bend me to her will.

But I'd always held out hope that one day Avril would finally see. That she'd finally land at rock bottom, and somehow it would make a difference that I was there to catch her when she fell.

I'd always believed our connection was stronger than the

addiction. Regardless of anything else, I'd chosen to believe our bond—our friendship and our devotion—meant more.

She left me.

To be broken. Violated.

Terror shivered down my spine when I realized just how deranged that man had to be. I didn't know his name. I only knew he somehow had brainwashed my sister into believing she owed him something. It was hard to even think about what would have happened to me at his vile hands had my deliverer not intervened.

I was still having a hard time processing the kind of control that monster had over my sister with just a low command.

I rested the phone on my pursed lips, fighting tears as the realization finally took hold.

Avril's fear was so much greater than all of those things. So much greater than our love. Maybe it had been bred by her addiction that still held her hostage, but those chains were controlled by that disgusting man.

Maybe it made me the biggest fool of all, but I'd never felt more committed to freeing her than I did now.

A shock of surprised air shot from my lungs when three sharp knocks sounded at my door, jerking me from the silence.

God, my nerves were frazzled. Shot. Which was so not like me.

I felt scared and vulnerable and timid. I usually embraced life, not ran from it.

Doing my best to shake it off, I inhaled, straightened my shirt, and ran my fingers through my bangs, as if fidgeting and stalling might straighten out the mess of emotions laying siege to my spirit. Then, I slowly moved across the floor.

A quiet dimness held fast to my living room, save the waterfall of light pouring in through the single bay window that faded into a pale, dusky glow as it spread out through the room.

Almost warily, I hiked up on my toes so I could peer out the peephole.

I stumbled back and my heart galloped out ahead of me.

An onslaught of emotions rushed and sped and churned at who was waiting on the other side, this mix of unknown gratitude and confusion that had chased me for the last three days.

I felt frozen by the fact he was there as another soft but pleading knock sounded at the wood.

Swallowing hard, I gathered my wits, twisted the lock, and slowly cracked open the door.

He was standing there on my small stoop. Larger than life and filling it full. Capturing sight and mind and reason.

I stood at his feet, staring at him while he stood there staring at me.

Brown eyes potent and kind and somehow unyielding and hard.

My knees suddenly felt weak as I was flooded with this foolish kind of fascination that made me want to reach out and touch his face. To explore him, body and soul and mind. This man, who'd rushed in to hold together all the splintering pieces of my world and forced them back together before they were completely destroyed and unrepairable.

Maybe this feeling was purely gratitude. Or maybe it was wholly due to the trauma. How I felt bound to him in an unfathomable way.

As if when he'd been holding those splintering pieces together, the man had managed to chip away a small piece of my soul. A piece that would permanently belong to him.

He rushed a hand through his hair, a hand that was big and tattooed. His arm muscular and covered in ink.

I had a fleeting thought that I should be terrified of this stranger standing in front of me and shouldn't relish in this confused comfort that struck my bones and touched those secret places in my spirit.

"Alexis," he said. The word might have been a question had it not glided across my skin like familiarity and warmth.

I barely nodded, my response a whisper as my heart fluttered and sped. "Alexis."

His gaze dipped for a moment, tracing me head to toe. As

if he needed reassurance I was there.

Something about it felt so intimate and private. As if maybe he was aware he now held that piece of my soul he'd chipped away.

His tongue swept his lips.

My eyes dropped to follow it, a slow heat lighting in my belly as they roved. I took in his face, glancing across the short beard I had the urge to scratch with my nails, memorizing the way his cropped light brown hair was really bronze when it was struck by the sun.

It was a little longer on top, and a silky lock flopped over the lines on his forehead that I ached to reach out and smooth away.

"I hope it's okay I'm here," he said, forcing my attention back to his eyes.

A lump grew heavy in my throat and I swallowed around it, nodding as I tried to find my voice. "Of course it's okay."

Maybe I should have been hearing warning bells. A thousand caution flags tossed in the air and raining down around me. Because there was something about this brilliant boy that screamed trouble and mayhem. Undoubtedly, he wore his own beautiful brand of destruction.

And I was the fool who always seemed to run straight for it. Diving right in to the middle of it without having the first clue what was waiting for me.

"I'm Zachary Kennedy. Friends call me Zee," he said, shifting on his feet as if he were wondering what he was doing on my doorstep.

I could feel the pull of the soft smile at the side of my mouth. "I know who you are."

"Is that so?" he asked. Something about it rang with a tease.

I nodded.

Of course I did. He was the drummer for one of the biggest rock bands in the world.

And I realized that probably put both of us at a disadvantage. No doubt he had women throwing themselves at him any time he walked off a stage or into a room. Wanting a taste of fame or maybe a name to drop, I could only imagine the number of women who salivated over this boy simply for who he was.

It didn't help he had to be the most gorgeous man I'd ever seen.

But this was different. The staggering need I felt to know him more. Not the boy pinned to Pinterest boards labeling him a sexy, tattooed bad boy. Not the boy splashed across the tabloids with their speculations and judgment.

The real man.

This man made up of flesh and bone. The man who rushed into an alley in the middle of the night to defend a complete stranger. The man who'd tenderly rocked me in his arms while I'd felt the controlled rage radiating from his body.

The one who stood in my doorway, spinning my mind with how he could both look so powerful and vulnerable.

My insides shook, and I took a step back and widened my door. "Would you like to come in?"

A smile crept to his mouth, this tug of full, soft lips framed by his beard. God, that expression alone would be my complete undoing. He tilted his head to the side. "You're awful brave to be inviting a complete stranger into your house."

I lifted my chin and met his gaze. "A complete stranger who put his life on the line. A stranger who stood between me and a gun. You could have died, and I very well might have if it weren't for you. Trust comes in a lot of forms, and I'm pretty sure you've already earned mine."

His strong throat bobbed as he swallowed, and he looked down at me with those brown eyes that should be nothing else but plain. All except for the flecks of bronze that perfectly matched his hair. They shimmered and flashed in the sunlight, like treasures secreted away. I had the urge to discover them all.

His tone dipped in severity. "What if I don't deserve it?"

"What if you do?" I challenged.

He shook his head as if he couldn't make sense of me. His gaze stole a little more of my breath as it grazed my skin like a rough caress, and his slow perusal sent a scatter of chills down my spine.

Tension rose between us. Bottled and shaken. Questions churned in the air. Each of us in limbo.

Somehow, I knew we were standing at either the beginning or the end. Neither of us seemed to know whether we should stop or start.

What had happened between us wasn't normal. I knew that. And maybe everything I was feeling was a result of it. Maybe every single emotion rushing through me was dependent upon the fact that this man had saved me.

But standing in front of him, I didn't care where it'd been born. The only thing that mattered was I felt it stronger than I'd ever felt anything in all my life.

I widened the door even farther, taking my stance.

I wanted to start.

"Please come inside."

Maybe I shouldn't have noticed the way his jaw clenched and all those muscles bristled, as if he were holding himself in restraint, or maybe he was cursing himself, because something dark moved through those eyes before it was gone.

He angled his wide shoulders to the side as he stepped inside, the movement sending a flash of heat against my skin when he passed and stepped into the quiet sanctuary of my home.

I latched the door shut, pulling in a steadying breath while I faced away, before I slowly turned to find the man standing in the middle of my living room with his back to me as he looked around. I got the distinct sense he was studying, learning little bits of me.

Silently, I watched him there, larger than life in my small, small space.

He was tall. Arms masculine and thick. His back strong and wide. A white tee was stretched across the expanse, hugging his sculpted shoulders and tapering down to his narrow waist and his perfect ass, his dark jeans snug in all the right places.

No. The Pinterest boards weren't wrong.

This gorgeous man was the epitome of sexy. Tempting. Tattooed with a tapestry of ink littering the entirety of his exposed skin.

Delicious and dangerous.

Attraction heated my blood. It was an onslaught of need that had me itching to run my fingertips across every inch of him, to discover, reveal, and unearth.

That desire felt forbidden. As if my thoughts had strayed into territories that might be dark and perilous.

He turned to look at me, his arms lifting up at the sides, a soft puff of air escaping between those full, full lips. "This is exactly what I pictured."

He stared back at me with his captivating face, almost catastrophic in its beauty.

At least that was what I felt when standing beneath the intensity of it.

Destroyed.

Wrecked and unsettled in a perfect, absolute way. Every inch of the man was a sublime contradiction.

His entire demeanor serenity and war.

Peace and strife.

As if the man bore the scars of a thousand battles and still managed to look past the brutality of the world.

I fumbled through a self-conscious laugh. "You were picturing my house?"

He gave a short nod. "Yeah…I guess I was. Trying to imagine what I'd find when I came here."

I wrung my hands. "Are you pleased or disappointed?"

The smirk that curled his mouth was self-deprecating, laced with something bitter. "Only in myself."

I blinked. "I don't know what you mean."

He laughed low and rubbed a hand across his bearded jaw. "Nothin'," he mumbled.

Uneasily, he glanced around before he looked back at me. He seemed to struggle to find words. "I was worried about you. Spent the last three days trying not to be. Trying to stop thinking about you."

As if it frustrated him, he shook his head. "In the end, I couldn't stay away."

Emotion clogged my throat, and I warred with how much to give him, with what to say. Wondering if it was too soon or maybe it was already too late.

But I was a girl who'd never been afraid to take a chance.

No fear. Just life.

"That's good. Because I'm really, really glad you're here."

eight
ZEE

Energy brimmed and bristled in the atmosphere, so thick I was sure I could see it carried on the motes that floated and danced in the bright rays of light slanting in through the only window in the room.

The rest of the modest space was dimmed, the lights cut, all except for the girl shining like a beacon where she remained by the door, wringing her hands. Like maybe she was physically restraining herself from reaching out and sinking her fingers into my skin.

Didn't matter.

I could feel them piercing me, anyway. Forging a bond that never should've been established.

God, what did I think I was doing? Chasing down something I couldn't have? Taking a chance that wasn't worth the risk?

Yet, there I was, staring at this girl who was just about the best damned thing I'd ever seen.

I turned away when I spoke, wandering deeper into the

room. "You think it's just because of what happened?"

I could sense her confusion, the shift of her feet as she contemplated taking a step forward. "What?"

A low chuckle rumbled in my chest. I swiveled a fraction, enough so I could gesture to that space between us that came alive every time we were in the other's presence.

"This. The fact I can't get you off my mind. The fact there was nothing I could do to stop myself from coming here. You think it's only because of what happened, the stress and trauma of it all? Or do you think if I'd run into you at a bar it would be the same?"

All of it bled out in some kind of frustration. But I figured if she was talking trust, I owed her the same.

"I honestly don't know," she finally admitted as a flush of red touched her cheeks. This sweet simplicity that coalesced with the greatest kind of courage.

There was no missing it where it welled from the depths of those mesmerizing eyes, twilight and the deepest sea.

Amusement made its way into her tone. "Considering I don't frequent bars all that much, I'm not sure I'd be the best judge."

I chuckled again, this time lighter, feeling the tease that touched her words. "Are you implying something, Alexis?"

She glanced to her bare feet, which were just about as fucking cute as the rest of her, and her bottom lip got caught up in her teeth again. When she peeked back up at me, the sweetest smile hinted on her face. "You do run with a crowd that has quite a reputation."

A grin tugged at my mouth. "And that didn't change your opinion of me?"

She laughed, a tinkling, self-conscious sound, and a delicate shoulder lifted to one ear. "No. Not at all."

"That's awful brave of you." There was no missing the implication behind it, the silent question I was desperate for the answer to.

What the hell were you doing down there?

Her head shook. "I wouldn't call it brave. I was just doing

what I had to do."

"You want to tell me about that?"

Couldn't help pushing, unable to keep from digging deeper.

She sighed and looked to the wall like she was contemplating. Then, after a beat, she returned that powerful gaze back to me with some sort of resolution on her face. "Why don't I make you a cup of tea?"

"Why do I get the feelin' I'm not going to like this story?"

Her voice was small. "Maybe because it's not a story I like to tell."

"How about I do my best to listen?"

She nodded, this shaky gratitude quivering in her chin as she did. "I think I'd like that."

She headed toward the arch cut out at the far end of the room that led to the kitchen. The girl kept peeking over at me the whole time, something strong yet shy about her as she went.

Her white hair was again piled on her head in some kind of messy twist, and she was dressed in a thin sweatshirt and sweatpants—all of it pink. It hugged her curves and made her appear innocent and sexy at the same damned time.

Standing there, I was left without doubt.

This girl was pure and soft.

Good and grace.

Angel.

Then I caught sight of the tiny star tattoo that dangled on a string that ran down the base of her neck, starting at her hairline. I had the itch to reach out and brush my fingertips over it. Wondering why the sight of it touched me like a brand.

She paused at the entrance, words muted but sure. "Make yourself at home."

"Awful brave." My voice was gruff but not the least bit hard as I teased her some more.

For a flash, she smiled this smile that nearly knocked me to my knees. "I try to be."

Then she shook her head and disappeared through the arch.

Shit. What was I doing? Better question was why the hell was I staying?

I'd been fighting with myself for the last three days, one side of me arguing every reason I needed to keep away.

Of course, the other side had slowly but surely convinced every part of me it was my responsibility to check on her. Make sure she was fine. That she was whole and happy and not broken down with fear.

And there I was. Staying.

I tried to rein in all the thoughts and ideas racing out ahead of me. I gathered them up and tied them down, a firm resolution set in place.

I'd stay and listen because obviously she needed someone to talk to, then I'd be on my merry way. I'd go back home where it was lonely and too damned quiet and those walls echoed all my mistakes back at me.

Fuck. Maybe I was the one who needed someone to talk to.

Shaking it off, I inhaled deeply and attempted to relax, my footsteps tamed when I let myself wander the room.

Her house was one of those older, pint-sized boxes that had been refurbished and refinished. Everything about it was cozy, light, and warm. Beneath my breath, I chuckled. It basically looked like a Pottery Barn catalog had exploded in it.

Couldn't help the way I was drawn to the big bookshelf nestled in the corner of the far wall. Curiosity held me, and I edged closer, needing to get a closer look into this girl. To dig a little deeper. Once I got started, I found I couldn't stop.

The square slots were cluttered with trinkets and stacked with books that were obviously well-worn and well-loved. All of it was mixed with a scatter of picture frames that tightened my stomach and sent this foreign feeling through my chest.

Because there was this girl I couldn't get off my mind, smiling out from every frame, face shining with belief and ambition. With courage and faith.

Wasn't sure I'd ever met someone who shined so much light. So, how the fuck did she end up in that kind of darkness?

Dishes clinked in the kitchen, and I took a step closer,

letting my gaze drift across the faces that obviously meant the most to this girl. It took all of a second to realize it was her family.

The breath punched from my lungs because they were everywhere. Three faces showcased again and again. Alexis with the same woman who'd been with her outside the station.

Then there was another—a face identical to hers.

My hand was shaking when I reached out and picked up a frame. Two little girls with white hair were grinning at the camera, smiles exact, eyes the same.

I jerked from the pained voice behind me. "That's Avril."

I glanced back at Alexis, torment shifting through her features, those blue eyes a storm of grief and love.

"Your twin."

She nodded slow. "Yes."

I couldn't stop my smile, even though I knew it probably came across as sad. "It always feels amazing to me…that two people can look exactly the same. Have always wondered if their souls are the same, too."

She sucked in a sharp breath, and my jaw clenched when I realized I'd just stepped out of bounds. "Fuck. I'm sorry. Didn't mean to say something I shouldn't."

I set the frame back in its place.

"No. It's okay. I'm just surprised you'd think something I believe."

"Yeah?"

"I do."

Unease spun around us, this awareness that was never missing when she was near, all mixed up with questions and confusion.

"Why don't we sit?" She gestured to the loveseat situated in the middle of her living room.

"That'd be nice."

Far too nice, which was probably why I should have refused, but there I was with my boots thudding on the hardwood floors as I edged to the loveseat piled with a bunch of mismatched pillows.

I settled on one side, and Alexis handed me a cup. "Thank you," I said.

"You're welcome." She curled up on the opposite side, her back on the armrest so she could face me, one knee drawn to her chest.

She blinked at me with the power of those eyes, intricate, keen, and knowing, her lashes so dark the almond shapes appeared to be rimmed in black.

If I stared too long, I was afraid I'd get lost. Fall right inside, never to be found.

I twitched with the shock of lust that pulsed through me as I took her in, my eyes tracing the slight quiver of her throat and caressing across the delicate collarbones exposed where her thin sweatshirt draped off one shoulder.

Everything about her was so simple and sexy.

The sight of her sitting there spun through me like the makings of a song.

Apparently, this girl inspired me in a way that should be impossible, because threads and wisps of beauty rose in the confines of my mind and shivered through my veins, twisting and winding until it became something powerful and magnificent.

It itched my fingers with the need to play. Itched my fingers with the need to touch.

That was a sensation I hadn't experienced in such a long damned time. A sensation that was dangerous. But it didn't matter how hard I tried to shake it off. Shun it. It was right there.

Didn't know what it was about her.

I'd been tempted a million times and in a thousand different ways.

But she had gotten under my skin.

She blew at the steam billowing from her cup, her voice soft. "How did you know where to find me?"

I laughed a little. "Let's just say I have friends in high places."

She buried another one of those sweet grins in her cup.

"That sounds sketchy."

My brow rose. "And now you're gonna start asking the questions you should've asked when I showed up at your door?"

"Trust, Zachary, trust." I could feel the mischief playing through her words, though there was something more about it as she made the statement. Like she wanted me to know something.

She cleared her throat as a little of that heaviness leaked back in. "I'm glad you came. I…I know they're just words and they really don't mean much. I know there's no way I could ever repay you, but I need you to know how grateful I am for what you did for me that night."

Anger tightened my chest, that feeling that consumed me every single time my mind strayed back to the girl pinned to that grimy wall, the girl sobbing on the dirty ground. "What else could I have done?"

Her lips tightened. "There are so many people who would have turned a blind eye."

My hand fisted. Guess that pissed me off, too. "And how the hell could I have slept at night if I had walked away? Knowing you needed me?"

Her voice was hoarse. "I did…I *needed* you. And I'm sorry I did, that I put you in that position. I chose to go down there, and because of it, I put you in danger."

"And I *chose* to help you."

Emotion brimmed, so fucking profound I was sucking it down with every shaky breath I inhaled.

Moisture glimmered in her eyes. "I'm so grateful you did."

"You ready to tell me about it?"

So maybe it wasn't any of my business, needing to know, but I didn't think I could force myself from that spot until I understood what had led her to that obscene place that night.

She looked across at me. Honestly. Openly. "There's a part of me down there I can't leave behind."

Their souls are the same.

"Your sister…Avril."

Her nod was jerky. "Yeah."

And I got it. I fucking got it on a level I wished I didn't. That helplessness of loving someone and having to watch them whittle and erode until there wasn't anything left but destruction.

Agony trembled her lips, and she clutched her teacup like it might have the power to shield her from all the pain. "Sometimes the people we love most end up in the places we never imagined they'd go."

"And no matter how much we want to stop it, there's nothing we can do," I said, the words nothing but gravel.

Guilt sped and singed, skating just beneath the surface of my skin and consuming everything. I'd wanted to stop it, with all of me, and the only thing I'd done was push Mark over the edge.

A tear streaked free, racing down her angel face. "Our whole lives, we were inseparable. I know it sounds stupid, but we were more than sisters. More than blood. I was the one who wanted to experience everything, and she was the one who was reserved."

She wiped the wetness from her cheek. "But together, we were a team, me rushing out to meet the day while she followed me everywhere."

She trembled, her gaze dropping to somewhere on the floor. "When we were fifteen, I convinced her to sneak out to a party our mom had told us we weren't allowed to go to. She'd tried to warn me it was a bad idea. That the only thing we were going to find was trouble."

Gutted, she looked back at me. "She met a boy there that night. It was so unlike her, but she took off with him without telling me. When I realized she was gone, I searched everywhere for her, screaming her name as I ran in and out of every room of the house we were at."

She touched her chest, right over her heart. "I had this horrible feeling I wasn't ever going to see her again. That I'd lost her. The most important part of me. And I did, Zee. I lost her that night. Lost her to a world I never could have imagined she'd go, and I've been searching for her ever since."

She blinked over at me. "That's my truth."

I couldn't stop myself from reaching out and grabbing on to the closest connection I could find. I squeezed her calf, the feel of her inciting that battle that waged inside me.

Right and wrong.

And this was definitely wrong.

"You were fifteen. It wasn't your fault."

She shook her head. "It never would have happened if I hadn't taken her there."

"You can't know that."

Her head angled, eyes dimmed. "Can't I?"

Hardest part was sitting there and knowing exactly what she was talking about. The awareness that one decision you'd made had changed the course of everything.

I wanted to reach over and erase it from her consciousness. Because if I knew one thing, this girl didn't deserve that kind of burden.

She hesitated, all those questions moving around us like misshapen pieces trying to figure out where they fit. "What were you doing down there?"

Hefting out a sigh, I pulled my hand from her leg and roughed it through my hair. I had the inclination to just…tell her.

Lay it out.

Which was so goddamned stupid, I was certain during that fight I'd lost a piece of my mind.

"Let's just say sometimes the wrong roads lead us to the right place. I'm just glad I was walking it."

My answer only stirred up a thousand more questions, the girl watching me with so much belief and trust, without all the disappointment she should feel.

I couldn't stop the vision from assaulting me. One of me setting my cup aside and crawling over her and tugging her down the loveseat so I could press my body against hers. So I could touch her and taste her and explore her.

Every inch.

Remember what it was like to embrace something good and pure.

I had to get the hell out of there. I was walking the most dangerous kind of terrain. A place that ran rampant with disloyalty and betrayal and shame.

Agitated, I rubbed my thigh. "I should go."

There it was—the disappointment.

Her brows tightened before she seemed to nod in understanding. "Okay."

I stood, set my cup on the small whitewashed table, and walked toward the front door. I could feel every movement she made, the ripple of energy when her bare feet hit the floor, the sway of her body, the taste of her breaths.

Fuck.

I opened the door, blinking against the stark sunlight shining down, and stepped out onto her stoop, knowing I needed to run. This needed to be goodbye.

Instead, I swung around.

She stood in her doorway, so goddamned pretty and perfect. Brighter than the sun. Every single thing I'd want if I hadn't fucked away my life.

"You know him?" I demanded.

The shock from my question jarred her back.

I couldn't shake the sense that encounter hadn't been chance. The way the investigator had been pressing, there had to have been more.

She wavered, before she shook her head. "Just his face."

"Same guy from that night? When you were fifteen?"

For a flash, she squeezed her eyes before she opened them back up to me. "No. He's just another in an endless string she's gotten wrapped up in. They just get worse and worse with time."

Rage shook through me with the power of a freight train. Knowing she had gone there and put herself in the line of fire to confront that piece of shit. She had been willing to lose if it meant her sister might have the chance to win.

"You want to repay me?" I found myself suddenly saying.

She jolted, again caught off guard. God knew I probably looked deranged. Like I was barely clinging to reason. Still, she nodded, this girl who didn't even know me.

"Then stay away from him, Alexis. Stay far, far away. Avril calls? Call the police. Tell them where she is. Just…stay away."

I knew I was fucked when the only thing I wanted was to tell her to call me.

Another tear streaked free. "She's my sister. I don't know how you can ask that of me."

Fingers trembling, I reached out and gathered the line of moisture that tracked her defined cheek.

Sparks and fire.

They flamed between us.

Something unseen but clear.

"Stay away from him, Alexis. I'm asking it of you because I can't bear the thought of something happening to you." It came out low, harder than it should have, because I didn't have the right to make that demand.

I knew it.

So, I did the only thing I could do. I turned and walked away.

Giggles lifted beneath the warmth of the sun that blazed from above. Liam ran ahead of me, little feet pushing him as fast as he could go, even faster than the last time I'd seen him.

He squealed as I chased him close behind. I caught him, letting us somersault to the grassy ground. He clutched me at the sides, me on my back, staring up at the sky with his face in my chest.

Holding him.

The best feeling in the world.

I could feel the weight of his free, uninhibited smile as I ran my fingers through his silky brown hair.

"Why you been gone so long?" he said. He was just beginning to lose that adorable lisp, the boy growing faster than I ever could've imagined.

"Because I had to work."

"Why you got to do that?"

I tugged him closer, my chest so goddamned full when I angled him so he was looking down at me, this kid filling all those vacant places that throbbed when we were apart. "Because that's what mommies and daddies do…we work so we can take care of our families."

He frowned. "Mommy doesn't work."

Anger cinched tight. Had way too many things I wanted to say about that, but the last thing I was going to do was take part in poisoning his mind. He was the only good thing that came out of this nasty, heartbreaking mess. The innocent one bred of the worst kind of disaster.

And there I was, keeping Mark's kid hidden like some kind of dirty secret. But it was me that was filthy.

I touched his chin. "That's because your mommy spends her time taking care of you."

That was the one thing I'd always been able to count on from her. That she would always take good care of him. Protect him when I couldn't be there. Never once had I questioned it. Not until recently.

His smile touched that black place in my soul, dimples denting his chubby cheeks. "I like it when you take care of me, too."

I ran my hand down the back of his head, wanting to wrap him up and hold on to him forever. "I like it, too, buddy, I like it, too."

My phone buzzed in my pocket, and I pushed out a sigh when I pulled it free and read the message, again having to bite my damned tongue.

You've been gone for two hours.

"That's your mom. We need to get you home."

"But what if I want to go home with you?"

The adoring expression on his face was a reminder of why I was doing what I was doing. Of what I stood to lose. Of why I needed to remember where my loyalties lay.

I had to pretend I wasn't feeling all the things I was feeling. Pretend like my heart wasn't calling me across town and this worry about Alexis wasn't eating me alive.

I tucked all of it away and focused on what mattered.

Liam.

"How about on Sunday we spend the whole day doing whatever it is you want to do?"

Nothing like a diversion.

He hopped to his feet and shoved out his hand. "Deal."

I couldn't help the chuckle that was somehow both proud and utterly sad. The kid was growing up so fast. I shook his hand like the little man he was. "Deal."

I tried.

I fucking tried.

But I couldn't shake the twisted sense of dread. Couldn't shake the worry. Felt like I hadn't slept in days. Weeks, really.

Things were getting more fucked up than they'd ever been. Veronica sketchier than ever. I practiced every day with the band, living that half-life. All the guys and their families had made it into town and our preparations for the tour were in full swing.

In the middle of it all, this mesmerizing girl had taken my mind hostage.

My life felt like it was barely hanging by threads, and it was only a matter of time before every last one of them was snipped and I'd find myself in a free fall.

I knew what was important. Knew what I was fighting for. Knew what I was living for.

But there I was, trailing her from her house like some kind of deranged fuck, keeping tabs on the white ponytail bobbing through the crowd so I didn't lose her.

Anger twitched my muscles and turned my stomach as she headed deeper and deeper toward the shady part of town.

I'd asked her to stay away. Had basically begged her. But most of us just didn't know what was for our own good.

God knew I didn't know it myself.

nine

ALEXIS

"Just…come home with me." Fear crawled along my skin, my gaze darting around, hating that I had to be afraid.

Avril stared back at me where we were tucked up close and hidden in the shadows against the side of a building. Far too close for comfort to the depravity she'd pulled me into three weeks ago. I had to be an idiot I was there again.

Her eyes were the exact color and shape of mine. But hers…they were drawn and sunken. Vacant. A vast emptiness haunted by ghosts and horrors that I couldn't even begin to fathom.

Uneasily, she shifted her feet, her voice dropping low like she was terrified anyone else might hear her confession. "You know I can't do that."

Grief gripped every cell in my body. "That man…I don't know who he is…but he's…dangerous. Don't you know what he was going to do to me?"

I reached out and took her by the wrist, tugging at her and praying there was a chance the physical connection might draw her closer to me. "I know you're scared, but I'll help you. Protect you."

Her laughter was sad. "You know better than that." She pulled free of my hold, her body twitching with anxiety as she glanced over her shoulder before she turned back to me. "I really need to go."

"Avril—"

She shook her head, cutting me off.

"I love you," I whispered. My last reserve. What could I do when she'd left me with nothing left to say?

A brittle smile wavered on her lips. "I know you do."

Sorrow bottled in my throat, and I found myself nodding at the same second I was digging in my pocket.

A fool. That was what I was. Because I handed her a wad of cash where we were partially obscured by the building.

Somewhere inside, I knew it was my own fault. I'd trained her that if she called, I'd come running. Without question or reason. Knowing she was only going to trample my heart all over again.

Because when she reached out a shaky hand and clutched the money in a desperate fist, I knew where it would be spent. But how could I ignore her cries when she begged that she was hungry? That she had no place to sleep?

Almost frantically, she stuffed it in her front pocket and began to back away.

A pained panic slammed me from all sides, and I took a surging step forward, my voice a plea. "Avril."

"Thank you," she whispered before she turned her back and started walking away from me.

I took a lurching step forward, overcome with the impulse to chase her. "Avril…please."

She rounded the corner before I could stop her. She never even stopped to look back.

Defeated, I slumped forward, fighting the tears in my eyes and the unbearable ache in my chest. That place that throbbed and moaned every time she walked away and took another piece of me.

I dropped my head, sucking in breaths as I tried to get it together. It seemed the only tough love in this situation were the brutal blows Avril dealt me at every turn.

Straightening, I inhaled toward the sky, needing the sun on my face, the reminder that there were so many beautiful things in this world in the midst of all the ugly and depraved.

Then I froze, awareness shivering through the air, chills prickling across my flesh. I swore I felt my axis tilt, bending and bending and bending until my direction had been altered.

Sucking in a breath, I peeked over my shoulder. My heart trembled and shook.

Staring back at me were brilliant brown eyes that raged and stormed and promised they were getting ready to wreak a new kind of havoc on my life.

On the opposite side of the street, he pushed from the wall where he'd been watching. He didn't hesitate. He came straight for me. His gaze only broke from mine to dart back and forth at the small street before he began to cross it in long, purposed strides.

A frenzy lit. A quiver of attraction that rocked and provoked.

I was fixed to the spot, gaze enraptured as I watched the intricate ink dance and play over the corded muscles that bunched and flexed in his thick arms. So much strength in his body and so much beauty in his being.

I swore he stole the air when he stopped two feet away. Hands fisted, he glowered over me.

I stumbled my way through the choppy words. "What…what are you doing here?"

His were hard. "Think I could ask you the same question."

I shook myself out of the stupor. "Are you following me?"

It came off as an accusation that was somehow half-pleased and half-offended.

Standing in front of me was a man who was little more than a stranger, who had been tracking me, and I couldn't stop the excitement that thrilled in my bones. I couldn't stop the comfort that washed through me at his concern.

But I knew it was even more than that.

Over the last three weeks, I'd spent too much time wondering if I'd ever see this beautiful boy again.

He'd come to my house, and I thought we'd formed some sort of connection, even stronger than the one we'd forged that night.

And then he was just…gone. But not before he'd confessed that he couldn't stand the idea of something bad happening to me.

So, I'd given into the fantasies.

Remembering the way his hand had burned through me like bliss when he'd simply grasped my leg as he'd sat on my couch staring at me. The way his hungry gaze had dipped and roamed, and I was sure he'd been thinking the same thing I was.

Wondering what it might be like if he were pressing me into the couch.

Bodies tangled.

The sad thing was those fantasies had also filled me with a bolt of insecurity. Again, it was something so unlike me. Because I didn't want any man who didn't appreciate what I had to give.

But this boy was a rock god. A legend shrouded by his own brand of mystery. The kind of boy I didn't have the first clue how to handle.

I knew he could reach out and have his pick of just about any woman. I knew I wanted him to pick me.

"Maybe." Frustration laced his tone. At him or me, I couldn't tell.

I blinked at him, tongue-tied, my confusion and surprise tumbling out. "That's just…weird."

God. I was brilliant.

But what was I supposed to say? This boy caught me unaware at every turn, always at the advantage.

He almost laughed, this sound that was exasperated and filled with disbelief. "Weird?"

I bit at my lip, fighting a smile that really shouldn't have been there. But he was *here*, again finding me when I felt helpless and vulnerable.

I nodded emphatically, clutching the lightness that whispered through the air. "That's right. Weird."

With his index finger, he scratched at the back of his head. He chuckled low, this sound that rumbled through my senses and warmed my belly. "I'm sure there are plenty of other things we could call this other than weird, don't you think? This is just…"

I frowned when he trailed off and took a step in his direction. "What?"

Helplessly, he looked back at me. "I can't do this, Alexis. I've got a shit show getting ready to blow up in my life, and the only thing I can think about right now is you. Can't go to sleep at night because I'm fucking terrified you might be sneaking off and doing something that's going to land you in trouble again. That I might not be there to save you next time. And when I do finally nod off? I wake up in the morning panicked, praying you're okay and having no way to make sure."

His tongue darted out to wet his lips. My gaze followed, entranced by the thick bob of his throat as he swallowed.

"I don't have the first clue what you've done to me, but I'm not sure I can handle whatever it is I'm feeling."

A knot twisted in my chest. A mess of affection and remorse and gratitude. "I hate that I make you worry."

His expression hardened. He glared over my shoulder as if he wanted to destroy the street that had suddenly become his worst enemy. "Obviously, I wasn't worrying for nothing, was I?"

I rolled my bottom lip between my teeth. "I told you…she's my sister. I can't just cut that tie. And I didn't go back there. I made her meet me here. Where it's safe."

Frustration blew from between his lips, a big hand tugging at the long part of his hair as he looked around. "Where it's safe? This isn't safe, Alexis."

I shook my head at him. "I don't exactly live in Beverly Hills, either."

He rubbed his strong chin. "You know that's different. Your place is…good," he seemed to settle on.

My heart fluttered at his words. At the way he said it with this shot of affection. "Thank you for caring about me. For worrying. And I know I unwittingly dragged you into the middle of it, and I'm sorry I did, even though I can't express how thankful I am that you did what you did."

I blinked hard. "But you can't come into my life and tell me to give up on my sister."

He rubbed his face with both palms then dropped them just as fast. "God, I know that. But this makes me crazy, you coming back down here after what happened."

"I promise, I'm trying to be careful. I just…"

I bit my lip and looked into the distance, gathering my thoughts before I looked back at him. Completely honest. "I need to get her out of there, Zee. Make her see there's more to life than the one she's been living. It kills me that she's wasting it."

He blew out a strained breath, looking to the ground. "I get it, Alexis. You and I are more alike than I think you know."

I wanted to stop him, to ask him, to find out why those brown eyes that glimmered and glinted with bronze were suddenly dimmed with grief and regret.

Instead, he distracted me with the expression on his face, this boy so beautiful when he smiled. "This is crazy, you know that?"

"What?"

He gestured between us. "This. Us. Me following you down here when I don't have the right. That is some seriously unhealthy shit."

Would it be wrong to tell him how much I liked it? To admit it pulsed a warmth through my veins I hadn't felt in a long, long time? Maybe in forever.

Because he felt different. So different from all the men of this city who were always after one thing.

And there I was again, wondering if there was more to this than just a warped sense of obligation. More than just the burden I'd placed on his shoulders that night when I'd inadvertently sucked him into the most destructive part of my life.

The part that threatened to be my ruin.

He looked over at me. Sincerely. "I would never hurt you. You know that, right? Following you…"

My older sister Chelsey had always accused me of having zero self-preservation. She always teased that I rushed into every situation heart first, my brain nowhere to be found.

Maybe she was right.

I cocked my head and took a chance. "Are you hungry?"

Surprise widened his eyes, and he massaged the back of his neck, big arm bulging as he did. "God, Alexis, you are more than I know what to do with. I'm the freak who just followed you five miles on foot like some kind of fucked-up stalker, and you're asking me if I'm hungry?"

"I already told you trust is earned in a lot of different ways."

Something heavy moved through his features, and somehow I knew he was warring with something unseen.

Then he smiled. A smile that flooded through me, filling up my spirit. "You're insane."

My lips curved, heat touching my cheeks. "No fear. Just life."

ten

ZEE

No fear. Just life.

I'd never met a girl quite like the one sitting across the table from me. The one inciting all kinds of chaos in my already fucked-up world. But I hadn't been lying. There was absolutely nothing I could do to stay away.

Had felt like I'd been losing my mind. Day by day. Hour by hour. Consumed with worry about her because I understood her situation better than she could ever know.

Didn't matter how hard I'd fought it. I hadn't been able to ignore the bond that'd been established between us without my permission.

So, there I sat, out in public with this girl, knowing it was the absolute worst thing I could do.

Sure. We were on a side of town where I was less likely to be recognized. There was little chance of someone taking note of me. So, I'd told myself another lie to make this okay.

Pretended like I wasn't hooked on every single word that came out of her pretty mouth. Pretended I didn't love the way she made me smile without effort, that blinding light shining all around her.

I could blame it on the arrows of sunlight shooting through the windows, the way they sparked in her almost white hair and burned in her eyes.

But I knew better.

"Tell me you aren't over there complaining about being a rock star." The tease weaved into the words only amplified the intensity. A contented energy that swam around us like a drugging joy.

"What?" I feigned offense. "I'll have you know it's a hard life out there on the road. City after city, never knowing which one to call your own."

"Because you have houses in too many cities, you actually forget where you live? I can't fathom the atrocity." The mocking in her voice was the sweetest kind. Nothing malicious behind it. Just this casualness that had seeped into the mood like it'd always belonged.

Nothing like the shit Veronica had given me for years.

Always wanting more and more, never satisfied until there wasn't anything left.

Quiet laughter rolled from my chest, and my voice dropped like there was even a chance I could be upset by the ribbing. "Look at you sitting over there, thinking so little of me. I'll have you know, I only have one house that I can call my own. Just bought it last summer. Considering I'm twenty-seven, a whole ton of people would actually consider that kind of pathetic."

I wondered what she'd think if she knew why. The reasons I'd been holding off, hoping for something to give. And when it gave, praying it'd give in my direction.

"No?" Those blue eyes danced, soft with mirth.

"Truth."

"So…this place you bought…is it here in LA?" I could almost hear the hope behind it. And I was wondering if she might be wishing I could give her the things I couldn't.

Was it messed up that part of me was wishing I could?

"Yeah. A loft down in the revitalized area in Hollywood."

She took a bite of her burger, chewing slowly as she studied me, watching me like she knew whatever I said was going to be important. Like she truly cared. "Why now?"

I sucked in a breath, wishing I could lay it all out, give her everything. Let her hold it and make her own decision.

But I knew better than skating that direction. Giving more than I could. Didn't matter how badly I might want to share that part of my life with someone. Especially someone like her.

Like I always did, I settled for the half-truths I could afford. At least they weren't a lie. "Ash…Sunder's bassist?" I said it like a question, not sure what she knew about the public part of my life.

She nodded for me to continue.

Clearly, she knew exactly who I was talking about. Seemed crazy who I was seemed to make no impact on her perception of me. Zero pretenses set between us because of what I could give her. There was none of that sleazy lust gleaming in her eyes like so many of the chicks who so clearly wanted to sink their claws into me.

She just sat there all lit up. So fucking gorgeous that every time I looked at her she stole a little more of my breath.

An angel.

The brightest light in the midst of my darkness.

Starshine.

I swallowed around the emotion that suddenly clogged every cell.

Fuck.

I couldn't get lost in this girl. But there was a part of me that wanted to do it anyway. Give up and give in.

My voice was rough when I forced myself to continue. "He got married last summer."

A soft smile played at her mouth and something shy worked into her admission. "I might have read something about that."

I chuckled, low and with the affection I felt for Ash and Willow. "They have their first kid coming in just a couple months."

I shook my head, still so grateful the guy had finally found what he'd been missing. "Ash was the last of my crew to finally give it up and tie the knot. Honestly, I never thought I'd see the day. For the last handful of years, while the rest of the guys had been getting married off, I'd been hanging with him at the house the band owns here in the Hills, and then whenever we were back in Savannah, we crashed at the place he owns there. But once he got married…"

Red splashed her cheeks when she leaned in and whispered, "Things got awkward?"

I chuckled. "Yeah. Could only walk in on them so many times before things got weird. Figured it was time to man up and get my own place. Most all the guys and their families are settling back in Savannah, but each of them bought a house here for when we're in town. All except for Lyrik and his wife, Tamar. He has this super cool kid, Brendon, who lives half-time across the city with his biological mom, so they spend as much time here as they can swing."

I gave her a casual shrug like it meant nothing at all, even though I was giving her more than I'd ever given anyone else. "My family's here, too, so it only made sense this was where I'd finally put down roots."

Both the family who'd raised me, my mom and my dad, and the one none of them knew a thing about.

Veronica had done a bang-up job of keeping me close and still a galaxy away. It'd been an easy decision to stick around LA more. Trying to earn more time. Even though she seemed intent to take more and more away. Coming back and finding she'd sold the house I'd bought her was proof enough.

Anthony had warned me it was stupid to put it in her name, but I'd done it as a peace offering. A treaty.

Guess I should've listened.

A tiny scowl tightened her brow. "Sounds complicated. Going back and forth. Houses in two different cities. Trying to keep up with each other."

I couldn't stop my grin. "Told you it was a hard life."

Alexis laughed, this tiny, lilting sound that trickled around me like a melody. Could almost see the notes of an emerging song dancing through the spikes of sunlight that slanted all around her.

This girl was like music.

Harmony.

Settling into silence, she nibbled at a fry. I could see her contemplating. When she finally spoke, her tone was laced with caution, like she might be ashamed she knew something so personal about me when I hadn't given her the key to that lock. "I'm so sorry…I heard you lost your older brother…I heard that's why you're in the band? You took his spot when he passed away?"

Old grief slammed me, regret and pain and every mistake I'd ever made. "Yeah."

"You always knew how to play the drums?" The creases in her brow cinched tighter.

A humorless sound rumbled in my chest. "Yeah…I always knew how to play the drums."

Memories flashed. The aspirations that'd been the single focus of my life. I just didn't know which of my mistakes had been the one that had stolen them. The catalyst that had set me on a path I'd never expected to go. Guess it was the sum of them. A string of hurt and betrayal and regret that had destroyed both my and Mark's lives.

Something soft eased into her expression, and she sat back in her chair with her head angled, exposing the delicate, milky flesh at the side of her neck.

A shock of lust belted me in the gut. I wanted her.

Maybe it'd just been too goddamned long. Maybe I was just a man. But this girl had me spun up in a way I'd never been before.

"My little drummer boy." She murmured it like a tease.

Didn't matter. Because something about it went sailing through me like a thunderbolt. Like I could feel those small hands on me. Touching and healing and inciting.

Unable to stop myself, I angled forward, suddenly needing

to get a little deeper. A little closer. "Tell me your truth, Alexis. If you could do absolutely anything, what would it be? And I don't mean something for someone else, because I know what you're getting ready to say. I mean for you and only you."

She choked out a laugh. "Well, that's out of left field, isn't it? How is it you always manage to catch me off guard?"

I forced a smile. "I like to keep people on their toes."

"You're crazy," she said.

"I thought that title belonged to you?" I tossed it back, loving the way her skin lit up with a flush.

She looked down as she shook her head. Self-conscious and good.

I edged in even closer. "Tell me. I want to know."

Because I was the fool who suddenly wanted to know every single detail about her. I wanted to explore and discover. Slip right inside her beautiful mind and sift through her thoughts.

Vanish in her body.

For a flash, she looked away, out the window to the people milling on the sidewalk outside. Then she turned those blue eyes back on me, a collision of sky and sea.

She hesitated, seeming to need to work up the courage to give me her answer. "If I could do one thing for myself, I'd learn to play piano. I've wanted to since I was a little girl. I would beg my mom for lessons, but we never had the money. Then I was putting myself through college and then pouring myself into work. It just never happened."

I just stared.

Redness flushed that stunning face, and she started fiddling with the spoon at the side of her plate. Like this brave girl was suddenly shy. Like there was any kind of possibility she could say the wrong thing.

"It's kind of silly, I know." It was a whisper beneath her breath.

"No. Not silly. Not at all." My voice was gruff. "There's no song like a song played on a piano."

Ideas were thrumming through my mind. Dangerous, dangerous ideas.

I needed to put a lock on them and fast.

She must've caught onto the undercurrent of my last words, because she sat back in her chair. A spark of excitement flashed in her expression. "Tell me you don't play piano, too."

I shrugged. I wondered if she noticed the hesitation behind it. Because I was traversing rocky ground. Getting closer and closer to those boundaries I couldn't cross. Letting her into a place that'd been barren for a long, long time.

As much as I knew I shouldn't, I couldn't stop the admission from sliding from my mouth. "I play about everything."

Speculation lifted her brow. "What do you mean, everything?"

I shrugged again, this time self-consciously as I slanted a nervous hand through my hair and glanced out the window. "It's not a big deal. It's just if there's an instrument lying around, I can usually pick it up and play it."

Disbelief filled her soft words. "It's not a big deal? Zee, that has to be the most amazing thing I've ever heard."

Words like prodigy and genius spun through my mind, words that had been tossed around me when I was just a little kid, having not a clue what they meant. Not until it'd meant everything.

It was just another door that had been slammed in my face seven years ago.

"I got lucky, I guess."

She stared across at me. The expression on her face spoke of hurt and understanding. Like she got something about me maybe I couldn't even see.

That air shivered around us when she leaned over the table, getting as close as she could. Found myself edging closer, too, erasing that space that churned and begged.

"If you could do one thing for yourself," she said, "what would it be?"

Guess I shouldn't have been surprised the girl would turn the question on me.

I'd set myself free.

The confession scraped from my throat, hard and pained. "I'd go back and change everything. Both for him and for me."

So slowly, she inched back, stopping just far enough away so she could fully meet my gaze. My chest tightened, this needy clench while we sat there staring, breathing each other's breaths.

"Your brother?" she whispered.

"Yes. I'd go back to the day when I made the worst mistake I ever could've made." My voice was nothing more than shards and dust as I let her in a little further. Further than I'd ever allowed anyone before.

Blue eyes searched my face, a storm that built at the edge of a blazing sky.

I got the distinct feeling this girl would give up anything to hold a little of my pain. That she was sitting there wishing she could sink into me, discover all my secrets the same way I felt desperate to discover hers.

"What were you really doing down there that night? People are only on that side of town after dark for two things." Her chin trembled, the words cracking somewhere in her throat. "Drugs or sex. Usually both."

Grief bottled at the base of my throat. "Wasn't down there for either, Alexis. I promise you. A friend needed me."

I felt strangled by the lie, because Veronica was a lot of things, but she definitely wasn't my friend. But I pushed right past it, our faces too close, the need spinning through me almost too much to bear.

My lips just brushed her cheek. "Turned out you needed me more."

That potent gaze flamed and brimmed, her words hushed. "Have you ever wondered if each day of our lives is purposed? If every step we take is exactly where we're supposed to be?"

She dropped her attention, her fingers trembling when she reached out to the ink etched on the back of my hand. She traced the shooting star that blazed before it burned thin.

Fragments charred to dust.

I shivered, trying to hold it back, hold it in. This need that flickered and boiled in my blood.

My voice was grit. "I'd like to imagine that. But then I'm left wondering about the bad things. The horrible shit that goes down and the terrible things people do to each other."

She caught that bottom lip between her teeth, and my dick twitched. This girl just sucked me in further and further. Taking me deeper and making me question every single thing I knew as truth.

"What if the good moments are reprieve? Mercy that's been granted?"

God. This girl was good. Flush with grace.

Like she'd been sent as a sustaining breath in a world that threatened to suffocate.

Transparency in a life full of confusion and doubt and questions.

I pressed my hands against the table and pushed away. Like it might put enough distance between us to extinguish the smolder. Douse the coals growing hotter and hotter.

And there it was again. The beginning strains of a song. I could hear it. Notes weaving and spinning. Lyrics knitting together to make something whole.

For the first time in years, my fingers itched with the urge to sit down and bring it to life. To create and compose.

This song?

It would be soft and sweet and tender.

Exactly the kind of love this girl would be.

I knew it.

Felt it bursting in that space between us.

Sweet.

Uncomplicated.

True.

My guts clenched, knowing I was walking too thin a line. It was time to end this before I did something else I couldn't take back.

Resigned, I pushed out a strained breath and stood, dug out my wallet, and tossed a stack of bills onto the table. "Let's get you home."

Surprise flitted through her expression before it dipped into something that looked too close to rejection. Reluctantly, she nodded. "Okay."

I did my best to ignore the way she trembled when I set a palm at the small of her back. Did my best to ignore the flames that smoldered and lapped. To ignore the way our breaths came shorter and harder when our skin touched.

I ushered her out the door and onto the busy sidewalk. The second we stepped out, agitation lit. Anxiously, I looked left then right, because the last thing I needed was a camera shoved in my face.

God, this was stupid.

Warily, Alexis shifted around so she could look up at me. It was like she sensed that I was pulling away. Because that dark storm in her eyes was begging me to stay.

My fingers jerked, my pulse an erratic thunder hammering through my veins. I wavered, trying to talk myself down. Should've known better because all it took was the softest smile gracing that mouth to send my willpower crumbling down around me.

Because there was something sorrowful in her expression—a goodbye.

"Thank you so much for lunch. For worrying about me today. I know you don't know what it means to me, but if there was any way I could show you, I would."

Panic bubbled to the surface. I couldn't stand the thought of letting her go. I needed to know she was safe. That she was taken care of and protected until that bastard was locked away.

I ignored the fact that it was clearly more than that. That standing there, I wanted to give this girl everything.

So I caved.

My hand was shaking like a bitch when I reached out and cupped her cheek. Heat sped across my skin. All those cold, dark places lit up. Desperate and needy for her warmth. My voice dropped in a way to match. "You really want to learn to play piano?"

She stilled at my words, this brave, gorgeous girl looking up at me with kindness and trust. She nodded against my hand. "I want it more than anything."

No doubt there was something more in that simple statement.

Fuck, I was a fool. Because my offer was out before I could stop it.

"Let me teach you, and in return, you let me protect you until that bastard is off the street."

She stared up at me. "What does that mean?"

"That means you stick close. Your sister calls? You call me. You think you need to meet her? I come with you. You let me *be* there. Simple as that."

That energy thrashed around us like an approaching storm.

"Then why does it feel so complicated?"

eleven

ALEXIS

The interior hall was deserted, the entire place completely quiet as I stood in front of two big metal doors. My heart raced, alive with this thrill that had followed me through the last four days.

I could have sworn when Zee had abruptly stood from the table that day at the café that it was the end. That whatever obstacles standing between us had become too much for him. That maybe I'd pushed him too far.

But I'd never been the type of person to tiptoe. Had never been one to keep my tongue tamed when I felt I had something important that needed to be said. And offering all those truths to him had *felt* important.

Vital.

Sucking in a steeling breath, I rapped my fist against one side of the door. That nervous energy magnified when I heard movement on the other side, thrummed and sped when the door unlatched and one side opened to reveal the man standing there.

The man who had to be the most intriguing I'd ever met.

Carved in mystery and sculpted in secrecy.

"Alexis." His voice grazed across my skin, and his gaze made its own electrifying path, sweeping me from head to toe.

A shiver rolled through me when I did the same, taking in the man dressed in a pair of soft worn jeans and an even softer tee.

I had this foreign urge to reach out and press my hands against him, to feel the strength I saw bristling beneath the fabric.

"Hi," I whispered.

He stepped back and widened the door. "I'm really glad you came."

"You didn't think I would?"

His head tipped and he scratched at his neck. One side of his mouth arched into an affected grin. "No. I didn't really think that. I just thought by now you might've come to your senses."

"And why on earth would I go and do something like that?" I almost teased, though I realized I was clutching my big bag tight to my chest as if it might act as a shield. As protection against what this boy was gaining the power to do to me.

Which seemed insane because I was the girl who was never afraid.

A low chuckle rippled through the air, and he eyed me with the slightest grin. "The girl who'll give up anything to save the world but won't stop long enough to save herself."

I could almost hear the warning behind it, but I chose to ignore it and stepped into his loft.

"Wow."

Articulate, I knew.

But I didn't think there was another word sufficient to describe his home.

"You like it?" His voice hit me from behind. "Ash's wife…Willow. She helped me decorate it. Helped me make it feel like home."

"It's incredible."

Both luxurious and warm, the loft was one massive, open space. The floor was an expanse of dark gray hardwood and the ceilings two stories above remained open, the ductwork and metal framing left exposed.

Four concrete support columns stretched between the bottom floor and the ceiling. Leather couches and plush lounge chairs were set up in the middle, all mixed up with restored, rustic antique tables and decorations.

My gaze wandered to the far right where a set of stairs led to a bedroom in an upstairs loft that jutted out over the custom kitchen below. It was enclosed only by metal railings, and a huge bed sat in full view, overlooking the living area below.

But the two-story wall of windows on the left was what completely captured my attention. I wandered toward it, drawn to the undoubtedly million-dollar view of the sprawling city beyond.

The sun was just beginning to set, sagging low on the horizon, sending a scatter of twinkling glitter across the buildings and cars below.

My fingers brushed the glass, struck by the beauty, almost floored by it when I glanced over at Zee standing in the middle of the room. He was staring at me. As if I might be a hallucination in his living room.

"Look at you, my little drummer boy, living like a king." I forced the tease, though it cracked beneath the effort. I wondered how it was possible I thought I could so easily claim him as my own.

His head shook. "Hardly."

I studied every movement on his face, the words almost a question. "You're the drummer for one of the biggest bands in the world." I lifted my arms out to my sides. "You have this amazing place. And then you offer to do this for me? To give me something I've wanted for so long? It feels backward. I should be the one doing something for you."

My voice grew small. "But what do you offer the boy who has everything?"

"None of that means anything when I don't have anyone to share it with. And you being here?" He paused, and my heart clenched. Then he dropped his face toward the floor as if he didn't want me to find what would be written in his expression. Desperate to hide the things so visible in his eyes.

Lifting his head, he looked back at me, throat heavy when he swallowed. "You being here for a day is more than enough. Sometimes it gets old, living in the shadows. Somehow they're not quite so dark when you're around."

"Is that what you feel? Like you're invisible?" That connection I didn't understand flamed within my chest. Building and intensifying. "Because you're the only thing I see."

He flinched. "That's the problem with all of this."

"This?"

"The fact I can't stay away from you when I know goddamned well that is exactly what I need to do. I just…"

He rubbed a knuckle across his pursed lips. "I can't fucking stand the thought of that piece of shit out there, Alexis. That he's still on the street. A danger to you. I need you here…with me…until I know that threat is eliminated."

Emotion gathered fast. "So…I'm here because you want to protect me?"

I didn't know whether to be disappointed or overjoyed.

His voice turned gruff. "You're here because this is where I want you. Fact I can give you something you want so badly on top of it? Let's call that the cherry."

His confession took possession of the air. Desire throbbed, crackling between us and throbbing between my thighs.

I was in so much trouble.

Blinking, I tried to bring us back to common ground. "So…" I said, looking around and forcing a smile. "How do we do this? I'm actually kind of nervous."

It was the truth. I'd wanted to play for as long as I could remember.

He took a step forward, as if he were stepping out of that thick knot of tension that kept him rooted to the spot. His tone shifted, turning so sexy it sent another shot of attraction tumbling through me. "What are you nervous about?"

My teeth caught my bottom lip, and I bit down, trying to fight the flush I could feel climbing to my cheeks.

"How could I not be? I haven't a single clue what I'm doing, and you, *this rock star…*" The last of my words changed course, veering into something incredulous. "You want to teach me how to play. It shouldn't come as a surprise that's a little bit intimidating."

He came closer. So close I caught the faint murmurings of cedar and spice. The scent radiating from this beautiful boy was distinctly man.

Overwhelming.

I inhaled a shaky breath, his presence rippling through me when he took another step in my direction. He was so close I could reach out and fall right in.

His voice turned hoarse. "Don't ever want you to feel intimidated by me."

Too late.

I forced myself to look at him where he towered over me.

"Okay."

He edged back a fraction, angling his head away as he muttered quietly, "I'm the one who doesn't know what he's doing."

I got the impression that statement had nothing to do with music.

"Come on," he said. His big hand settled back to that spot at the small of my back. The second he touched me, my breaths became shallow.

He led me around the living area to the far wall where a baby grand piano was situated between the long island bar that separated the kitchen from the rest of the living space and the bank of windows.

I couldn't stop from reaching out and running my fingertips across the gleaming wood. The instrument wasn't the normal glossy black. Instead, it was a deep red. Mahogany dipped in chocolate.

Zee released a shuddered breath, and my attention darted to his face.

Panic and fear.

"What's the matter?" I whispered.

He roughed an agitated hand through his hair. "It's just…been a long time."

A frown pulled at my brow. "You don't…play?"

His smile was pained. "Not in a lot of years."

I blinked at him, trying to see through the veils and secrets and mystery. I settled on the obvious. "But you miss it."

He nodded. "Yeah."

I turned back to face the piano. "And still, you brought me here."

"Yeah," he repeated.

How was it possible to make sense of this conflicted man? I could feel it, his spirit being cut in two, as if he were desperate for one thing and terrified to claim it.

And again, he was taking a leap for me.

He cleared his throat, breaking up the intensity. "So…have you ever taken any sort of lessons before?"

"Fourth grade music. Mrs. Lindstrom. I could play a mean recorder." I smiled at him, wishing it might hold the power to erase whatever was tormenting him.

He chuckled. "Impressive."

"I thought so."

"She teach you how to read music?"

I cringed. "A little, but I honestly don't remember much about it."

He nodded. "That's okay. If you know how to read, you can learn how to read music. It's like learning another language. It just takes time and commitment."

Time and commitment.

I was all too willing to give it if it meant I got to spend more time with him.

"That sounds…difficult."

Movement twitched that gorgeous mouth almost into a grin. "And here I thought you were up for the challenge."

"I am…I just…I don't want to disappoint you."

A sound of frustration jutted from his nose. "Don't think that's a possibility, Alexis."

He sighed again before he reached down and pulled out the stool. "Sit," he said, and I complied. He rested his hands on my shoulders. A shiver raced down my spine.

What was he doing to me?

"I'm going to give you some things to study at home before I see you next time. But for today, the thing I want you to take away is music is all about feeling. Yes, there are techniques and rules, and you're going to learn all of those. But music lives above them. Beyond them. Despite them."

His breaths were all around me, his presence eclipsing me from behind.

Energy lapped and pulsed, his heart erratic where it pounded at my back. He leaned in, arms caging, fingers poised at the keys. His muscles twitched and bowed, and I swore I could see the ink imprinted on his skin begging to play.

The shiver of that bleeding star.

"Lay your hands over mine."

My breath was a rasp when I did. Everything came alive, zapping and sparking in the air.

I could feel his sharp inhale, the way his big body trembled where he stood behind me, the quake of his hands as he played a single chord.

A gush of air rushed from his mouth as soon as he did, as if he were staggered by the sound echoing against the walls.

I felt it the moment he gave, the enormity strike in the room when he began to play.

Talented fingers flew across the keys, taking mine with them.

They spun a web of beauty.

A maze of sorrow.

I shuddered, wanting to beg him to sing the lyrics. To show me it all. What lived in his mind and dwelled in his spirit.

His voice grated in my ear. "Do you feel it, Alexis? It's about tapping into the emotion. The pain. The joy. The love.

The lust." Those last words were rough, spinning through my senses. Heat pounded through my body.

I moved with him.

With the feeling.

With the ebb and flow of his body.

His fingers flew. The song growing in intensity. Something magical.

"Do you feel it?" The words were a pant, as if he were captured. Removed. Lost in a place that, for a time, only belonged to me and to him.

"It's alive. A light shining somewhere in space, just waiting for us to harness it. To capture it. To give it a voice and life. Tell me you feel it."

"Yes." It left me on a needy rasp.

Because I could.

I could feel it.

I could feel the intensity. I could feel the beauty. I could feel his talent.

A tremble of desire vibrated through my being, and I could feel his erection pushing into my back.

Maybe it was only that, the lust that bled from the song.

A song that was somehow both desperate and bittersweet.

Foreign and somehow known.

But I wanted to get closer. Turn and find what would be on his face. The passion and need.

"Does it always feel like this? Every time you play? Every time you're on a stage?"

The song slowed, his heart still a thunder, his breaths choppy and short. He hesitated before he finally said, "Only here…when I'm in front of a piano."

I couldn't stop myself. I angled around the side of him so I could see his face.

It dizzied my senses that were already overwhelmed. "Then why the drums?"

Those brown eyes raged in a full-blown war. As if he were trapped in a vacant space between the power of that song and the shackles of his reality. "Because I owe my life to my brother."

At his admission, a breath parted my lips. I knew he was offering me a veiled part of himself. A glimpse into that place that too often went dim. Part of his truth.

Bewildered, I searched his face and his expression and those hypnotic eyes. My mind raced with all the questions that seemed silenced on my tongue.

Warily, he reached out, his hand splayed wide. He cupped the entire side of my face.

I trembled, couldn't breathe.

"Lex." It was a murmur that twisted my belly into a thousand intricate knots, while every other part of me came undone.

Completely at his mercy.

I swore I could see it, the desire that crackled in the atmosphere.

A shrill ring sliced through the intensity.

Zee jerked back as if he'd been burned. I blinked, fighting the flash of rejection that welled too fast and stung my eyes.

How did he manage to make me question things I'd never questioned before? I'd never been the kind of girl to doubt my value or merit, yet there I sat with my head spinning.

I had no clue where I stood, if I was falling, and if I was, where I was going to land.

Because I found the only thing I wanted with him was to *start.*

And every word out of Zee's mouth pointed at the temporary.

He raked a hand down his face. "Fuck. I'm sorry."

"What are you sorry for?" I pressed, digging deeper, desperate for *something.* Desperate for him to let me into the place I could feel him steadily taking me to, whether he wanted me there or not.

The words left his mouth like a dirty confession. "I'm sorry I can't seem to stay away from you."

My voice was the softest plea. "What if I don't want you to?"

Bitterness curved his mouth, words tight with regret. "And what if I don't have anything good to give you?"

"Everyone has something to offer, Zee. *Everyone.* Living is a choice. *We* decide how we wake up each morning and face the day. Either we're led by hope or ruled by fear. And I won't let circumstances define me. Maybe I'm a fool, because I will stand or I will fall, but I will never, ever allow fear to clip my wings."

I glanced back at the piano, my spirit still dancing with the magnitude of his song that had been held back for too long, with the stark, blinding reality that for some reason this man had stopped living for himself.

I turned back to look up at him. "Maybe you've just forgotten how to fly."

Pain lashed across his face. "No man is free if he's already condemned."

His words struck me like sorrow, and I wanted to reach out. Hold him. Touch him. Beg him to touch me.

His phone rang again. Cursing under his breath, he glanced at it, gripping it so tight I thought he would crush it in his hand. "I'm sorry. I need to return this."

Disappointment slowed my nod. "I guess that's my cue, then."

Feeling like I'd run a marathon, dragged and pushed and pulled, I stood from the piano, reached down, and grabbed my bag. Slinging it over my shoulder, I headed for the door.

"Shit," he muttered quietly from behind me before his heavy footsteps were suddenly moving across the floor. "Fuck, Alexis, don't go."

I sped up, that nonexistent self-preservation finally kicking in.

He snatched me by the wrist and tugged me around, forcing me to face him. His expression a map of conflict and turmoil. His voice dropped lower. "Don't go."

Sadness clutched my chest. "If I give myself, Zee, I give myself with all I have. With everything I have. I give and I give, and I let people take and take. But with you? I'm not sure I can handle you not giving in return, because I have no idea what it is you want from me."

Honesty. Sometimes it was brutal. Sometimes it was hard to confess. Sometimes it made you vulnerable and small.

I was transparency. He was fog and mirrors.

He fisted a hand, pushed it against his mouth as if he were trying to keep the words in.

The second he dropped it, they rushed out. "I…I want to teach you. I want you to come back. I want…" He trailed off, leaving his intentions hanging in the air.

He blinked. "Most of all, I need to know you're safe. Until that bastard is behind bars, I need to know you're safe."

I raked my teeth over my bottom lip, searching for ground when he'd already knocked me off my feet. "You confuse me."

A regretful smile pulled at his mouth. "Believe me, gorgeous, you confuse me, too."

twelve

ZEE

"So that means an additional three months?"

From behind his desk, Anthony rocked back in his chair, attention jumping to each of us who were sitting in his office. "That's what it would require. Some of the big cities will be two shows. They expect every stop to sell out. Nothing but coliseums and stadiums. The money is…" Anthony shook his head. "It would be insane to pass it up."

Crazy this was everything we'd ever wanted. What we'd worked and strived and fought for. The bullshit my crew had endured. The life my brother had been dragged into.

The devastation and destruction. The victories and the triumphs.

I'd been there for the lowest lows. Now we were sitting at the highest high.

And I was certain I'd never sat through a heavier meeting.

Lyrik looked at the ground where he rested his forearms on his knees. He rubbed a tattooed hand over the back of his neck, weary when he looked back up. "That's a lot of time away from home, man. We were already gonna be gone for four months. Now you're asking for seven?"

Could feel the agitation churning through Austin where he sat to the side of me, it even clearer with the way he scrubbed both hands down his face. "Seven months. More than half a year."

Austin was our lead singer, and just like me, he had stepped up to take his older brother's place in the band. Though their circumstances were entirely different since his brother Baz was sitting to the other side of him, there to support us through every decision we made.

The guy was still just as much a part of this band as he was the day he'd stepped down to spend more time with his family and started producing our albums rather than standing out in front of them.

He'd said his heart couldn't take it, being out on the road and leaving his family behind.

Which led us to the crux of things.

Tension bounded off the walls, the room far too small to contain the friction that clashed and contended. The loyalty and devotion and commitment that was spinning and raging.

Problem was, none of us really knew exactly what that meant anymore.

Austin gave a harsh shake of his head, something like grief striking in his hoarse voice. "God…Sadie will probably be walking by the time I get home."

Austin's wife, Edie, had given birth to Sadie three months ago. The baby girl was the light of his life.

Grief got me by the throat. I totally understood. My days were always like that.

Limited. Just glimpses and flashes into what could've been.

Lyrik sighed and looked in Austin's direction. "You think I don't get it, man? You think I want to take off and leave Tamar and Adia behind for that long? Barely get to see Brendon as it is. This is just…brutal."

Anthony cleared his throat, his tone riddled with his own hesitation. "You know the only thing I want is the best for each of you. The best for your families. But I've also watched you work your asses off for years to get to this point. I've seen the dedication and commitment to your goals. The blood, sweat, and tears that came with it. The *sacrifice.*"

His gaze bounced around to each of us. "I know what it is you've told me you want, and this is it. The culmination. And it's not like you won't be able to come home on breaks, or your families can't meet you wherever you are. I promise you, we'll make this work."

I knew it was hard for him to push us in this direction. But he'd also always done what was best for the band. After all, that was what we'd hired him to do.

Lyrik shook his head, dark hair in his face. "You know it's not that simple anymore. We have babies we don't need to go jetting into foreign countries. The girls…they have their own ambitions. Don't want Tamar to think it's her duty to follow me around the world just because I'm living my dream."

Baz lifted his chin to Lyrik. "But you know she'd do it for you if you asked her to."

Affection deepened Lyrik's tone. "Of course she would. Just like any one of our girls would. Which is why I don't want to uproot her when she's happy. Settled."

Anthony thrummed his fingers on the desk, filled with his own agitation. "I'll make sure there's time for you guys to get a break at least once a month so you can come back home for a few days. Some of them I know we can fit in a week or two."

Lyrik tilted his face toward the ceiling, rubbing his throat, contemplating.

Austin sighed and sat back in his chair.

Everyone turned to Ash who'd remained silent the whole time. Dude was leaned over like he might be sick to his stomach, holding his head.

He suddenly jerked his head up. "Is this what everyone wants?"

Austin banged his head back on his leather seat. "It's our fucking job."

"Yeah," Lyrik agreed. "Nothing none of us didn't expect.

Just fuckin' sucks when it sneaks up on you."

My knee bounced a million miles a minute, hating the idea of being gone that long. Not with the shit that was going down with Veronica. Not with her going off the rails and shunning the agreement we'd made.

Not with Alexis.

The thought hit me unbidden. It should've been warning enough. An omen I was treading on thin ice. The fact I was even considering her in the midst of everything I was already trying to balance was straight stupidity.

Because this was my life. What I lived for. My duty.

My brother's legacy.

I wouldn't ever let that go.

I blew out a strained breath and turned my focus on Ash. Dude was big and burly, covered in tattoos, menacing if he wasn't always sporting a grin. But right then he looked like he was about five seconds from losing it.

He swiped an agitated palm over his mouth. "You've got to make sure I'm here when the baby comes, man. Need to be here for at least a couple of weeks. Can't leave Willow alone. I mean, fuck…if I missed it?" His expression was bleak. "Promise me, Anthony. Promise me you make sure that window happens."

Anthony rocked forward, leaning on his desk. "God, of course, Ash. You think I'd ask anything more of you?"

He glanced around at everyone. "You know I hate even making you all decide. If I could make it simpler, I would. But it's my job to look out for you as a band. It's my job to present it to you when there's an opportunity unlike any you've ever had. Now it's on all of you to decide."

I just sat there silent, letting everyone else take the lead the way I always did. Maybe it was the feeling I never quite belonged. Or maybe it was simply because I never felt I'd earned the right.

"Okay then, we're decided?" Austin asked.

Lyrik nodded. "I'm in."

Ash shook his arms out, like he was pumping himself up.

"Okay."

Anthony lifted his chin toward me and all eyes shifted my direction. "Zee?"

I figured it wasn't even a question. "You know I'm game."

I always was.

After the meeting, Anthony pulled me aside, his voice hushed. "Any news on what's going on with Veronica?"

I expelled a frustrated huff. "She's still maintaining she can do whatever she wants with that money. Isn't telling me anything." I shook my head. "Still can't believe she's back down in that shithole. That she'd take him there."

Anthony eyed me where we had our heads bowed together, our conversation muted. "Are you really surprised? She's been manipulating you from day one, Zee."

Anger swelled. "You think I don't know that? I didn't have a whole lot of choices, though, did I?"

"Didn't you?" he challenged.

Old rage, compiled for too many years, fisted my hands, the thought of it more than I could take. "You know what she would've done."

"And that very well may have been another lie, too. You know nothing comes out of her mouth that you can trust."

"Then what the fuck do I do?"

"You need to decide what it is you want, Zee. You have to keep going along with all her bullshit demands or stand up and demand a change."

Anger and worry thrummed through my blood. "God…I hate the idea of confusing Liam. He loves his mom, Anthony, and up until I got back from Savannah this last time, I would have sworn she loved him more than anything else."

Up until then, I hadn't really given a shit how she'd treated me. Only thing that mattered was the way she treated him.

"Are you worried?"

I ducked my head, scratching my fingers through my short beard, before I eyed him straight. "Yeah…I'm fucking terrified. You know she's always been a wild card. But in the end, I could always trust her to put him first. Care for him the way he deserves to be."

Anthony shifted in agitation and doubt. "You think she's slipped?"

Terror threatened to seize my heart. "Don't even want to contemplate the thought."

That was the one promise I'd made clear there would never be any breaking. She had to stay clean.

For good.

Compassion lowered his voice. "You might have to."

Looking toward the ceiling, I blew out a breath. "I know, Anthony, I know. And now I'm looking at being gone for seven months?" Worry doubled at the thought. "I've left so many times before and was able to trust her. Not sure I can do that this time."

"Just…lie low while you're here. She's probably only looking for something else to hold over your head. Don't give the paps anything juicy to talk about. Smile for the camera. Sign some autographs. Your reputation is squeaky clean. Keep it that way and she won't have anything to say."

I rubbed a hand over my face. "Feel like I've been lying low my whole damned life. Been stuck in the same spot since I was twenty, pretending I'm someone I'm not. Don't know how much more of it I can take. I'm going out of my mind, man. I need to know he's safe."

Grief pressed and vied for dominance, itching at my skin and nagging at my spirit. Could barely force out the declaration. "It'll be seven years next month. I'm not sure I can keep going on like this."

Understanding dawned on Anthony's face. "I know, Zee, I know."

thirteen

ZEE
SIXTEEN YEARS OLD

Zachary shouldered into the packed house. Music blared, and his heart rate increased as he stepped into the dense fray. Bodies were crammed wall to wall, and voices shouted to be heard above the heavy bass pounding from the speakers.

Chest tight, Zee's uneasy gaze roamed. That discomfort grew as his attention traveled over girls wearing next to nothing, red cups clutched in their hands and even redder lipstick smeared over their lips. Men hovered on the outskirts. Like predators on the hunt, ready to strike.

That apprehension only intensified when his sight landed on a guy who sat on the couch, leaning over the coffee table and cutting lines, two over-eager chicks salivating at his side.

A warning flared at the forefront of his mind. It was that spot inside that told him to just turn around and go. He wasn't supposed to be there. This was so not his scene. At least not anymore.

It wasn't like he hadn't ever witnessed it before.

For years, he'd tagged along behind Mark, clinging to his coattails and praying one day he might get the chance to be even half as cool as his big brother. Growing up, Mark had been the greatest thing in his world.

That hadn't changed.

But it'd finally come to the point where Zee had to make a choice. He'd known he couldn't continue to hang with this crowd.

Sure.

Music was music.

But that didn't mean they weren't two entirely different worlds, and Zee couldn't be a part of both of them and expect to reach his dreams and aspirations.

Everything came at a cost.

With a sacrifice.

But tonight that didn't seem to matter. He pressed on, maneuvering through the crowd.

He'd promised.

And the truth was, Zee wanted to be there for him.

"Zee, there you are."

Relief barreled through him when he saw his brother sitting at a high top table just off the kitchen. A cigarette hung from between his lips, and one hand was waving Zee over.

He rushed that direction.

Mark slung his arm around his shoulder and stubbed out his cigarette in an ashtray. "About time, asshole. Thought you weren't gonna show."

A smile pulled at Zee's mouth. "Told you I'd be here."

Mark squeezed him, jostling him at his side. "Then I really shouldn't have had any doubts, should I?"

With the hand not hanging around Zee's shoulder, Mark pointed at him, voice elevated as he talked to the group of people crushed around the table. People Zee hadn't ever seen before.

"This guy right here? My baby brother? Best dude in the world. Can count on him for absolutely anything."

Affection pressed against Zee's ribs. It was that same feeling of belonging that engulfed him whenever he was around his brother.

"Yeah, yeah, yeah," Zee said, grinning at his brother who was always playing him up. Making Zee a bigger deal than he actually was.

Mark shook his head, his voice too eager, his pupils nearly obliterating the brown of his eyes. "Seriously, man. You're the fucking best. Don't know what the hell I'd do without you."

He looked back at his friends. "Goddamned brilliant, too. This asshole?"

Mark was back to jabbing at him again. "Got accepted into some kind of genius school. Kid's a prodigy. Can play a piano like none other. Sits down and composes a song like he's been working on it for years. Has been doing it since he was about three. It's like some kind of Beethoven shit. Next to him, I look like a pathetic hack."

Mark smiled at him. Too wide and reckless. Zee knew he was fucked up. High on something. He didn't know what, but it seemed like lately he always was.

Zee hated it. Worried about him nonstop. It was better when he was around. When he could keep tabs on his brother and make sure he wasn't getting himself in too deep. Guilt grew in his chest, and there he was again, wondering if it was worth it, stepping out of the world he understood and into one where he wasn't sure he would ever quite fit.

Remnants of the song he'd been working on churned in his mind and twitched like an unfed hunger in his fingers.

He had to believe making that choice was right.

But right then, neither of those things seemed to matter.

The only thing that mattered was that Mark's pride in him was real. Almost as real as the pride Zee felt for his brother. "Stop it, man," Zee told him. "What I have going down in my life doesn't mean anything tonight. We're here to celebrate you."

Zee tightened his hold on Mark's shoulder, his voice low as he muttered it toward his brother's ear. "You guys made it.

You did it. Nabbed yourselves a label. That's legit. I'm so fucking proud of you…don't think you have any clue how proud I am."

He wanted to tell him to guard it. Protect it. To revel in it, but also to make sure he didn't let it slowly kill him, either.

Because everything good also had a flip side.

An underbelly.

And Zee couldn't stand watching Mark waste away in it.

But he didn't say anything, and instead kept it to himself. He didn't want to ruin the moment.

"Not too bad, right? Now it's gonna be you watching me on the big stage. No more of that dive shit." Mark squeezed him again. "Gonna take care of you, man. Always. We've got this."

Zee held tight to his brother. His best friend. The guy he'd always wished he could be.

"We've got this."

Mark grinned as he rocked back, arm still slung around Zee's shoulders as he jabbed his finger at him again, voice lifted too loud. "Someone get this kid a shot and someone to fuck."

"Shit…Mark…come on," Zee muttered, wanting to throttle his brother for being so damned crass all the time. But he guessed he really didn't mind when he tossed back the shot glass that swirled with shimmery black liquid. He minded it even less when a chick wound her way over to him and slithered up to his side.

No.

He was sure he didn't really mind it at all.

fourteen

ALEXIS

"Are you ready to talk about it?"

I glanced over my shoulder and found Chelsey sitting at the small round table tucked beneath the window in my kitchen. Midmorning light poured inside, and shimmery silver rivers splashed across the table and tumbled onto the floor.

My older sister stared at me, fiddling with the string of her hot tea bag.

Worry.

It was blatant.

I wondered if it was backward that I was in a constant state of worry over Avril, and Chelsey seemed to be in the same constant state for me.

Or maybe it was perfectly normal.

A typical hierarchy.

I turned back to the dishes I was loading into the dishwasher. "What do you want to talk about?"

"Come on, Alexis. You know exactly what I'm talking about. More than three weeks have passed, and you haven't said a single thing to me about that night since I dropped you off here after we left the station."

Our mother had worked two different jobs to support us when we were growing up. Mom had relied so much on Chelsey to be there for me and Avril, and the four of us had become a team that had to work.

Somewhere inside, I knew Chelsey felt just as responsible for Avril straying from our tight-knit flock as I did. She just chose to handle it in an entirely different way.

A sigh filtered free. "I'm not sure there's anything more to say."

Her cup clanked behind me, adding to the weighted tension climbing into the stagnant air. "Has she called you since then?"

I hesitated.

"Damn it, Alexis. Tell me you haven't gone back down there. God…did you give her more money?"

Setting the rag aside, I slowly turned and leaned back on the counter.

I loved my sister. I did. She wanted the best for me. But it seemed what she'd forgotten was *we* wanted the best for Avril, too.

A shot of defensiveness rose in my chest. "I did give her some money, but I didn't go all the way back down there."

Thoughts of Zee sprang into my mind. The heat of his stare as he'd leaned against that wall. A shiver shook through my body.

Shaking her head, Chelsey's gaze dropped to her tea. "She's not only putting you in physical danger, Alexis, but also she's *robbing* you. Robbing you of your security, of the things you might want to have or do. You work hard at a job I know you really don't even like, and then you turn around and *give* it to her. That is so messed up."

"I like my job." Why did my argument sound so weak?

"You tolerate your job," she disagreed, finally lifting her eyes back to me as she tilted her head to the side. "You think I don't know you'd rather be doing a million other things than working in an attorney's office?"

"I don't know how my job has anything to do with this."

"It has everything to do with it. It's just another example of you always doing what benefits everyone else instead of yourself. You make great money, but you do it so you can support your deadbeat sister. Before Mom moved to Iowa, you gave up most of your weekends to visit her, and you don't go out because you volunteer your time."

I started to defend myself, but she held up a hand. "Before you say something, I'm well aware there's nothing wrong with wanting to help other people whenever you can. But when was the last time you did anything solely for yourself?"

My gaze dropped to my fuzzy white socks. Maybe it would hide what I knew was ripping through my expression.

The redness and heat and vestiges of the man who'd steadily staked claim after claim.

Stealing my thoughts and my dreams and my breath.

I should have known she'd catch it.

"Oh…" It slid from her like an *aha*, curiosity blazing free. I wasn't even looking at her, but I totally knew she had that smile on her face. The smug one that said she'd caught me red-handed.

"Alexis." She said my name like a prod.

Warily, I peeked over at her.

She was grinning and circling her finger in my direction like proof. "Tell me what that's all about."

I cleared my throat, but the words still cracked. "I…I am doing something for myself."

Her brows rose, a nudge for me to continue.

"I'm…learning how to play piano."

"You are?" Her smile widened. "Why didn't you tell me? That's amazing."

"It's new."

"Where are you taking lessons?"

This was the part I wasn't sure I wanted her to know.

Chair legs skidded against the tile. Chelsey stood, taking the three steps it took for her to cross the kitchen. She jutted her hip into the counter two feet away from me. "Why do I get the feeling there's more to this story than you're letting on?"

I chewed at the inside of my cheek, wondering how much to give her. Because she was going to want answers, and I had no idea what any of this even meant.

She touched my shoulder. "Hey…I'm your sister. You can tell me anything. You know that, right?"

I turned to look at her. "I do know that." My tone was cautious. "The guy who saved me…"

Her eyes flared with surprise. "The drummer?"

I nodded.

"You're kidding me." It was a dumbfounded breath.

I wrung my hands. "He came to check on me a couple of days after everything. And…we kind of became friends. He offered to teach me how to play."

Skepticism seeped into her chuckle. "Your expression isn't exactly saying friends."

I clutched the counter with both hands, as if it might support me. "Because I'm not sure that's what I want us to be."

Concern climbed back to her face. "That's a gorgeous man, Alexis. Believe me, I get the attraction. That morning outside the station was kind of…intense between the two of you. You obviously went through something together. But chasing a guy like that? It doesn't seem your style. And the rock star drummer actually plays piano? I just…" Her words trailed off with her own questions.

I understood the paradox. The way that boy looked, so bad and bold on the outside, covered in ink and that mystery each day I wanted more and more to discover. But what she didn't recognize was the vulnerability that glowed from the inside.

My head shook. "He's different."

Incomparable to anyone I'd ever met.

"You need to be careful, Alexis," she murmured the quiet warning. "You always run headfirst into everything without thinking through the consequences."

Softly, I scoffed. "You're always telling me I need to get out and do something for myself, then the second I do, you start telling me to be careful. I'm twenty-five. I'm not a child anymore, Chelsey. You have to stop thinking you need to question and criticize everything I do."

She touched my shoulder, the words winding with the lightest tease. "But you'll always be my baby sister."

My smile was slow. "I know. But you have to know sometimes taking the chance is worth any consequence."

She eased forward and wrapped me in her arms. "I love you."

I squeezed her tight. "I love you, too."

She rocked me and laughed, something wistful in her tone. "How about we make a deal? You stop chasing the dangerous things and I'll stop worrying about you."

Soggy laughter rolled from me as I squeezed my eyes shut and buried my face in her neck. "I'm not sure I can make that deal."

Because sometimes the best advice was the hardest to take.

fifteen

ZEE

Crossroads.

They were always there. On the horizon. With each second that sped by, they got closer and closer until they were right in front of us.

Obstacles littering the way. Distracting and diverting us from the direction we knew we needed to travel. Slowing us down when there wasn't anything we should be doing other than barreling forward, full speed ahead.

I knew where I was supposed to be going. The direction I *had* to go. Yet there I was—distracted.

Guilt scraped at my insides, this feeling that was achy and raw, goading me for being so damned selfish that I couldn't just cut ties with the girl right from the start.

I knew better. I fucking knew better. But that knowledge sure as hell didn't seem to stop me every single time I got in her space.

She'd be at my place soon for her next lesson.

The fact that was the only thing I could think about all day should've been warning enough.

A heavy sigh pilfered from my lungs, riding out into the silence like a reprimand. Because taking this kind of risk was just about as stupid and selfish as I could get.

That reality was mixed with the fact that not taking the risk for her felt like some kind of mortal sin.

The waning day burned through the windows as the sun crashed toward the horizon.

The world on fire.

I found myself standing in front of my piano. The piano that had been my grandmother's. The piano where I'd basically spent my life growing up. Countless hours at her keys.

A shiver of unease slithered across the surface of my skin and then prickled with the need.

Alexis had nailed it. I hadn't played in years.

Not since it had all gone down, and that comfy, cozy rug had been ripped right out from under my feet.

Dreams shattered.

Aspirations lost.

Hearts broken.

In all that time, I'd never itched or yearned or felt that stirring rise from deep within me.

The inspiration had died.

Until she had somehow brought it back to life.

Last Saturday, she'd incited something in me. And it fucking terrified me, the way it had felt to be wrapped around her body when I'd given in. When her song had come pouring out the exact same way as I'd heard it in my head.

A knot grew in my throat, and I shook, compelled by that same kind of need as I sat down at the bench. My eyes dropped closed and my fingers found their mark.

Hesitation trembled in the cage of my chest before I gave, for the moment letting it loose.

Her song.

The chords and the strains and the melody.

Harmony.

I bit back the lyrics that spun on a circuit through my mind, demanding to be released, and instead, I let my fingers sing her words.

Need.

Lust.

Belief.

So many questions and too much confusion.

It poured from my fingers as my body bowed and curved and swayed. The piano like an old lover. My first friend.

And that energy…it lashed and hammered and pounded.

Alive.

Too intense. Too much. So close.

A burst of warmth crashed over my skin. Eliciting chills. Overpowering heat.

Alexis slid onto the bench beside me. So full of that good and grace, and my fingers stilled on the keys. I struggled to draw a breath into my lungs that burned from the exertion of playing her song.

"I'm sorry I startled you." Her words were quieted, like she didn't want to break the passion knitted through the room.

"I knocked, but you didn't answer. I could hear you playing…the door was unlocked, so I let myself in." She fidgeted in that innocent way. "I hope that's okay."

Carefully, I nodded. "Of course it's okay."

My gaze traced the exquisite lines of her body. She was wearing these super tight skinny jeans that instantly had my mind running wild, and a delicate blouse that teased my thoughts into wicked things.

Lust.

It tangled in my stomach and pulsed through my veins.

A scatter of glittering golds struck against her porcelain skin like a torch.

But it was the girl who was lighting up the room.

My chest tightened. She was some kind of miracle. I wanted to reach out and take a little magic for myself.

Sheets of white hair framed her sweet face, her cheeks flushed, her lips lush. But it was her eyes that staggered me. They were a storm that had gathered on the Caribbean. The deepest, most destructive kind of blue.

Her voice was a plea. "Sing it to me."

I sat there dumbfounded, and she continued like a prayer. "It's so beautiful. The song you were playing. It's the same you were playing the first day I came here, isn't it? Sing it to me. I bet you have an incredible voice, don't you, little drummer boy?"

Her voice was muted, so quiet in the backdrop of the setting sun.

Chest heaving, I struggled against the desire that bounded and churned. My cock was so goddamned hard it neared on painful, begging for her touch. "Those are words I won't ever get to sing."

"Why?"

"Because they hurt too much."

She fluttered her fingertips over the star on the back of my hand. Soft, soft encouragement. "Outside…I stood and listened. The song…it sounded both like sorrow and hope. It's sounded like you want to believe."

God.

How did this girl manage to see straight through me?

My tongue felt heavy and thick. "It's the culmination of every wish and every regret, Alexis. So yeah, there's hope in it. But I guess the part that makes it sad is that I won't ever get to have it."

My hands lingered on the keys, and she reached out and set her hand on top of mine.

Warmth and light.

It invaded my senses. Clouded my judgment.

My hand flipped over, palm up, and she threaded her fingers through mine. Her head angled, so soft, this girl so fucking good.

"What is it you want, Zee? What is it you can't have?"

You.

You.

You.

Flames leapt into that space between us. Alive and dancing

and inciting.

A siren's call.

My tongue darted out to wet my lips, and I was shaking as I lifted our entwined hands. I brushed my knuckles along the silky flesh of her cheek. I swore I saw the trail of pink it left behind, the simplest touch affecting this girl.

She released a shuddered breath. It mingled with mine.

Our mouths were close—too close—and our noses just touched as we hovered in that space.

"I want things that will only ruin me, Alexis. But you…you make me want to wish for them anyway. Make me believe there's a chance that maybe they could belong to me."

Tension tethered us, this rigid band that had me rocking in indecision, every second getting closer and closer as I fought the foolish ideas that tried to take root.

Giving in would only destroy me. But none of that seemed to matter when I leaned in and brushed my lips at the corner of her mouth.

Her fucking delicious mouth.

Because fuck. I just needed a taste. Something to take with me. Something to tuck away, even when doing it felt like some kind of brutal tease.

Alexis gasped at the contact. I edged back the barest fraction, and she was panting these tiny breaths.

Breaths I was breathing.

Her eyes locked on mine. Hungry and pleading. Brimming with belief and hope.

I ran my thumb over the corner of her mouth where my lips had just been. "You are so beautiful. I've never met a girl quite like you."

Something so genuine took hold of her expression. "I hardly know you…and somehow you make me feel like I am. Like when you look at me…you see the person I always hoped I'd become."

Everything stilled at her words.

At her confession.

Because that's what I wanted.

For this amazing girl to know the way I saw her. That in her space, I felt something different from all the bullshit I'd dealt with for all my life.

I felt like someone different. Someone better. Like the person I'd once hoped I'd become.

I clutched her stunning face in my hands, searching for resolve. For that dedication that right then somehow felt out of reach.

"Zee," she whispered.

That was all it took for that band to snap.

My hands drove into her hair. And my mouth? My mouth was devouring hers.

Frenzied in its demand. Pleading the same way as her eyes had been pleading with me. Saying all the things I couldn't ever say.

Our tongues tangled, and my spirit coiled. Heat spread in a flashfire of need. Lust rose in the knitted air, like this intangible greed we both were grappling for, searching for the fastest way to get to the peak.

Our hands searched and clawed and explored. We were a mess of limbs as we struggled to get closer to each other where we sat side by side on the bench.

"Zachary…Zachary," she whimpered, grasping me by the back of the head. She crawled forward so she could straddle me.

Motherfuck.

My hands sank into her hips, and she edged up and pressed those gorgeous tits against the wild beat thundering in my chest. A groan rumbled out from somewhere in my soul.

She felt so perfect. So good.

I wanted to touch her. Explore her. Claim her.

My dick raged against its confines, all that delicious heat at the apex of her thighs grinding against my jean-covered cock.

It'd been too long. Too damned long. I was goin' out of my mind.

"Fuck…Alexis…Lex. I need you…God, I need you so bad I can't fucking see."

"I think I want you more than anything I've ever wanted. Not in all my life." It was all a manic whimper between this frantic kiss, her words and her breath rushing over me.

What am I doing?

What am I doing?

My hands slid up her sides before they fisted in her hair. I kissed her deeply—madly—before I forced myself to pull back.

Alexis panted and gasped. Blue eyes wild. Raging with need.

Blinking, I attempted to clear my head of the lust distorting all my loyalties. I cleared my throat, loosened my hold in her hair, and slowly edged back.

"I…" I trailed off.

"Did you feel that?" she murmured into the air, her voice like the remnants of that song that kept trying to take possession of my spirit.

Carefully, I set her aside and climbed to my feet. I had to put some distance between us before I went and did something I couldn't undo. Before I made any more mistakes than I already had.

It left Alexis sitting there at my piano, watching me cautiously. Reflecting all the confusion I felt. Wondering if she might've done something wrong.

Problem was, all the wrong was on me. It always was.

Her hand fluttered my direction. "Zachary…tell me what's wrong."

I swiped the back of my hand over my mouth like it might be able to erase the sweet ache she'd left behind.

Impossible.

"I just…I need a minute, okay? Uh…why don't you practice a little of what you practiced during the week. You watched the videos I told you to, right?"

I was rambling, but I was looking for a different sort of distraction. A detour that wasn't perilous. A road that wasn't fraught with hazard signs.

Hurt and disappointment were clear in her expression, but she nodded. "Yeah. I watched the videos and practiced some on my keyboard like you asked me to."

Damn it. Couldn't stand that I'd put that look on her face.

I brushed my thumb beneath the hollow of her eye, needing to reassure her. To encourage her she hadn't done anything wrong. Or maybe I was just the fuckup who was looking for any excuse to touch her again. "Good girl. I'll be right back, okay?"

She swallowed hard, and I backed away and let the space between us grow.

I needed a moment of clarity outside this attraction that pulled and pulled and pulled.

Before I let this go any further, I needed to remember my resolutions. Remember exactly what it was I was fighting for.

Chains were a bitch.

But sometimes they were the only things tying us to what was most important.

I backed the whole way to the staircase, watching her watching me, before I turned and jogged up to my bedroom.

I went straight for the bathroom separated from my bedroom by a high partition wall. I closed the door behind me, though it did nothing to mute the tentative, tinkling sound of fumbled keys floating up to tickle my ears.

I set my hands on the countertop and stared at my reflection as she pushed all the way through the boundaries.

Touching that cold place in my heart.

Seven years and I'd never been tempted.

Seven years and I'd never questioned.

Seven years and I'd never *failed.*

And there I was, staring down the bastard in the mirror who was itching to commit the greatest kind of betrayal. But how could I stop myself from wanting her? Not when her simple song lifted and danced and teased.

It was a song I'd learned to play when I was three.

"Twinkle, Twinkle Little Star."

I looked down at my hand fisted on the porcelain sink, at the star that'd burned for a few fleeting moments before it'd disintegrated.

Just dust and ash and decay.

But beneath it, I felt something smolder.

A spark to a dying ember that I'd believed lost its flame.

Harmony.

And I had no idea what the hell it was this girl was doing to me.

sixteen

ALEXIS

The energy shifted the moment he stepped back onto the bottom floor. I could feel it, the way the tension increased and pulsed with every move he made. How it grew and grew the closer he came.

The man had already brought me to my knees with his mind-bending kiss.

By the heat of his touch and by the need in my body.

And then—just as fast as it'd started—he ended it. Ripped himself away. As if touching me was something wicked.

Hurt tried to crawl up and take shelter in my chest, and I struggled around it as I tinkered my way through the song on the piano, pretending as if I didn't feel more emotionally vulnerable in this moment than I had in all my life.

"I think you're a natural." His words were a coarse caress that blasted across my skin.

A tiny sound climbed my thickened throat, landing somewhere between a self-deprecating laugh and a cry. "It's a child's song, Zachary."

I could sense him behind me and off to the side, as if he didn't want to step too close.

"No song is less important than another." Voice so low it was dangerous to my sanity.

He inched forward, the air pulsing with each uncertain step. "How many lives do you think that song has impacted? How many souls has it touched? How many mothers have rocked a child to sleep while they hummed this song? It's a child who believes. Never, ever take that fact for granted."

His breath barely kissed along the bare skin of my shoulder, and I ached for him to again breach the space. I wanted to feel him.

Everywhere.

I'd always chased after experiences. I'd always loved the feel of the sun on my face and believed in the power of a falling star.

This boy felt like both wrapped into one. Life and death. A beginning and an end.

I fumbled across the keys, trying to make it through the song before I finally broke and jerked around to face him. "What is happening between us?" Wildly, I gestured. "Between you and me? Because it feels like something important."

His voice was rough. "I wish it could be…something important."

"Why can't it be?" Desperate confusion flooded from the words.

Something bleak edged his expression. "Because we can't always have the things we want."

I blinked up at this complicated, perplexing man. "What is stopping you from taking what you want? Because it's not me."

And there I was. Running toward danger. Heart-first, just like Chelsey said.

"That's the thing, Alexis. I see you looking at me the way you do. Like we could be somethin'. And I want it so fucking bad. To be something to you. To be good for you. But I ruined that possibility a long time ago and I'm not sure there are enough pieces left to give any of them to you. That's my truth."

As if he could no longer stand, Zee dropped down to his knees in front of me. Like an offering.

I shifted the rest of the way around on the bench so I could meet him eye to eye.

Reaching out, I ran my thumb across the tense lines on his forehead, my head angled as I studied him, searching for an answer. "Who do those pieces belong to?" My head shook. "Who do you belong to, Zee?"

Low, gutting laughter rolled out from some place hidden within him. "I belong to my mistakes. To the choices I made a long time ago. Now, it's a matter of remaining loyal to them. Remembering what I owe."

His gaze shifted to the windows before he looked back to me and edged forward an inch. My knees shook with the urge to drop open, to make room and beckon him to me.

"Doing this…inviting you here…is probably the most reckless thing I've done in years."

My heart sank. Why did him admitting that have to hurt so much?

Both for him and me. Because I could see it, written all over his gorgeous face. His expression was riddled with pain and regret.

"Then why am I here?" I pushed.

Humorless laughter rolled from him as he moved forward to hold onto the bench on either side of me.

Those bronze eyes pinned me to the spot.

Mesmerizing. Intoxicating.

"Because I can't seem to stay away from you, even if I know doing so is only for my own good. For your own good. But I need this, Alexis. Just as much as you do. I'm giving you the sliver I have left. A few moments in the midst of the bullshit that I made my life. And yeah, it's stupid and reckless and careless…"

He scooted forward, and I could feel him giving. Just a fraction. His big body barely prodded at my knees as he climbed between them to invade my space.

That self-preservation was nowhere to be found when I breathed him in.

Cedar and spice and sex.

I wanted to lean forward and inhale. Memorize everything about him. Because somewhere inside me, I knew one day he would simply disappear.

His hands landed on my waist, and he tugged me forward. Low and desperate, the petition spilled from his mouth.

"But I need this, Alexis. I need to know you're safe and, for a little while, I just…I need you. I need to remember what it's like to be a part of something beautiful. And I fucking know it's about the most selfish goddamned thing I could do…to ask you to stay when we aren't playing for keeps. But I know you need a little bit of this, too. This feeling. So for the little bit of time we have, let me stand by your side. Let's pretend like this is something we could possibly have."

My entire being trembled. "What happens when you break my heart?"

His fingers dug deeper into my flesh. "You don't give me that power. When that bastard is behind bars, you walk away. You find someone who can give you all the things I can't."

Part of me wanted to be relieved to have any piece of him. Willing to take whatever he would offer.

The rational side of me resisted. The part that rang with a warning my conscious couldn't ignore. "Why does this…us…being here…feel wrong? Why does it feel like we're doing something wrong?"

He wound one of those big hands up in my hair. "You could never, ever be wrong, Alexis. What you have to remember is I am. And there are some things I can't tell you and the public can't know about us—about this—but I promise, I won't ever lie to you."

I bit at my bottom lip. "You want me to be your dirty secret."

His face blanched, and his fist constricted in emphasis. "God. No, Alexis. It's not you who's dirty."

And I knew it then. It was him who held all the secrets.

Dark, deep, and destructive.

If I were smart, I'd get up and run. But that didn't change the fact I felt desperate to get behind those secrets, to see what they meant and why they caused him so much pain.

"The tabloids…they say you've never been spotted with a girl. They're always speculating…coming up with reasons why you've lived a life so different from the one the rest of the guys used to. Is that true…that you've never been with anyone since you've been a member of Sunder? Or do you keep secrets like *me* everywhere you go?"

I didn't want it to come out like some kind of accusation or pathetic jealousy, but even if he didn't realize it, he was asking me to put my heart on the line.

He already had me so mixed up, questioning everything. Who we were and who I wanted us to be.

"I haven't been with anyone in a long, long time, Alexis."

"Why now?"

Frustration jetted from his mouth. "Why now? Why? Because of you, and you couldn't have come crashing into my life at a worse time."

Tears threatened to gather, but Zee…he looked at me so tenderly that it tugged at all those secret places inside me.

He cupped my chin. "You came at the goddamned worst time, Alexis. But I guess it's true what they say—the best things always do."

"Then what do we do?" I gulped around the affected words. "I feel like you're asking me to have a temporary relationship with you. That it ends the second that monster is in a cell."

"We can't have a relationship, Alexis. The only thing I know is I want to steal as many moments with you as I can until there aren't any left."

Choked laughter rolled off my tongue. "So, you're going to keep your hands to yourself?"

The faintest smile pulled at his mouth. "All I'm saying is I can try. You make me wish for things I don't deserve to have. To believe in wishes coming true. To believe in us… even when I know it's just pretend."

"This is crazy." The words sounded like submission.

He fiddled with a strand of my hair, rubbing it between his fingers. "Well, since we already established you're insane, this should be easy."

"Goofball." It came out soggy with affection. This boy was doing things to me he shouldn't have the power to.

Tucking the piece of hair behind my ear, he sighed and glanced toward the giant clock that hung on the wall. "Shit," he muttered as he edged back an inch. "Hour has already passed. I have to go. Guys are expecting me for practice tonight."

"Oh." I didn't mean for it to come out so disappointed.

Apologetic, he rubbed his palm over his mouth, and I watched in wonder as his demeanor changed course and this light affection climbed into his eyes.

It was right then I saw two sides of him clash.

"Next tour kicks off in about four weeks. Last year, we took it pretty easy with all the family stuff going on, but it's time we got back on the road before the fans go and forget about us. We're working through a few kinks for the set, trying to grab onto the vibe. Get our hearts back in the music. All the guys and their families are in town to prepare, so it's kind of a mandatory thing. I don't show and they'll basically come over here and round me up anyway."

"That's okay. It's your job," I told him.

"Yeah, but it's more than that. We might not have the same blood flowing through our veins, but we're family. A team. Even if it wasn't part of my job to show, I'd want to be there."

His smile was softer than I'd ever seen. "Their wives kind of like to mom me considering I'm the loner of the bunch."

Affection. It was so apparent. Easy in his eyes. I couldn't help but feel happy for him, that he had people who clearly meant so much to him.

"Honestly, it's fine. I completely understand." I glanced behind me at the piano. "We kind of got sidetracked."

He chuckled. "Yeah, guess we did. Not sure I have it in me to complain."

It would probably do us good to put some space between us anyway. Some time away to figure out what all this meant.

Standing from the bench, I leaned down and grabbed my bag from where I'd dropped it on the floor. I could feel Zee rising behind me.

Could feel him deliberating. Contemplating.

"Come with me."

Shocked, I spun around to face him. "What?"

"You heard me. Come with me." It was so gruff that I couldn't tell if it was a request or a demand.

I blinked up at him. "I feel like that might send mixed signals. You just told me we couldn't be seen together."

He shrugged. "Let my crew think what they want to think, but this is about that sliver of time we have. With the shit that's getting ready to go down, I'm pretty sure that time's going to run out and fast. And if there's anyone I trust to have my back? It's them. Things are calm enough out at their place, so we don't have to worry about paps hopping out of a bush to snag a pic. It'll be cool."

"Are you sure?" Because I wanted this. To be in his space. A part of his time. Even if it was fleeting.

I watched the heavy bob of his throat when he swallowed. "Yeah, I'm sure."

"Okay…what's the address?" I started to rummage through my bag to find my phone so I could input the address.

His expression shifted. Something powerful flashed behind that dark, dark veil.

Then a smirk climbed to his mouth. That mouth that had been on mine less than twenty minutes ago. That mouth that had consumed and drugged and made me want things I was sure I'd never before desired.

His tongue darted out to wet his lips. I took a fumbled step backward.

Oh God. This was the side of Zee I wasn't sure I could handle.

The wicked side that promised mayhem and chaos. A side that was wild and reckless. The side that decided if he was giving in even a little, he was going to take everything he could while it was there.

Hungry. Greedy. Possessive.

"Oh no, Alexis. What kind of man would I be if I let you drive over there alone? Think tonight you ride with me."

Why did that sound like a threat?

My eyebrows rose to my hairline, and there I was again, clutching my big bag as if it were a shield. "Ride?"

Zee reached out and unwound the straps of my bag from my shoulder and then pried it out of the clutch of my hands. He tossed it to a nearby chair.

Sweet, seductive arrogance. It played around his lips and danced in the ferocity of his eyes. "You won't be needing that."

A flare of excitement flashed through my being, this rush of exhilaration that stampeded through my veins.

Chelsey had always warned me I had zero self-preservation.

She was right.

Because there was no way I wanted to miss this experience with him.

seventeen

ALEXIS

It took less than ten minutes for me to become the happiest girl alive.

Could anyone blame me?

The big bike ate up the ground below us, the gleaming metal pure power and pride. The pavement flashed by in a dizzying whirl of colors and lights as night steadily eclipsed the sun and possessed the sky.

My arms held tight around his waist, my chest pressed to the rigid strength of his back as he commanded the engine that roared as we flew down the street.

Air whipped in my face, and I inhaled the deepest breath.

Ingraining it in my mind.

Imprinting it on my soul.

Cedar and spice and the raw potency of this man.

Sexy and masculine. It was a scent that had invaded my mind and seeped into my dreams.

It was bold and distinct. Just as bold and hypnotizing as him.

Nerves wound through me as he confidently took the roads. The heavy metal beneath us rumbled as we sped. The insides of my thighs shook and shivered where they were pressed tight to the outside of his.

Those tattooed arms were stretched out, and the color strained and flexed over the muscles that rippled as his hands gripped the handlebars.

My awe only increased when he turned into a historic neighborhood that had to have been there for a century, as if he'd taken me through a portal and directly into the early glitz and glam of Hollywood.

Zee lowered his booted feet as he slowed and came to a stop. He killed the engine, and the roar in my ears was replaced with the sudden ring of silence.

My legs were shaking so badly I wasn't sure I could stand. The problem was I had no clue if it was from the adrenaline of the ride, or simply the staggering effect of Zee.

A big hand covered both of mine where they clutched the firm planes of his abdomen, the heat of him making me wild. "You okay?"

"I'm…that felt incredible."

He chuckled low. "Ah, you like my bike. My kind of girl."

My kind of girl.

"Yes, I definitely like your bike," I managed to say.

Did I tell him I liked so, so many other things? Did I admit there was just something about the mixed-up, conflicted equation of him?

It was easy to realize I wanted to be a factor. To count. Even when he promised this could only last for a time. But whatever *time* meant, I wanted it to matter.

Holding on to my hand, Zee helped me onto my feet. He towered over me, gently reaching out to undo the strap of the helmet he'd insisted I wear, his attention never wandering from my face.

Fingertips brushed my throat. Stoking the chills that never seemed to want to leave my skin.

I glanced at the vintage mansion in front of us.

It was two massive stories high, fronted by six white columns that rose to support the portico. The home was undoubtedly a landmark from the early era of Los Angeles, carefully renovated to maintain its character from long ago.

Yet, somehow it radiated welcome and warmth.

Comfort.

Zee gestured at it with his chin. "This is Ash and Willow's place. A few years back, Ash bought a house out in Savannah. Just as lavish as this one—maybe more so—and the fool thought he had to repeat it here. He just can't help himself. He's about as over the top and rash as they come, so fair warning. But he has a heart the size of the sun, so we pretty much let him get away with it."

For a second, he scratched at his head, as if gauging what to say. Dealing with his own nerves while trying to keep mine at bay. "They're all…amazing. You'd be hard pressed to find a better group of people."

"Intimidating people." I could feel the red rush to my face when I said it, teeth catching my bottom lip in their clutches when I peeked back at the house.

It seemed insane I'd ended up here. I was no tabloid junkie, but that didn't mean I lived under a rock.

For years, I'd seen their faces plastered on the front pages of magazines and trending on the gossip sites. I hadn't missed the scandal and speculation that had followed these wild boys everywhere they went. The trouble they'd incited had gained almost as much notoriety as the music they played.

"Are you nervous?" he asked.

"I'm trying not to be. Your friends are…" I took a deep breath. "It just seems crazy to be in their space, in your space. And I promise I'm not some kind of weird fangirl or something. It's just…weird."

He chuckled. "Weird, huh? You keep saying that."

I laughed under my breath and let my fingers fiddle with the hem of his tee, the smallest of smiles tweaking at the corner of my mouth. "It seems you bring about the strange, little drummer boy."

He laughed through the tease. "Oh, they're strange all right, gorgeous. Whole lot of them are nothin' but a handful. But I promise you that you won't be able to help falling in love with them."

Maybe that was what I was worried about. The falling part.

"So what are we in there?" There, with him, I felt confident. I just had no idea how Zee wanted to handle it once we stepped through the door.

He touched my chin. "We're us. As complicated as we are, I say we walk in there and *be* whatever feels right. How's that sound?"

My brow arched. "It sounds complicated."

Zee laughed, and he slung one of those strong arms around my neck and kissed the top of my head. "How's it you make every single thing better, baby?" he murmured.

Baby.

Oh God.

The boy had me in the palm of his hand. The only thing I could pray was for him not to crush me in the end.

Zee squeezed my hand where we stood in the archway that led into a quaint sitting room that rested just to the right of the sweeping foyer. He cleared the roughness from his throat. "Guys, brought someone with me tonight that I wanted you to meet."

He glanced down at me with a tilt of his head toward the room. "Alexis, this is my crazy family that you're basically going to need to ignore."

Oh goodness.

I stepped a little closer to Zee. My protector. My savior. Standing there in the entryway of this incredible house with about ten different pairs of eyes staring at me, I was pretty sure I was going to need it.

A group of children were playing on the floor, and the men of Sunder were littered around a sitting room just off the foyer, so big and bold, radiating this striking aura of power and a dark, menacing kind of beauty and magnetism. They were surrounded by women who were even more beautiful than their pictures.

They all shifted from where they had been lounged back on plush sofas.

Ash Evans jumped to his feet, covering the ears of a little black-haired boy who stood in front of him. "Holy S-H-I-T."

The boy squirmed out of his hold. "Uncle Ash, you don't need to go covering my ears. You really think I don't know what you spelled? You're gonna have to get way better at that before you and Willow have that baby if you think you're gonna be foolin' anyone. Probably gonna need a money jar like my dad's got. Momma Blue is pretty much rich."

Brendon…this had to be Brendon, the son of the band's guitarist, Lyrik.

I had the urge to press my hand to my mouth to stifle a laugh.

I shifted, trying not to be shy, remembering I always faced every situation like the adventure it was.

But something about this felt different.

"You've got me there, Brendon," Ash agreed, shooting Zee a sly grin. "But sometimes men like me just don't know how to handle this level of surprise when they're in the presence of children. Things are bound to slip out."

Brendon shrugged as if it were obvious. "Money jar. Problem solved."

Willow, the woman I knew was Ash's wife, pushed to standing from one of the couches, her belly so round I thought this practice session might be interrupted by a surprise trip to the hospital.

She had a vibe about her, soft and sweet and encouraging. She ran her fingers through Brendon's hair. "I think that sounds like the perfect kind of plan, Brendon—a money jar it is. The last thing we need is this big oaf to be teaching our little man words he doesn't need to know."

Brendon nodded as if he was all kinds of proud of himself, and I found myself smiling into Zee's arm as I peeked out at his mismatched family.

Willow approached us. "Alexis…it's so good to meet you. Welcome to our home."

"Thank you so much for having me."

"Any time." She slanted a curious glance toward Zee before she turned her gaze back on me. "Any friend of Zee's is a friend of ours."

Ash clapped his hands, something wry in his smile. "That's right, Alexis. We couldn't be happier that you're here, could we, everyone?"

The entire group nodded, smiling as they stood to make introductions.

Zee filled me in on the names of the children, Connor and Kallie who belonged to Sebastian and Shea, Adia and Brendon who belonged to Lyrik and Tamar, and the tiny baby girl, Sadie, who was Austin and Edie's.

Ash caught me totally off guard when he suddenly swooped me up in an overbearing hug, flinging me around like a rag doll. "Welcome to the freak show, darlin'. Admission is free, but you don't ever get to leave."

"Oh my God, you did not." Willow shoved her husband in the shoulder. Her expression was a mixture of fond disbelief and sheer horror.

Ash jostled to the side, righting himself, stretching his hulking, tattooed arms wide, continuing with a story I was a little horrified of, too. But it was done with so much natural warmth it was hard not to fall into the comfort of it.

"What? It was our boy Zee's twenty-first birthday. What did you expect me to do? That was nothing but my own responsibility."

Zee had settled into some kind of mood I didn't recognize. So casual and calm. Laid back.

He glanced at me with a smile playing all over that mouth. I couldn't keep my eyes off it, the memory of his kiss still rushing like a river through my veins.

He looked back at Ash, this sparring sarcasm dripping from his tone. "Last kind of birthday present I needed, man. Last kind. Flip on the light to my hotel room, ready to crash since you assholes kept me out all night, and here's this chick tied to my bed."

Incredulous, Ash scoffed. "Last kind of birthday present you needed? What the hell are you talking about, man? I'm pretty sure it was the only kind, considering I hadn't seen your ass with a girl the whole year since you'd joined Sunder. It was the least I could do."

I peeked over at Zee, wishing I could ask him more. Dig deeper into the subject we'd only touched on back at his place earlier.

I wanted to make sense of it. He was the sexiest thing I'd ever seen, and yet, he'd chosen to shun the attention that was clearly thrown at him at every turn.

No one-night stands. No relationships. Nothing at all.

It seemed impossible.

There are some things I can't tell you.

That admission taunted my mind. A flicker of that self-preservation I was lacking urged me to take heed.

Instead, I smiled and let myself get lost in the relaxed vibe. Because like Zee had said, if our time was running out, we needed to savor the moments we had.

Shea's mouth dropped open. "A stripper? Ash, what is wrong with you?"

Shea, Sebastian's wife, was adorable. Everything about her screamed country, from the red boots to the cute drawl that continually came from her mouth.

Sebastian nuzzled his nose in her hair. With the way he kept touching her, I got the feeling the man couldn't get close enough. "Ah, baby, you should know by now that's nothin' but tame for Ash. Zee's just lucky the asshole didn't have a prostitute waiting for him back in his room."

Zee shook his head, that cool easiness gliding out. "Uh, pretty sure the two were interchangeable. Let's just say stripping was entirely unnecessary since she was already lying there naked."

Ash pointed at Zee. "Again, you should be thanking me."

Oh my God. These guys were out of control.

I floated on their joy.

"Thanking you?" Zee shook his head. "Only thing I wanted was to hunt you down and strangle you. You should've seen the girl's face when I opened the door and asked her to leave. She thought it was some kind of sick role-play that she wasn't sure she wanted to play. You know, since I was doing my best to remain respectful with a parting 'please' and 'thank you'. Don't think she'd ever heard the words. You know me…the generous one who sent her right back up to your room. On my twenty-first birthday, nonetheless."

Ash stretched out his arms. "Well, what did you expect? She got a good look at me and the poor thing was hooked."

Willow just shook her head. Apparently, she was used to it and accepted the way her husband used to live before she'd become the center of his life. The guy had come with quite the reputation.

But it was Ash's younger sister, Edie, who covered her ears. "Ah, stop it. I don't need to hear anything about the crazy stuff that goes on while you're all out on the road."

Austin wound his arm around her shoulder and leaned close to her ear. "Went down," he emphasized, smiling down at the baby girl Edie held in her lap. "I think the key here is this is all in the past. But let's just say before I took Baz's spot, I was witness to some unsavory shit. Pretty sure Sunder wrote the book on bad behavior."

Zee was absolutely right. I couldn't help but love them. Couldn't stop my grin as I listened to them spar and tease. Their true affection for each other was apparent in every word, and I wondered what it might be like to be a part of it.

Shea laughed her sweet country laugh, though it was tinged with the slightest reprimand. "If I'd been around, I never would've let them pull that stuff in front of you, Austin. Shame on all you boys for being such bad influences."

Austin grinned, but there was something soft about it. Rimmed in a gratefulness that rushed to his expression when he glanced meaningfully at his older brother then back to Shea. "Think the guys here did the best they could, considering the circumstances. Only thing that matters is I turned out just fine."

His gaze dropped to his wife, just as low as his words. "Better than fine, actually."

"I love you." Her voice was less than a whisper as she mouthed it up at him, their lips meeting for a flash.

My spirit danced. Throbbed with the sweetness of it all.

How many stars had I wished on that one day a man might look at me that way?

I dropped my head when Zee looked my way and caught me staring at Austin and Edie and the obvious love they shared.

He reached out, his fingers gentle where they brushed along the sensitive skin of my forearm.

Eliciting chills.

Stoking hunger.

His voice was a soft murmur intended only for me. "Thank you so much for sharing this time with me. You don't know what it means."

eighteen
ZEE

We finally made it into the music room about two hours after Alexis and I had shown. It was the way it always was, all of us getting caught up in memories, joking around, my family enjoying the crazy awesome life they'd been granted.

All the while, their kids playing at their feet.

Baz was slouched back on the couch where he'd been watching the four of us hammer out a song that needed to be tweaked before we hit the stage.

Just like every tour, we'd be kicking this one off here in LA at our favorite old theater. It was just about as much a tradition as the shots Ash had us tossing back after every show.

It was the theater where Sunder had been discovered. The theater where Anthony had first talked to Baz after Sunder had gotten their first big break and opened for a huge band back in the day.

It was the same night Lyrik's life had come crashing down.

Crazy how that old saying remained true. One door closes and another door opens. At the time, I seriously doubted Lyrik would've chosen the door his mistakes had led him through.

But ultimately, that door had led him to Tamar. Ties had been made that night. Aspirations set. Goals kicked into play.

It was where it all had begun. Always had seemed a fitting starting line.

Sweat slicked my back and brow, and I lifted the hem of my shirt to wipe it, trying to gather my breaths that had been pounded out during the session.

"Hell yeah, that was killer." Ash tugged his teeth over his bottom lip as he set his bass on its stand. "All that speculation about Sunder going dry? Getting too soft to kick ass? Washed up? Now that is just about the most offensive shit the paps have ever gone on about. If they know one thing about us, they should know we always, always kick ass. That's just one thing that hasn't and won't ever go out of style."

Lyrik roughed a hand through his sweat-drenched hair. "Yeah. Some things do indeed remain the same. And if that's our one constant? I'll take it. No complaints here, man."

Austin was all gloating grins as he chugged a bottle of water. "Hey, you assholes got me on board in place of the big brother. Did anyone seriously think we wouldn't be killing it for the rest of our days once I took the stage? Now maybe if Baz wouldn't have stepped down, we might be tellin' a different story."

Baz pointed at him. "Oh, you wish, little brother. I was the one who got the train barreling down the tracks. You just hopped on like a hobo snagging a free ride."

"Hobo?" Austin went for him, throwing a bunch of fake blows to the side of Baz's face that Baz deflected like an old pro.

"Who's calling who a hobo? Considering your lazy ass spends half your time at the beach on Tybee Island," Austin taunted as he jumped around, throwing those jabs and just missing his brother's face.

Baz lifted his hands, palms out. "Hey, don't be jealous I get to chill. I put in all the hard work at the beginning, and now I get to kick back and reap the rewards."

Lyrik scoffed, voice brimming with sarcasm. "At thirty-one. Man, all those strenuous years of hard work you put in…don't know how you survived it."

Baz chuckled. "Watch it, dude, or next time you all want to crawl to my place in Savannah to record your next album, I'm all of a sudden gonna be all booked up."

Ash gasped, hand over his heart. "You wouldn't dare."

"Oh, you know he would," Austin razzed.

You'd think with the way they went directly for the throat, there would be some hard feelings. But there was nothing but support bounding from the walls that were made for acoustics, their words an echo of encouragement as they bounced and played.

I was struck by a wave of regret.

Mark should have been here. A part of this.

I gritted my teeth, trying to hold back the rush of memories, but it was like sitting at that piano had set them free. The questions I'd done my best at dodging.

I'd accepted the path I'd been given and traveled it without question. Without any of those distractions or diversions.

Just like it applied to Lyrik? One door had been slammed in my face, and I'd been shoved through another by all the fucked-up mistakes I'd made.

Those mistakes pummeled me, right hook after right hook.

What if Mark were there? What if I hadn't pushed him over the edge? What if he had a *family*?

Regret burned hot, and I attempted to shake it off while I focused on reorganizing all my shit I kept here at Ash's. Made it easy, each of us having instruments at each other's pads so we could play whenever inspiration struck. Usually at the drop of a dime.

Same way as the music came.

As a feeling.

An emotion.

When we were pissed and dealing with heavy shit or when we were floating with the clouds, blissed out when something amazing had come our way.

I suddenly felt the stare burning a hole in the side of my face. "So…Alexis, huh?"

This from Ash, the bastard. Had no clue how the asshole had restrained himself this long.

I shrugged. "We're friends."

"Really?" It was all a challenge.

Did my best to pass it off with a shrug, reining in the urge to lash out and at the same fucking time finally come clean. "Yep. Ran into her a couple weeks ago."

And by ran, I meant I ran after her like some kind of twisted fuck. Like they needed that kind of ammunition.

"You 'ran' into her?"

So maybe that was obvious.

"Yep."

"And?" he pressed.

"And we just…kind of hit it off. She's super cool. She wants to learn how to play piano, so I'm going to teach her. Besides, that piece of shit is still out there running free after what he did to her. Wouldn't be able to sleep at night if I thought she was down there, getting herself into trouble again."

Silence struck the room like the ring after a bomb.

Deafening.

Baz looked at me like the dude was trying to climb right inside me. "You're gonna teach her to play piano?"

I gave a tight nod.

He roughed a hand down his face and glanced away before that gray gaze locked on me, voice laced with caution. "How long's it been, Zee?"

I turned away. "Doesn't matter."

Baz stood. "You're really gonna stand there and pretend it doesn't?"

Anger and regret and guilt bottled in my throat. A dangerous cocktail. "Just…don't, man."

Ash shook his head in some kind of pity. "Come on. You're really going to pull this after the bullshit we've all been through? You've seen us at our lowest. Stood by us when we were making every mistake in the damned book. And that whole time we were making those mistakes? There you were…sober. Taking care of us. Going it alone like it was your responsibility."

It *was* my responsibility, but he didn't need to know that.

"Never once since the day you stepped into your brother's shoes have I ever seen you with a girl, not since you broke up with whatever that chick's name was when you were just a kid. And don't pretend like you didn't have an endless string of women just begging for your attention. And then you bring a girl into the fold and you're gonna actually stand there and act like it's nothin'?"

Just the fact he was mentioning Julie made me want to crawl right the hell out of my skin.

"I didn't say it didn't mean anything."

Ash grinned, all teeth. "Now don't go and get me wrong, because I am one happily married man, but that is one smoking hot woman. And the way she's looking at you? Pretty sure the two of you are getting ready to go *BAM*."

Fucker actually clapped his hands together.

His smirk grew. "And then you go and leave her with our girls for the last two hours? You're in so much trouble, dude. Might as well hand over your balls, because I'm willing to toss down some Benjamins that girl has you by the dick."

Trying a new tactic, I forced a grin. "You should know better than that, Ash, considering I'm the one who always ends up with all your dough."

Austin chuckled from where he was leaning against the wall. "Except for the bedrooms, Zee…except for the pink and blue bedrooms. You totally blew that bet, brother."

Years back when Ash had purchased the mansion in Savannah, Shea had bet him he'd be painting all the upstairs bedrooms pink and blue and filling them with a herd of baby Ashes.

I'd been a fool to bet against her. But at the time, I sure as hell didn't think Ash would be settling down. It was a loss I'd gladly take.

Still, I played along, defending my bad bet through laughter. "Only one room so far. Shea has yet to win that bet—she said *all* the rooms. There are seven of them. Our boy Ash here has some work to do."

Lyrik laughed. "Give him time, Zee, give him time."

Baz set his hand on my shoulder. "Come on, Zee. Time to fess it up, because from where I'm standing, I don't see what the problem is."

Our conversation was cut short by the door cracking open.

Thank God.

I had no idea how to answer their questions. Had no response for what had changed or why I'd been that way in the first place. For years, they'd razzed me, giving me shit left and right. But it'd always been off-handed, in the end the lot of them letting me rest in peace.

Peace was about the farthest thing from what I felt.

Especially when in came a tumble of gorgeous women with even prettier hearts. They slipped into the attached sitting area off to the front of the big space that served as Ash's music room.

But it was the one who came in behind Shea that stole my breath.

Literally.

Her eyes found mine and she lifted her hand in a small, timid wave, just a curl of her fingers before she followed Shea the rest of the way in.

Seeing her standing there in the mix of the women who'd come to mean the most to me felt like that was exactly where she was supposed to be. Like she belonged.

Shea plopped into one of the plush couches. "Hope y'all don't mind us interrupting, but we figured if Alexis came all the way over here to spend the evening with us, she could at least get a glimpse at our sexy men doing what they do best."

Ash feigned a mortal wound, a stab right to the heart. Dude was always such a damned clown. "Oh, my poor, beautiful Shea. If you really think *this* is what we do best, then your boy Baz here is doing it all wrong."

Baz smacked Ash on the back of the head. "You only wish I had it all wrong. Shea here just didn't want to embarrass the rest of you assholes in front of your girls. You know, just being thoughtful. That's all. Though, I'm sure my wife has a hard time not bragging to her sisters about just how good my best is."

"Don't worry, baby, I always let the girls know how well my man keeps me satisfied." Shea didn't even hesitate to shout the flirt at her husband.

His lip curved at the edges, somehow soft and hard. "That's what I thought. My woman wouldn't know how to tell a lie that big, anyway."

She pressed her hand over her heart, country drawl dripping with the innuendo. "Oh, no…I could never tell a lie that *big*."

Tamar cracked up and raised her glass in Shea's direction. They clinked them in the middle. "Oh, yeah. Now that's exactly what I like to hear. Men that look like that and satisfy. I do believe we hit the jackpot."

"Heck yes," Shea agreed, taking a big gulp of her wine.

Willow and Edie giggled behind their hands, both of them turning red with the way Shea and Tamar went back and forth. Two of them should be used to it by now.

But it was the expression on Alexis's face that washed through me like a ravaging flood.

Overpowering emotion gripped tight between us. Pulling and pulling and pulling.

Something soft and tender and sweet.

Fueled by faith and conviction that all the good things in this world waited on the wings. Just waiting to be captured.

Like she saw all that good shimmering like dazzling flashes of light on the fringes of the room.

Got the feeling she was doing her best to pour that belief into me.

Urging me to see it.

To reach out and take it.

Fuck. I had no idea how to process it. The fact that I

wanted to, knowing I couldn't, and still dipping my fingers in for a taste anyway.

Knew full well this was going to lead to disaster.

Maybe it was selfish, but it felt like these stolen moments with Alexis might just be worth it.

"Think we're gonna call it a night. Need to get Alexis home."

Shea pouted. "So soon?"

I looked at the watch around my wrist. "It's midnight."

"See, it's early," Tamar added.

I widened my eyes at both of them. "And you're planning on keeping Willow up all night when she needs to rest and get up her strength for having that baby?"

Okay, so maybe that was a low blow. A little on the manipulative side. Because just like I knew he would, Ash jumped into action.

"Out. Everyone out." Ash was all spastic arms as he gave Baz and Lyrik a little nudge. "Know you all can't stand the thought of not being in my presence since a little Ash always makes everything better, but it's high time I carry my girl upstairs and tuck her in bed so I can rub her feet and her back and her belly. Then if she's up for it, I might show her a little more of what *I* do best."

Willow frowned at her feet. Well, in that direction at least, because I was fairly certain she couldn't see them. "But they're ugly and swollen."

Ash tsked. "Not even, darlin'. Every inch of you is as gorgeous as the day I met you, and I won't ever be able to look away."

Swore the girl swooned, and it made me fucking happy that the two of them had found each other. Also made me want to rip at my hair and grind my teeth, and the last thing I needed was for my brothers to catch onto the vibe I was feeding.

I lifted my jaw in Alexis's direction, wishing I didn't have the vision of stalking across the space and taking her in my arms rolling through my head. Kissing her like I had earlier.

This time not stopping.

"You ready?"

Her nod seemed reluctant. "Sure."

She said her goodbyes, hugging and talking with the girls like it was the most natural thing as she told them how amazing it was to meet them, how thankful she was she got to share in their night.

She whispered something quietly to Willow, her expression so soft, her hand a gentle sweep down Willow's belly as her teeth caught on her bottom lip.

Like she might be dreaming of the day that might be her.

Did it make me a bastard that the thought of it cut me to the core?

Jealousy fisted my hands. Couldn't even stand the idea of her with another man.

Shining all that goodness on him. Not when I felt desperate to keep all that light for myself. Like she could ever be mine to keep.

Jesus. What was wrong with me?

I huffed out a breath in an attempt to clear my head, clapped Ash and Lyrik on the back, then bumped Austin's fist as I told them I'd see them tomorrow.

Baz slowed my steps with a hand on my forearm. "You good?" he asked.

"Of course."

Motherfucking lie. It always was. And I think it had always been Baz who'd known it ever since the day I'd shown at his door with a pack slung on my back and agony in my heart.

Baz narrowed his eyes to study me. Finally, he gave me a reluctant nod. "See you later."

"Yup." I headed toward Alexis. As I approached, she turned in my direction. Like she could feel that connection tighten. Drawing us closer. A tense, keening wire.

She smiled up at me. Softly. That expression alone hit me square in the chest.

"Let's get you out of here."

I weaved her fingers through mine, not having any clue where we were gonna go from there. But for just a little while,

I was going to embrace it, her, every fucking thing.

No fear.

Just life.

I led her back through the rambling expanse of Willow and Ash's house.

Without saying a word, I clicked open the front door and she followed me out into the night. It was dense and dark and heavy.

Something foreign thrummed through my veins, an exhilaration and joy I hadn't felt in a long time. So long that I wondered if it could even be real or if I was just getting caught up in a trap that was only going to ruin me in the end.

Because I had two loyalties. And this girl couldn't be one of them.

But that didn't stop the purpose in our footsteps as I led her down the big concrete steps. The night sky opened up like a dark, magnetic sea as we stepped out from beneath the cover of the veranda and down onto the walkway.

I could hear her gasp in a breath. Could feel the tension of her hand as it squeezed against mine.

When I turned, I found Alexis with her face upturned, basking in the beauty as she watched the faint trickle of a star burning out.

"Did you make a wish?" My question grated out.

Alexis dropped her face back down to look at me, wonder in her eyes. "Don't you know falling stars aren't for wishing on? They're a wish finally falling free. Somewhere out there…someone has a wish coming true."

That statement alone was almost enough to drop me straight to my knees. Could barely form the admission as I wondered how the fuck this girl was so damned perfect. "Used to think that…back before I realized they were just people's wishes coming to an end. Fizzling out."

She stared up at me in that way that tightened my guts and made me feel like I was standing on uneven ground. "Maybe you've just forgotten how to wish."

That space between us swelled, and her voice dipped in this

wistfulness that cut me straight through.

"If we don't believe in miracles, then what do we have left?"

"Lex…" I pulled her toward me. "Why is it you feel like a miracle?"

She buried her face in my shirt, both her hands clinging to me, her voice the softest praise. "You are the miracle, Zee. You were there in the moment I needed you most."

I ran my fingers through her hair, let them brush down over that star tattoo I knew was etched on her neck, and murmured the words at the top of her head. "I want to be, Lex. I want to be there."

"Thank you so much for bringing me tonight. You were right. I…loved your friends. Every crazy ounce of them."

"Guess it means you fit right in, doesn't it?" My heart ached with just how perfectly she did.

She laughed a soggy sound and hugged me tighter. "Goofball."

I rubbed her back, both loving and hating how standing beneath the stars with her felt so natural.

Finally, I shook myself out of it and helped her back into the helmet. I straddled my bike and kicked over the engine. Never letting go of her hand, I helped her on and tucked her close so that sweet, sweet body clung to mine.

Warmth and heat and all things right.

The bike rumbled, just as deep and fierce as the rumble rolling in my chest. I clutched her hands to my stomach that quivered with need.

"Hold on tight," I told her.

Her answer came as a breath across the shell of my ear. "I won't let go."

Something about the way she said it sounded like a promise. A promise I ached to keep but could never receive.

I took to the street, cool night air whipping at our faces. The girl clutched me a little tighter. Like she couldn't get close enough. Swore I could feel her heart hammering at my back, just as sure as she could feel my heart hammering in my chest.

It thundered and roared and increased.

I needed to get away from her. Take her home and drop her at the door where I couldn't hurt her. Before I got too close to those places that I couldn't go.

But her car was back at my place. Another bad move I'd made in this no-win game.

Fifteen minutes later, I slowed in front of my building, fingers quick to punch in the code to the ground-level garage. My bike vibrated and grumbled as I slowly edged inside.

The garage door automatically slid shut behind us as I pulled into my reserved space, stretched out my feet, and killed the engine.

Silence.

It was a silence so thick and charged I felt like I could see it weaving around us, echoing back with lust and questions and need.

Alexis shivered when I helped her stand. Her legs were shaking, and with the way my blood went pounding, I knew it wasn't just from the ride. She was feeling this, too.

I climbed off my bike, and my fingers brushed the silky softness of her skin as I again helped her free of the constraints of the helmet. She released a breathy, needy sigh. The warmth skated my skin and sent a thrill rushing through my veins.

"My bag is still inside your loft." It sounded like both a warning and a confession.

"Yeah," I uttered.

I swallowed hard like it might hold back some of this emotion threatening to spiral out of control. I clutched her hand, trying to remind myself of all the reasons I couldn't give into this. Of all the reasons I couldn't step over the line.

I tried to remember exactly who I would be betraying and exactly what I had to lose.

Neither of us said a word as we climbed into the elevator. Metal doors slid shut, closing us in, and with it, closing off air. Closing off sanity and reason and the fading sense of wrong and right.

Keep my hands to myself.

That was all I had to do.

I'd told her I'd try.

But this girl? She made me crazy with need, the way I was breathing her staggered breaths and she was breathing mine.

Energy lifted around us.

Shimmering and bright.

Alive and demanding.

Just as demanding as the plea of my body when I suddenly spun and pinned her against the mirrored wall. My hands were planted above her head, and her tight, sweet body was flush with mine.

A rush of shocked air gushed from between her lips. Blue eyes wide and needy as she looked up at me and locked those tiny hands in the fabric of my shirt. "Zachary."

She begged it like a plea.

Like devotion.

Flames leapt between us.

Hot.

I gripped both sides of her neck, this girl in the palm of my hands.

Her pulse ran wild, and my dick grew hard. Just as damned desperate as the rest of me.

Her voice was a whisper. "No fear. Just life."

No fear. Just life.

And God, just for a little while, I wanted to know what it would feel like to be alive.

My mouth crashed against hers. Hard and demanding against all her sweet, sweet belief.

She opened and gave.

nineteen

ALEXIS

Warm, insistent lips pressed against mine, his body hard and big and straining as he pressed me harder against the elevator wall.

My head spun and my hands tightened in his shirt. Desperate to hold on to this moment.

My heart sped and careened, and I lifted up on my toes in a bid to get closer. To fall inside and get lost in that sacred place where I might discover all his secrets.

Where I could live on his brilliance.

Zachary groaned, and his touch became urgent, as if he wanted to erase every inch that separated us. Connect us in every way.

Those big hands were on my neck, gliding up and leaving a streak of chills on my skin as he took me possessively by the jaw. He held me steady as he nipped at my bottom lip. The plush warmth of his mouth coaxed and pled. He turned to do the same to my upper lip.

Commanding. Taking. Demanding.

Reservations gone.

Desire bloomed, bright and blinding.

It pulled a gasp from my lungs, and every part of me gave when he deepened the kiss.

His tongue stroked against mine.

Fire and consuming light.

Different from earlier.

Because while that felt like an accident, this felt like giving in.

Every intention became frantic. A chaotic need surged in the air and lit in our blood. I grappled to get him closer, my fingers frenzied as I attempted to touch him everywhere.

I traced across the ink on his arms, over the strength of his shoulders, and down the expanse of that wide, wide chest.

Right over the roar of his conflicted, captivating heart.

Did he feel mine? The way it thundered and kicked and begged?

Stomach tight with want, I wound my arms around his neck. He hitched me higher and pinned me to the wall with his hips. Fingers sank into the flesh of my thighs as he wrapped my legs around his waist.

A needy whimper left me when he rocked against my center, his cock hard and prominent as he ground against me, coaxing me into a frenzy of desire.

We reeled.

Both of us staggered by the sudden power of that irresistible connection that had steadily built.

A breaking point.

A chasm that couldn't be crossed.

So instead, we fell.

The elevator dinged and the doors slid open.

"Hold tight," he muttered, still kissing me madly, refusing to let me go.

He fumbled in his pocket, freed his keys, and twisted the lock. He kicked one side of the metal doors open, then kicked it closed just as fast, carrying me into the darkened depths of his loft.

Never breaking that kiss.

A hazy light filtered in from the huge bank of windows overlooking city and sky, and somehow I knew he was drawn to it, his footfalls guiding us in that direction, to the beauty that abounded and waited in the heavens.

Waiting for him to reach out and take it.

I shivered when cool glass hit my back.

"Zachary," I whispered against his lips, still kissing him just as wildly as he was kissing me.

It was as if something inside him had been unhinged. Freed. Something he'd been missing and had somehow found in me.

"Lex…God…Lex."

His dick pressed eagerly against my jeans. I felt like I was burning up, from the inside out, flames lapping at my spirit, at my soul, while this boy's possessive touch singed and marked my skin from the outside.

I moaned when he dragged down the collar of my flimsy shirt, yanking down the cup of one side of my bra at the same second. Cool air hit my skin, and my nipple pebbled, tight with anticipation.

Zee edged back and took the flesh into his mouth.

Hot and wet and perfect.

Sensation spun, a live wire that stroked the desire that consumed me, every cell. I writhed against his solid length while he lapped and sucked until his hand was back on my face, his mouth on mine, kissing me like he meant it.

"You are so beautiful. So goddamned beautiful." The words lived in the middle of our kiss. Meshing and twining with every lap and lick. "Can't get you out of my mind, Lex. Doesn't matter how hard I try, I can't get you out. You've gotten under my skin. So deep. So fucking deep."

My fingers sank into the bristling muscle of his shoulders. "Why would you want to stop thinking of me? Don't you feel this?"

His voice was pained. "Don't you get it yet? That's the problem. I feel *everything.* I want you so goddamned bad, and I can't ever have you."

I was swept up in a sudden overwhelming emotion.

This boy.

This boy.

This giving boy who I knew would have given his life for me. Without a name or a reason or any proof I might deserve his mercy.

My kiss turned tender. So tender as I caressed the lines and curves of his gorgeous face. "Why wouldn't you deserve me? You *saved* me."

His hold cinched tighter on my hips, his body rocking in a slow, needy arc. His teeth ground as he rubbed his cock against the heat burning at the center of my thighs. As if it caused him physical pain while I was certain I'd never felt anything so perfect.

"Tell me why you can't have me," I panted.

Grief struck in the depths of those bronze eyes. "Told you there are things you can't know. And fuck, Alexis…there are things you deserve that I just can't give you."

"Like what?"

He threaded his fingers in my hair. "You deserve someone who can love you the way you should be loved. Someone who can walk out the door with you on his arm and know he's got the best girl at his side and show the fucking world how great she is. You deserve a relationship. A man to come home to. Tell me that isn't something you want. Tell me it isn't something you've been looking for. I know you well enough, if you deny wanting those things, it'll only be a lie."

I blinked at him. "Of course it's something I want. Something I've been looking for my whole life."

"And you haven't found that guy yet?" Was it anger that flashed through the storm in his eyes?

I gulped around the emotion that suddenly clogged the base of my throat. "No. I've just always known I'd feel when it was real. I've had boyfriends…a couple who were kind of serious. But none of them have ever made me feel the way I knew I'd feel when I met the one who was meant for me."

Zee kept rocking against me. A needy, desperate sway.

So close to driving me out of my mind. And I was feeling all those things I'd anticipated when I just knew…this breathtaking sensation that I was falling. Falling fast and hard.

What I never anticipated was the fear that would come with it. I guess I'd just never known what it would feel like for my heart to truly be at risk.

I was torn between begging him to bridge the gap between us and pushing him away as a wave of horror swelled in my chest as that nagging question I tried to disregard refused to be ignored.

I forced out the raspy words. "Before we move any further, I need to know one thing. Tell me this isn't cheating."

His strong jaw trembled. "No."

Relief. It hit me on all sides.

Should I feel it?

I didn't know. Because something about his response and reservations felt off. Wrong. While everything else felt perfectly right. This road ours. Purposed.

I cupped his face, forcing him to look at me when I kissed him softly. Reverently.

Before I took a leap of faith because I'd always believed faith would catch me. "Then I don't care what's standing between us as long as we have right now."

He roughed his hands up the outside of my thighs, his heart slamming at his ribs as his fingers sank into the soft flesh of my ass, pulling me closer to his straining body.

He groaned, and I swore his eyes rolled back in his head. "Fuck…you feel so good. Too good."

The softest giggle rolled up my throat, something awed and confused and elated. My voice was a trembling, breathy mess of lust and emotion. "You're barely touching me."

Somehow, that felt like a lie. I could feel him everywhere.

Low laughter rumbled in his chest, and there was something dark about it, something both regretful and amazed when he buried his face in my neck and murmured the words, "You have no idea, Lex. No idea what just touching you like this does to me. I could die a happy man right now…but we need to stop."

The frenzy had worn off, and my senses slowly came back into focus. I chewed at my lip, finding restraint in a moment I wanted to let go most. "You're probably right. We should slow down. I'm not exactly a one-night stand kind of girl."

And I was sure once I gave that part of myself to him, I'd never fully recover when he was gone.

Guess I had a little self-preservation, after all.

Chuckling, he ran a knuckle down the side of my cheek. "No?"

My head shook, and I could feel the soft smile playing around my mouth. "No."

"That's good, because I'm not much of a one-night stand kind of guy."

I looked up at his stunning face, my insides trembling with the need to know him.

Would he ever let me?

"What kind of guy are you?"

His teeth ground, hands tensing on my hip, as if warring over what to give. Slowly he lowered me to my feet, his touch so tender as he helped to resituate my clothing. He peeked up at me as he straightened my blouse back onto my shoulder.

"If I could be, I'd be a forever kind of guy. But I gave up my forever a long time ago."

Affection brimmed inside me, all tangled with hurt and worry for this broken boy. Wishing there was a way to fix it, whatever it was.

I cleared my throat and stepped away from him. "I should probably get going. It's late."

He stepped back to put more distance between us. "You probably should or I might not let you leave."

I headed for my bag, peering back at the man who watched me softly as I went. I could feel his eyes tracing me, caressing me just as sure as his hands. Remnants of desire trembled beneath the surface of my skin.

My body already hooked.

Needy for his touch.

I nearly jumped out of my skin when my phone started ringing from my bag. "Oh…crap…I didn't even realize I'd left it."

I guess that's what happened when you got wrapped up in a hypnotizing boy—you forget yourself.

I fumbled through my bag to find my phone. It glowed where it sat on the bottom, and all that desire I'd been feeling scattered in a bluster of wind like the last of autumn's fallen leaves.

Avril.

I swallowed hard in attempt to steel myself for her call. I never knew what was going to be waiting for me on the other end. What I did know was it never was good.

Hands shaking, I accepted the call and pushed it to my ear, turning away from Zee because somehow I couldn't stand to see him watching me as I took this call.

"Avril," I said, voice low.

Sobs echoed on the other end. "I need you."

Of course she did.

"I told you, you need to stop doing this." I'd been telling her for years.

"I just need something to eat."

My head dropped, fingers on my temples, knowing her excuse amounted to nothing but a lie. "At one in the morning?"

"Please."

"Damn it, Avril." It was a sigh of surrender. She knew it well.

She started to ramble. "Thank you so much, Alexis. After this time, I won't ask you anymore. I promise. I just…need something to get me through the night."

Agony clutched every cell in my body.

I knew what she meant. Where she'd slipped. What it was she really was needing.

Guilt locked in my chest when I told her to meet me at the same intersection I'd met her at the last time—the day Zee had followed me and somehow set all this in motion.

I ended the call.

Silence swamped the open space, filling it like black waters that lapped and churned and raged.

Goose bumps lifted at my nape when I felt the puff of air exhaled at the back of my neck, blowing through the matted strands of my hair as his rage trickled down my spine like a warning.

"That was your sister?"

Shivers rushed.

I should feel fear. But the only thing I felt was safety in his anger. Comfort in his dread.

"She needs me," I whispered, hating that I sounded so helpless. But in this situation, that was exactly what I was.

He snaked an arm around my waist so his hand was against my stomach as he yanked me back against the hard planes of his chest.

His mouth was at my cheek. "And what if I need you? What if I need you safe? What if I need you to stay out of that side of town so I don't end up in prison?"

I felt the truth of his threat.

The words were thick. "I feel her, Zee. When she hurts, I do, too, and I know exactly what it is she's feeling. I can't ignore that. Not for me. Not for you."

Torment. I felt it. His and mine. As if he somehow could understand what it was like to be in this position, he tightened his hold, every inch of him still hard, maybe harder as his muscles bristled with this barely contained storm that threatened to spin out of control.

"I won't let him hurt you. Told you that night. Not ever again." His second hand wound around me, belted around my waist. "You know I'm coming with you."

There was no question behind it.

And I think I knew right then—If Zee made a promise, he was going to keep it.

twenty
ZEE

I pried the keys out of her trembling hands. Shocked, she looked up at me. Anguish swam in the deep wells of blue that were normally so bright.

I opened the passenger door. "Get in."

"I can drive."

I grabbed her hand, pressed it flat across my chest where it vibrated and quaked. "No way, Alexis. You actually think I'm going to let you get behind the wheel when you're in this state?"

Problem was, I'd put down bets she'd done it a hundred times before. All that time, this girl hadn't had someone to stand by her side.

Her gaze swept over me as she edged forward, and she nodded slow as she folded herself in the passenger seat. I leaned in, buckling her seatbelt as this insane sense of protectiveness swelled.

A storm building in the distance. Ready to consume.

Every inch of me tightened, my jaw clenching as I started to lean back out and instead got tripped up on her gorgeous, trusting face.

I cupped her cheek. "You really think I'm gonna let you go out there alone?"

Her head shook. "No."

"I just…I'm not normally like this when she calls. So shook up. I…" She trailed off, her gaze dropping to her lap.

"You what?"

Her eyes fluttered back up. "After that night—"

She swallowed, her confession raw. "It changed me, Zee. He made me fear things I'd never stopped long enough to fear before. I hate feeling this way."

Anger bristled and burned and twisted my guts. I wanted to hunt the fucker down. Take him out. Wipe his stain from the earth.

I hated for even a second he'd held power over her belief and faith.

I framed her sweet face in my hands, my mouth an inch from hers, our stares locked. "No fear. Just life."

A single tear slid from the corner of her eye. "You're the one who gave it back to me. Ensured I didn't lose it at the risk of your own. Words don't contain the power to describe what that means to me. How it affected me."

She grappled for my hand and set it over the thunder of her heart. "How you marked me right here."

My spirit thrashed the lyrics of her song. One that was hard and confused and so utterly soft. Where the words held too much power and said all the things I'd never be allowed to say.

"I know, Lex. I know. That night changed me, too."

And there was no chance in hell I'd ever let something like that happen again. Not to her.

Not ever.

I rounded the back of her car and hopped in the driver's seat, turned over the ignition, and took to the street. Darkness blew passed the windows like the rush of a nightmare as we headed in the direction of what had gone down that night.

Memories of my brother inundated my mind, slamming me with a violence strong enough to cut me in two. Part of me had hated him for what he'd put me through. For the worry and the sleepless nights and the betrayals that I'd taken like a personal insult.

Funny how, in the end, my treacheries had been so much greater than his.

There'd been no time for apologies. No time for explanations. No time to tell him I'd take it all back.

Because all his time was gone. Just like time was fleeting for me and Alexis.

I fought against the onslaught of it all, knuckles white where I death-gripped the wheel, teeth grinding so hard I was sure they'd be nothing but powder.

A soft hand touched my forearm. "Don't blame her."

How could Alexis know? Could she feel that I wanted to shake her? Scream at her that it was no fucking use and tell her never to give up in the same breath?

Did she know?

Every nerve in my body was on edge when I jerked her car into a parking lot in front of a shitty 24-hour convenience store. It sat like some kind of twisted portal into a pit filled with nothing but the vile.

God knew I'd been down there too many times.

That possessiveness and protectiveness lapped into a flame as I thought of how many times this girl had traipsed down to this side of town in the middle of the night.

She clicked open her door. My hand shot to her arm. "Don't move."

I got out and went to her side. My attention was sharp, darting around the area, calculating every face and every intention.

It finally landed on the worn-down girl huddled against the wall of a building across the street, her silhouette just outside the reach of the streetlamp.

She stepped from the shadows, and I tried to rein in the anger I felt that Alexis had to deal with this bullshit, too.

When Alexis saw her sister, she unlatched her door, and I held it open while she stumbled out.

Avril crossed the street with her hands stuffed in her pockets. "You came."

Grief shivered through Alexis. Palpable and ripe. "One day I won't. But the fact that I'm here means I haven't given up on you."

Avril's chin quivered. "I don't know what will happen to me that day. When you give up on me. Stop loving me."

Emotion charged between them.

God. This was brutal.

Alexis fisted her hand over her chest. "You know I won't ever stop loving you. But I don't know how much longer I can keep doing this. Every time I see you, you take a little piece of me with you. I can't keep going until there's nothing left. I can't keep putting myself in danger just because that's where *you* are."

Avril shrank into herself, voice small. "You know I don't want to be this person."

Alexis took a pleading step toward her. "Then don't be. Come with us. Right now. We'll get you out of here, and you don't ever have to come back."

Jerking like she was struck with a sudden bolt of fear, Avril peered over her shoulder, into the shadows she'd stepped from before she turned back to Alexis.

Nervously, she whispered even lower than she had before. "You know it's not as simple as that. He'll find me."

Rage punched me in the gut.

It was that moment when I finally realized what Avril was saying. How abhorrently tied she was to this piece of shit.

Dread sank to the pit of my stomach.

Is that why that scumbag had Alexis pinned against that grimy wall in the first place? Thinking he might be able to draw her into that life. Or was he simply willing to guard his *possessions*, at any cost, thinking his best bet was getting Alexis out of his way?

I gripped two handfuls of hair, trying to keep it in check

when I turned to look over my shoulder. Searching and seeking.

A breeze rustled through. A beer can clattered as it rolled along the deserted lot across the street, the only sound breaking up the thick haze of silence.

I looked back to see Alexis grip Avril by the forearm. "He doesn't own you."

Sadness spun across Avril's features. "That's where you're wrong."

Avril swallowed hard and held out her hand, palm up.

Sorrow filtered out with Alexis's resigned sigh before she turned and sifted through her bag and came back out with a wad of cash. She set it in Avril's hand but didn't let go.

Motherfuck.

This was too much.

"I love you," Alexis finally said before she released her hold and Avril took a step back.

"I know. I love you, too."

Avril took two more steps backward, eyes locked on the girl who sank deeper and deeper into my spirit with every selfless piece she revealed.

This gorgeous girl who allowed herself to be used up just like her sister, though in an entirely different way.

I couldn't stomach it. Not for a second longer. I took a step toward Avril, my voice low and urgent. "Come with us. I'll take care of you. Protect you. I won't let that bastard touch you. Not ever again."

Avril finally looked up at me, like she just realized I was there. I was just another inconsequential face in the many that passed her by in her quest to survive. She laughed. Cold and hollow. "That's not how it works."

She turned away, quickly looked both ways, and darted across the street.

We watched her in silence until she disappeared. The second she did, I rushed for Alexis, held her up when she slumped in my hold. She clung to my shirt, tears seeping into the fabric. "It hurts, Zee. It hurts so bad."

I ran my hand down the back of her head. "I know, baby, I know."

My attention moved around the lot, back to the store. There was a tweaked-out guy hanging out against the hood of his car, watching us with too much interest. "Come on, let's get you out of here. You don't belong down here."

"Neither does she."

"No," I agreed. But right then, it didn't seem to be anything Avril was willing to change.

Alexis let me help her back into the car, and I quickly shut her door and rounded to my side. I hopped in and turned over the ignition.

Putting it in gear, I flipped the car around. Our headlights sprayed out ahead of us, tossing light on the shadows where Avril had disappeared.

A damned spotlight that sent a scatter of rats running from the sewer.

Two men took off one direction, while three women cowered against the wall.

Avril was in the middle of them.

Rage burned hot when my sight landed on the bastard standing off to the side of them, eyes lit up like a demon in the flash that cut through the night. My muscles ticked and jerked, ready for a fight, my foot itching to slam on the gas.

He was right fucking there.

Alexis set her hand on my forearm, fear clogging her voice. "Don't. He's not worth it."

I squeezed the steering wheel tighter, trying to contain the violence spinning the axis of my world. The instinct to protect.

The asshole lifted his chin and an arrogant smirk took hold of his mouth.

Sickness clawed at my senses.

Because the bastard knew. He knew Alexis. He knew her car. He knew she'd come.

And without a doubt, he knew it wouldn't be the last time she came running back.

Nausea spun when I realized what it was he really wanted

from her.

He wanted to bind her and tie her. Make her a pawn in his sick, twisted world. Use up her body while men slowly killed her spirit and mind.

That was how these assholes worked. They saw someone who was vulnerable and innocent and viewed them as an opportunity.

I tore my attention from the piece of shit across the street and turned it on Alexis.

She stared back at me, blue eyes wide and frantic, an overpowering collision of sea and sky. Her hair was a mess from my fingers, her cheeks pink and stained with her tears.

"He might not be, but you are."

twenty-one

ALEXIS

Zee pulled my car into my narrow driveway. He'd brought me straight home, telling me he'd figure out how to get himself home.

I'd wanted to tell him I would drop him off. That after what he'd done for me, it was the least I could do. But how did you repay someone when you owed them your life?

Besides, right then, he didn't exactly seem like a man to be argued with.

He put the car in park and cut the engine. A hushed quiet filled the atmosphere. Darkness swept in. I was sure the tension bounding between us had become more powerful than it'd ever been.

Savage and stormy and somehow sweet.

He cut his eye toward me.

The boy was so severely beautiful it struck me like an arrow. Piercing and exquisite.

My body hummed as I was assaulted with the memory of the way he'd felt pressed against me. The weight of him. The feel of him. The magnitude of his kiss.

Sitting there, I felt as if I'd been on a rollercoaster with him tonight. Climbing the highest highs and diving to the lowest lows, twisting and turning and jerking and spinning.

Now I was experiencing that odd vertigo that set the entire world askew when the ride jolted to an abrupt stop.

I had no idea where it left us.

"It's late," he rumbled in that dark voice.

"Yeah. It is."

I snapped open my door, and he did the same. Quickly, he rounded to my side. I could feel him towering over me as he kept a step behind, his footsteps heavy as he followed me to my front door.

The night danced around us, sultry and mild. The exterior lamp hanging beside the door warmed the stoop in a golden glow, and my breaths became shallow when Zee reached around me and slid my key into the lock.

He turned the knob, and the door slowly swung open to the stilled darkness that waited on the other side.

I gazed back at him, wanting to see, to experience a little more of who this man might be.

His expressions were like a map that led directly to his conflicted heart. Turmoil rippled and rushed across his face, played across his lips and trembled in his fingers. Fingers he ran down the edge of my cheek.

"You terrify me, Alexis."

Drawn, I slowly shifted around to face him. Heat burned across my flesh. I could feel it radiating, seeping into the space between us. "I hate that I dragged you into my mess," I told him.

I hated more that I'd needed him there. With me. Beside me. I had no idea what would have happened tonight had he not been there. When Avril had called earlier, she had promised it would just be her. That I'd be safe.

Maybe I shouldn't have been surprised that, rather than her drawing me into the gulf of her sordid world, she'd brought it closer to me instead.

"And I hate you keep getting yourself deeper into it," he rumbled, erasing another inch between us.

My gaze was drawn to the heavy bob of his muscular throat when he swallowed. "You would've gone down there tonight by yourself had I not asked you to make me that promise."

In reluctance, I nodded. Not because I didn't want him to know, but because I wanted the truth to be different. "She calls…and I…I think about her out there alone. Scared. And I know I should refuse, tell her it's her own fault, but it seems tough love is tougher on me."

His stare touched deeper than anyone before him.

And I wanted it—him to see me.

"Does that make me weak?"

Fingertips traced across my lips. "What it makes you is the bravest, most selfless person I know."

He trailed them down, grazing my jaw and caressing down into the hollow of my throat.

My stomach fluttered, and the edge of his mouth kicked up. It would have almost been a teasing grin if it weren't for the rough protectiveness that slid out with it.

"It also makes you the most reckless person I know."

His jaw ticked. "You can't be putting yourself in danger. Not even for her. There are other ways to help her than to drop everything and run down there every time she calls you."

Everything swelled. Affection and worry. "I feel like I've done everything. I don't know what to do. I feel so…stuck. Helpless."

A strike of anger burst in his gaze. "The guy, the one who attacked you…"

Fear knotted in my chest, and I felt the tears gathering in my eyes. "I can't believe she had him with her. That she'd put me in that situation after what happened. She knew, Zee. She was there that night…before you got there. She saw what he was going to do to me."

"We need to go to the police with this. With a name. There has to be something they can do. That asshole was right fucking there, Alexis. Right there."

My chest clenched tighter. "You know we don't have a name. I have a face, and I described him to them. They said they'd do everything to find him, but I get this feeling it's more. That they're waiting on something. Trying to pin something bigger on him than what happened to me."

I could only imagine what kind of drug ring he was involved in. How deep his connections might go.

I could see it. His rage at my confession, and his hand tightened on my neck.

Possessively.

A quiver rocked through me.

"I just want it to end, Zee," I admitted through the exhaustion of it all. "I just want her to be okay. I don't want her to waste the life she's been given. Too many people do. It kills me she's making that choice."

Grief passed through his expression. "And it kills me you keep putting yourself in danger because of it. That you're taking chances with *your days*, Alexis."

Understanding coursed between us. "I don't want to waste them, either."

I meant it in more than one way.

I meant it for me, for him, for us.

I didn't want to waste whatever this was.

I thought maybe he felt it, because his palm flattened and slid lower so it was splayed wide across my chest, as if he were pulling energy from the beat of my heart and allowing it to sustain a part of him.

"Lex," he whispered. "What're you doing to me? Whatever it is, I can't stop it."

Flecks of bronze and gold shimmered in his dark, dark eyes. They appeared almost black in the shadows of the night.

Need spread beneath the weight of his hand, billowing out and sliding free.

I whimpered, and Zee shifted me, my back to his chest. His arm wound around my waist and he buried his face in my neck. "You make me fucking crazy, Alexis. Do you know that? I want to make you feel good. Just for one night…let me make you feel good."

He edged me forward. My door stood wide open. A beacon.

A shiver rolled down my spine as Zee bunched my hair up in his free hand and pressed kisses to the junction of my shoulder and neck, moving across the star I'd inscribed there as a reminder to never stop believing.

His voice was a rasp across my skin. "First time I came here, I knew it. Knew you were different. Knew I wasn't ever gonna be the same."

He kicked the door shut behind him.

His hand splayed wide across my belly that shivered and shook, the darkness swallowing us in its warmth. It was only broken by the swath of moonlight pouring in from the window.

He kissed behind my ear, teeth raking the lobe.

That desire that'd been subdued to a smolder flamed back to life.

I gasped when he suddenly turned me again and pushed me down onto the loveseat.

I clung to the fabric, squirming as the man stared down at me in the shadows.

"You were sitting right there," he said, so low, like a threat. "There I was, showing up to check on you, and the only damned thing I could think about was crawling over that tight body, pushing you back against the couch, and *sinking in*."

I shivered and my mind spun. "Take your shirt off."

Oh God. Where did that even come from? But I wanted it. To see him.

Because my own fantasies had been there, too.

Zee slowly reached down and pealed the tight tee up his body. He yanked it over his head and dropped it to the floor.

I swallowed around the lump that throbbed in my throat as my gaze stroked and caressed over every beautiful inch of him.

I'd said it before. This man was brilliant. Magnificent.

Inside and out.

His shoulders were wide and his skin was smooth where it

was stretched taught above the rigid, defined muscle that bristled underneath. His abdomen was flat and cut, lines carved and distinct as it tapered down to his narrow waist.

My mouth watered as I imagined tracing my tongue along those lines, tasting and touching and exploring.

But it was the ink etched on his skin that made my spirit lurch in a bid to bring him closer.

It was the first time I'd been able to take in the designs in their entirety, to understand what he had etched on his body like tribute and praise.

One arm was a tapestry of life, stars and a perfect, endless night.

The other was death. A dragon at the bottom of the deepest sea, the skulls of its victims piled like trophies at its feet.

Curved around one side of his collarbone was a simple tattoo that somehow felt incredibly profound, written in an almost medieval script

Relentless.

It was easy to see which of these two worlds he was chained to.

"You are beautiful." I could barely form the words.

The lowest chuckle slid out from his mouth. "If you saw everything hiding underneath, you'd know better."

"I don't believe you," I whispered where he towered over me in the shadows of the night.

He set both hands on the back of the couch on either side of my head, leaning in close and murmuring, "That's because *you are belief.*"

He slowly sank down to his knees.

Everything shivered. My body and the air and the foundation of my heart.

He set his hands on my knees. "That's because you're everything that's good. You think I don't see it, Alexis? Feel it? And I'm the bastard who can't stay away. Desperate for a taste."

He slid his palms higher, riding up the top of my thighs.

My belly trembled, and I sucked in a breath when his hot hands landed beneath the fabric of my shirt. He drew it up. A trail of goose bumps were left in his wake as he dragged the blouse over my head.

He tossed it aside and then slipped his hands behind my back, freeing the clasp of my bra, inching the straps free.

"Zachary."

"I'm going to make you feel good, Alexis. After tonight…I need to make you feel good." His fingers were on the button of my jeans, and I was gasping as he pulled them down, taking my underwear with them.

The man exposing me, inch by inch.

Chills lifted, that energy suffocating, almost too much to bear as his gaze washed over me.

Wonder.

Awe.

He tugged off my shoes and leaned back to pull my jeans free from my ankles. And there I was, spread out for him across my couch like an offering.

That was exactly what I wanted to be.

"You are the best thing I've ever seen. Can't believe I get to see you this way. That I get this chance."

I heard what was behind his words. That it was going to be the only one, the only chance.

He edged up, his waist barely breaking the boundaries of my knees, one hand pressed to the couch beside me to hold him up. His eyes latched on to mine as his fingertips traced the skin of my thigh, up and over my hip, tapping out a soft beat across my trembling belly.

My back arched from the tease. "Oh God…Zee."

"Shh, I know, baby, I know."

His fingers trailed down, barely making contact as he brushed them over the short crop of hair that covered me, before he parted my lips and dipped his fingertips into the wet flesh.

He teased and tortured, just barely touching my clit.

My hips jerked, desperate for more. "Zachary…"

He met my eye, his gorgeous face carved in stone and etched in restraint. "Do you need me? Tell me, Alexis. Do you need me?"

I touched his face. "I need you."

He growled before his hands were back on my knees, forcing my legs apart.

He drove his tongue into my folds.

My hands flew into his hair. "Zee."

He licked deep and long. His hands glided down the outside of my thighs, gripping and caressing and stroking, before they slipped under to grab hold of my ass to yank me closer to the edge of the couch.

He inched back, piercing me with his hungry gaze. "You are the miracle, Alexis."

His fingers kneaded my flesh, and I squirmed, hips jerking in a plea. He let his thumbs brush at the skin just at the juncture at the inside of my thighs and my center.

Teasing.

Taunting.

"You make me remember."

My hand was shaking like crazy when I cupped the side of his head, fingers still threaded in his hair. "What did you forget?"

He dipped down and pressed a simple kiss at the juncture, whispering at the sensitive flesh. "You make me remember what it's like to feel. What it's like to want someone in a way that makes me feel like I'm going out of my mind. Coming out of my skin."

"And you've made me feel that way for the very first time."

He clutched me tighter to him, his fingers searching, dipping into my sex and running along the crease of my ass, his breath a flame as he exhaled slowly across my clit.

My heart stuttered and heaved. "Zachary…please."

"Please what?"

"I need you."

As soon as I uttered the words, the man let go. His tongue drove deep, fucking deep, his groan vibrating through my body like the crackle of a forest fire before he turned his focus to my clit.

He laved and lapped.

Everything burned.

He clutched one ass cheek tight in one hand as he shifted up higher on his knees, and with the other hand, he sank two fingers inside my body.

I moaned through a gasp, my walls clutching at his fingers as he plunged them deep. He picked up this devastating pace with his tongue and his fingers.

And that energy.

It spun and spun as he lifted me higher, pleasure gathering fast. Ecstasy tightened in my belly and threatened at my clit. I panted and gasped while Zee propelled me to this place where air was gone. Where my only breath was him.

This man.

This man.

Everything split.

Shattered.

A blinding bliss that scattered like stars.

Burning as they fell and poured and shone.

My legs gripped his head just as tight as my fingers gripped his hair, and I swore my entire body floated six inches from the couch.

I cried his name.

Wanting to *reach* him and never feeling as close to someone as I did right then.

And he was whispering things I couldn't hear, kissing the inside of my thighs as I gasped toward that hidden, starry sky.

Where I slowly fell.

Zee was right there to catch me, his big hands holding me, massaging and coaxing and saying all the things he thought he shouldn't say.

I struggled for a breath, trying to still my heart that battered and raced and drummed.

I felt dazed. Stunned. Like I would never be the same.

He inched back. "You are fucking stunning when you

come."

Heat crept to my cheeks as I edged forward and set my hands on his chest. I didn't understand how he could make me feel both brave and so incredibly shy. As if he looked at me differently than any man ever had. As if he saw things only he could see.

I nudged him back, and he slanted me some kind of grin that curved with lust and swam with adoration. My palm smoothed over the ink that lined his collarbone.

Relentless.

I kissed across the skin. "And just who are you fighting for?" I whispered against it.

He groaned and fisted a handful of my hair, twisting it tight as I kissed down the overwhelming strength of him, my tongue darting out to taste—to trace the defined lines of his abdomen like I'd been imagining.

He jerked beneath it, tightening his hold in my hair. "Fuck…Lex. I can't."

I climbed to my knees, peeking up at him as I worked free the button of his jeans. "Yes you can. I want to feel you. Touch you."

"Shit…baby."

And I could feel his restraint, the resistance fighting for some kind of control. Just as sure as I could feel it slipping away when I licked down the trail beneath his belly button.

Leaning his weight against it, he pushed back the coffee table to make more room, using it as support as he lifted his hips and let me drag down his jeans and his underwear.

His cock sprang free, bobbing against his belly. The sight of it twisted my stomach with some kind of delirious greed.

My voice was a whisper. A prayer. "You're…beautiful, Zee. Every inch of you."

My hand trembled as I caressed the velvety soft flesh covering his massive dick that was so utterly hard, the head throbbing, dripping with his need.

"I can't believe I get to touch *you* this way."

He tugged at my hair, winding it close to my head. "It's me

who can't believe you're touching me this way. That I get to have this with you. This moment, Alexis. I won't ever forget it."

An ache threatened to bind itself to that secret place within me that he'd touched, that place I knew would recognize *him* when he came.

This courageous, bold boy who was somehow broken.

I wanted to find the pieces, hold them until he found a way to put them back together.

Instead, I shifted to straddle him at the knees, and Zee kicked his clothing the rest of the way free as I took him in both hands, stroking him long and hard.

Zee jerked in my hands. "Fuck…it's been…too long, Lex. Too long."

Then I wasn't wasting any time.

I kissed him just at the tip, my tongue snaking out to lick, to taste. I edged up higher while my head sank lower, my body curled over him as I took him deep into my mouth, my tongue flattening at the back of his shaft.

Both his hands were in my hair, fingers in my neck, my name on his breath.

He hissed a slew of curses as his hips jerked from the floor.

Maybe I should have been concerned that it was me who saw stars when he came.

Maybe I should have been concerned that I felt elevated in that moment.

Removed.

That was one second before I was falling.

twenty-two

ZEE

EIGHTEEN YEARS OLD

Zachary was coming to realize it was the simple moments that often meant the most. The moments when next to nothing happened that made the greatest impact.

Who would have thought it could be a comfortable silence that spoke louder than words?

Sitting out in the backyard under the drape of the darkened sky during the deepest hour of the night, Zee knew this was one of those moments.

Relaxed back on a patio chair, Mark took a long drag of his cigarette and exhaled it toward the heavens. Smoke curled and twisted above his head. It climbed toward the infinite canvas strewn above them before it dispersed and disappeared, becoming one with the vast nothingness.

"How many of those stars do you think are still holding on to our dreams?" Mark's voice was quiet and full of contemplation when he finally broke the hushed stillness that bound them.

On a low chuckle, Zee sank deeper into the lounger. He wasn't surprised when his tone filled with some of that awestruck wonder he'd carried when he was a boy. "Does it count if I was always wishing for the same things?"

Mark smiled and scratched at his throat before he shifted to look over at Zee. "It was always all about that piano, wasn't it?"

It was almost a tease, all mixed up with the kind of sheer affection that would be impossible for Zee to miss.

Zee almost felt self-conscious when he answered, "Guess it mostly was. Sitting at the throne of those ivory keys started to feel like the most important thing in my world."

"It is important," Mark told him.

With a nod, Zee sat up and leaned his elbows on his knees. "Yeah. Doesn't mean I don't miss hanging out with you. Hate that I hardly get to see you anymore."

Mark lifted a shoulder. Not in carelessness. But in encouragement. "Things that are important take dedication and sacrifice, Zee. I get that. My world's a million miles away from yours. You want to make it happen? Then you need to do what you need to do. Just like what me and the guys have had to do for Sunder. Doesn't make you and me anything less to each other. You'll always be the most important person in my life."

Guilt ate his insides.

"But these last couple of years—"

"Were shit," Mark cut him off. He shrugged again, his words going quieter. "Yeah, things were bad, man. Fucking brutal. But just because my world stopped moving, didn't mean I expected yours to stop, too. You've been chasing after this for years." He cracked a smile. "Believe me, I'd knock you on your ass if you gave that up."

After a show in LA two years ago, Baz and Lyrik had gotten themselves into a ton of trouble. Baz had ended up behind bars for the better part of a year while Lyrik had fought to piece his life back together after he'd lost his family because of the mistakes he'd made that night.

That whole time, Zee knew Mark had struggled. Knew he'd been getting lost to those dark places more and more often. Pumping his veins full to cover up the fear and loss.

It'd seemed impossible for Zee to reach him.

But over the last year since Baz had gotten out, Sunder had regrouped for a comeback.

Their label had honored their contract, the same as their new manager, Anthony di Pietro. They'd laid down a new album and had been out on tour promoting it. Their popularity had seemed to gain speed with each day that passed.

Between those two things and Zee's own crazy schedule, he felt like he hardly had the time to connect with Mark.

But Mark was right.

Nothing could lessen their bond, because there they were, sitting under the stars. Same as they'd done when they were kids.

It was like a day hadn't passed.

But that didn't mean things hadn't changed.

Zee hesitated before he muttered what he knew sounded close to a confession. "Met someone."

Mark's attention jerked his direction, eyes wide. "No shit."

Zee rubbed a knuckle across his upper lip as he was hit with another rush of affection. But this was an entirely different kind. This was something that flooded his stomach and pulsed in his chest.

"No shit," he said.

"Is it serious?" Mark asked.

Zee lifted his head to meet his brother's stare head on. "I love her, man. Like crazy."

Mark laughed under his breath, grin pulling at the corner of his mouth. "So my baby brother went and took the tumble, huh?"

A short laugh rippled free, and Zee shook his head. "Guess I did."

Truth was, he'd tumbled hard.

Mark's brows narrowed in speculation, the words on his

tongue full of the same kind of ribbing he'd given Zee for years. "And you're just gonna give up on the girls that flock to you every time you walk through my door? All that easy lovin'? It's like you're the rock star with the way they go all starry eyed every time you decide to show. Tell me you aren't gonna miss it."

"Don't miss it," he said. Honestly. "Being with Julie is…easy."

The best thing he'd ever done.

Mark chuckled and sank deeper into his chair. "Falling in love is the easy part."

He took another drag of his cigarette and turned back to the sky. "It's picking up all the pieces in the aftermath that's the hard part."

twenty-three

ZEE

I jerked to a stop a little too quickly at the curb. So maybe I was still fuming that I had to leave Alexis's warmth to deal with this bullshit tonight.

For just one goddamned night, I wanted to pretend.

The second the texts had started coming through, I'd wanted to put my fist through a wall.

Last thing I wanted was to look at that good, good girl and give her some lame ass excuse about an old friend needing me.

But I'd just been asking for this, hadn't I? Taking the bits I shouldn't?

My passenger door flew open.

"Where is he?" They were the first words that left my mouth.

Anger ate through my spirit, this vicious ache that took me whole when I looked over at Veronica sliding into the front seat of my car.

I'd taken a cab home from Alexis', grabbed my car, and drove straight there.

She scoffed. "I don't even get a hello? Always such the gentleman."

Yeah. Because she was the epitome of class.

"Think we're a little past that point, don't you?" It was all a sneer.

She rolled her eyes. "Whatever."

"Where is he?"

"At my mom's."

"Good."

A scowl twisted her face. "What's that supposed to mean?"

Was she really that clueless or was she just playing me?

"It means at least I know he's bein' taken care of. That he's safe."

"I'm his mother."

I wanted to shout at her to act like it then. Demand to know what had changed that she'd all of a sudden think it was fine to take him into that hellhole.

But once I'd stopped to think about it, there'd been warning signs. She'd always been manipulative, doing whatever she had to do to slant things in her favor, like she got off on making me suffer. Previously, it'd never come at the cost of Liam's safety and happiness.

Over the last couple of years, I'd felt that sliding. Maybe I just hadn't wanted to fathom the idea of her slipping into her old ways. Truth was, I probably should have been expecting it all along.

This wasn't the first time I'd been in the same situation, driving across town to meet her in the middle of the night. She'd texted, saying she needed to see me immediately. It was an "emergency".

I rubbed a hand over my face to try to clear all the bitterness.

"You ready to tell me what this bullshit is all about? It's three in the morning, Veronica, and it doesn't look like you're bleeding."

So maybe it was a dick move.

A frown pulled tight across her brow. "You're supposed to

be here for me."

Right. Because we were just one big, happy family.

"Which is why I'm here. So spill."

She dropped her gaze, fiddled with her fingers. The innocent, helpless act. "I need rent."

Of course she did.

My laughter was hostile. "Funny, seems like there's a whole lot of money that went missing."

She shifted in the seat. "My momma needed help."

My jaw clenched. How many times had she used that excuse? Anthony had his guy digging, seeing if it was true.

"How much?"

"A couple thousand would be good…to cover rent and utilities. Food and stuff." She was all defenseless and forlorn, playing it up.

Goddamn it.

I bit down on the edge of my bottom lip, drawing blood, wanting to fucking lash out. Instead, I sat forward a fraction and dug out my wallet. Already knew what her big emergency would be, so I was prepared.

It wasn't like this was something new.

I pulled out a fat stack of cash. "I'll give you a thousand. Your regular allowance will be landing in your account next week. Make this last."

She pouted before she caught my expression. The rage that floated just beneath the surface. Waiting to snap.

She snatched it out of my hand. "You make me sound like a child."

Then stop acting like one.

I gripped the steering wheel, and she reached out and touched my cheek.

Too softly.

I yanked my head back out of her reach.

She cracked a smile and something malicious broke out from beneath the façade, voice saccharin sweet. "You wouldn't go and cheat on me, now would you, Zee?"

My chest tightened against the manipulation, like she was

physically sinking her sleazy, skanky claws into my spirit. Twisting and twisting. The way she always had.

"Pretty sure you're the one who broke that vow a long time ago."

Her hand was on the door handle, words low with a threat. "I'm not the one who has to keep it."

Then she climbed out and was gone.

twenty-four

ZEE
EIGHTEEN YEARS OLD

Julie barreled down the aisle of the theatre and threw herself into Zachary's arms. He picked her up and whirled her around.

He was panting, still riding that high, floating in the clouds, trying to slow his heart rate and loving the way it raced at the same time.

Joy.

So much joy.

"You did it." Julie's words were a breath that spun around him, infiltrating the disbelief that still thundered and sped.

Reality was still trying to breach his consciousness.

"I can't believe it," he said.

She pulled back to look at him when he set her back on her feet. "You didn't really think it'd turn out any other way?"

"Considering the fact I couldn't sleep for the last week, I think maybe that's exactly what I was worried about."

Julie beamed at him. The girl was always wearing fitted sweaters and perfect hair and her grandma's pearls. So damned pretty in a conservative kind of way. So different from the girls he'd grown up around, the one's always hanging around his brother and his crew.

"I'm really proud of you," she said before she hiked up on her toes and whispered in his ear. "Just how tired are you?"

Zee chuckled and wrapped an arm around her waist, pulling her flush, because he loved when she undid a few buttons and let her hair down. When she went from straitlaced to pliable and soft. "Don't think I could ever be that tired."

"Good. Because I think this calls for a celebration."

"We've got that thing with my brother first."

Julie dropped back down, nerves taking her whole. "I don't know if I'm really comfortable going over there."

"Hey, I know it's a different vibe than what you're used to, but I promise you, they're good guys," he told her, his hand on her face and his thumb running the hollow beneath her eye. "And this is my brother we're talking about. He's important to me."

She pressed her lips together, her fingers threaded through his. "I know he's important to you. I just…that crowd isn't the type I want to get mixed up in."

He tugged her closer and placed a kiss on the crown of her head. "I get it…and we're not getting mixed up in it. But he's throwing a party for me…because he cares about me. He's doing it because of this."

Zee waved a hand at the piano. The piano he'd just poured his heart into during the audition. The piano that had felt like a lover. A caress. Perfection.

Sitting behind it, Zee had never felt so alive.

Just like Julie, Mark hadn't questioned the outcome. He'd simply texted Zee before the audition.

> **You own this, baby brother. Haven't ever met anyone as talented as you. I'm back in town at 8. Tonight we celebrate.**

Zee threaded his fingers through Julie's long brown hair,

loving the way she felt in his arms. "Don't worry, baby. I promise that I'll take care of you. Today was the best day of my life…I need you there with me."

Julie nodded, her fingers twisting in his shirt. "I don't want to be anywhere else."

Zee's response was simple. "Good."

Because he didn't want her anywhere else, either.

twenty-five

ZEE

Lunch?

I sent off the text as soon as I left Lyrik's place in the Hills. I hadn't seen Alexis in a week and…I needed to.

I was kind of going out of my mind, the memories of that night back at her house taunting me through the days and haunting me in the nights.

She'd had to work throughout the week, and I'd spent almost every waking hour practicing with the guys. We'd shared a few texts during that time, skating around the subject, neither of us quite knowing where we stood.

That was what happened when you blurred the lines.

Resisting it had become too much.

Thirty seconds later, my phone buzzed.

Sure! Where?

I tapped out a quick response.

Why don't I pick you up. Give me fifteen.

Perfect. I'll get ready.

Less than thirteen minutes later, I rounded the last turn into her neighborhood, struck with another rush of anticipation at being with her again. I just couldn't fucking help it.

Not when she came skipping out her door looking like sweet, sweet sunshine, hair a white blaze of shimmery rivers running down her back. She was wearing a short, flowy dress, baby blue and printed with red flowers, thin straps over the shoulders.

There probably wasn't supposed to be anything sexy about it, but on her, it was close to obscene. The kind of temptation that made my fingers itch and my dick twitch.

She didn't even wait for me to get out of my car before she was swinging the passenger door open and jumping inside. An effortless smile rode those full lips and just a shade of pink tinted her cheeks.

This girl was a damned knockout, and I wasn't sure she had the first clue.

"Hi." She pulled her seatbelt on.

When she glanced over at me, her teeth tugged at her lip. "I missed you," she said, clearly not sure if she should say it.

"I missed you, too."

I was damned sure *I* shouldn't say it, but it was already there, making its claim in the air.

That energy was compounded in the small space, and I did my best to pretend it wasn't there, demanding attention, instead trying to keep things light. "Tell me you've kept your word and haven't gone on any dangerous rescue missions since the last time I saw you."

A giggle slipped out beneath her breath. "No…I promise. Things have been pretty quiet in my neck of the woods for the last week."

Relief gusted through my spirit. "That's good to hear."

Her eyes widened. "It's good to hear that my life is

boring?"

I laughed. "Hey, sometimes boring is safe."

She feigned a pout. "That sounds boring."

My head shook as I turned onto the main road. "You're insane."

She smiled one of those smiles that knocked the breath from my lungs. "This we already know."

Twenty minutes later, I was ushering her inside the quaint, quiet café, a little off the beaten path and out of the way of prying eyes.

The floors were a light blue stained concrete and the ceilings were pitched and made of glass. Rope lights draped from them and potted trees were situated around the space, almost giving it the feel of being outdoors.

Alexis glimpsed at me from over her bare shoulder. "This place is amazing. How did you find it?"

The hostess led us to the very back, and I held out her chair for her before I slid into the opposite side. "Guys and I used to hang out here every once in a while when we wanted to lie low. Get all of us together and things all of a sudden become a little more conspicuous."

Those blue eyes played a rhythm of comfort and ease. "I can only imagine."

"That, and they have about the best cheesecake in a thousand mile radius."

"Ah…a man with a sweet tooth, huh?"

A grin ticked up at one side of my mouth. "What kind of man would I be if I didn't have one? My mom used to make me clean my plate if I wanted dessert."

"I'm assuming it's safe to say it was a good tactic?"

"Uh…yeah. I would say so." The chuckle that slipped free was wistful, the memory of the smile that used to grace my mom's face stabbing the raw wound deep inside that would never heal.

Alexis unfolded her menu. "Then cheesecake it is. But what do we eat first?"

We ordered and the waitress brought us iced teas

sweetened with real berries. Alexis took a sip of hers, peering at me from across the table, her voice turning into a breath as some of that redness flushed. "Is this…awkward?"

The slightest chuckle tumbled out. "No, Alexis. I think this is just about as far from awkward as it could be. If anything, it's much too comfortable."

Too easy and right.

An affected, shy smile pulled at her mouth and she dropped her chin a fraction. Locks of that white hair fell over one shoulder as she tilted her head and played with her straw, jabbing at a blueberry with the end of it like it was a dagger.

"Tell me about, Avril…before. About what it's like to have a twin."

Surprised, she looked up at me. A flash of sadness struck across her face before it quickened into tenderness. The smallest laugh left her mouth, and she swirled the straw in her tea, getting lost to the memories.

"We were inseparable, as you can imagine. It was like always having your best friend over to play. A friend who never had to go home and was exactly like you."

"You both liked to do the same things?"

She gave a slight nod. "Yeah, but like I told you before, I was a little more adventurous, always coaxing her along when she got scared. But she always got this look on her face… It was different from the one I got. It was when I knew she was happy. Free. Experiencing something she'd never thought she'd be brave enough to do. "

She looked straight at me, her voice lowered like a confession. "I think maybe that's why I pushed her so much. I wanted to see her face like that because it made me feel amazing inside to see it. Lit up that place where I felt our connection most."

Her tone turned wistful. "I can still see her…we were about seven and Chelsey had taken us to the park. Avril didn't want to get on the merry-go-round. I hopped on, begging her to come with me. I told her I wouldn't let her fall. She was terrified, but finally she climbed on. We both hung on to the same bar, our arms wound around and locked together, facing each other, while Chelsey spun us round and round."

A tiny grin pulled at my mouth. "I can picture it. Bet you two were adorable."

She gulped around the emotion as she continued, "I could see it the moment she started to realize how much fun it was. When she realized what she would have been missing if she hadn't gotten on."

The saddest smile rimmed her mouth as she looked across at me. "I was always coaxing her to go faster and farther, and she was always encouraging me to stop and look around. To appreciate what was already there."

"And together you both experienced the best things in life." I went for reassurance, but somehow my words were filled with longing, yearning for the days that'd been lost.

Both for Alexis and Avril and for me and Mark.

"Exactly." Something pleading climbed into her expression. "I know you see this horrible person, Zee. But I still see the person she used to be…that person who's hiding underneath. That's who she really is, and I can't stop believing that person exists."

I reached out and threaded my fingers through hers where they rested on the tabletop. "No one should ever ask you to stop believing in that. The only thing I'm asking you is to protect yourself along the way. You're living for her, and you deserve to be lived for, too."

Maybe I meant more by it. Maybe it felt like I was exactly like Avril. Taking all the good I could get from Alexis while I could.

I cleared my throat. "So…it was just you and Avril, your older sister, and your mom?"

She seemed to try to shake the heaviness off, even though I could see the remnants clinging to her. "Yeah. Mom had to work a lot to support us, so it was Chelsey's job a lot of the time to watch us and keep us in line. She really hasn't stepped down from the position."

I chuckled. "She's protective of you, yeah?"

I could've sworn she rolled her eyes a bit. "You could say that."

I laughed a little harder. "Nothing wrong with someone looking out for you."

"Oh, she takes it to a whole new level."

"I like her already," I said.

Alexis giggled. "Between the two of you, I don't know how I even make it out my door. I'm surprised one of you didn't show up to escort me to work this week."

"That sounds like a great idea."

Her head shook. "Goofball."

My chest squeezed. I loved it, the way she talked to me. Like I was just another guy.

No. Strike that. Not just another guy—her guy.

The kind of guy who might be good enough for a girl like her. I ran my thumb over her knuckles, our fingers still wound, hooked on this connection, for just a little while, refusing to let it go. "So…was it hard without your dad?"

Her gaze dropped in contemplation, the girl so open when she looked back up at me.

"It was hard in the sense that we didn't get to spend as much time with our mom as we wanted to. She is great…like amazingly great. So, it was hard with her being gone so much, on her because she didn't want to leave, and on Chelsey because it gave her so much added responsibility. But otherwise?"

"Yeah?" I asked.

Her shoulders lifted to her ears. "No. We were all better off without him. He left when Avril and I were barely walking. I could have let it bother me. Turn me needy for attention. But I don't really think I ever felt that void. The love I received from all three of them…it was enough…and I can only hope now it was enough for the rest of them."

God.

This girl.

"You are unlike anyone I've ever met, Alexis."

Redness flared, and she dropped her chin, fighting one of

those grins that tugged at all those strings inside me. Strings that were getting more and more attached to her.

She squeezed my hand. "What about you. Are you close to your parents?"

I guess I wasn't prepared for her to turn the conversation on me, and I sucked in a breath before I turned my gaze to a spot on the ground, trying to gather myself. To find an answer to give her that wouldn't be a lie.

Just a bit of the truth.

"I used to be."

I stared at her fingers, fiddling with them as I spoke. "We were really close. Like yours, my mom worked a lot, but our dad was there, working just as hard."

A pained chuckle knocked loose from somewhere in my chest. "Mark and I…we kind of ran wild. We were boys, so I don't think our parents worried about us quite as much. Figured as long as we were outside and not starting fires, we were free to run around and tear up the countryside."

Her smile was gentle with encouragement. "Why do I get the feeling you two started a few fires?"

I choked on a laugh. "Oh yeah, we started a few fires."

Wistfulness tweaked the corner of my mouth. "Mark was five years older than me. You'd think he'd try to get rid of me…think I was a nuisance. But he always wanted me right there at his side."

Sympathy swept across her features. She brushed her fingers across the star on the back of my hand, and I trembled. "I'm so sorry you lost him. He sounds amazing."

Emotion clotted my throat, words thick. "He was. He was my best friend."

Blinking back tears, she averted her gaze. When she looked back, she wasn't looking at me. She was looking in me. "And now…are you still close with your parents?"

I scratched at my beard, trying to keep it together. "Don't see them all that much. It's difficult…going over there after Mark. It's like there's this void in them that I feel responsible to fill, and I know that won't ever be possible."

A frown edged between her eyes. "But I thought you said you settled here since it was near your parents?"

But that was the thing. I was always just on the outside, watching in on the good things of my life and never being able to quite take part.

"Not sure I'm that good for them."

She leaned over the table, coming closer. "How could you not be good for them, Zee? I bet they miss you terribly."

The waitress showed with our food. Alexis sat back, and I did the same. But it didn't matter. I could feel that connection all the same. This girl's spirit pulling and tugging and demanding all the things I couldn't give.

I was beginning to think there wasn't anything I could do to stop it.

"Thank you for lunch. It was delicious."

"I dare you to tell me you've tasted better cheesecake."

Walking beside me, she shot me a smirk. Pure flirt with a dash of sex. "You haven't tasted my cheesecake."

I nearly buckled over. A shot of lust straight to the gut. "Woman, don't tease me."

"Hey, you dared me. It seems with you I'm always up for the challenge."

That was it, I needed to touch. My hand went straight to that sweet spot at the base of her spine, fingers splaying wide in hopes of copping a feel of her delicious ass. We were both smiling when I pulled open the door and guided her out and into the afternoon sun.

We chatted quietly as I led her to my car that was parallel parked at the curb. I opened the passenger door for her, helped her in, and closed it when I heard the gasp, the telltale vibe that suddenly radiated from someone who had stumbled to a stop three feet away from me.

"Oh my God…it's you…you're Zee Kennedy, the drummer. Oh God. I seriously can't believe it. This is crazy. My friends are never gonna believe it. Can I get a picture…and…and…um…can you sign this?"

A girl who couldn't have been older than fifteen shoved her backpack at me as she stood there stammering.

While I stood there floundering.

A flood of panic surged through my being. Saturating every cell. Overpowering. I tried to blink, to focus, to hear through the sudden ringing in my ears.

You idiot.

You fucking idiot.

I swallowed, barely able to hold the marker she'd pulled from her backpack. I scribbled my autograph across the front pocket.

My smile was nothing less than a grimace when I leaned down close enough so she could snatch a selfie of us.

At least I had enough sense to make sure it was angled the opposite direction of my car.

"It was nice to meet you," I mumbled the second she clicked, not stopping to let her say another word as I raced around to the driver's side, breaths labored and my heart this manic thunder of dread.

I turned over the ignition and slammed it in gear, at the same second gunning the accelerator and taking to the street like doing so might stand the chance of letting me leave all these foolish mistakes behind.

I pounded the heel of my hand on the steering wheel, my teeth clenched as I fought the nausea threatening to rise in my gut.

What were you thinking?

Discomfort pressed and pulsed, laying siege to that energy that refused to let go. That energy that'd gone dark and ominous, filled with questions and confusion, this throbbing chaos of outright hurt and grief.

I weaved through traffic like I was some kind of madman, swerving as I changed lanes, car skidding as I took too sharp of turns.

I slammed on the brakes in front of her house.

Not a single word had been uttered the entire ride home, and that bottled silence echoed back, somehow amplified by the rumbling idle of the engine.

Alexis reached out a trembling hand and set it on my forearm. "You're upset that girl recognized you?" I could feel the hurt riding on her question.

I made the mistake of looking at her. At the girl who'd done her best to ruin me in the best of ways, heart and body and mind.

All that white, shiny hair falling around her face.

So fucking pretty.

Stunning, inside and out.

Angel.

"Tell me what happened back there," she demanded, her voice cracking on the emotion that ran heavy in the air. "Why you're so upset about it. Please."

My jaw ticked in anger. Anger directed entirely at myself. I could feel it bursting, busting out at the seams.

"You want to know what happened back there, Alexis? That was me, making mistake after mistake. That was me fucking everything up. That was me, disregarding the things I need to protect most. Just like I told you I would."

Confusion shook her head, lines pinched between her eyes. "What does that mean?"

My skin itched, this feeling crawling over me like a dirty rash. Sickness sinking in as memories flashed.

Too vibrant. Too close. Too much.

"He's gone, man…he's fucking gone."

Disbelief. Horror. Grief.

I fell to my knees, couldn't breathe. I gripped my head in my hands as I wept.

What did I do? What did I do?

"It means I can't do this. This was a mistake." It flew out harder than it should have. This hatred I couldn't contain.

She jerked back like I'd slapped her. "That was about me?

About the fact I can't be seen?" She sat there blinking as she came to her own twisted conclusion.

But it wasn't about her. Not even close.

It was about me.

But it was better this way. This needed to end.

Before it was too late.

twenty-six

ALEXIS

"What a jerk…what a total, complete jerk." I muttered the words under my breath, hands still shaking as I yanked at the weeds in my tiny flower garden at the side of my house.

Even as I said the words, my consciousness whispered it wasn't true.

A sensation fell over me. Gutting me. Crippling me in a way I didn't quite understand.

Zee had used my shock as a tool to get me out of his car as quickly as he could. So he could get away.

Run. Escape from whatever was chasing him.

Or maybe his intention had been to run straight back to his chains. To submit himself to whatever kept him bound.

Because I'd felt it—the agony that had radiated from him.

A vacuum.

A black hole.

Nothing left in the wake of this tornado that had torn this boy to shreds.

Tears streamed hot down my face, and I wiped them with

my forearm, gasping for a breath as I sat back on my haunches. "Shit," I whispered, sniffling and looking around as if I'd find the answer to what could have caused his sudden shift.

Our lunch had been…magical. All week, I'd missed him like crazy, the emptiness of my bed never feeling quite so vacant since that mesmerizing man had made his mark on me. I could only hope that somehow, in some way, I was making my mark on him.

It wasn't until I was sitting across from him at lunch that I was struck with a realization. He understood me in a way no other person ever had. He saw my strengths and he didn't judge me for my weaknesses. Just as I saw his strengths.

So why would he think I would judge him for his weaknesses?

Disappointment and this thick, drenching sorrow swam inside me. I pushed to standing, my footsteps sluggish as I rounded to the back of my house and climbed the three steps that led up to the backdoor. I entered my kitchen, which was dimmed with the late afternoon light, and trudged over to the sink to wash my hands.

I turned the faucet on high, scrubbing the dirt from my nails and trying to convince myself to let him go. To ignore the nagging that thrummed with every beat of my heart. But it was too loud to disregard.

I guess I'd never been one to turn away.

Anxiety fired in my nerves as I paced the hall, whispering toward my feet, reminding myself of why I was there. I just needed to let him know I was there for him. That if he ever needed someone to talk to, I wanted it to be me.

Maybe I wanted more, but that was okay. I'd be honored to be considered his friend.

The heavy metal door swung open, and Zee was there,

clinging to both sides of the frame to support himself.

Distressed and tormented.

Pieces of that light brown hair stuck up every which way, as if he'd spent the entire day ripping and yanking at it.

But it was his eyes—emblazoned in bronze and secrets and significance—that shattered my world and sent a rush of affection rushing through my blood.

"Tell me your truth," I whispered.

On the way over, I'd practiced what I was going to say, but maybe it was my own truth that came sliding out. I wanted him to know he could trust me. That I would keep his secrets safe.

"Alexis." It was a growl of relief and restraint.

A severity rose in the air, and I gasped when he rushed for me.

His mouth crashed against mine.

Devouring. Destroying. Demanding.

Taking everything I had to offer.

His tongue parted my lips, claiming more. He pulled me inside and slammed the door shut. He pushed my back against it in the same second he pressed his big body against mine.

I wanted to weep with relief, with the feel of him in my arms.

This beautiful, confusing man.

"Lex. Thought I would die after I left you….saying those things to you. How could you be a mistake? How?"

The words were half past mad. Delirious. Just as delirious as the rush of insanity that spun through my mind when he rocked against my center.

"Zachary," I whispered. "I don't want to let you go. Don't let me go."

He spun us, hiked me up higher as he began to carry me across his loft. My legs were fastened around his waist and my breasts begged at his chest, nipples tight and flesh on fire. My fingers sank into his shoulders, holding on as I kissed him recklessly.

Unable to get close enough.

Shock jutted from my mouth when he suddenly had me

against the metal railing of the staircase. My back arched over it and my head dropped back when he wedged a knee between my thighs and ran a path of needy kisses down my throat.

He held me at the waist while the other hand rode the length of my thigh. "This dress," he moaned as his fingers brushed the lacy material of my underwear aside.

I gasped when he plunged two fingers into me.

Possessively.

No hesitation.

My nails scraped at his chest as I writhed against his fingers that continued their perfect assault. "Zee…oh…God."

"This body, Alexis…"

He kissed lower, his mouth moving over the neckline of my dress and running to just above my breasts.

He breathed through the thin fabric, pressing a scatter of kisses over the spot that thrummed and sped and raced. "This heart…this fucking miraculous heart. You make me want to be better. You…you make me forget. Make me forget who I am."

His words were a frantic rumble as he continued to drive his fingers into my sex.

Tingles rushed, my words nothing more than pants as he kissed down through the valley of my breasts. "Maybe you're just remembering who you are. Who you were always supposed to be."

I felt as if I was so close to knowing him. This boy whose beauty had been muted.

He groaned, half pained, half demand. "You almost make me feel like him."

Yanking me away from the railing, he pulled my body tight against his and carried me the rest of the way to the upper loft. To this magical place where twilight touched every corner, whispered its secrets and danced in its shadows.

He'd barely tossed me to the bed when he was over me, shoving my dress up and ripping it free, my fingers just as frantic as I tore his shirt over his head.

I searched him, hands racing across his chest, feeling the wild beat of his conflicted heart, hearing the struggle that whimpered from his spirit.

He angled down and captured my mouth again. He kissed and bit and nipped as he held my face steady in the frame of his hands. Then he edged down, driving me wild with murmurs of kisses at my jaw and ear and neck.

My head rocked back, and a scream of unexpected pleasure ripped from my throat when he bit down on one nipple and drove his fingers into the well of my body.

"So tiny and tight and perfect. Just like every inch of you."

"Zachary…please."

I writhed, dizziness rushing as I stared up at him towering over me.

His body was brimming with hard, cut muscle. Muscle that jumped and ticked and flexed, as if the desire thrumming in his veins stalked back and forth, a caged predator, searching for a way to be released.

My gaze traveled across the tattoo on his collarbone.

Relentless.

"Fight for me," I begged.

He groaned when I said it. He scrambled to the side of the bed and onto his feet, ripping my underwear down my legs as he did.

And I felt it. Something came alive in that second. Something gave beneath the intensity that glowed and flamed between us.

Zee seemed almost frantic as he fumbled to get the button free on his jeans. He shoved them down his legs and kicked them from his feet.

The man was bare, and my chest stuttered beneath the magnitude of him. This gorgeous, gorgeous man.

"Tell me you need me, Alexis. Tell me you need this as fucking bad as I do. Tell me it's okay. Tell me I'm not the only one who's losing his mind." The words grated, rugged and fueled by need.

Emotion thickened in my throat, so heavy, so right. "I need you."

The last threads of whatever was holding Zee back

snapped.

He was back over me, faster than I could make sense of it, his hands everywhere. Frantic and frenzied as they searched me out.

He ducked his head, snatching a nipple between his teeth, biting down before he lapped at it with his tongue.

I clutched at his hair, at his neck, at his shoulders, both of us in this desperate struggle to get closer to the other.

He edged back for the barest second, blowing air across the nipple that had just been in his mouth. That ball of need in my belly shivered and shook as he turned and did the same to the other.

Desire throbbed between my thighs. So bright. Too much. Overwhelming.

I was desperate for this man.

For his beauty and his touch and his everything.

"Tell me," he said again, licking up the hollow of my throat.

I squirmed as his fingers tickled across my belly, the boy magic, inciting a storm. "I need this. I need you."

Did he know?

I needed him to. "I need you more than anything I've ever needed."

"Goddamn it, Alexis." He rubbed himself at my center, my knees dropping wide, jagged pants escaping his mouth, my face back in his hands. The edges of everything shimmered with light.

He moaned, rocking, teasing me with bliss while he tortured himself with the unknown. "Tell me you're on the pill. Tell me, Alexis. Tell me this is right. Tell me this is okay."

I nodded frantically, gripping him by the sides of the face. "No fear. Just life."

A growl pulled from somewhere deep inside him, and in a flash, he'd shifted, taking his cock in his hand, before he was there, the big head of him breaching that space I felt desperate for him to take.

A sharp cry jutted from my mouth as he took me whole in a single thrust.

Taking everything.

Light. Sanity. Mind.

Sucking me into that darkness that rimmed and rolled and spun around him, drowning me in the blackest night.

He was so big and overwhelming he burned, and I struggled to catch my breath, to adjust, to make sense of this feeling that swept through me with the power of a shock wave. This feeling of utter belonging that strummed through me like the passion of that song.

His song.

"Fuck." Zee's hand tightened on the caps of my shoulders, his chest quaking in spasms, jerking up and down in some kind of twisted restraint, those chains giving and giving and giving until the shackles fully snapped.

Broke.

Zee grasped me behind the knee, spreading me wide. His expression was savage. His eyes fierce.

He rocked his powerful hips.

Owning.

Taking.

Possessing.

My walls desperately clutched around him, the feel of him almost too much, too great, while the greedy part of me knew I would never get enough.

I grasped his shoulders as I struggled to meet him. His hips snapped and thrust and fucked, eyes narrowed and tight, holding me hostage beneath the demand of his stare.

He never looked away as he dominated every inch of me.

Relentless.

I understood it then. This masterful boy with his skillful hands, pouring every single thing he had into me. My body lit up beneath it, pleasure building with every surge of his body.

His pants were deep, guttural, wild.

He suddenly rolled us, pulling me on top, and jerked up to sitting in the same second. He twisted one hand up in my hair, the other burrowing into my hip as he guided me. Harder. Faster.

I panted as our bodies rocked and pitched, and my heart soared to heights too great, pleasure climbing right along with it.

"Lex…you…you feel so good. Too good. I can't…"

Zee was back on his knees, taking me with him, both of us too lost to care we were at the edge of the bed, tumbling over onto the rug on the floor.

He pushed up on his hands, sweat slicking his skin as he drove us both toward the edge, his gorgeous body working over mine.

I'd always chased experiences. Wanted everything they had to offer. But somehow, I knew I'd never again have an experience quite like this.

"Alexis…baby…I—"

"I know." It was a whimper.

He wedged his hand between us, fingers precise and perfect as he circled my clit. He coaxed me with those brilliant eyes while the rest of him coaxed my body into bliss.

Higher and deeper and faster.

And we spun.

Falling through a vacant space that belonged only to us.

Where the stars burned so bright they blinded.

Where the only thing I could see was this boy.

This brilliant, beautiful boy.

Zee increased his pace, every inch of him tight and rigid. His hips rocked mercilessly, and he clutched me by the shoulders, a shudder taking him whole as he thrust and held, his groan so deep as he spasmed and jerked.

My name a prayer.

He slumped forward. Both of us gasping. Panting.

Staggered.

Softly, I threaded my fingers through his hair.

I could feel him swallow. Could sense the wariness that threatened to seep back in.

He inched back to look at me, so tenderly it hurt. "Lex," he whispered, as if maybe this too caused him pain.

The best things always did.

He shifted and pulled me to his side, adorning a bunch of kisses across the crown of my head, my hand resting on his chest against his erratic heart.

I peered up at him, and he laid one of those kisses against my forehead, his big hand running down the back of my head.

"Lex," he whispered again, this time lower. Touching those secret places inside that he had just claimed as his own.

He took my hand, wound it in his, lightly brushing his lips across my knuckles. Those lips almost tweaked into a smile. "I lose my head when I'm with you."

A wilderness of lights slowly flickered to life outside the bank of windows that overlooked the sprawling city below. They glowed against the canopy of night that hung like a warm embrace of protection.

In Zee's bedroom loft, removed from the rest of the world, that was the way I felt—protected.

Suspended somewhere between earth and sky.

"And I find myself when I'm with you."

A rumble echoed in his chest. "You know that wasn't supposed to happen."

"I don't believe that's true. I think you and me…we were supposed to happen all along."

I felt his sigh against my head. But I also felt his smile.

He pressed a kiss there. "Come on, let's get you cleaned up. I bet you're starving."

Zee was right. I *was* starving. I sat on the island in his kitchen with my legs swinging over the edge, wearing one of his tees and my underwear. This was all while I watched the man cooking me dinner, wearing only his underwear.

I felt dazed. Still trying to come down from that high. And seeing him this way wasn't helping. Not at all.

I wrung my hands, the memories of what we'd just done

heating my cheeks and pooling like warmth in my belly. How was it possible to feel so intensely satisfied and desperate for more at the same time?

"That smells so good."

He stirred the creation he was whipping up in the skillet as he glanced back at me.

"Garlic and butter. You can't really go wrong with that. And by can't go wrong, I mean this is about the simplest dish of pasta you're ever going to eat. Don't get too excited over there. It was kind of a mandatory thing back in the days of barely scrimping by. Easy and cheap."

I found myself shaking my head.

"What?" he asked, not even fighting that grin that moved through me like a caress.

My curiosity got the better of me. "What is that like…going from struggling to get by to having everything?"

He grunted and dumped the box of spaghetti into the boiling water. "Don't have everything, Alexis. Not even close."

"You know that's not what I meant…what I mean is the success. How does it feel after you guys worked so hard for it? I have to imagine that's incredible."

Spinning around, he leaned his back against the counter and crossed his arms over his chest. "It is incredible. The guys…they've worked for it for so long. Dreamed about it since they were kids back in middle and high school. They made a commitment and didn't stop until it happened."

Creases pulled at the corners of my eyes. "And you?"

On a sigh, he turned away to stir the pasta and added a can of sauce to the sauté in the skillet. His explanation was filled with caution. "Playing with the guys is my home. It's what I'm supposed to do."

"But do you love it?" There I was, pushing again. I didn't know how to stop when I was around him.

He surprised me by smiling over at me as he walked toward the massive fridge on the other end of the kitchen. "You are just full of questions, aren't you, Alexis Kensington?"

I fisted the collar of his tee that I was wearing, brought it up over my mouth and to my nose, fighting a rush of modesty that flushed across my skin and mixed with the swell of giddiness. "That's just me, Zachary Kennedy. If you like me enough, you'll get used to it."

He chuckled under his breath, shaking his head as he set one hand on the freezer door and opened the refrigerator with the other. "Guess I'm gonna have to get used to it then, huh?"

That giddiness bloomed. "I think that would be a good idea."

"You want something to drink?" he mumbled as he rummaged around inside.

"Do you have white?"

He peeked back at me. "Wine?"

I was suddenly unsure. "Yeah."

He shook his head. "Nope. Sorry. No wine. I've got soda, water, and just about every juice known to man. Pick your poison."

It kind of struck me then, and I remembered all the guys and girls had shared a couple bottles of wine that night we'd been at Ash's house. I'd had a couple glasses myself. Zee had refrained.

Regret tightened against my chest as realization took hold. "I'm sorry… You don't drink, do you?"

Another grunt. "Not really. Definitely don't keep it in my house. Though, there is kind of this tradition—like a pact that goes way back—with the band. Everyone does a shot together either before or after the show. I partake in that. That's about it."

Uneasiness had me shifting on the counter. "Is it okay if I ask why?"

He grinned over at me. "Doubt I could stop you."

"I don't mean to pry…I just…I want to know you."

Zee crossed to me, his hand on my face, thumb brushing the curve of my cheek. Even with that simple connection, I could feel a spark.

"I know you do, Alexis. You don't have to apologize for that. And you're right. I don't drink. The reason I don't is because it's just not worth the risk. Horrible choices and mistakes are made when we aren't in our right minds, and I'm not willing to ever put myself in that position again."

Again.

Awareness hung in the air.

He cleared his throat and pulled away, moving back over to the stove where he stirred the pot and the sauce.

"A Coke would be nice," I said quietly, letting him know I was letting him off the hook. That I respected him and his privacy.

The tension in his shoulders eased. "A Coke it is."

He filled a glass with ice, grabbed a soda, and set it on the island next to me before he went back to finishing our dinner. He moved to the sink, dumped the noodles into a colander, and piled them on our plates.

"So…piano…when did you learn?"

He laughed outright. "More questions?"

I raked my teeth over my lip, trying to hold back the giggle that wanted free. "Oh, come on, that's an easy one."

He was back at the stove, covering the noodles in sauce when he answered. "I kind of always knew."

He gestured with his chin to the piano where he'd been teaching me. "That was my grandma's. She said she found me when I was three, sitting on the bench, tinkering out the theme song to a cartoon I'd been watching while she babysat me. The rest was kind of history."

"What kind of history?"

He glanced to the floor, hands on his hips, contemplating, before he looked up to answer. "Lessons. Tons of them. Playing night and day. Then I was accepted into this pretty prestigious music school when I was sixteen. Playing that piano was pretty much my life."

"What? Wow…" It was so easy to say, but I knew to him it was more. That there was so much wrapped up in his answer. That it was part of that war that burned through him when he sat in front of that piano. The reason he no longer played.

"So, what did you see coming from it? From the school?"

He leaned back on the counter, shrugging his shoulders as if it didn't mean anything. "I don't know, maybe I'd imagined moving to New York. Writing for plays. Or maybe I would've stayed here and composed for movies. Guess I imagined being a part of a feeling that could be brought to life in people's imaginations and eyes."

Do you feel it?

That severity rippled through me, just as strong as that day. "And you gave it up…to take your brother's place."

He wasn't looking at me when he nodded.

On a sigh, he grabbed both steaming plates, carried them over to the island, and set them next to me.

He pressed both his hands to the counter on either side of me, gazing at my face. He looked so vulnerable.

"My little drummer boy," I whispered, fluttering my fingers across the tattoo etched on his chest.

"Lex," he murmured, wedging himself between my knees. He twisted my hair up in his hand. And he kissed me. Slowly.

This wasn't a plea.

This was a promise.

Then he edged back, plucked two forks from the drawer, and handed one to me. "Eat, sweet girl."

twenty-seven

ZEE

I sat at my piano.

Silence swam through the stilled darkness of the loft. Like waves lapping at my bare skin. Cool and soft. It was almost enough to convince me I wasn't submerged. Suffocating where I drowned.

Seven years.

Seven years I stood on the foundation of my loyalty.

Now the evidence of my treachery lie twisted in my sheets upstairs.

My perfect torment.

A faultless penalty.

In the end, I knew I was gonna lose her, too. It was the way it always went down. Coming so close to something great right before it was ripped away.

Joy nothing but a cruel-hearted tease.

But I couldn't help but feel some of it—joy.

Wrapping me in ribbons just the same as her caress. This girl who'd been breathing all that vibrant life into me.

Her belief.

No fear. Just life.

A huff of a breath pressed from between my lips. That energy—a steady rhythm that beat through my blood—hadn't abated since I'd held her in my arms six hours ago. She'd drifted into the most peaceful kind of sleep, stealing mine and affording it, too.

The stark conflict of what she made me feel was mind-bending.

But it didn't matter how hard I tried to shun it. It was right there. Nipping at my heels and prodding at my spirit.

My fingers twitched as the faintest whisper of that song glided through my veins.

Life.

I pulled in a breath, drawn, fingers at the keys. Emotion knotted tight in my throat, and I set my foot against the soft pedal to keep it muted.

I rasped out a gush of air from my lungs when I pressed my fingers down, the strike of the chord like a flash fire across my skin.

I played, the sound subdued against the darkness of my loft, amplified in her spirit that seeped down from above.

There was nothing I could do. Nothing to keep it from pouring out.

The overflow.

Spilling.

Crashing.

Flooding.

I got lost in it, gliding through the feeling.

In the music that danced all around me, waiting on me to reach out and take it. Make it mine. Give it life and beauty.

That beauty and the unrelenting pain.

Two always seemed to go hand in hand.

Everything intensified, and I gave myself over to the song. To the lyrics that twisted and grew. The words meant for her, murmured silently on my tongue.

Written in the skies

Bleeding stars and broken hearts
Scattered wishes and shattered dreams
Never knew you were strewn
Right there with them

They felt real. Just like she said. Meant to be.

They flowed through my mind like the chords flowed through my fingers.

That space between us alive.

Bigger than before.

Consuming.

Everything sizzled and the hairs at the nape of my neck stood on end. Attention rapt. Hunger throbbed in my gut and became a thriving entity when I felt fingertips glide down the bare skin of my back.

The ground fucking shook.

She was the first girl who'd ever given me chills. The first one to make me think there might be something better out there than the constant disappointment. Than the torture of the day to day.

She wrapped the comfort of those slender arms around me, her lips pressing fast to the top of my shoulder.

"Magic," she murmured. "You play the drums for the world to see, and they have no clue about the talent that's hiding inside you."

She leaned in closer, the words a promise against the shell of my ear. "My little drummer boy."

A groan climbed straight out of my spirit and dove into the atmosphere. I snatched her wrist and swiveled around.

Alexis stood there wearing nothing but my sheet wrapped under her arms. A torrent of that white hair fell all around her in soft, seductive waves, making her glow, that knowing shimmer that glinted and danced within the passion and strength of those striking blue eyes.

A clash of the deepest sea and the darkest heavens.

Starshine.

"And you are a fucking vision."

I slowly stood and Alexis took a step back. I was wearing nothing but my underwear, my cock raging like a beast as it fought against the thin fabric.

If I was giving in, I might as well take it all.

Her attention dropped to where I was straining for her like a madman. Like she felt the weight of my body's demand. A rush of that red crawled across her chest and climbed the delicate slope of her neck.

I couldn't see it in the shadows, but I felt it. Could feel the heat. The attraction that flamed.

The need and the confusion that lapped in that space that came alive every goddamned time.

Maybe it was what had finally thrown me over the edge. Maybe it was what had me edging her back, stalking toward her as she clutched that bottom lip between her teeth, one of those affected, sweet smiles fighting to break free.

She kept backing up with every step I took in her direction. A tiny gasp escaped her when her back hit the windowpane. I pressed both my hands over her head. Trapping her.

Because fuck.

I didn't want to let her go.

She was lit up by the cityscape, like the girl was the focus in some kind of precious portrait. A shimmery silhouette. A light in the darkness that held me captive.

And I was thinking foolish thoughts.

Wondering if I just might find my way out of the darkness and finally break free if she lit the way for long enough.

"Do you have any idea what you're doing to me, gorgeous? Are you trying to send me straight outta my mind?" I followed the curve of her jaw with the tip of my index finger.

She shivered beneath it, head tipping up as I trailed it down. I let it glide the length of her delicate neck and across her collarbone.

I leaned in closer, two of us breathing the other's breath.

"I hope so, because I'm pretty sure I've already lost mine," she murmured.

"Alexis." It was a groan. I pressed her tighter against the

window. "Now that I've had you, I don't want to stop."

She lifted that brave chin, making more of those demands I had no idea how to heed and even less of an idea of how to resist. "Tell me you need me."

I gripped a handful of the sheet covering that tight, sweet body. "I've never needed anyone…anything…the way I need you."

I gave it a tug, and the satiny material pulled free, pooling like a beggar kneeling at her feet.

This angel that was nothing but temptation.

Bare.

Soft.

"Lex." I splayed my palm across the beat of her heart, right between those gorgeous tits. I cupped the right one, thumb brushing her pretty pink nipple, fucking loving the way it pebbled and grew tight.

Loved the way she panted when I trailed down, brushing the delicate skin of her soft belly before I cinched my hand down tight on her hip.

She gasped. "Zachary."

"What do you need?" It was all a demand.

She didn't hesitate. "I need you."

I spun her around, her hands flat to the window. I wound the long locks of her hair into my hand, mouth at her ear. "You are so goddamned sweet. So gorgeous."

My opposite hand rode the path of her spine, that damned star taunting me with its promise. Her ass jutted out as if on command, and I palmed her round bottom.

She shuddered, her sweet voice going rough with desire. "Zee."

"I know, baby. I know exactly what you need."

I shouldn't. It should be so fucking foreign that I didn't have a clue. But somehow, this girl made me remember myself, exactly the way she made me remember my piano.

I tightened my hold in her hair, guiding her lower, demanding all she had to offer.

"Perfection."

Knees shaking, her breaths came harsher and harder as I tugged her hips out and closer to me, her hands pressed to the window to keep her standing.

I was overcome with the reality of it.

I didn't ever want to see this girl fall. Never wanted her to darken or dim.

Wanted her to shine forever.

Which meant what I wanted most was to snuff out her threat.

Keeping hold of her with one hand, I twisted out of my underwear, kicked them free from my feet. I held my dick at the base, rubbing just the tip through her slick heat, so wet and ready for me.

Lust gripped me everywhere, spirit crushed by a devastating need.

I drove home, and Alexis screamed.

Like she wasn't anticipating the full intrusion of me. Like she was just as unprepared as I'd been for the chaos that had devastated me when I'd found her standing at my door earlier this evening.

That had been the moment she had loosed something intrinsic in me.

Now I didn't know how to hold it back.

So, I took her the way I could feel her taking hold of my heart, my hands splayed wide and gripping her ass while I pounded into the sweet, tight clutch of her body.

Her walls grasped at my cock.

It spun my mind with earth-shattering bliss.

I fucking loved that she let me take her bare. Like this precious girl needed me as close as she could get me. Like it might erase some of the bullshit fighting to separate us.

I let my thumbs run the crease of her ass, teasing her into a frenzy of need as I fucked her wild. She begged my name.

Zachary. Zachary. Zachary.

I fell into the spellbinding power of it. Into the feel of her body and the sound of her gasps. Got lost in that energy that pitched through the air.

Alexis tumbled over the edge.

I could feel her sinking in everywhere as she took me with her.

My body bowed as I came. Exploded. Mind-blowing, earth-shattering pleasure.

My fingers dug deeper into her hips because I didn't ever want to let her go.

If I could, I'd let this girl take me wherever she went.

Finally, her knees went weak, and she sagged forward. I held her up, one hand scooping up the sheet in the same second I swept her into my arms, carrying her back to my bed.

Without a doubt, I was the biggest fool who'd ever lived.

Because that was exactly where I wanted to keep her.

My cell vibrating on my nightstand pulled me from sleep. I groaned and blinked into the breaking day.

Blindly, I swatted for it. Truth of the matter? I didn't want to move. For a second, I just wanted to relish in the feel of her curled up in my hold, her head on my shoulder and that sweet body tucked up close to mine.

I finally focused on my phone when it rang again.

Baz.

I accepted the call and pressed it to my ear, voice gruff with sleep. "This better be important, asshole. Not even six in the morning."

And I was getting about the best damned night of sleep in my life. Last thing I wanted was to get roused from the dream. This fucking perfect, impossible dream.

"Got a call from Ash a half hour ago. Willow's water broke in the middle of the night. They've been at the hospital for a few hours. Looks like it's happening soon. Shea and I are heading that way. It's family time, brother."

A shot of fear jolted through me, worry I could never

shake. The need to keep this family tight. Safe.

Alexis stirred and shifted to look over at me with concern.

"It's early, isn't it?" I asked him.

I could feel Baz's easiness through the phone, his own anticipation blazing through. "Nah, man, like three weeks. Shea says that's cool. If he's ready, he's ready."

That fear shifted to excitement, and that feeling of commitment pounded through my veins. "All right. Be there in a bit."

I ended the call and let the phone drop to the bed.

My world skidded to a stop when I glanced over at the girl who was staring at me from where she was propped up on her elbow, at the ready to be at my side the same way I wanted to be for her.

She was so fucking pretty. Gorgeous in that humble way, and that feeling tightened in my chest. That feeling I couldn't allow her to make me feel but she was pulling from me anyway.

I should tell her I needed to go. That I'd see her later, all the while knowing I was shutting her out.

Because I couldn't afford for her to get any closer to me. Couldn't afford whatever the fuck was happening between us.

I should've ended it right there, because after last night things were more intense than they'd ever been.

I should.

Instead, I smiled and patted her sweet ass. "Come on, we have a baby on the way."

twenty-eight

ALEXIS

"Are you sure it's okay I'm here?"

Zee clasped my hand in his as we climbed into the elevator. He squeezed me a little tighter and tossed me a glance that breezed through me like the calm after a ravaging summer storm.

His expression was the kind that made you want to look toward the sky in wonder. To memorize the moment—engrave it on your heart—because you were sure you'd never experience anything quite so beautiful again.

"I want you here."

I was still reeling after last night, still staggered by the fact that he had given in.

I'd felt it, the shift in our worlds as everything tipped and became something brand new.

Something better.

This connection profound.

I nestled a little closer to him. "Good, because this is exactly where I want to be."

Four people climbed into the elevator with us. Affection pulled at my spirit when Zee didn't pull away or try to put space between us. All this time, he'd seemed terrified someone might look at us and put two and two together—add us up as one.

I'd tried not to allow it to offend me. Struggled with the facts he'd given me and attempted to understand and not take it as a rejection.

But it was hard when the man you wanted to stand beside kept you hidden in the shadows. When that man made you another of his secrets without revealing to you the reason to keep them in the first place.

It hurt and always came like a slap to the face.

A stark reminder that all of this was going to end.

So, when he reached out and framed my face in both his hands, it meant…everything.

"That's good, gorgeous, because right here is exactly where I want you to be."

His mouth tugged at the side, and something cocky and sure glided into his features. Leaning down, he murmured in my ear, "Thing about last night, Alexis?"

Chills skated my skin. I could barely nod.

"It was the best damned night I've had in a lot of years."

I stared up at him, my truth sliding out. Because I refused to tiptoe. To make it less. "Last night was the best night I've ever had."

I wanted to ask him what his had been. If he could remember the moment when his life had changed permanently for the better, or if the secrets and shame had overshadowed that second, scratched and scratched and scratched at that sacred space until it was dull and dim.

Zee brushed his thumb along the hollow beneath my eye. His gaze flickered with fondness and fear. "You shouldn't even be real, Alexis Kensington. You're a gift. A treasure."

I wanted to tell him gifts were to be received. Given. Taken without penalty or concern. Somehow, as I stood there, I got the feeling he was terrified I might come at the greatest cost.

I lowered my voice to shield my confession from the other people on the elevator. "You came as an offering to me, Zee. Complete and whole and willing to give up everything. Do you have any idea what that means to me?"

I reached out and tapped my fingers at the roar that drummed in his chest. "I cherish you...I cherish this giving heart…more than you could ever know."

The words were right there, spinning in the atmosphere, magnified in the tight confines of the elevator.

I adore you.

I am lost to you.

I'm in love with you.

I kept the confessions tamed, devotion on the tip of my tongue.

I thought maybe with him towering over me, staring at me with the potency of his gaze, he knew it anyway.

The elevator dinged. It jumped us back, and I couldn't stop the giddy sensation from sweeping through me when he sent me a knowing grin. My teeth clamped down on my lip as if it I could keep it contained.

Keep it forever.

"Come on, I think we're this way."

We followed the signs that directed us to labor and delivery. The hall opened up to a large waiting room, which was full of people.

Sunder had taken over.

They looked completely out of place, the appearance of these boys so menacing and bad and bold. But there was no chance of missing the excitement that bounded from each of them as they waited on something so precious.

As precious as their children who were gathered around them, the older two, Kallie and Brendon, sharing an iPad where they sat on the chairs, the younger two, Adia and Connor, were on the floor, playing with toys.

Shea, Tamar, and Edie, who was holding Sadie, were engaged in their own eager conversation.

When I'd left Willow and Ash's house that night, I'd

thought I understood the love this stitched up, patchwork family had for each other. The strength of the devotion they had for one another.

But I didn't think I really got it until that moment.

Not until I literally felt the loyalty pulse through Zee when he stepped into the fray.

Baz shot to his feet. "Zee, man, you're here. About time."

They went in for a handshake, both of them clapping each other on the back. "Well, if you would've given me a little more heads-up, I would've gotten here earlier."

Baz slanted a knowing glance at me, a wry grin taking to his mouth. "Looks to me like you were otherwise occupied."

My gaze dropped as I pressed my lips together, trying to hide the flush of embarrassment that made a straight ascent to my cheeks.

And I thought Zee might step away. Put space between us.

Friends.

Instead, he cast me the most tender kind of smile. "Yeah, guess I was."

Emotion clutched me everywhere. Affection, warmth, and hope.

Shea climbed to her feet. "Oh my God, Alexis, you're here." She hugged me tight as she rocked us. "It's so good to see you again."

"It's so good to see you, too."

It was true. True when I said hello to Austin and Lyrik. True when I hugged Tamar and Edie.

The truth of the matter was, I'd fallen a little bit for all of them.

I caressed my fingertips over Sadie's tiny fist and her even tinier fingers, this sweet, sweet girl with her pouty pink lips and cherub face.

My hammering heart shot into a frenzy when Zee dropped to a knee beside Adia and Connor, bringing me with him. He ran a loving hand over both of their heads as I whispered my hellos.

Some things were so adorable they physically hurt.

Zee straightened back to standing, keeping hold of my hand. "How's it going in there? Any news?"

Lyrik shook his head and roughed his palms down his thighs, his tattooed hands pressing into his jeans. "Who knows, man. They've been back there for close to five hours now. Only experience I have on the matter is Adia, and she sure didn't seem to want to give up her hold on my Blue."

Tamar grinned at him. "Stubborn, just like her daddy."

His expression was nothing but adoration as they looked at each other. Clearly both of them were right back in the middle of that day.

"Heck yeah, she's just like her daddy. Look at the little thing…little spitfire isn't about to let boys push her around, either."

Adia was rambling incoherent orders to Connor where they played with a pile of wooden bricks on the floor.

Lyrik looked back at Zee. "Think it was something like thirty hours we were in there. Pretty much was about to go straight out of my damned mind with the worry. Can't even imagine how our boy Ash is handling it right now. Surprised all the nurses on the floor aren't running for the hills. Be willing to throw down some dollars Ash is back there being an overprotective beast."

Austin chuckled, his glance a soft caress against his wife where he watched her hugging their daughter. "And my Edie barely made it to the hospital. Thought I was gonna have to pull over and deliver that baby girl in the backseat."

Edie scoffed, though it was tender. "I'm pretty sure there would have been no delivering where you were concerned. You just about passed out as it was."

Baz laughed, all tease. "Ahh, baby brother, just couldn't man up and handle it when things got messy, huh?"

Shea nudged his arm. "Oh, you're going to sit over there and give Austin a hard time?"

Shea hooked at thumb at her husband. "Y'all should've seen the way this guy was sweatin' in that delivery room when I had Connor. You'd think he'd just run a marathon when I was the one trying to squeeze out a kid."

Baz was all grins and affection. "Hey, I'm not too big to admit when you all have us outdone."

"Survival of the fittest, baby." Shea winked at him.

Tamar threw up a high-five to Shea. "Exactly."

Lyrik held up his hands. "No arguments here."

Zee shook his head. "Well, let's just hope this one is as painless as it can be…both for Ash and Willow."

He smiled at me, tugging at my hand. "Better get comfortable…this could be a while."

I curled up next to Zee on a chair. Tamar and Shea were on the other side of me. I felt like a part of them, their quiet murmurings of encouragement, the low laughter that rang with support.

I couldn't keep my eyes from the children. From the way Zee watched them with outright reverence. His demeanor was so soft.

But there was no missing the way it carried some of that grief each time his gaze landed on them.

Softly, I brushed his leg, my voice even softer, dipping my toes in a little deeper, trying to get inside him. "Do you want that someday? A family?"

His fists clenched, but still he looked at me, eyes so intense. Unyielding. "Definition of family means a lot of different things to different people."

"What is your definition?"

"Commitment." He said it without reservation, gesturing with his chin around the room.

"These people…I'd die for any one of them, Alexis. I'm committed to them. I don't share blood with a single one of them, but that doesn't matter in the least. They're my family. Tried and true."

I kept my voice discreet, our conversation private. Knowing I was pushing and not having the first clue how to stop myself. "But what about what they have? Love? Marriage? Children? Do you ever want that for yourself?"

He surprised me by grasping my face and forcing me to get

up close to his. "You think I don't, Alexis? You think if I could have it, it wouldn't be the greatest fucking honor? But I already told you…I have my loyalties and they're set in stone. I'm bound to them. It doesn't matter how much I want more. *He's* my life."

We both froze the second he said it.

I blinked at him. Searching. Pleading.

Tell me.

Everyone's phones dinged with text notifications at the same time.

Baz hopped to his feet with a huge grin on his face. "He's here."

All the couples took turns going back to meet the new baby. An hour later, I was at Zee's side as we made our way to Willow's room.

Zee tapped at the door that was already open a crack and popped his head inside. "Still a good time?"

"Yeah," a deep voice uttered.

Zee nudged the door open a little wider and held it open for us to enter. Inside, the lights were dimmed, and Willow was propped in the bed.

Exhaustion rimmed her entire being. Though she glowed with a happiness unlike anything I'd ever witnessed before. It glimmered around her like a halo, as if she'd been lifted to another plane.

Her attention was fully on her husband, who sat in the chair next to her, holding the tiniest creature I'd ever seen in his massive arms. His head was dropped.

In a daze, he looked up when we approached.

Ash was such a big, burly guy. The couple of times I'd met him, he'd been full of laughter and quick with a tease. So it was a shock to see tears in his eyes, glinting with devotion, love, and wonder.

He blinked, words raw when he turned back to the child. "I have a son."

Zee released my hand, intensity running wild as he edged deeper into the room. He set a hand on Ash's shoulder and looked down at the baby, his voice rough. "He's beautiful, man. So perfect."

"I can't believe it, Zee. Can't believe I'm holding my son. Colton."

My attention drifted to Willow, who was watching them through bleary eyes.

"Congratulations," I whispered, not sure where I stood in the middle of this but humbled to be a part of it all the same. "I'm so happy for you."

Her smile was soft when she glanced at me. "It's the only thing I ever wanted."

She turned back to them, her voice a breath of reverence. "A family."

Ash looked at her. "I never knew it was exactly what I needed until I met you."

Need.

I swear everything punched me in the gut. The overwhelming devotion. The belief that there were good things waiting all around us. I had so much to be thankful for in my life.

But what I'd been missing was someone to believe in *me.*

Until Zee.

This mesmerizing man who set his big hand so tenderly on the top of Ash and Willow's son's head. Affection and love poured from him. "You deserve it, man. You and Willow. Take it and cherish it and don't ever let it go."

Overcome, Ash nodded up at him, a silent understanding transpiring between the two.

I felt like a foreigner peeking in at something great. Missing the details. No question, their stories went deep, but that didn't mean I couldn't see the big picture, and I wanted to be a part of it.

Zee straightened. I took a step back when I saw his expression, staggered by the amount of emotion he held there.

Love and grief.

Fear and life.

He reached over and squeezed Willow's hand. "You did good, Willow. So damned good."

She nodded, and he released her and strode toward me. He took my hand without a word, and I mumbled a goodbye, wondering how I'd lost footing in those few moments.

We stepped outside into the hall where the rest of the guys had gathered.

"Ever think you'd see the day?" Baz asked.

Zee shook his head. "Nope, but I'm sure as hell glad I did. Anyone deserves it, it's Ash."

Baz punched his shoulder. "Maybe it's time you started to believe you deserved some of this, too."

I got the feeling Zee didn't want to look at me. I squeezed his hand. A silent *it's okay.*

The door opened behind us, and everyone turned to see Ash stepping out. He ran a hand over his face. Nerves seemed to shake him through. "Can I have a word with you guys?"

I didn't even wait for someone to ask me to leave. I just brushed my fingers against Zee's arm and said, "I'll be right over there."

I slipped over to the corner, wishing I was out of earshot and feeling like a snoop when Ash's words floated to me.

"I can't do it…I'm so fucking sorry, but there is no way I'm going back out on the road and leaving them."

Anxiety took to the air.

I backed a little farther away, knowing I shouldn't be privy to something so private, but unable to get far enough away that I couldn't hear them before I backed into a corner.

Lyrik shook his head. "You can't just bail like that, man. Give it some time. You have a few weeks to process. Figure out how to make all this work. You just went through the most intense moment you'll ever experience. Let it settle."

"A few weeks?" Ash's voice was incredulous. "I didn't

bring a kid into this world so I could have a few weeks with him before I left him behind."

Something dark flashed through Lyrik's face. "And you think I was ever wantin' to go and leave Tamar and my kids behind? Not ever. Not once. But I did it because I had an obligation to the band. An obligation to you."

Austin paced in a circle, agitated, his words suddenly flooding out. "I've got Ash's back on this. We've got newborns. *Newborns,* man. Being on the road isn't the way to raise a family."

Lyrik's laughter came across as scorn. "So, it was all fucking fine when I had to hit the road and leave Tamar and Adia? She was *two months old.* It nearly fucking destroyed me."

"Then you get exactly why I can't do this," Ash shot out.

I didn't want to see it, but I was watching wide-eyed when I saw the outright pain split Zee's expression.

Baz set a hand on Lyrik and Ash's shoulders. As if he were keeping them apart in the middle of a boxing match.

"How about we drop this right now, yeah? Think it'd do us well not to go causing a scene in the middle of the hospital on the day Ash's kid is born. Let's meet next week and we'll talk it out. Figure what's best. For everyone."

Lyrik rubbed his face with both hands, dropped them just as fast. "Fuck…I'm sorry, Ash. Just hit me wrong, that's all."

Ash shook his head. "You think I want to do this? Hurt any of you? I just—"

He looked back to the room, as if he were tied in some elemental way. A band stretched between him and what waited for him behind the door.

Tugging and tugging and tugging.

No doubt that kind of draw left a man with zero resistance.

Baz gestured that direction with his chin. "Go. Be with Willow and your son. Enjoy this moment. We'll deal with the rest of this shit next week. I don't want you even giving it any consideration right now. You got me?"

Ash nodded as he backed away. "Thanks, man." His gaze bounced to each of the guys. "All of you…you don't know what it means to me. That you're here. That *my family* is yours."

Everyone nodded. All except for Zee, who still hadn't said anything.

Pain leached the color from his face. Worry and questions spun. I started to go to him, but he was already on the move, stalking down the hall and out the double doors we'd had to be buzzed through to enter.

I followed. I could feel the surprised stares from Tamar, Edie, and Shea who had retreated back to the waiting room to sit with their children.

Zee stormed right by, not even offering a parting glance.

Panic bubbled up in my spirit. "Zee," I called.

He increased his speed, only stumbling a fraction when he got to the elevators just as a man was stepping from it. The man was wearing a suit and carrying a big teddy bear in the crook of his arm and a bouquet of flowers in the other.

Familiarity flashed.

It took me only a second to realize he'd been with Zee that first day when I'd run into him outside the police station.

He muttered a few words I couldn't hear at Zee, but Zee only shook his head, didn't say anything as he hopped on the elevator.

I was right behind him.

Shock widened the man's eyes when he saw me before his expression downshifted into anger and worry.

I hated the feeling of being out of place. The feeling that I might not belong. Insecure was something I'd never wanted to be.

But I couldn't stop it under the weight of his stare, the stare I felt boring into me when I called for Zee again and rushed to get into the elevator with him before the doors shut.

Zee was panting, pacing the enclosed space.

"Zee," I whispered.

His hands fisted, and he sped up again, a building cyclone of energy.

The doors opened at the first floor, and he flew out. I rushed behind him, out through the two sliding doors and into the sun. Zee stormed down the walkway that led down the side of the hospital building, only slowing when he got to an area with shade trees and benches.

He came to a stop facing away, his hand reaching out to support him on the trunk of a tree.

Warily, I touched his back. "Zee. Tell me what's happening."

He flinched, every inch of him rigid. "I can't let this happen, Alexis. I can't. I promised. I fucking promised."

Agitation swirled through our connection, and I inched around him. Slowly. Carefully. Terrified he might push me away.

I wanted to hold him a little, the way he'd been holding me. I nudged him back, wedging myself in his space. I felt desperate to look into the depths of his eyes.

So I could see where Zee held his secrets.

So I could witness where he held his truths.

"What? Who did you promise?"

"Mark." The word broke, and his hand fisted on the bark. "I promised him. Promised him no matter what, whatever the cost, I would keep this band together."

I blinked up at him. "How could that ever be your responsibility?"

Bitterness shook his head. "It is my responsibility, Lex."

He hit a fist against his chest. "It's all on me. This band…these guys…they almost lost everything because of me. And when Mark died…I promised him I would keep them together. For him. That I would make sure they found those dreams they'd been living for."

His lips pinched in torment. "I've spent seven fucking years, Alexis, *seven years* watching their every move. Trying to keep them out of trouble. Praying they'd make it home at night when they were out doing whatever they did."

My brow pinched. "How was that on you?"

Mocking laughter ripped from his chest. "I was always the outsider, Lex. Always the one on the outside looking in. All of them treating me like a little kid when I was sitting there desperate to keep the pieces together."

"Zee," I attempted, but he pushed on, agony flashing in his eyes.

"And I thought maybe…maybe now that they were all growing up—now that they were getting married and finding families—I thought maybe that pressure was gonna ease up."

"Hasn't it?" I asked.

He shook his head. "I just…I thought Mark might be looking down, watching me, and I'd know I made him proud. Thought maybe now I could finally start working for those things I needed to make right in my life."

Grief slammed me from every side.

He was so full of sacrifice and shame.

I reached out and set my palm on his rugged cheek. "What if Mark is looking down? How could he not be proud of you and what you've become? How could he not be looking down at the guys…his best friends…his family…and not be at peace, knowing every single one of them has found happiness? The good kind of joy?"

He trembled against my palm, that energy potent with the connection. "They had a pact, Alexis, a pact that they were going to make it no matter what. Nothing was going to stand in their way. Sunder is what Mark wanted more than anything in his life."

I could feel the frown that pulled at my brow. "And how do you know that wouldn't have changed for Mark? How do you know he wouldn't have found love like the rest of the guys?"

He flinched with that.

Pain. It was so damned intense. I wanted to caress it away.

"Priorities change, Zee. Don't you see that? We grow and we learn and we find out some things are so much more important than the things we originally thought were the most significant. Sometimes we find they aren't significant at all."

Helplessly, he looked down at me. "I gave up my whole fucking life, Alexis. Everything. Everything I ever wanted. Every goal I ever made…every love I ever had…to keep that promise."

"Zee," I whispered, edging closer, letting the warmth zap and fire between us.

His breaths became shallower with every inch I erased. I tipped my face toward him. The man towered over me.

Caging.

Consuming.

Obliterating everything but him.

"Do you really think this is what Mark would want? You running around trying to keep things together? Terrified a piece is going to slip through the cracks and you aren't going to catch it in time? What about what the rest of the guys want? What about what *you* want?"

His throat bobbed. "I owed him this, Alexis. Owed him everything."

"How could he ever ask that of you? Expect that from you?"

Zee's hands landed on either side of my neck. I could feel the wild thrum of my pulse beating against his palms. "Because I took everything from him."

Bitterness shook his head, and he gritted the words as he studied his feet. "And I sound like some kind of pussy asshole…complaining when I've got the rock star life. When I've got more money than I could ever spend. Have more experiences than I ever thought I'd have. When I inherited this amazing family."

He cut his gaze to me. "And all I fucking want is for them to be happy. For them to live the good life, whatever that looks like for each of them. I'm just not sure I know how to keep it all together any longer. Can feel it slipping away and, when it does, I'm going to be left without anything."

The words broke, as if the thought of it broke his heart.

"Keeping them together doesn't have to mean keeping them together as a band. What about family? And what about me? You have *me*," I pleaded.

"Goddamn it, Alexis." He grasped me tighter, a war in his gaze.

Am I worth the fight?

His mouth collided with mine. Dominating and devouring. His tongue fevered and his touch demanding as he pulled me closer, hands in my hair and gripping down my back.

I let him possess me right out there in the open. Beneath the sun and the trees. And I thought maybe, just maybe, I had my answer.

twenty-nine
ZEE

"Where are we going?"

Alexis struggled to keep up as I eagerly hauled her along behind me. Seemed it'd been that way a whole lot of late. Me pulling her along. Wanting her with me no matter where I went.

I was unable to fight back the full smile that broke free. "Figured you could use a little fresh air."

She giggled, a tinkling sound that bounced off the closed-in walls of the stairwell. "Fresh air? In the middle of Hollywood? Don't tell me you're confused and think you're back in Savannah."

Grinning, I kept climbing the stairs to the building rooftop. A tease found its way into my voice. "Isn't it you who's always going on about making the best of the things we've got?"

"I guess I am, aren't I?"

"Yeah." I glanced at her from over my shoulder. "You've just got this way of seeing all the good through the bad. Figured you might wanna take a peek at this, as well."

A flush rushed to her cheeks, anticipation swelling with that shyness that had her chewing at her lip.

There were few things I liked more than that. The humbleness radiating from this tender girl. The grace and the good that emanated from her like a lullaby.

Harmony.

Her voice softened. "I'm not sure I don't see the bad in things, Zee. Sometimes I just choose to look at them differently."

"Case in point."

Confusion slowed her and a line dented her brow. So damned cute. "What?"

Light laughter filtered free. "You just keep proving my point, again and again. You're better than me. Better than this…what I've been giving you."

She blinked up at me. "When are you going to realize you've given me more than anyone ever has?"

"Lex," I sighed, smiling at this girl who kept tripping me up. Distracting me. Leading me astray.

Wanted to follow her everywhere.

When we made it to the top, I wedged open the heavy door. A gust of warm wind blasted across our faces as we stepped out onto the rooftop.

Alexis gasped and immediately wandered out toward the railing at the edge. "Oh my God. It's incredible up here. I had no idea this was even here."

"Best part of the whole place, in my opinion."

Her smile was so bright when she looked back at me, those locks of white whipping around her face as another gush of wind came barreling through.

"I would have to agree," she whispered as she turned back to the view.

A summer storm was on the horizon, the city alive on the streets below, and up here, you couldn't help but feel removed from it all.

Like you were looking at it through a different sort of lens. A lens that obscured and bent and distorted. Made things look better than they were.

Night wrapped us tight from above, sinking so low it felt as if we could reach out and dip our fingers into its murky depths.

Hidden in the darkness was a blanket I'd come up earlier and spread out on the ground. I had a bottle of wine chilling in a bucket, fruit and crackers on a tray, pillows spread about.

All that shit that was supposed to be romantic.

Because I wanted to share that with this girl. Something normal. Give her something good. And having a glass of wine with her sure wasn't any worse than the traditional shot I always took with my crew after a show. Maybe she and I were making our own little pact.

I couldn't help but find an extreme contentment in that.

Alexis looked over at me. A gasp parted her lips when she noticed where I was kneeling on the blanket. Something so damned simple. And there she was, looking at me like I might have given her the world. "Zee…you did all this for me?"

I pulled the wine from the ice and focused on removing the cork. "This is nothing, Alexis."

She edged my direction, wearing a thin, loose-fitted dress, white like her hair that whipped all around her.

Chaos and light.

Angel.

Temptation.

I swallowed hard as she approached.

"It means something to me." There was no missing the undercurrent. That she meant more. That *I* meant something.

Just like she was coming to mean something to me.

Too much.

"And I think you know it does, because if you didn't, you wouldn't put in the effort." The smallest of smirks lifted to her sweet mouth. "You know, since I'm already kind of a sure thing."

Surprised laughter jetted from my lungs.

This girl.

She took me by surprise at every turn.

"You are, huh?"

Slowly, she settled onto her knees on the blanket. "Mmhmm…considering every time I get around you, I can't seem to keep my hands to myself."

I inched closer, my mouth just brushing hers. "I'm thinking that's just fine. I kinda like those hands on me."

She blushed, dropping her gaze for a heated second before she looked back at me with this adoring expression on her face. "Zee."

I pushed out a sigh. "Get over here. Seems when I get around you, I can't keep my hands to myself, either."

She released a giggle, and I settled to the ground, pulling her between my legs and letting her back rest against my chest.

I reached around her, finished working the cork from the wine, and poured us each a glass. "Something tells me you like it sweet."

Just the way I liked her. Pink and sweet and luscious. Every delicate, lust-inducing inch.

She took a sip. "It's delicious."

My mouth was at her ear as I wrapped an arm around her waist. "Exactly what I was thinking."

She released a contented sigh, and I leaned back a little more so we could turn our gazes to the weighted sky that rippled with the glow of the city below, while we sipped our wine and nibbled at the food. Relaxed in a moment's peace, as if nothing mattered other than this.

"It's gorgeous out here. You were right, I needed some fresh air."

I pressed my lips to her temple. "It reminds me of you, you know."

"What?"

"The sky." My voice was a throaty rumble. "Beautiful and deep. I look up at it, at the massiveness of it, and it feels like anything might be possible."

Fingertips fluttered across my forearm. "I like to believe everything is…if we want it badly enough. Believe in it strongly enough."

"And that's exactly why I can't stop looking at you."

She shifted deeper into my hold, like she felt safe there and wanted more. Of all the things I wanted to give her, safety was the one thing I could actually deliver.

Silence swam around us. Palpable like that space that came alive. Though there was so little distance between us, the energy had gathered to a sharp point. Compressed and amplified. Like her spirit was slowly becoming a part of mine.

"I wish we could see the stars from here," she whispered.

She didn't even have to look, her eyes still attuned to the sky, her fingers attuned to me. Tracing over the star on the back of my hand. "To me, that's what love feels like."

A shudder rocked through my being. This girl too keen. I should have shut it up and shut it down. Instead, I was murmuring the words, coaxing her deeper. "What's it feel like?"

Her voice was a wisp of emotion. "The falling part. Like you can't catch yourself, no matter how hard you try, even if you wanted to. And I don't want to."

I clutched her tighter. Maybe if I held her tight enough, I wouldn't ever have to let go. "Don't. Fall."

"I think it might already be too late."

My chest hurt from the pressure. From all the things I wanted and everything I wanted to give her. I wanted to say something, but any words felt bottled, these overbearing chains of restraint that tugged and pulled and struggled to keep me from falling right along with her.

"Have you ever been in love?" She whispered it like it was a secret. Treasured. Like the answer wouldn't hurt and she'd embrace it like the beauty she was.

I tried to form the lie, but the lie wouldn't come. The admission was dust. "Yeah."

I could sense her sad smile. "What was she like?"

A quiet shot of disbelieving air puffed from my mouth. "You really want to talk about this, Alexis?"

"I told you, I want to know you. I want to know everything about you. Tell me your truth, Zee."

But that was the problem. When she really knew, she'd run.

She'd find no beauty in my truth and all those slivers I had left would be gone.

Emotion throbbed in my throat, my voice turning soft as I let myself get lost in the memory. "She was pretty. Ambitious. That music school I told you about? I met her there. She played violin."

Those fingers were trailing across the star on the back of my hand. "While you played piano."

"Yeah," I said.

"My little drummer boy."

God, this girl was undoing me. Ripping me up and turning me inside out. I didn't even have to tell her playing the drums for Sunder hadn't ever really been me.

She already got it.

Waves of that old grief rushed and surged, pushing at my heart, taunting at my spirit. I chuckled a little. "She was kind of stuffy. Expected things a certain way. Not a whole lot of wiggle room in the world we came from."

The softest giggle rippled out and became one with the wind. "It's hard to picture you that way."

I squeezed her. "What way?"

"Not a badass rock star, all dressed up for a performance. I only have the pictures of you in my head from a different kind of stage."

I buried my laughter at the back of her neck. "I was always a badass. Believe me, I can own a suit."

Light, light laughter, playful and good. "Are you sure about that?"

"Oh, yeah. Girls couldn't get enough of me."

"Now that I can imagine." Alexis sobered. "What happened to her?"

Regret puffed out with my exhale. "I happened, Alexis."

"Do you miss her?"

I hefted a weighty breath. "Used to think I did. It killed me at the time. But I just had to add it up to another thing I'd lost. I can't help but wonder, if I had loved her enough, if she'd have loved me enough, would things have happened differently. Maybe then, we would've stood by each other, made decisions for each other, instead of letting it ruin everything."

Alexis was barely breathing while she absorbed what I said. Processing. Tucking away the few bits I'd offered. I wondered when she was going to hold everything—all of me.

I sucked in a breath, my insides shaking with possession, fighting the feeling that she was mine as I asked her, "You…have you ever been in love? You said there were a couple of guys…serious guys."

She seemed to waver, contemplating her feelings. "I think I've gotten close. In high school, of course I thought I was in love a thousand times and it was over just as fast, and I had a couple guys I dated in college. Then there was Sam…"

I didn't mean to fucking flinch. But I did.

"He was good to me…treated me well, and I liked him a lot. I wanted to love him. But it just wasn't there. Because being in love…it should be something more."

"What is it you want?" I suddenly murmured, right up close to her ear. "What have you been wishing for?"

I could feel the tremble skate her spine. "I don't know, Zee. I just know I want more."

Her voice dropped to a murmured wish. "I want to fall. I want to *feel* it. I want to see stars. Float with them and fall with them."

She burrowed herself deeper. Closer. "*I can feel it.* Can you?"

thirty

ZEE
TWENTY YEARS OLD

"Can you just be cool for one night? It's my brother's birthday."

Julie sat in the passenger seat of the car with her arms crossed over her chest. Over the last couple of years, it'd gotten harder and harder to talk Julie into hanging out with his brother and his crew.

It seemed to be Zee and Julie's single point of contention.

The place where they always seemed to clash.

"I told you I don't feel comfortable around this crowd." Her voice was pleading.

Frustrated, Zee swiped a hand down his face. "If you'd just give them a chance, you'd see they're all really good guys. Yeah, they've made some mistakes, but we all have and there's not a single one of us that is perfect. You know that."

Tears pricked at her eyes. "Give them a chance? Every time we show up to a party, there are drugs all over the place—and before you say something, I know your brother has been trying to stop. That the rest of the guys have. But that doesn't mean it's not right there, in my face."

She pulled in a frantic breath. "Not to mention every single time, there is some slut trying to steal you from me, acting like I'm not even there. Do you have any idea how that makes me feel?"

Searching for patience, he looked to the ceiling. "And you really think that's ever going to work, Julie? That I'd step out on you like that? Mess up my entire life for a night of fucking around? I think you know me better than that. "

He squeezed the steering wheel. "I grew up with them. They've always treated me like a brother. They're family to me."

He loved Julie. He did. So fucking much. But ever since they'd gotten together, he felt like there was a little bit that had gone missing in his life.

Friendship and brotherhood.

That sense of really belonging. That bond to his brother had always been tight, and it was time to take the steps to make sure it didn't weaken.

Julie touched his forearm. "I just worry if you hang around them too much, they're going to influence you into doing something you shouldn't do."

"I'm not twelve."

A frown pulled between her brows. "Why do you have to be like that? This is a legitimate concern. You don't know when you step through that door what kind of situation you'll find yourself in. I care about you. I care about *us*, and you know that isn't the type of crowd we need to be associating ourselves with. You know the kind of reputation it could earn."

Disbelief and frustration flooded the short laugh that Zee released. The problem was, he understood her point, too, and wholeheartedly disagreed at the same damned time. "You're concerned about my reputation? These guys aren't just insanely successful, they're also insanely talented."

She rolled her eyes. "You don't need to pretend like that's music."

"Are you joking right now? Do you think the songs they write are any less important than mine?"

"You're brilliant, Zee. Brilliant. None of them can touch what you do."

"I can't believe you'd say that, Julie. You of all people should know there's importance in everything. In every art, however it's created. Only thing different is how people react to that art. Art touches people in different ways, and each of us is drawn to the different forms of it."

She dropped her head, the words a whisper. "I know that…I'm sorry. I just…"

With wide eyes, she looked over at him. "It scares me, Zee. What they do. The way they live. I don't have room for that in my life."

"But Mark is part of mine."

Nodding, she unlatched her door the second Zee pulled to the curb, like she needed to do it before she changed her mind. "Okay."

Cars lined the streets, and he could already hear the heavy metal blasting through the walls.

"Hey," he called softly.

Before she climbed out, she shifted to look over at him.

"I promise you…none of this even entices me. I want no part of it other than to hang with my brother and his friends."

"Promise?"

"Promise."

Killing the engine, he climbed out and went straight to Julie's side.

He took her by the hand. "Come on, baby, this will be fun. Just…let loose a little bit. Enjoy yourself."

"Okay, I'll try."

He framed her face and kissed her hard. "Thank you for doing this for me."

She brushed her fingers down his chest. "You know I'd do anything for you."

Zee hugged her, so tight. "I love you so fucking much."

She burrowed her fingertips in his waist. "I love you…more than anything."

Ash lifted his shot glass. "To Mark, the birthday boy. May this year be the best yet, brother, full of songs and full of life. And let's not forget the ladies. May there ever be a long line of the lovely, lovely ladies."

Mark lifted his glass and shouted, "Here, here," before he looked down and winked at Veronica, a chick he'd apparently been hooking up with for the last couple of months.

Baz had filled Zee in. He wasn't a fan.

Veronica joined in on lifting her glass.

A slew of glasses clanked where the toast went up in the middle of the packed kitchen, arms stretching wide to make sure they were right in the middle of the festivities.

Zee was laughing as he clinked glasses with everyone in the room before he tossed back his shot. It seemed crazy a freezing cold liquid could light like fire in his belly, warming him from the inside out as it spun his head and slowed his senses.

Still, everything felt heightened.

Good.

He tightened his arm around Julie's waist and nuzzled his face in her neck. "You smell delicious."

Giggling, she pushed at his side. "And you smell like a bar."

"And you smell delicious."

"You already said that. I think someone has had too much to drink." She laughed again, lifting her chin and granting him better access as he kissed up her throat.

God, he loved it when she was like this. When she opened herself up and stepped out from behind the barricades of safety where she liked to stay. When she allowed herself to see where he came from. Who he was outside the tuxedo sitting at a piano to entertain a prim and proper audience.

He was both of those things.

A part of both worlds, and he loved each of them equally.

He thought maybe their last barrier was Julie realizing and accepting it.

"Hey now, hey now." Ash was suddenly right there, breaking the spell. "We never get to see our Zee around here anymore. He finally shows, and here he is, all his focus on this girl he can't seem to get enough of."

Zee pulled back and grinned. "You're exactly right, my friend. I can't get enough."

Ash slammed his hand over his heart. "You just love to destroy me, don't you? Here I thought you came to see me, and look at this atrocity. I'm over here. All. Alone. By my lonesome. Without any lovin'."

Zee gestured with his chin around the house crammed wall to wall, chicks everywhere, on the prowl just the same as the guys. It was a familiar scene Zee recognized all too well.

"Take a look, man," Zee said. "The pickings are a plenty. Don't think you have anything to worry about."

Next to him, Julie cringed. Zee just hugged her tighter.

Ash grinned at her. "Ah…it's all good, Zee. We know why you decided to go break all our hearts and ditch us. Got someone a hundred times prettier to keep your attention."

He was all cocky smiles when he angled his head at her. "Can't really compare to someone as gorgeous as you, now can I?"

Redness flushed Julie's face.

Mark's laugh bounded from across the kitchen as he shouldered through our direction, Veronica in tow. "Better keep an eye on your girl, little brother. Ash here will be trying to steal her away."

Feigned horror struck all over Ash's face. "Never. What kind of delinquent do you think I am?"

Mark chuckled. "We've all seen you in action, asshole. We know exactly what kind of delinquent you are."

Mark squeezed his arm tighter around the girl at his side. "Veronica, don't think I had the chance to introduce you. This is my baby brother, Zee."

Mark's eyes sparked in that old way, full of life, a smirk pulling to his mouth. "Although, he's obviously bigger in all the ways that count. Thanks for outgrowing me, man. That's just not cool. Not cool at all."

Under his breath, Zee laughed. Leave it to Mark to put him on the spot. "Hey, you know I spent my childhood cleaning my plate because the only thing I wanted was to be taller than you." Zee stretched out his arms. "Sweet, sweet success."

Mark's grin softened into a genuine smile. "Now that is something to celebrate. Sweet, sweet success."

Zee turned to Veronica. "Nice to meet you."

Veronica was pretty in a wicked way. She was tall and slim, and thick, super long waves bounced around her shoulders, the edge about her just as dark as the clothes she wore.

"It's great to finally meet you. Your brother never stops talking about you."

"Ahh…I guess that could be awkward."

Maybe he had had too much to drink.

Of course, it was Ash who cracked up while Julie cringed. Again.

Zee was moving to soothe her, his arm locking around her waist as he tugged her close. "This is my girlfriend, Julie."

The only acknowledgement was a mumbled hello, and Zee was wondering why it was chicks were always so damned competitive around each other, sizing each other up.

Like it mattered when it didn't matter in the least.

Ash clapped his hands together. "All right, assholes, I do believe this shindig calls for another round. It's Mark's birthday. You know what that means…doubles."

"How's it you always find a reason for doubles?" I tossed out.

Ash backed away, hands held up with his palms out. "Hey now, hey now, I'm neither a glass half empty nor a glass half full kind of guy. I'm a full then empty then fill it right back up kind of guy."

"Of course you are."

"No shame, man, no shame."

Mark slung an arm around Zee's shoulder. "Glad you're here, little brother. Today wouldn't mean anything without you being by my side. What do you say we celebrate…we never know what day might be our last."

Julie tore out the front door. Zee was right behind her. "Julie, come on. Don't do this."

She didn't slow when she looked at him from over her shoulder. Tears streaked down her face, and her eyes were wide and horrified. "Stay away from me."

Panic bubbled beneath his skin. "It wasn't what it looked like. Please…just…wait."

It didn't take all that much effort for him to catch up. He reached out and snagged her around the wrist.

Rounding on him, she yanked her arm free and kept backing away. Music echoed from the house, the windows lit up, the night all around as Julie edged farther down the yard.

She was in shadows, but that didn't mean Zee could miss the hurt written on her face. The piece of trust that had gone missing.

"It wasn't what it looked like?" she accused.

"It wasn't. I went to take a piss, and she was waiting for me when I came out. She caught me off guard."

"You were kissing her."

Zee roughed a shaking hand over his face, his buzz gone, shot the second he'd stepped out into the hall into what amounted to a trap when Jen, a chick he barely remembered, was waiting for him outside the door. "I wasn't kissing her, Julie. Fuck…you really think I would kiss her? Let alone while you were waiting for me at the end of the hall?"

She pressed both her hands to her chest. "Tell me you haven't slept with her before."

Zee gulped around the regret that threatened to suffocate him. Choices. You left them littered behind you everywhere you went. Time never made them obsolete. "It was years ago, Julie. Before I ever met you."

He watched grief strike her like a lightning rod. She stumbled back and Zee pushed toward her.

"Years ago," he said like a demand, "and it didn't mean anything. Nothing meant anything until I met you."

"I just…" A sob tore up her throat, and she turned away, her hands yanking at clumps of her hair. "I can't…I can't do this, Zee. I know he's your brother, but the girls…and…and then I walked in on him shooting up with his girlfriend."

She turned back toward Zee, her shoulders slumping in helplessness. "It's not me. It's not who I ever want to be or who I want to surround myself with. I'm sorry, Zee. But it's me or it's them."

Relief bounded through his body. It was physical. Palpable in his blood. He lurched for her, wrapping her in his arms, his mouth on her forehead, her cheeks, her lips. "You. I choose you. I will always choose you."

thirty-one
ZEE

Sitting around watching everything you devoted your entire life to crumble around you was kind of surreal. Foundations splintering and walls collapsing.

Like I was watching it implode from a distance, and there wasn't a goddamned thing I could do about it.

Ash leaned forward with his elbows on his knees where he sat in one of the big chairs in Anthony's office, rubbing an anxious hand over the back of his head.

Like maybe he was rubbing at a genie in a bottle.

Making a few wishes so he could set everything right. A solution that worked to the benefit of everyone so each of us could walk out of this room and all those goals and aspirations and loyalties would be set straight.

Problem was, I wasn't sure that any of my crew knew what those loyalties were anymore.

Everything had become convoluted.

Confused.

Those dedications and fidelities had all of a sudden taken a sharp turn, shifting all the focus to a new end game.

"Fuck…you guys don't know how messed up I am over this. Making this decision. Know it leaves you all hanging, scrambling to find a replacement."

"Now you know what that shit feels like." Even though Lyrik's words were hard, there was no resentment. "Letting your crew down and knowing there isn't another choice in the world you can make."

Apparently, he'd had time to cool down since we'd left the hospital two days ago.

Ash shook his head, regretfully staring at his hands that he continuously rubbed together. "Funny how I was the one who hounded you for months until you gave in. Look what that got you. My fault, too."

I hadn't been a part of Sunder in those days. It was nearly ten years ago when Lyrik had tried to leave the band with the intention of leaving the lifestyle behind—the drugs and the parties and the women—so he could focus on what was right.

But I'd been close enough to all of them to get the gist of the tragedy Lyrik had suffered. The loss that had come at the cost of his mistakes.

Had been around to witness the aftermath.

I'd also been there to witness his resurrection.

The man had come back to life the moment Tamar had stepped into his.

Lyrik sighed heavily. "It was shit, man, those days. Everything falling apart. But you know damn well these circumstances are different. We've fought through the bullshit and made something out of it. Found something good. Both with the music and with our families."

Austin sat forward. "Doesn't make any of this easier, though, does it?"

Baz kneaded his fingers into his thigh, knee bouncing a million miles a minute. "I know I don't have the right to say much in the matter, considering I was the one who bailed first. Only thing I can do is offer advice. My own experiences now that I can look back."

Meaningfully, Ash looked at him. "You regret it? Stepping back? Leaving the stage that you love?"

Point blank, Baz stared back. "How could I ever regret a single second spent with my family?"

Ash nodded, knowing he'd be looking back in a few years and thinking the same exact thing.

Anthony was behind his desk, attention bouncing around between everyone, unsettled and uneasy. But just like he always had been, I knew he was there to have the band's back. Ready to step up and fight for whatever was right for us.

I just didn't know how the fuck that included me.

Austin cleared his throat. "I haven't been an official member of Sunder for all that long, but I've felt like it…all those years living with you guys." His lips pursed. "I don't know how all of us can keep going like this. Leaving our families behind. Gets harder every time, and now that there are kids involved..."

Lyrik nodded in agreement. "I know, man."

Austin rubbed the back of his neck. "Know too well that life is a gift. That we don't know how many days we're going to be granted. And the time I spend, I want it to count. *I want it to matter.*"

"Think it's safe to say we all do," Baz agreed softly.

Austin blinked. "I fucking love bein' on that stage. Playing for our fans. Being a part of something bigger than the rest of us. But Edie and Sadie matter more, and I don't want to waste the time I'm given with them."

Lyrik yanked at his hair, agitation burning through his body. "Crazy thing is, this band brought all those amazing things into our lives. Wouldn't have met Tamar if it hadn't been for this band. If it hadn't been for the fact that Anthony sent us out to Savannah to lie low while the dust blew over for Baz after the trouble he got himself into out here in LA."

"And I wouldn't have met Willow," Ash added thoughtfully.

Austin laughed under his breath, glancing over at Ash. "And I definitely wouldn't have had the chance to go sneaking into your sister's room if she hadn't come to spend the summer with us."

Ash pointed at him. "Hey, asshole, I still haven't forgiven you for that."

Austin's brow lifted. "Really?"

Ash laughed. "Nah, not really. Would've kicked your ass at the time, but there isn't any doubt in my mind now that some things are just meant to be."

Meant to be.

Those words tightened my chest and threatened to take hold.

Disbelief filled Baz's chuckle. "Funny how things just work out, yeah? At the time we think everything is fallin' to ruin, only to find out in the end we'd been diverted exactly to the place we were supposed to go."

Lyrik nodded. "Yeah, but what about the music, man? Music's in my blood. Just don't know how to let that go."

Austin hefted a shoulder. "Who said we have to let it go? Maybe we just do it on our terms."

Everyone nodded while that emotion knotted in my throat.

Anthony glanced around. "So, what's this mean?"

Lyrik looked over at him. "Means we do everything how we want. I say we do the show here. End this where we started it. Axe the rest of the tour. Make music when it fits and do some shows around that. But our families always, always come first."

"You assholes are lucky I started the label and I'm gonna let you out of your contract." Baz was all teasing grins.

Everyone laughed while Anthony tapped the back of his pen against his planner. "You guys are certain this is the direction you want to go?"

All of them agreed. Everyone except for me. Because I'd given up my life for this.

For a promise.

My penalty.

My penance.

And now I had a debt I didn't know how to repay.

thirty-two

ALEXIS

The doorbell rang three times in quick succession. Surprised, I rushed for it and hiked up on my toes to peek through the peephole. I sucked in a quick breath when I saw him waiting for me on the other side.

I quickly worked through the lock and opened the door.

He pushed in the second it was unlatched, his big hands on my body as he tugged me against him. He didn't hesitate, his mouth capturing mine.

Desperate.

Hungry.

Impatient.

My fingers sank into his shoulders, trying to make a connection, to break through the haze. Pulling back, I latched on to the confusion in that bronze gaze. "What's wrong?"

Those arms tightened around me. "Tour is cancelled, all except for the show here. Guys say we're gonna do things on our own terms."

I buried my face in his chest. "What exactly does that

mean?"

He hugged me to him, madly, as if I might have the power to hold him together. To help him stand. "It means everything is changing." He sucked in a breath. "Don't know who the fuck I am anymore, Alexis. Don't know who I'm supposed to be. Don't know who I am outside the band."

I pulled back and threaded my fingers through his. "Come here."

I led him to the couch and curled up at his side, our fingers still bound. "Are you okay?"

He shook his head. "I don't know."

"Is this about Mark?"

The sound that huffed from his lungs was unsure. "Think it's always about Mark."

I hesitated as my heart rate picked up a notch, knowing I was pressing, but needing to understand him better. "Tell me about him. About what happened to him."

Zee gulped for air, the pain that ripped through him palpable. "Mark…he was always there for me. Always had my back. Because that's what family does. They stand by you no matter what. But when shit went down and he needed me the most? I wasn't there. Mark needed me, and I didn't have his back. I failed him. God, in so many ways, I failed him."

I squeezed his fingers as I peered up at him. "How?"

He hesitated as if he were searching for what he could share with me, those secrets churning in the depths of his eyes. "A bunch of shit went down right before he died. He was leaving on tour and we had this big blow out, things going to hell between us. He called me a couple weeks later. Told me he was in trouble. I didn't listen."

Horror climbed into my chest. "What kind of trouble?"

He lifted a shoulder. "I thought it was the same old shit. Drugs. He said he needed money. It wasn't a few days later that I got a call from Baz telling me he had OD'ed. He was just…gone."

Zee's gaze drifted toward the window, lost in the memory as his voice went quiet. "I got this agitated, unsettled feeling, knowing something was off. Deep inside, I knew it went deeper than that. I told Baz, but Baz…Baz was the one who'd found him. He was certain it wasn't anything more than an overdose."

I curled up closer to him, wishing to take some of his pain as he continued. "It wasn't until four years ago that we found out it was more. You live a corrupt life, and you're bound to get messed up with corrupt people. Apparently, he'd found out some shit he wasn't supposed to know about a girl this bastard Martin Jennings had planned on taking out."

I clutched him tighter, my pulse thrumming in my ears, terrified of what he was getting ready to reveal.

"Turned out it was Shea."

I gasped. "What?"

"We didn't know the connection until Baz and Shea had gotten involved. Mark knew about it and stepped in to stop it. He saved her, Alexis. He saved her and no one fucking knew it. Everyone assumed he'd filled his veins too full when it was that piece of shit Jennings who'd had him erased."

"Oh my God," I whispered, unable to fathom the atrocity of it all. "I'm so sorry."

He looked over at me. "It fucking destroyed me, Alexis. Both times. The lies and the truth. But part of me is glad he didn't die for nothing."

"But then I can only imagine there's another part of you who wishes you could change it," I said softly.

Bitter laughter ripped free. "Sacrifice is a bitch, isn't it?"

Zee shook his head. "But I set it all in motion, Alexis."

"And now you think you owe him."

He sighed. "I do owe him. I—"

Zee cut himself off, as if he couldn't say more, refusing to let me in further, the corner of his mouth tipping down as he murmured, "Don't know what the fuck I'm supposed to do now. Who I'm supposed to be."

"Who is it you want to be?" I edged back, holding on to his forearm as I stared up at him. "What is it you want to stand for?"

thirty-three

ZEE

Anthony tossed the stack of glossy sheets to the middle of his desk.

"What are you doing, Zee? You know better than this. All these years, and you don't slip up once, and then this?"

I fought the panic that welled in every cell in my body, coalescing into a hot point of anger and fear right in the center of my chest.

It wasn't fair. It wasn't fucking fair.

I was looking at picture after picture of me and Alexis from the last couple weeks. Her coming into my place and her leaving. A couple of me in front of her house.

What got me were the ones of us outside the hospital, that sweet, trusting girl staring up at me with all that belief.

My hands on her face. The girl in my arms where she belonged. Kissing her like she was breath. Air. Sanity.

Killed me to look at it as if it were something dirty. Something bad.

"You know the definition of lying low better than anyone,

Zee, and then you go and pull this? Veronica will ruin you. It's a goddamned miracle she's kept to the agreement this long."

I scoffed. "You think she would've if it weren't for the money?"

"Of course she's only kept it a secret because of the money. And you know how much she loves holding that secret over your head."

"Like taking care of my family is some kind of sin." Disgusted, I spat the words.

Lines dented Anthony's brow. "You were the one who didn't want anyone to know, Zee. You can't have it both ways."

That was what I'd been terrified of all along. Walking this shaky balance. Trying to juggle these two worlds and dreading when they collided.

"Just…don't know that I give a fuck anymore, Anthony. Not if it means letting her go, too. Not sure I can do it."

Cautious, he stilled, like he was bracing me for his words. "But what about for him?"

Grief cut me in two. I bent over, trying with all of me to hold together the threads of my life that were unraveling faster than I could repair them.

Or maybe they'd just been lit at the end.

Burning out.

I fisted my hand with the tattoo.

Just like the stars.

Regret had taken me hostage. Pain throbbed with each vapid pulse of my heart like those little bits that had sparked to life had suddenly been dimmed.

When the doorbell rang, I slowly moved across my loft, wishing I could ignore it, pretend like I hadn't made that call to Alexis saying I needed to see her right away.

But I had to end this before it got any messier than it already was. Before I went and fucked up the last good thing I had in my life.

Before this hurt Alexis any more than I already knew it was going to.

I had to remember what was important. Why I was doing this in the first place.

I fumbled with the heavy metal lock and slid it free, opening one side of the massive doors. I jerked back when I saw it wasn't Alexis on the other side.

"Veronica…"

It was all shock before a rush of anger came raging in. "What the fuck do you think you're doing here? You know you aren't supposed to be at my house."

She strutted right past me like she owned the place, wearing high heels and tight black leather pants, slinking in and taking in my home like she were calculating exactly what it would be worth when it belonged to her.

Probably wasn't that far off the mark.

She looked back at me with all that innocent wrath. "Hmm…well, I figured since you were breaking the rules, I might as well, too."

My hands fisted. It took all I had to keep myself rooted to that spot, every part of me itching to drag her right back out. "You're not welcome here."

She tsked and wandered deeper, over near the sofas. She picked up a framed picture of me and the rest of the guys, studied it, and caressed her finger over the faces. Then she looked over at me. "It's such a shame your brother's not in this picture, isn't it?"

I ground my teeth. "I'm warning you, Veronica."

She set it down, so casually. Too casually. I shook, fucking hating that she held all the control as she strolled around my loft. "You know, I'm really not the fangirl type. Living in LA all my life, I know better."

Right.

Like she hadn't hunted my brother down.

"But some headlines are just too big to miss, especially when they're splashed all over the front pages of everyone's favorite tabloids."

She sighed as if it actually hurt her and she wasn't over there doing her best to cinch that noose just a little tighter around my neck.

"I signed into Facebook this morning, and guess what was trending? Zee Kennedy. Sunder prince. The boy who'd always worn the innocent crown, never dipping his fingers into all the…let's say…unsavory offerings like the rest of his friends."

Sadly, she shook her head. "And there he was, caught with a lover, right outside the hospital."

I was at my end. "What fucking difference does it make?"

She turned on me, spewing venom. "What difference does it make? You took him from me, and we had an agreement. You *promised*."

"And you're gonna stand over there and pretend like you weren't responsible, too? You're the one who came to me."

She blinked, feigning offense, like there wasn't any chance she was guilty of the same goddamned sin. Slowly, she wound back my direction. "We were both hurting."

Resentful laughter tumbled out. "I wasn't anything but prey. Just like my brother. As far as I'm concerned, you can go fuck yourself."

She ran her fingers down the front of my shirt. "I actually prefer when it's you."

I gripped her by the wrist, probably squeezing too hard. "You are nothing to me, Veronica. I don't belong to you. I haven't in a lot of years. Get out."

She hefted a shoulder as she passed me by. "Liam says hi."

That was the thing about Veronica. She knew exactly where to get me. I blew out a breath, trying not to completely lose my cool. "He doesn't have anything to do with this."

Scorn rolled from her when she turned back to look at me from out in the hall. "He always has. You want to see him again? It's going to cost you." Then she headed for the elevator.

Of course, it had to be at the exact same second Alexis was stepping off.

thirty-four

ALEXIS

Anxiety twisted through me as I stepped onto Zee's elevator. He'd been strained since he'd shown up unannounced at my house five days ago. Questions so evident in his eyes. His direction unclear. His path obscured.

The thing was, I could see it shining all around him. Beckoning him forward. Calling to all his brilliance and talent that I felt bleeding from his soul and through his fingers every time he sat in front of the piano.

I wanted him to embrace it. Find it.

I jabbed the button for the sixth floor, maybe a little too eagerly as I waited for it to carry me to him.

The metal doors slid open, and I started forward only to stumble on my surprise when a woman shouldered past me, a grin on her face.

A grin that was pure menace.

Like somehow I'd been caught red-handed and she was all too happy to be the one to bring me in.

I held her malicious glare as she climbed onto the elevator, her smirk widening as she punched at the button and the doors slid closed.

Warily, I turned back to where Zee was standing in his doorway. Every inch of him was rigid, muscles bulging and bristling with throttled rage.

I blinked at him, hating the way my feet fumbled as I forced myself to take a step, the sinking fear that seeped through the surface of my skin as I tried to process the scene.

His jaw ticked beneath his beard when I stopped two feet in front of him.

"You said to come," I forced out, every emotion I was feeling exposed when the words cracked.

It seemed to snap him from the wall of fury, and he looked down at me.

Grief lashed across his face as he stepped back. "Please, come inside."

Something fierce and severe climbed into the air.

So thick it made it difficult to breathe as I dropped my head and entered his loft. I swallowed around the thick knot of emotion, moving toward the windows, to the light that poured in like a crashing, ravaging wave.

I stood in the midst of it, panting for the breaths the mood had stolen.

"Alexis." He whispered it from directly behind me. My hair was up in a high ponytail, and his fingertips trailed the star dangling down the back of my neck.

"Who was she?"

"No one." It was hard.

Slowly, I turned to face him. To watch his lie. "Don't tell me she is no one when she's so obviously someone."

This had gotten complicated.

Because there I stood, making demands I'd promised him I wouldn't make. But it didn't matter. It didn't change the fact that I'd fallen.

Fallen hard and fast.

I was terrified of hitting the ground.

His jaw tightened. "She's the past."

I reached out and fisted my hands in his shirt. "Then tell me I'm the future."

He flinched. "You know I can't do that."

"I don't understand."

"I already told you I couldn't do this, Alexis. You already knew this was temporary. Fuck…it never should've even gotten started. Told you I couldn't do this…and here I am."

"What if *this* is exactly where you're supposed to be?"

"And what if it ruins me?"

"What if you're breaking my heart?"

He edged me closer to the window. Heat blanketed my back and poured into my spirit as he wound an errant piece of hair around his finger, brushing at the side of my neck.

It made the room spin and my breaths heavy. How did one man exert this much control over me? I was supposed to be the strong one.

The brave one.

Instead I was trembling at his feet.

He murmured rough words at the side of my face. "Last thing in the world I want to do is hurt you, Alexis. I was supposed to protect you. Take care of you."

Right then, I knew the only thing in danger was my heart.

"What if I want to take care of you, too? Do you think I don't feel it, Zee? Do you think I don't know you need me, too?"

"Sometimes the things we think we need only hurt us in the end."

I felt the warning behind it.

I placed both hands on his waist. "And sometimes those things are exactly what we've been waiting for."

His eyes closed, as if he needed to shield himself from this. From us. From this out-of-control train we were riding.

Unstoppable.

I had no idea how to prepare myself for the devastation of when we finally crashed.

He buried his face in my neck. "What I *need* to do is let you go, and I don't fucking know how to do it."

Anguish rose in his throat, so thick when he grated the words. “Last show is next week. I need you there, Alexis. I need you there when I tell it all goodbye. You make it real again. You make me *feel* it. Tell me you’ll be there.”

I let him wind me in his arms, my cheek pressed to his chest. “Why does it feel like it will be our goodbye?”

thirty-five

ZEE
TWENTY YEARS OLD

Zee cracked open the door. His chest tightened when he found his brother on the other side. He hadn't seen him in three months. Not since that night. His words were thick. "Mark...hey…what are you doing here?"

Telling his brother he had to cut ties had been about the damned most difficult conversation he'd ever had in his life. Keeping to that decision? It'd been close to impossible. Eating him alive. He'd contemplated driving over there a thousand times.

Uneasily, Mark shifted on his feet. "I'm sorry for just showing up, but I really need to talk to you."

Zee craned his head so he could look at Julie who was reading on the couch. She looked so peaceful sitting there, and he knew he was about to throw a bomb right in the middle of the tranquility.

But there was no way he could turn his brother away.

Zee widened the door. "Yeah, man, you should come in. We can go out back and talk."

Mark's relief was visible. "Thanks."

Julie's attention jerked up when Zee rounded from the entry, Mark ambling along close behind. Confusion and worry sprang to her eyes, her lips pursing as she slowly shook her head.

Zee sent her a pleading look. "Mark needs to talk to me. We're going out back on the balcony."

He watched her swallow, the way her hand shook as she turned back to her book and flipped the page.

Zee chose to ignore it, needing to be there for his brother. He pulled open the sliding glass door and the two of them stepped out into the muggy night. Mark slumped down in a chair, forearms on his knees as he bent over, and Zee sank into the opposite chair with a sigh.

He hated the tension that ricocheted between them. Hurt and questions roiled in the air, the damage he'd done visible, the rejection and the abandonment.

Mark eyed Zee, and Zee shifted, nervously rubbing his hands on his thighs.

"Thanks for letting me come in," Mark said.

Zee roughed a hand over his face, like it might break up the apprehension. "You're my brother, man. What did you expect?"

Mark's laugh was close to a scoff. "Considering the last time I talked to you, you told me you had to sever ties, I wasn't entirely sure what to expect."

Anxiously, Zee rocked. "You have to know making that decision has been killing me. But fuck, Mark…Julie doesn't deserve to witness that shit. I have to protect her from it. And I'm sorry if you can't respect me for that." His head shook. "Hell, I'm not sure I can even respect myself. Makes me feel like I'm going crazy, torn between two sides, belonging to them both."

Mark blinked over at him seriously, his brown eyes earnest.

"I respect you more than anyone I've ever respected in all my life. Look at you, brother. You have all your shit together. Composing. Have a girl you love and building a home. You think I don't look at that and know it's better than anything I'm ever gonna have?"

The smallest smile tugged at the corner of Zee's lips, his words trying to lighten the mood. "Come on, Mark, no need to make me feel better when you're the one out there living the rock-star life. Traveling city to city. Playing music. All that money and all those women? Don't act like you're not eatin' it up."

Mark chuckled, but it was sadness that climbed into the air. "Beginning to realize none of that means anything. Not if you don't have something that's important to live for at the end of the day. Something to work for. Someone to come home to."

"What about that Veronica chick?"

The sound that left his mouth was half groan, half affection. "Don't know. Can't seem to stay away from her, even if I wanted to try. Guys can't stand her, though. Think she's a snake. Just using me for what I have to give. They think I can't stay clean because she keeps dragging me back into it, which is kinda bullshit, since it's pretty much the other way around."

"You care about her?"

His shrug seemed hopeless. "Yeah…guess I do. Not sure what difference it makes, though."

Zee could feel the frown tugging at his mouth. "What does that mean?"

A heavy sigh bled from Mark. "I'm surrounded by people. Constantly. People who want to get as close to me as they can, looking at me like I'm something I'm not. Like I have something to offer that just isn't there."

His tone dropped with the admission. "In the middle of it? Don't think I've ever felt so lonely. Not in all my life."

Mark's voice drifted into something wistful. "Remember when we were kids…always out running wild? Getting into all sorts of trouble? But we always did it together."

Zee roughed a hand through his hair. "You'd have thought since you were older, you'd have tried to ditch me."

"Nah, man. We were partners in crime. Thick as thieves. It's you who taught me to love music, you know? Walking with you to your piano classes. Way you'd be all lit up and excited when I'd pick you up afterward. The magic you were making in your room. It seeped in and became a part of me. I hope you know that."

Zee rocked back in his chair and looked at the sky, wondering about all the dreams he and Mark had made upon those stars. Wondering just when they were going to start falling free and coming true. For so long, they'd seemed so close.

But Mark was right.

They didn't mean anything if the people who were most important to you weren't close.

And his brother was who he'd been missing.

Silence hovered around them before Mark broke it as he looked at his boots planted on the ground. "Think it was those days—back when it was just you and me—that might have been the last time I felt real. Like I knew who I was. I can barely remember that person now."

Mark rocked, his mood suddenly shifting. He rubbed at the back of his neck as he looked away. "I got myself in deep, man…with some bad people. Some really bad, fucked-up people. Not sure how the hell I'm going to get myself out of it."

A slow dread seeped across Zee's skin. "What do you mean, got yourself in deep?"

"Means I know shit I shouldn't."

Fear prickled across Zee's flesh, this burning, freezing cold. "What do you know, man? Tell me…we'll figure it out. Just like we always have."

Mark's chuckle was dismissive. "Didn't come over here to get you involved, Zee. No way am I getting you anywhere near that kind of trouble. I got myself into this mess…now I need to figure out how to get myself out of it. I just needed you to know…in case something went down…that I love you. That no matter what happens, you'll always be the person in this world who means the most to me."

Zee could barely breathe beneath the disturbance that seethed in his chest. "You're scaring me, man. Tell me what the hell is going on."

Mark grinned. Zee knew it was forced. "It's nothing, little brother. Just needed to get it off my chest. Put it out in the open. Now that I said it aloud, I'm pretty sure I'm just being paranoid." He scratched at his forearm, eyes glancing to the marks imprinted there. "Mixing all this shit will do that to you, you know. Either way, it's all on me."

"Mark, come on. Don't shut me out. Tell me what's going on."

Instead of settling in, Mark suddenly stood and smacked his hands together, no joy in his too-wide smile. "What I should do is get the hell out of here before Julie comes out here with a broom to run me off."

"Dude, she's not that bad."

Mark laughed. "Oh, I know, brother. I think the girl just knows a rat when she sees one."

Regret pulled tight across Zee's ribs. He pushed to his feet, beating down the need to demand that his brother tell him what he was talking about. Chances were, Mark was right. He was just overreacting.

Besides, they had a bigger issue to tackle.

"I'll talk to Julie, Mark. Honestly, I fucking hate this wedge between us. I miss you. Maybe you can make that U-turn. Get back to who you used to be."

"That's the hope, isn't it?"

Zee followed Mark back through the small living room of the apartment, stepping out behind him and onto the front stoop. The second they were out there, Mark flew around and pulled Zee into a hug. He squeezed him like he didn't want to let go. "You turned into a good man, Zee. A fucking good man. Don't let anything or anyone ever change that."

Zee hugged his brother tighter. Hoping he could feel it.

Love.

Belief.

Hope.

"Take care of yourself, brother."

Mark nodded. "Yeah."

Julie slowly stood from the couch when Zee stepped back inside and locked the door behind him. Her voice trembled. "What was he doing here? You promised."

Zee turned to look at her, stricken by grief and hope. "He's my brother, Julie. Love doesn't give up that easily. I don't know that I have it in me to choose."

He knew she was hurting and scared. She rubbed both hands over her arms as if she were trying to keep herself warm. "I…I have a horrible feeling about this, Zee. I don't want you to have to choose, but if you don't, my gut tells me I'm the one who's going to lose."

"I can't just pretend he doesn't exist." His voice was pleading, and he erased the space between them and pulled her into his arms. She sagged against him, her knees week. "Please don't make me choose," he begged.

thirty-six

ALEXIS

Colored lights whirled and danced through the heavy duskiness of the old music theater. They struck like flares against the faces of eager fans that pressed and vied to get closer to the stage.

To witness Sunder's final show.

They'd made an official statement that it wasn't the band's end. They promised they would be back, although in a different capacity. They would continue to play on their own time and on their own terms.

Fans had still billed the show a final farewell.

Music blasted from the huge speakers that hung from the cavernous ceiling. It was heavy and thrashing like the music I knew Sunder played. It was so not normally my thing, but I couldn't stop the shiver of excitement that blistered across my skin as I weaved my way closer and closer to the stage.

Drawn.

The way this boy had made me feel since the second he crashed into my life.

Zee had wanted me backstage where I could watch safely from the side. But I'd wanted to experience this through the fans' eyes. Feel their energy and their exhilaration.

It was as if there were two distinct sides to this mysterious man.

One half so powerful and intense. An extension of the mayhem that hummed against these walls. The other half was something so vulnerable and quiet and profound, acute in the skill of his hands.

Together they were magnificent.

Imposing.

Everything I'd ever wanted.

People crushed against one another, adding to the frenzy that sizzled and hovered in the air.

Like a match that ached for a strike.

The lights went dim and there was a collective gasp. My breath was officially gone when the entire stage lit in a flash of blinding light.

Zee was there, big body taking to the stage, so powerful and sure as he lifted his drumsticks to the air.

Cheers roared through the space. Deafening. His face was upturned and his eyes squeezed closed.

My chest heaved. Because I saw it so clearly.

The tribute.

The respect.

The grief.

Mark was written all over Zee when he strode across that stage and climbed the riser to take his place. The riser hidden farther in the back and in the shadows.

But he was the only thing I could see.

Ash strode out, cocky and sure. A fresh rustle of energy burst in the crowd. It only grew when Lyrik sauntered out from the side, so dark and menacing, fitting that stage as if he'd been formed from its mold.

Everything went wild when the final member stepped out on the stage—Austin Stone.

Lyrik strummed a reverberating chord on his guitar in the

same second Zee began to tap out a mesmerizing rhythm on his drums.

Then the entire place ignited in one thrashing beat.

Austin jumped into action, screaming the lyrics I couldn't begin to understand. But I could feel them all the same. The intensity. The meaning.

Zee pounded and beat and played.

Fiercely.

Savagely.

My little drummer boy.

Overwhelming in his beauty. Destructive in his talent.

I wondered if he knew he was absolutely stunning in that moment, just as breathtaking as when he sat at his piano.

If he knew that this gift was just as great.

Or if he believed this was only a penance.

Punishment.

I got lost in Sunder.

In the music. In the connection that was so clear in the four of them.

The crowd thrashed and slammed at the base of the stage, each song only propelling it higher.

It rose into something that verged on violence, a chaotic disorder that somehow felt like freedom, as if the entire place was riding that sharp edge of beauty that at any moment might slip and shatter.

It became more intense, so intense that I felt myself losing my footing. So wild I couldn't tell if it was my spirit or my feet that had truly been swept away.

I felt staggered when the set came to an abrupt end.

Vibrations of their last song still rang through the air, knitting with the roar of the crowd.

Austin thrust a fist in the air and exited the stage, and both Lyrik and Ash tossed their picks out into the crowd before they followed him off.

How it was possible that energy grew when Zee climbed down from the risers, I didn't know.

But I felt it stirring, building fast as he made his way down and came closer to the edge of the stage. He tossed one drumstick out into the crowd, then the other toward the other side. He was so mesmerizing I could've sworn I was floating in the remnants of the song.

I thought he'd exit the side of the stage like the rest of the guys. But his gaze scrambled across the faces that cheered and stretched out their hands to get closer to him. The same way I felt desperate to.

Bronze flecks gleamed in his eyes when they finally tangled with mine.

And this boy…this magnetic boy leaned down toward me, hand outstretched.

Oh God.

He'd warned me we had to be careful. That the paps were watching. That we had to keep our distance and play it cool.

Maybe I'd been a fool to agree, to give in. But I was chasing those slivers of time that I could feel winding down, clinging to the moments before they came to an end.

It was what had led me to stand at the base of the stage, my heart going haywire. Erratic beat after erratic beat.

I fought against the bodies that crammed toward him, eager to get closer. He touched a few of the hands lifted in his direction.

The second I touched him, his hand curled around mine. He hauled me up through the demanding crowd, the muscles in his arm bulging as he lifted me onto the stage.

Giddiness swept through my consciousness. Dizzying and sweet. I gasped out in shock when I was suddenly on stage with Zee.

It felt like a statement.

It felt like a promise.

It felt like perfection.

"What are you doing?" I rasped through the surprise when both his hands landed on either side of my neck.

His voice was gruff where he murmured it close to my lips. "I need you."

"What about people seeing us?"

"I don't care anymore, Alexis. Can't go a second more acting like what we have is wrong."

And that was it. I was gone. There was no longer any question. I belonged to him.

"Come with me," he demanded.

Didn't he get I was already there?

Cheers turned to chants that rose from the floor as he hauled me behind him. He led me to the opposite side of the stage than the rest of the band had exited. He pushed aside a thick black drape that hung from the ceiling and pulled me into the well of darkness waiting backstage.

Members of the crew darted around the narrow space, shuffling cords and rushing on stage as they moved equipment around.

The chants grew fainter though more demanding the deeper we went into the depths of the theater.

"This way," Zee said, keeping a tight hold on my hand as he took a right turn down another hall.

My heart thundered, this thrill shivering through my senses and taking me whole.

Zee turned the knob of a door and ducked us inside. He flipped a switch.

A light flickered on, breaking the wall of darkness and lighting the room in a dusky glow.

If I had to guess, it had once upon a time been a small dressing room, the space currently cluttered with boxes and old equipment.

Zee spun around in the middle of it. For a beat, he stared me down, pinning me with the stunning potency of those eyes. Those eyes that consumed and ravaged and devastated.

"Alexis." He said my name like praise.

A strike of lust exploded in the air. A frenzy lit.

He pushed me against the wall, big hands on my neck, fingers driving into my hair.

He groaned the deepest groan when he seized my mouth, his tongue hot and his kiss unyielding. He pressed me tighter against the wall, the strength of his body overpowering mine, my knees weak and my spirit bounding.

"Zee," I mumbled at his mouth. I clutched his shirt and lifted to my toes in a bid to get closer.

His hands moved down my neck and over my shoulders.

Chills spread.

I panted, and he splayed his hands wide, dragging them down my sides until he had hold of the hem of my lacy tank. He edged back and tore it over my head.

My chest heaved, bare, no bra underneath.

"You've ruined me, Alexis Kensington. I know all the shit I'm supposed to do, but then I catch a glimpse of you, and it's all over. Done. Finished." It was a growl. "No power left in me except what I'm gonna do to you."

I threw myself at him, locking my arms around his neck and kissing him with everything I had.

With everything I felt.

Did he feel it, too?

Was it possible?

Fall with me.

He ripped open the button of my jeans and yanked down the zipper.

He spun us in the same second he was dragging my jeans and panties down my legs. He kept edging me back, lips still touching mine. "What the hell have you done to me? I'm so lost, baby. So damned lost."

A thunder vibrated the floors, the heavy beat of music as it thrummed from the other side of the theater, the chants of the fans a throb that pulsed against our ears.

I lifted my face, the man a fortress over me. I flattened my palms beneath his shirt. "And with you is where I'm found."

His defined abdomen trembled as I drew up his shirt, and he leaned down so I could pull it free.

Needy pants jetted from my mouth. He was so gorgeous in the glow of the light, his body glistening from the exertion of the set.

Muscles solid and tight.

Relentless.

My fingers shook as I trailed them over that mark before I turned and dragged them to his fly. I ripped it down, and it was Zee who shoved his pants to his thighs. His cock sprang free, just as massive as the rest of him.

Begging.

Demanding.

Straining toward me.

I took him in my hand, pumped him twice. Zee groaned, so deep and dark it echoed through the room. Like a chord added to rumble that vibrated the floors and shook the walls.

I gapsed when he grabbed me by the waist and hiked me up, shoving boxes out of the way and setting me on the edge of a table.

I clung to it, barely keeping myself upright when he gripped me by the knees and spread me wide before dropping down in front of me.

Desire flooded.

A river. Liquid. Hot.

"Alexis," he murmured against my flesh before he drove his tongue in, taking a sharp dive through my center, deep, penetrating, before he angled, sucking and licking at my clit.

Pants rose in the air, my stomach in knots as sensations flew.

He set my thighs on his shoulders, his hands running up and down. Driving me higher with each caress. Higher with each stroke of his tongue.

"Zee…oh…God."

Flames leapt beneath the surface of my skin, tingles building.

Everything shivered. Tightened. The threat of bliss.

And suddenly he was there, a big hand on the back of my neck to keep me supported while he gripped the mass of himself in the other. He guided the swollen head of his cock to my entrance. Barely touching.

A tease.

I whimpered, so turned on I couldn't see. "Zee…please…I'm so close."

"What do you need?"

"You."

He surged forward, and a scream burst from my throat.

So big. Too much. Never enough because I would forever want more.

He ground his teeth, barely clinging to a thread of control.

I could feel it.

The tension that ran on a circuit through his body. Energy alive. The space between us one.

"Zee."

He rocked and fucked and stole my sanity, a hand on the back of my neck to keep me steady.

Every restraint decimated.

He took me in a way he never had.

Manically. Desperately. Unhinged.

Falling.

Gravity too great to resist.

His and mine.

Colliding.

Edging back, he pulled out as far as he could. His cock was slick as he withdrew, our breaths shattered as we both watched where we were connected.

Wild eyes flicked to mine, and he pressed his thumb into my mouth. I sucked desperately, and he tugged it free, dragging our attention back down as he swirled it around my clit as he drove into me as deep as he could take me.

That was it.

I flew.

Gone.

Bliss.

It blinded and bounded and shot me to a place that shouldn't exist. A place where darkness and light were one and the same.

Weightless.

Stars.

Zee sank his fingers into my ass and dragged me off the edge. He fucked me with wild, uneven strokes before he roared when his orgasm hit him, full speed.

My name.

My name.

My name.

Uncontrolled, I crumbled in his hold. The world alive, the walls a thunder of energy.

Someone was suddenly pounding on the door. "Zee…asshole…are you in there?"

Zee jerked back. "Shit," he muttered. He threaded his fingers through his sweat-drenched hair as he wildly looked around.

More pounding. "Zee."

"Yeah, give me a second," he hollered over his shoulder as he set me on unsteady feet. He kept a hand on me while he quickly resituated his pants and moved us back to the other side of the room and helped me into my clothes.

A fist hammered on the door, and Ash's voice bled through. "Not joking, Zee. We've been looking for you for fifteen minutes. We should've been back on stage for the encore five minutes ago. Crowd is about to lose their shit, man. You know the routine."

My heart raced as I frantically struggled to get back into my clothes. Shaking, I smoothed them out just as I tried to work out the knots in my hair.

"How do I look?" I whispered beneath my breath, feeling the flush of redness hit my cheeks.

Arrogance filled his smirk. "Like I just fucked you."

I chewed at my lip, dropped my gaze. "Zee."

He set his palm on the side of my face and forced me to look at him. "You look like a fucking vision, just like every damned time you walk in a room."

He gripped me tighter. "And what you look like right now? You look like you belong to me."

Emotion clogged my chest.

More pounding. "Now!"

Zee shouted toward the door, "I'm coming, I'm coming." He tugged his shirt back over his head while I slipped back into my shoes.

Then Zee slanted me a smile, unlocked the door, and threw it open.

Ash was on the other side, the guy appearing half pissed, though a knowing grin slid to his face the second he saw Zee towing me out by the hand.

"Now, you know I never want to get in the way of the lovin'…because there's no reason to tell any lies, we all know that's the most important thing…but we're just about to have a riot on our hands. Need to get our asses back on that stage. Pronto, baby. You two can get back to the good stuff after."

"Let's do it," Zee said.

Ash reached out and squeezed his shoulder. A statement passed through his eyes. Something that looked like encouragement. Maybe approval.

Still, Ash's expression brimmed with all the same questions I needed answered as well. It passed just as quickly, and the three of us were racing down the dank, dark halls.

We headed in the opposite direction of the one Zee and I had originally taken. It looped around to the other side where there were a handful of dressing rooms and a big room to the back with a bar and sofas.

The noise level grew, and we increased our pace. Heading down another hall, we broke into an open area where the crew was bustling around, and a bunch of people were gathered at the side of the stage.

The emotion that had almost exploded back in that room softened when I saw who was waiting in the wings—Tamar, Shea, and Edie.

Only Willow was missing from this group of women who'd somehow so quickly become important to me.

Zee led me right up to them as if that was exactly where I belonged.

Tamar saw me first. Her striking face twisted into a wry grin, eyes wide with suggestion.

"Well, look who we have here." Her grin grew as it landed on Zee. "If I wasn't so proud of you, I'd tell you that you're grounded for the rest of your life, going around and causing this kind of trouble. The audacity."

It was pure affection.

Zee pointed at her. "I don't have time to tell you to watch yourself…so take care of my girl, will you?"

He dipped down and pecked me on the lips.

Twice.

So sweet.

God.

"Gladly," Shea said, catching on while Zee walked backward, keeping his gaze on me, before he quickly spun around and joined the circle where the band was huddled.

They all took to the stage, Sebastian included. There for the encore, a mandatory piece of this momentous farewell.

Everything went wild. The screams and the cheers and the crushing wave of energy.

Because these bad, bad boys meant something to these people.

They had created something no one else could. Had a chemistry that could only be found in their bond. This mixed up, mismatched family.

My lips parted in awe.

Because this…this was beauty.

It was belief.

It was love.

Shea slipped her fingers through mine. Gently, she squeezed. "I'm really glad you're here."

I squeezed back, my voice a whisper as my gaze locked on these brilliant boys. "I really am, too."

Zee drove us back to my house. He parked in the driveway, and everything went still when he clicked open his door and came around to my side.

He helped me out and then into the welcoming darkness of my tiny house, down the short hall, and into my room. The only illumination was the small bedside lamp he clicked on that radiated a dull, dim light.

He glanced back at me, gently tugging me into the attached bathroom where he turned on the shower, slowly undressed me as the room filled with steam, my movements even slower when I helped him from his.

Savoring.

Relishing.

We stepped under the warm spray, our bodies bare, and I swore I thought maybe it was that moment when our spirits were freed.

His kiss was slow and tender as he washed my hair, his touch even gentler as he lathered a washcloth and carefully ran it over my body.

Something about it felt…cleansing.

As if we were leaving old promises behind and stepping into new truths.

Our truths.

We rinsed, and I could feel the moment slow as he turned off the shower and reached out to grab a towel.

He ran it over every inch of me.

In praise.

In adoration as he knelt at my feet.

I clung to him by the shoulders. "Zee."

"Alexis." It floated over me like a song. He straightened, swept me into his big arms, and carried me to my bed where he slowly crawled over me.

He threaded his fingers through mine and held me close as he nudged my legs wider and pressed into my body.

Every movement felt in opposition to earlier when we'd both been undone.

That was a plea.

This was a promise.

He looked down on me while the world spun around us. Shifting and changing and binding.

"Fall with me," I whispered.

He leaned down, lips just brushing mine, and Zachary Kennedy murmured his truth.

"I already jumped."

thirty-seven

ALEXIS

I jerked up in bed, disoriented, blurry eyed as I squinted and tried to make sense of what'd pulled me from the most perfect kind of sleep.

Zee was in the middle of my bed, spread out, face down, naked.

So insanely sexy.

Totally out and completely at peace.

I bit my lip, overcome by the well of emotion rushing to the surface at seeing him next to me.

I tore my attention from him when I was prodded again by the sound I realized had pulled me from sleep—my doorbell ringing again and again.

Quickly, I eased off the side of the bed, grabbed a robe, and slipped it on. Tying the belt into a slipknot, I padded across the hardwood floors and clicked the bedroom door shut behind me so Zee could remain asleep.

Once in the hall, I hurried to the door and popped up on my toes to see through the peephole.

Shock stumbled me back two steps.

Then I shot into action, working the lock and ripping open the door.

"Avril, what are you doing here?"

She wasn't even supposed to know where I lived. But still I was surging forward and wrapping her in my arms. Hugging her tight.

She hugged me back before she unwound herself and put a few inches between us. Her face was pale, body too thin, clearly anxious. "I needed to talk to you."

I shook my head. "Why didn't you call? How did you even know where I live?"

This was the one privacy I'd asked of her. My sanctuary away from the ugly realities of the rest of the world. My safe haven.

"I'm sorry…I went to the library and used a computer to find your address. I needed to talk to you. In person." Anxiously, she peeked over her shoulder. "By myself."

"Why?"

"Craig." She whispered the word like a dirty confession.

I sucked in a shocked breath.

She'd never once said his name. She didn't need to explain or clarify who she was talking about. I already saw it in her eyes.

"What did he do?"

She twitched. "He…he keeps asking about you. Asking me to call you."

Guilt blanketed her expression.

"It's always been money, Alexis. When he makes me call you."

Horror filled the harsh breath of air that pitched from my lungs. "You…it was never for you."

She looked so frail in my doorway, her shoulders slumped and her body worn from the lifestyle. "Everything I have is his. Don't you get that? I keep trying to tell you."

I blinked through the torment. "What did you do, Avril? What did you do?"

Her laughter was empty. "I sold my soul to the devil."

Grief nearly dropped me to my knees. "Avril."

She shook her head and backed away. As if she needed to keep space between us. "I just…I needed to warn you. To tell you he keeps talking about you. Asking questions. He sees an opportunity, and I think…I think he's looking for a weak link. For a way to get to you. For a way to draw you into that world and keep you there. And I'm pretty sure he knows that's me."

Fear twisted through my spirit. "What does he want from me?"

Her mouth pinched in regret. "I don't know. I think he's angry that you got away that night. That he didn't make you pay for what he believes you owed him. And if he looped you into this life with me? That would be quite the jackpot, wouldn't it?" The words on her tongue were sharp with disgust.

Nausea pooled in my stomach.

Never.

Shaking, I stretched my fingers for my sister. My twin. This broken girl who had always been my other half. "Just stay…we'll figure it out. Whatever you think he has over you, he doesn't. It's not right. It's not legal. He *can't* own you."

Sadness rippled through the dawn as she looked away. "I could stay, Alexis, and you would do everything you could to help me, and you know I'd just end up right back down there, anyway. I'm not worth it."

She looked back at me. For the first time in a long time, her eyes were shining with resolve. "Just…stay away. I call you, don't listen. Know it's a lie."

The energy shifted, building in intensity, fierce and savage.

I jerked my head to look over my shoulder.

Zee was standing at the entry to the hall, wearing nothing but his underwear, every inch of him straining with the clear need he had to protect me.

I had thought this house had been my reprieve, but it was Zee who had become my safe place.

Avril startled. "Oh."

I looked back to her. “We can protect you.”

She stumbled back, her gaze wary as Zee started across the floor.

“Avril,” he said, “let us help you.”

She fumbled a couple more steps back. “Protect her.”

Then Avril turned, stumbled down my steps, and bolted.

thirty-eight

ZEE

"I need to see him. Know he's safe." I squeezed the phone so tight I was pretty sure I could hear it crack.

"Ten thousand."

I was done. So fucking done.

"You think I'm just gonna hand over ten grand? Always knew you were nothing but a greedy, selfish bitch, but this time you've gone too far."

Pretty sure she'd crossed that line when she'd sold her house. The house I'd bought for them. To keep them safe.

"You know everything comes at a cost. You want to see him, it's ten."

I gritted my teeth, gripping at the back of my neck as I stormed around my loft, trying to rein it in. "He's not a fucking pawn, Veronica."

"You know how it works."

"Not anymore, it doesn't. I'm done. I'm going to see him, and you aren't going to stop me."

She laughed. "Don't fuck with me, Zee. You should know better than that."

The line went dead.

A roar burst from somewhere in my chest, fury and anger and this fucking brick wall she kept landing me against. Rage had my phone flying across the room. It slammed against the hard floor, tumbling as it slid.

I gripped handfuls of my hair, storming back and forth.

Losing it.

Forgetting the promises I'd made.

Because that girl…that sweet, sweet girl had me wanting to make different ones.

Would she get it?

Would she understand?

Could she ever look at me the same?

It didn't matter. I was finished letting Veronica control the situation. Yeah, I was fucking fed up. But I wasn't doing it for myself.

I was doing it for Liam.

That precious kid.

The one thing that'd been the permanent light in my life.

Now Alexis glowed all around me. Adding and amplifying.

Maybe the two of them together were enough to finally purge the dark.

I jerked my car to a stop out in front of the shitty building, propelled by the frenzy that pulsed through my veins.

They say there's only so much a person can take before they finally break. Mark and Veronica and all the fucked-up choices I'd made had broken me a long time ago.

But I was ready to change it.

Shift paths.

Take all the pieces that had fallen around me and put them back together. Build something solid.

I was ready to stand.

I jumped out of my car. My attention shot around the area, vigilant of my surroundings and every shady looking motherfucker lingering in them.

That ball of anger pulsed. Fucking hated she'd brought him here. Before I left, I was going to make sure she was packing her shit and moving back to where it was safe.

Yeah, I was terrified what this was going to cost. What the guys were going to think. How they were going to react to what I'd done.

Because after this?

No chance could it remain concealed.

But I was finished doing her bidding. Thinking it was somehow protecting him and providing for him when the only thing it was doing was exposing him to the vile depravity of this seedy world.

He deserved better than this.

The building was five stories of dingy gray brick. Trash littered the sidewalk out front, and weeds encroached on the sidewalk.

I jogged toward the building's entrance. The lock on the main door was still broken.

Surprise, surprise.

I took to the stairwell, bounding up three flights to Veronica's floor. Voices shouted from behind the thin walls and babies cried from behind the doors.

I skidded to a stop in front of apartment 317.

I pounded on the door.

"Who is it?" Veronica's voice shouted from the other side.

"Me." It was nothing less than a growl.

"It's a bad time."

I pounded again. "Seems like a pretty damned good time to me."

"You can't just show up here."

Hostility wound tight. "Open the fucking door, Veronica. I'm not leaving without seeing him."

"No…I'm…I'm busy. Come back tomorrow."

"Open the door or I will bust it down."

"I'll call the cops."

"Good."

Metal screeched, and the door just barely cracked open, one of those chain locks keeping it from coming all the way open at the top. "Please…just go away."

I thought maybe it was the first time I saw real fear on Veronica's face. Guess maybe this time she had a real reason to be afraid.

"Open it."

Cries echoed from somewhere inside.

Liam.

Devotion pumped fast, and I thought maybe Veronica saw the resolution written on my face, because she scrambled to slam the door closed. My hand was already on the knob, ramming it forward. It caught on the chain.

I didn't even hesitate. I reared back, lifted my foot, and kicked it in.

The chain snapped and the door flew back, banging into the interior wall.

Veronica screamed.

My eyes jumped around the trashed out space, my heart going wild where it slammed against my ribs.

No. There wasn't anything concrete lying around, no needles or bags, but it wasn't like I hadn't been around long enough to know the signs. I knew exactly what I was looking at.

Fear and hatred slicked like ice down my spine. I should've known. I should've fucking known.

My head cocked as I shifted to stare her down. "You're using?" It was a spew of revulsion that slid from my tongue.

Memories spanning the last couple of years assaulted me. The shady, sketchy shit she'd been pulling that had gotten worse and worse. The secrets. The lies. The manipulation.

God, how long had this been going on?

"You don't know anything," she spat.

Biting laughter rolled from my mouth. "Oh, I think I know enough. Where's Liam?"

I started for the hall, stepping over the clothes strewn about the floor.

Veronica was right behind me. She grabbed onto my back, her nails digging into my shoulders as if her pathetic attempt might stop me. I shrugged her off just as I tossed open the first door I came to.

I froze in my tracks, a shock of horror rushing from my lungs.

Two women were inside on twin beds. One was passed out, face down.

The other was curled on the opposite bed, her back pressed against the wall and her arms wound protectively around her knees. Bruises covered one side of her face, and there was a huge cut that was starting to scab on her upper lip.

Avril.

I blinked, trying to process. "Avril…what the hell are you doing here?"

She scrambled onto her knees, her eyes wide when she saw me. "You."

Frantic, I looked around, gaze quick to land on the sheer terror sculpted in every line of Veronica's face.

My lips pinched. "You're involved in this shit?"

"No," she begged.

I swung back around to Avril. "Come with me."

She shook her head. "Hurry. Leave. Get out of here."

"I'm not going anywhere without you. I'm calling the cops."

Veronica's voice went hard behind me, floating around like a dark warning. "She fell down the stairs. Lucky for her, I found her at the bottom."

"That's bullshit."

Veronica looked at Avril. "Tell him that's what happened."

Avril nodded through the tears blurring her eyes.

The girl looked so much like Alexis, it damn near destroyed me. "Avril, come with me. Right now."

She shook her head. "I can't."

Muted cries bled from behind the next door.

Liam.

It struck me like an arrow. I pointed at Avril. "I'm coming back for you."

I jostled Veronica aside, and the second I turned away, she was on me again, pounding at my back and clawing my skin. I shook her off and tore open the door to Liam.

Mark's son.

The boy on the floor with his knees pulled up to his chin, rocking.

Blameless and innocent and caught up in a mess where he shouldn't be.

My entire foundation cracked by the force of my anger. By the force of the protectiveness that combusted somewhere within.

Rushing in, I scooped him into my arms and ran right back out, because I sure as hell wasn't wasting any time.

Veronica's voice was desperate. "You can't just come in and take him. I'm calling the cops."

I flew out her broken door. "Good, call them, Veronica. Let them see the shit you live in. The things you're involved in."

Liam's little arms clung to my neck as I hurried faster, jogging down the hall and bounding down the steps.

"You can't take him. I won't let you!"

I didn't take the time to spare her a glance. "He's not safe, Veronica. You know it. For once, think of him."

In a frenzy, she scrambled down the steps behind me and out into the blazing light of day.

I ran for my car with Liam in my arms and then all the breath left me when I skidded to a stop.

thirty-nine

ALEXIS

"Pick up, pick up, pick up."

I paced in front of the bay window that overlooked my garden, listening to the phone ring and ring on the other end.

It went to voice mail for the fourth time.

"Crap," I muttered, resting my cell against my lips as I tried to fight the mounting worry.

Zee and I had spent the morning together, curled up on my couch watching a movie.

Like we were just a normal couple.

He'd been there to support me through the sadness my sister always left behind. He'd held me and brushed me with a million tender kisses to my temple as he whispered promises that had come alive in my spirit and taken root in my mind.

He'd left an hour ago, and I'd finally gone back to my room and grabbed my phone where it'd been charging on my nightstand.

Avril had left me a frantic message. "He's so pissed, Alexis. So pissed. He knows I went over there. He knows. I messed up. I think I messed up bad."

Now she wouldn't answer.

Panic crawled into my senses. Growing and building into this terror that I knew from experience was unwarranted.

This wasn't the first frantic call I'd received from Avril.

But there was something about it that gnawed at me.

Once again, I listened to her voice mail, and again I dialed her number, but it kicked me straight to the robotic voice, asking me to leave a message.

"Shit."

I lightly drummed my phone in my palm, knowing better, that I should let it be. My sister had done this to herself. Gotten herself into this mess.

She'd been doing it for years. Twisting and manipulating. But my gut warned me this was different. The way she'd shown up this morning was so out of character, and she hadn't asked anything of me but to stay away.

"Don't do it," I muttered to myself. But when it came to Avril, I never seemed to listen to that voice of reason.

I thumbed into my phone and activated the family locator.

I was the one who paid for Avril's phone. I'd rationalized I needed to be able to get in touch with her and she with me. We never knew when there might be an emergency.

This qualified, right?

The little red silhouette with Avril's name popped up on the map. Right back in that crummy area where she'd kept leading me.

God this was stupid.

So, so stupid.

But I couldn't ignore this feeling.

This intuition.

I dialed her again as I grabbed my purse and keys and headed out the door, leaving another voice mail. "I'm coming to get you, Avril. No more excuses. This has to end."

I ended the call and pressed the fob to unlock my car, jumped into the driver's seat, and backed out into the street.

I pulled up Zee's number and pushed call in the same

second I put my car in drive.

Voice mail again.

Frustration and a shot of fear attempted to climb into my chest, but I sucked it down, focused on what I needed to do.

"Hey, it's me. Avril called…something's wrong. I need to go over there. I know you just left, but you told me to call you. Do you think you could maybe meet me down there? I'm driving, though. Doors locked. I won't do anything stupid. Promise. Call me back if you get this."

I ended the call and connected the Bluetooth to Maps.

I needed to get to my sister.

Shock paralyzed me, and I clutched the steering wheel where I had pulled to a stop in front of the run-down building where Avril was supposed to be.

Hurt twitched through my body, and I started shaking. Shaking and shaking and shaking.

I couldn't focus beneath the force of the blow.

I guess it was autopilot that had me reaching out to unlatch my door. Or maybe it was just finally coming face to face with the reality of what he'd been hiding that had me floundering to my feet out on the sidewalk.

Zee careened to a stop.

Guilt on his face and a child in his arms.

The same woman from his loft that day was behind him, screeching and tearing into his flesh, demanding that he give the little boy back to her.

Our gazes were locked.

Horrified.

Telling.

I took a step back as I felt everything crack. Splinter and crash.

I stumbled and tried to hold myself up on the door of my

car. "You lied to me?"

"Alexis…just…I can explain, but this isn't the time. You need to get in your car and go straight home."

My head shook.

Stunned.

Speechless.

Destroyed.

He was suddenly right there, a hand on my shoulder, his voice a warbled echo against the ringing in my ears as he tried to force me back in the car. "Go home. Now. Lock your door and don't open it. I'll call you as soon as I can. It's not safe."

It's not safe. It's not safe. It's not safe.

I'd always known it was really my heart that was at risk.

"Avril," I mumbled, incoherent.

Zee touched my face, the child clinging to him with fear and panic in his eyes.

"I know," he said. "I know…but you've got to go. Trust me. I'm going to fix this. You need to get out of here, and you need to do it now. I'll call you later."

The woman was still flailing and screeching behind him as she tried to rip the boy from his arms, screaming that he'd betrayed her. That he'd promised.

Trust. That was the thing about it.

When you broke it? It was gone.

forty

ZEE

Anthony was already waiting for me back at the loft when I barreled inside.

He shot to standing from the couch. "Zee."

I held my hand against the back of Liam's head, holding him close and bouncing him like the few times I'd gotten to do when he was an infant, trying to get him to settle down.

To get him to stop crying. Praying he'd feel safe. Begging him to understand I would protect him, even if it cost me my life.

When I'd taken him out of the car, I'd done a quick check for visible injuries, thanking God I didn't find anything.

Still, I knew not all scars were visible.

I needed to think of him first. Make sure he was comfortable before I started bombarding him with questions I knew would be difficult for him to answer.

"I've got you, little man, I've got you," I kept telling him while I eyed Anthony from over his shoulder.

No. He wasn't a baby anymore. But he felt the same way

he'd felt the first time I'd held him.

He felt like devotion.

He felt like love.

He felt *right.*

The second I'd held him in my arms, I'd just known. I felt a connection to him in a way that should have been impossible. It was an intense bond that could never be fractured.

Like my brother's presence was right there, filling me with purpose.

Anthony quieted his voice. "What is going on?"

"You call Kenny?"

Kenny was the attorney who was always at the ready, fighting to get us clear of the trouble Sunder always seemed to find itself in. Without a doubt, this was going to be our greatest fight. The culmination of it all.

Every mistake each of us had made coming to a head.

Sunder's end.

Guess it'd been coming all along.

"I got in touch with him and asked him to get over here. He said he was dropping everything and would be here as soon as he could."

"The guys?"

"Texted them. Said it's an emergency. Everyone's on the way. Police have been called. I gave them the tip with the address you sent. You ready to tell me what the hell is going on?"

Protectively, I tightened my hold on Liam, keeping one of his ears against my chest and covering the other with my hand.

Like it might stand the chance of protecting him from all of this.

"Veronica was demanding more money for me to see him again. Ten thousand. I was done, Anthony. Just done. I decided I didn't care who knew, and if she ran with him like she's been threatening, I would hunt her down."

I sucked in a breath. "I couldn't keep going on this way. I've been feeling it in my gut that something bad was going down. That she was going back to her old ways. I finally realized that until I was ready to take a stand, nothing was going to change."

I swallowed hard. "She wouldn't let me in when I showed up at her place, so I kicked in the door. She's been using, man."

Anthony set both hands on his hips, face toward the ground. "Shit."

"Not the worst of it."

Guess he heard the urgency in my voice, because he looked back to meet my face. My tongue darted out to wet my dried lips. "There were girls…two of them…being held in one of her rooms. One was passed out…the other beat to hell."

He covered his mouth with a hand, wiped it across his lips like he could rid himself of the bitter taste.

I shook all over. "It was Avril. Alexis's twin sister. The one who got Alexis in trouble in the first place. She keeps telling Alexis that she *can't* leave."

"Goddamn it, Zee. This is a disaster."

I jerked around when my door banged open. The whole crew rushed in, wild eyed and fists clenched.

Ready to fight.

They had always been there, ready to have my back. I just prayed that remained the case this time.

They all stopped like they'd run into a brick wall when they saw the kid I held in my arms.

Liam flinched, having no clue what was happening. I kissed the top of his head.

Baz stepped forward, shaking his head, words cautious. "Zee, what's going on?"

forty-one

ZEE
TWENTY YEARS OLD

Zee shouldered into the dusky club. Strobes flashed. Bodies were packed wall to wall, the seedy, lusty crowd lit up in bursts of white, blinding light for the briefest of moments before they fell back into darkness.

Again and again.

It set the scene to slow motion.

Zee felt like he was wading through a dense fog that fought to hold him back as he pushed through the crowd.

Relief slammed him when he saw the group huddled in the far corner around a booth.

Distinct and sharp.

Familiar faces and the same goddamned scene. Just when he thought maybe Mark was pulling it together, shit like this had again become routine.

He knew Julie was trying to be understanding. But there was no chance of missing her concerned judgment when he'd slid out of bed and tugged on a pair of jeans after he'd gotten Baz's text.

Zee stormed that direction, giving zero fucks about the sneers and annoyance of the people grinding against each other as he barged through the middle of the dance floor.

Baz spun around when he felt Zee approach. "Zee, thank God you're here."

"What's going on?"

Baz ran a weary hand over his face. "Sorry to drag you out in the middle of the night. We tried to handle it, but he was insistent. Said he needed you."

Zee shook his head and took another step forward. Mark was slumped back in the booth, fading in and out of lucidity as his head rocked back against the leather seat.

His eyes fluttered open, pupils pinpoint. They shot through Zee like a goddamned spear. His voice dropped in worry, muttering mostly to himself because it seemed not a soul listened to him. "Fuck, Mark, man, what the hell are you doing?"

Mark's fingers fumbled across the collar of Zee's tee. Like he was searching for something to hang on to. "Little brother, you're here."

"Of course I'm here. You said you needed me."

A smile fluttered at the edge of Mark's slack mouth. "Always need you, man. You're my best friend. Always there for me. Love you…love you like crazy. You know that, right? You're the best."

Zee sighed. Of course he knew.

Lyrik, Ash, and Baz crowded behind Zee, peering over his shoulder at Mark like they didn't have a clue what to do with him.

"Come on, Mark, let's get you out of here," Zee said. "Do you think you can stand?"

"Think so."

He helped his brother slide out from behind the booth and onto his feet. The second he did, Mark canted to the side, nearly toppling over.

Zee grabbed him before he face-planted, hauling him back up and slinging Mark's arm around his shoulders, hoping he could at least support some of his weight. Zee belted his arm around Mark's waist. "I've got you," he promised.

Ash rushed forward to take the other side. "Got him?" he asked.

"Yup," Zee replied.

Baz and Lyrik took the lead as they worked their way back through the crowd, down the dimly lit hall, and into the back parking lot where Zee had parked. Ash and Zee maneuvered Mark into the front passenger side of the car.

The second he hit the seat, Mark nodded out.

Zee slammed shut the door, gusted out a strained sigh, and leaned his back against the door. As he pressed both palms to his face, he tried to rein in his frustration. The pain and hurt and worry that was the root of it all.

Unease sifted through the night as the club pulsed on behind them.

"He's bad, man," Baz said.

Zee dropped his hands and gave a tight nod. "Yeah, I know. It's getting worse."

Lyrik paced in the distance, the dark, dark silhouette a squall of turmoil where he raged.

A storm.

Baz's voice dropped low. "Listen…Mark's our brother…just as much as he's yours. Doesn't matter we don't share the same blood. He's family. But we're trying to get our shit together. Things are finally really happening for the band. Ash, Lyrik, and I…we all kicked, but Lyrik's still struggling bad, trying to get his life together after all the shit that went down. Can't have Mark spiraling like this. Worried he's gonna drag the rest of the crew right back down with him."

A wave of helplessness crashed over Zee. "What the hell do we do? I mean…I've been trying, begging him to see reason. He's good for a few weeks, and then it's this all over again."

Zee toed at a pebble on the pitted pavement, wary of what to say, wondering if he should bring it up or let it lie. He glanced up at Baz. "He came to me a couple months back…said he'd gotten himself into some trouble. Involved with some bad people. You know anything about it?"

A frown cut a path through Baz's expression before he anxiously rubbed at his chin. "Nah, man. Don't know what's been going on with him. You know Mark. He's always quiet. Keepin' to himself. But anytime someone's dealing in that world? You can rest assured the people he's gonna be hanging with aren't gonna be saints."

Zee's nod felt reluctant. "Yeah…probably." Hands stuffed in his pockets, he lifted his shoulders to his ears. "So what the hell do we do? How do we help him? He can't keep going on like this."

Baz blinked at him. "He's got to want to. Problem is coaxing him to that place."

Zee's head rocked back against the top of his car, face turned toward the sky, the stars obliterated by the city lights.

But he knew they were there.

Waiting with all their promises.

With all the good things the world had to give.

His brother deserved it all.

Zee made a silent wish.

Please, give me back my brother.

forty-two
ZEE

Hostility rippled through the air like heat waves. Baz was standing at the window, looking out on the city while Lyrik sat on a plush chair across the room, rubbing his palms together. Ash was in the kitchen, banging shit around.

Each of them trying to come to terms in their own way.

Liam sat on the rug at my feet, wearing headphones and watching a kid's movie on the iPad I'd given him to keep him entertained.

It wasn't like I had any toys lying around, considering part of the deal was Veronica would never let me bring him to my place.

We needed to remedy that, and soon.

First, I needed to wade through all the mistakes I'd ever made, find a solution, and pray to God the guys would forgive me for what I'd done.

If they didn't, it would rip out my fucking heart, same as the way Alexis's reaction left me feeling tattered and torn.

My heart didn't matter. My focus needed to be on this kid.

This kid I'd done my fucking best to be a dad for. To take care of him the way he deserved. No question, I'd failed miserably. He deserved so much better than being caught in the middle of this.

Baz spoke toward the window. "All this time…all these years…and not a goddamned word, Zee. Not one?" Agony was written on his face when he turned to look back at me.

Nervously, I sat forward, scratching at my beard as I struggled to find an explanation for the choices I'd made.

"It was the only way Veronica let me have a relationship with him. She said if I was stepping up and taking Mark's place in the band, she didn't want him anywhere near that kind of life. That it'd stolen Mark from her, and she wouldn't allow her son to be ruined by it."

Should've known better than all of that. The girl acting the victim. Needing money to get out of the bad side of town.

Was pretty sure she'd been running back down there all along.

From the kitchen, Ash scoffed and banged shut a drawer. "And I'm sure that's exactly how that bitch kept you eating out of her hand, isn't it? Making demands? Twisting things to go her way? Knew it the second she came waltzing in behind Mark that she was no good. Not all that hard to put a finger on her type."

"Yeah," I said. "We knew from the start none of you would ever go for it which was why we kept it a secret."

Baz turned all the way around. "We could've helped you. Why the hell did you ever think you had to go this alone?"

My gaze darted to Anthony, back to Baz, and I prepared to make my confessions. "Because it was my fault."

"What was your fault?"

"All of it."

forty-three

ZEE

TWENTY YEARS OLD

"You have to show. We hit the road tomorrow. Need to see you before I go."

Anxiously, Zee peered back through the bathroom door, through the murky light and into the bedroom where Julie was asleep in their bed. He'd crept into the confines of the bathroom so he could take the call and not disturb her since it was close to midnight.

He kept his voice quieted. "Don't know that I can make it this time. All this last minute, late night shit has been putting a stress on Julie."

"Forget Julie tonight. I'm gonna be gone for the next six months. She won't have to worry about putting up with me."

Zee rubbed a hand over the top of his head. "Who's over there?"

"Just a few friends. Rest of the band are off spending time with family before we hit the road."

"You're not high?"

"Do I sound like I'm high?"

Zee hefted a regretful sigh, hating that he even had to bring it up. "No, you don't."

"Then get over here."

Zee peeked out again at Julie's silhouette, before he blew out a resigned breath. "Fine…I'll be over there in a few."

"There's my little brother."

Zee ended the call and slinked back into the bedroom, silent as he pulled on a pair of jeans and a shirt over his head before he quietly snuck out the door.

He just hoped he didn't regret it.

Zee shouldered through the house packed with faces he didn't recognize, searching for the one face he wanted to see. The one person who held the power over him to drag him out in the middle of the night without telling his girlfriend where he was going.

Pushing through the pulsing crowd, Zee knew that compulsion was greater than just obligation. There was something special about him and Mark. Their brotherhood was something that mattered.

Mark would always be Zee's hero and Zee would always be his rock.

Zee found Mark and Veronica slung back on a couch, the girl draped around him like some kind of shiny, overpriced trinket. Gorgeous, but by the look on her face, never worth the cost.

Mark rushed to stand when he saw Zee approaching. "Hell yeah, the little brother is here. We can officially get this party started."

Mark wobbled on his feet, his smile free and wide, though he was missing that obliteration Zee had come to recognize so well.

Zee chuckled beneath his breath, slanting his brother a wry grin. "Looks to me like you already started without me."

Mark slung his arm around Zee's shoulder. "Guess we need to catch you up."

Four shots later and Zee was feeling just fine. Too fine. Too good and too loose. He joked with his brother in a way they hadn't in a long, long time. Like they'd done back when they were kids and their lives weren't filled with complications and obstacles.

Back when the only thing that mattered was them.

Mark clung to Zee as the night grew deep. Both of them were swaying where they hung out with Mark's friends in the backyard of some dude's house. He'd never even caught the guy's name.

Mark slurred his words toward Zee's ear. "Gonna miss the hell out of you. You don't know what it's like out there on the road. Gets so fucking lonely out there. Think I start to lose my mind just a little bit…start thinking crazy shit is going down, this paranoia I can't shake, like everyone is after me."

Zee squeezed the back of Mark's neck in some kind of an encouraging embrace. "Maybe it's time to ask yourself if it's worth it. If living this life is what you really want to do."

Mark's head shook. "Nah, man. It's my life. The one thing I've got going for me. Me and the guys? We worked our asses off, paid prices none of us wanted to pay, and we did it anyway. No way am I gonna ever let that go. Seeing this through with my crew is the absolute most important thing to me."

"I get that, Mark. I get it. But how are you going to know when you've had enough? When you want more?"

Mark's gaze drifted over to where Veronica was in the far reaches of the yard having a conversation with a guy Zee'd never seen before.

The two of them were barely shadows in the dusky light that stretched out from the house. Every once in a while, the dude's bleached-white hair struck in the light.

There was just something about him that screamed sleazy.

Trouble.

Like his brother needed any more of it.

Unease curled through Zee's gut. It almost seemed like they were arguing. Their words heated and lowered.

There was no missing Mark's suspicion, either. His brother swallowed and his spine went rigid. "Sometimes I think I might deserve something more. Want something more. But then I realize I always go looking for what I want in all the wrong places."

"You care about her?" Zee asked, chin barely angling toward the shadows.

"Too much, obviously." Mark seemed to shake himself from the heaviness. "Come on…forget this bullshit. Don't know when I'm going to see you again. Let's not waste it."

Zee's eyes narrowed as he tried to see through the fog, his vision blurry, and his limbs heavy. Darkness spun just as fast as the room while everything else felt slowed and distorted.

He blinked, trying to focus on the movement, the wispy silhouette that broke through the hush of the room he'd stumbled into where he sat sprawled back on a dingy, broken-down couch.

Hands were in his hair, a body straddling his waist.

He groaned.

He hated her. He knew he did. But he couldn't stop his body from reacting, couldn't stop his hands from going to her hips. Pushing her off. Pulling her forward. He didn't know.

"What the fuck is going on in here?"

Zee sucked in a staggered breath when a blinding light suddenly split into the room. He was completely disoriented and panting as he attempted to focus. To clear the stupor.

Veronica was off him in less than a flash. Her big brown eyes were wide, her mouth twisted with feigned innocence.

Disgust rippled from Mark in waves as he took a step deeper into the room. "What the fuck do you think you're doing, little brother?"

For a flash, Zee squeezed his eyes, trying to process. To make sense of what had just gone down. "Nothing."

Mark laughed. But it was lacking the affection it normally imbued. "Nothin', huh? Sure looked like something to me."

Mark rocked and took a lurching step forward, as fucked up as Zee, maybe more so. But where Zee felt nothing but confusion, it was clearly anger that raced Mark's blood.

"I was just checking on—" Veronica started to speak when Mark's phone rang.

"Don't want to hear a word, Veronica," he spat in her direction as he jerked his phone free. A sneer rode his expression when he turned the face Zee's direction so he could see who was calling. "Aww…looks like someone noticed you were gone."

Julie.

Alarms blared. Warp speed. Deafening.

Zee flew to his feet. "Dude…don't fucking answer that."

Bitterness rolled from Mark's tongue, and he was accepting the call, pushing it to his ear. Zee could hear the panicked dread in Julie's voice as she asked Mark if he'd seen Zee.

"Oh, he's right here, nothing to worry about. On second thought, maybe both of us should be worried, since I just walked in on *my fucking girlfriend* straddling my brother's lap."

Zee lunged for him. Mark fumbled back, killing the call and throwing his phone against the wall.

"What the hell, asshole?" Zee gritted.

Mark laughed. It was this senseless, hopeless sound as he stared back at Zee. "You're asking that of me? When I just walked in on you rubbing your dick all over my girl? How fucked up is that?"

Zee tore at his hair. "I wasn't…I wouldn't…"

"We weren't doing anything." Incredulous, Veronica shook her head, eyes wide as her attention darted between them. Like she was the victim and hadn't been the one to set off a bomb.

"I heard your brother getting sick, and I came in to make sure he was okay. He was getting ready to fall over, so I was helping him sit up. That's it."

Confusion pulsed through Zee's brain. Was that it? All she'd done?

Fuck. He didn't know.

The only thing he knew was he shouldn't have come. This was stupid and reckless and foolish. Not to mention the fact his brother had just thrown him under the bus.

Zee squeezed his eyes tight, fear tremoring through his body. "Julie."

"Julie," Zee begged, right behind her as she tossed a suitcase onto their bed.

Tears streamed down her face, her fingers shaking and frantic as she started yanking clothes from the closet and shoving them in.

"Julie…shit…shit. I'm so fucking sorry. I didn't do anything. I promise you, I didn't do anything. I wouldn't touch her."

Bitter laughter poured through her tears. "You didn't do anything? I wake up at four in the morning and you're gone, at a party, doing God knows what, and you didn't do anything?"

Her face pinched in grief, and Zee's insides twisted in agony.

"I told you I didn't want any part of that life." Sadness poured through her whisper.

"I love you, Julie…fuck, I love you so much. I'll do anything. *Anything.*"

Slowly, her head shook. "You already promised that. And if I can't trust you, then we don't have anything." Her expression grew somber. "And I don't trust you."

She quickly turned away and zipped the suitcase, wiping at her eyes as she dragged it from the bed and headed for the bedroom door.

Anguish gripped every cell in Zee's body, fear and horror and regret. "No…no…no…no…" he begged, chasing her out through the small living room. He grabbed her by the wrist, pressed it to his mouth. "Please."

She yanked it free, her own misery pouring down her face. "Let me go."

She pulled open the door and rushed out into the awakening day, the dusky sky grayed with morning's light.

"Julie," he pled.

She didn't turn around.

Zee dropped to his knees.

In the parking lot below, Julie's car rumbled to a start, and Zee swore he felt his heart crack when she backed out and drove away.

forty-four

ZEE

"Alexis, come on…please pick up the phone. I need to talk to you, explain what you rolled up on earlier today." I sighed before I dropped my voice and begged into the phone, "Most of all, *I need to know you're okay*. Just…call me back."

It was the third call I'd made to her. The third one she hadn't answered. I didn't blame her. I could only imagine what she was feeling.

I knew she had to be shocked.

I was feeling a whole lot of it myself. Trying to make everything add up and wondering what the fuck Veronica had gotten herself into.

My gaze wandered to where he was on his belly on the rug, doodling on a notepad with some markers I'd found him.

I contemplated.

Today had been hell for him, and I hated adding even an ounce of anxiety to what had already gone down. But I couldn't shake this feeling that rattled my bones.

Intuition.

Dread.

Before I could change my mind, I made the call. She answered on the first ring.

"Shea, I need your help."

I climbed down onto my hands and knees beside him. "Hey, buddy, what do you think about going to one of my best friend's houses and playing with their kids? They have a big backyard with a swing set."

Liam's eyes lit up. "Really?"

"Yeah. And one of those kids, his name is Connor, and he has a super cool room that's decorated with superheroes, and he has all kinds of superhero toys. I bet he would let you play with him."

"Superheroes are my favorite." He whispered it like it was a secret.

I ruffled a hand through his hair. "I know they are. We're gonna have to get you some for around here, aren't we?"

He nodded emphatically. "Uh-huh. 'cuz all my superheroes that you brought me are back at Mommy's house and I don't have any here."

Could feel the emotion clawing at my chest, the turmoil rising up from my spirit and gnawing at my being.

I stood and picked him up, knowing he wasn't a baby. In that moment, none of that mattered. I needed to hold him. Let him know he was safe.

"How would you like it if you and me got one of those big houses with a big backyard? Just like my friends Shea and Sebastian have for their kids?"

His little arms held around my neck as he tilted his head back to look toward the expansive ceiling of the loft. "You're house is already way, way big."

A chuckle rumbled free. "But not the right kind of big.

Think we need to have some place where you can run and stretch out those legs. Where you and I can go out back and toss a baseball. How's that sound?"

He squealed and squeezed my neck. "That sounds so good. I like that."

Excitement blazed in his eyes. "Does that mean I get to stay with you?"

"That's what I'm hoping. What do you think about that? Staying with me?" I rubbed a tender hand over his head when I asked it.

"I think that's the best idea ever. But what about mommy?"

A heavy sigh pushed from my lungs. "I'm not sure about your mommy right now, buddy."

Sadness and confusion hit him. I could feel it. This uneasiness that shivered through his little body. I held him a little closer, my voice dipping with emphasis. "You know you can tell me anything, right?"

He buried his face in my neck, and he nodded.

"Is there anything you want to tell me?"

His voice came out a whisper. "I don't like our new house."

I swayed him a little. Offering comfort. For both of us. "I don't like that house, either. That's why I brought you here…because I don't think that apartment is a good place for you. I would've brought you here earlier if I'd known it wasn't a safe place. You know that, right? That I won't let anything bad happen to you? That I'll keep you safe?"

He nodded again.

"Has anyone…hurt you there?"

His little shoulders scrunched up. Instantly, a ball of rage consumed me, threatening to burst, wondering exactly who I was gonna have to track down and kill.

"No…but sometimes people there are so, so mad."

"Who?"

"The man…he yells at Mommy. When he comes, Mommy tells me to go to my room and stay in there."

I kissed his temple, running my hand down his back.

That might have been the only good idea Veronica had ever

had.

"All right, let's go meet my friends. I'm going to leave you there, but just for a little bit, okay? I won't be gone long. I just have some really important stuff I have to take care of, and when I'm finished, we'll go do something super fun. Sound good?"

"I like that idea."

"Me, too, buddy. Me, too."

forty-five

ZEE
TWENTY YEARS OLD

"Need you, Zee. Please, man, you've got to listen to me. Told you I'd gotten myself in too deep. I don't know how I'm gonna fix this. They fucking know, they fucking know. I shouldn't have said anything, but how could I not?" Paranoia bled through Mark's tone.

Zee tried not to crush the phone in his hand as he pressed it tighter against his ear. Anger whirled around him like a windstorm. Howling and hot.

His teeth ground. "You really have the nerve to call me? After what you did? Because of you, I lost her. She's gone. Julie's gone."

Everything tightened and squeezed, and Zee couldn't breathe.

"I'm sorry. I fucked up, I know. I'd do anything to take it back."

Zee choked out sour laughter. "Yeah, funny how I told her

the same damn thing. Guess both of us learned the hard way there are some things you can't take back."

Marked stumbled over a sob. "Zee…I'm…I'm scared, okay? I need your help."

A rise of disquiet bristled through Zee's veins, that constant sympathy at odds with the hostility that flamed in his nerves. "And what is it you expect me to do?"

Zee heard Mark's hesitation. It was no match for his desperation. "Need money…fifty grand."

Zee laughed a hollow, disbelieving sound. He was so sick of this bullshit. So sick. So done. So hurt.

He could feel it all spiraling down around him. "Yeah, and I need my girlfriend back. Don't see either of those things happening any time soon."

Sitting alone in the vacancy of his darkened apartment, Zee tossed back another swig.

The bottle he'd cracked open thirty minutes before was half-empty, the dark, dark fluid sloshing down the sides as he attempted to balance it on his knee.

A fiery burn flamed down his throat, his stomach a pool of fire and venom.

He attempted to focus through bleary eyes, his head spinning against the weight of his heart.

Julie left him.

Mark threw him under the bus.

He didn't have anything left.

Sorrow pushed against the anger bottled tight in his chest. So damned tight he could feel it getting ready to blow.

So he drowned it.

He lifted the bottle and gulped another mouthful, fighting the surge of fury, blinking as he tried to make sense of the sound hammering against his ears.

Groaning, he tried to ignore it.

More pounding.

He clambered to his feet, quick to grip the arm of the couch when the room spun, the bottle clutched against his chest like a lifeline. He looked toward the floor, sucking in air as his mind tripped through a muddle of confusion and doubt and regret.

I just wanted my brother back.

I just wanted my brother back.

Instead, his brother had stolen everything.

Pound. Pound. Pound.

Floundering for the door, he fumbled through the lock and somehow managed to free it.

He reared back, caught off guard by the face on the other side. Tears stained her dazzling face, her brown eyes bright and pleading, one rimmed in fading black and blue.

She wrung her hands. "I'm so sorry to bother you…I just…I needed someone to talk to."

"Not sure I'm gonna be the best company right now."

Her chin trembled. "I think you're the exact kind of company I need."

The words were out before he could stop them. "What happened to you?"

Her throat wobbled as she fought a fresh round of tears. "He—"

Rage. He didn't know if he was feeling it for her or for the whole fucked-up situation. Either way, he couldn't control it, the way it lined his veins like steel.

Fingertips touched his chest, nudging him back. "Are you okay?" she asked.

Grief constricted Zee's throat, and he shook his head, too hard. It sent his world spinning again. Ground gone.

He tried to catch his breath.

"No…not okay."

"Me, neither. He…he broke up with me, Zee. I don't know what's going on in his head. First you…then me."

She edged Zee deeper into the hollow loneliness of his

apartment. Her voice was a soft whisper of understanding when she spoke. "I can't believe what he did to you. I'm sorry, Zee. You deserve so much better than that."

Emotion clogged his throat and burned his eyes. "I just wanted my brother back. I just wanted to be there for him. And Julie…she just fucking left. Didn't give me a chance to make it right. I can't make anything right."

It was all a slur of misery.

"Shh." She caressed his shoulders. She gave a gentle shove, and Zee slumped back onto the couch, looking up at her with his heart in his throat and his stomach on the floor as he clung to that bottle.

She edged forward, and Zee shivered when she slowly straddled his lap.

"Let's forget them. They don't deserve us."

A shudder ran through Zee's being.

This time there was no question of her intentions.

And again, there was no stopping his body's reaction as she fumbled with the buttons of his fly.

Veronica was right.

Fuck them.

forty-six

ALEXIS

Overcome, I dropped to my knees in the middle of my living room. I held both hands against my chest as if it might keep the torment from pouring out.

Since the moment Zee had come into my life, I'd thought I could feel something building every time I was in his space. The way that intensity had mounted and grown, continually gaining speed.

I'd thought it was propelling us forward. Forcing us in a direction that was good and right. Where the walls that had fought to separate us would be obliterated.

Turned to rubble.

Now I was left wondering who he really was. If everything had been a lie.

Tell me this isn't cheating.

Hadn't I felt it then? An unease warning me to take caution?

I just didn't understand how he could hide something so

important from me. Something intrinsic to him. Why didn't he trust me? That was the one thing I'd asked of him.

Had he been hiding another girl all along?

The thought nearly crushed me.

Broke me in two.

A sob tore up my throat and my chest heaved. Why did every time I got close to my dreams, they got ripped out from under me? Why couldn't I ever make anything better?

What good was belief when there was nothing left remaining to believe in?

My doorbell rang, and I gasped in surprise, rocking back on my knees. A spray of late afternoon light slanted through the room, lighting up the edges.

Nudging me with hope.

With the desperate need to find reason.

Answers.

I just needed to see his face and know I'd been right to *believe*.

I jumped to my feet and raced for the door. Without thought, I jerked it open.

I shouldn't have. I should have been so much smarter than that.

Apparently Chelsey was right.

I had no self-preservation.

forty-seven

ZEE

I drummed my fingers on the steering wheel of my car, anxious as I inched through the late afternoon traffic that crawled at a snail's pace.

It was kind of crazy how you feared the consequences of something so much that you carried an inordinate amount of dread as you waited for it to be revealed, all the while praying that moment would never actually come to pass.

Now that the time had come for me to pull it from the shadows, to take the stand and shine light all over my sins, I couldn't wait to finally lay it out.

To purge the weight.

To give it to someone else and beg them for the chance.

Praying that maybe she'd get it. That she might share it with me.

I zigzagged across lanes, trying to pick up time and distance. Worry needled at my senses.

I couldn't help but worry for Liam. I prayed the little man was fine. No question, he couldn't be in better hands than those of my family.

They would embrace him. Accept him. I knew they would.

He was every bit a part of this family as any one of us.

Funny how my entire focus shifted the second the total responsibility of something so utterly important was placed in the care of my hands.

Keeping him that way was gonna be a fight.

A fight I was willing to battle to the end.

That worry needled deeper at the thought of standing in front of Alexis and confessing everything.

Every sin.

My mistakes.

The secrets.

It would be a lot for anyone to take.

But this girl…she was good and grace. If there was anyone who would believe in me, it was her.

I breathed out in relief and anticipation when I finally took the last right into her neighborhood. Picturesque and quaint, light shined down through the lush leaves on the trees, like the sun was pitching daggers of warmth and faith.

I pulled up at the curb in front of her house and cut the engine. Jumping from my car, I rushed toward her door.

My footsteps slowed when I noticed the door was wide open. A knot of apprehension tugged at my gut, and my heart kicked an extra beat.

Breaths going shallow and quiet, I edged forward, angled to the side so I could peek inside. A frozen hush echoed back, everything completely still.

Too still.

I gulped around the panic that tried to work its way out.

"Alexis," I called, nudging the door open a fraction wider as I took a single step through her door, eyes darting everywhere.

Silence answered back.

A shiver of dread raced down my spine, and that was all it took for me to shoot into action, rushing for her kitchen, gaze frantic as I took in the area.

Quiet. Calm.

Completely opposite of what I felt.

I threw open the back door to her backyard.

Nothing.

I raced back inside, heading straight for the single bedroom tucked in the back and the bathroom attached.

Empty.

Panic tightened my chest, my tongue a rumble with the plea. "Oh God. God…Alexis…where the hell are you?"

I ran back down the short hall and into the living room, headed for the door. I stopped short when something on the floor, right up against the wall, caught my attention.

Alexis's cell phone.

The back was busted open and the battery had fallen out. Like it'd been dropped, shattered on impact.

And I knew. I fucking knew.

I rushed for my car, dialing 9-1-1 as I went. I shouted out Veronica's address, shoved the keys back into the ignition, and threw my car in gear, jamming on the accelerator. The tires squealed on the asphalt as I spun the car around and peeled off down the road.

Whatever was going down? No question, Avril was involved.

Had no idea how seriously they took me when I said I thought my girlfriend had been abducted, that I had no proof whether she was actually at this address or not.

It was nothing but a hunch. A hunch that felt a whole lot more like a premonition.

Ending the call, I dialed Anthony. He answered on the second ring. "Pretty sure we have proof of where Veronica has been funneling the money," he said before I had the chance to say anything.

Right then, I didn't give a fuck about the money.

"They have her." It scraped from my throat. There was no missing the fear. The fury.

I could feel his confusion. "What?"

"Alexis…I went to her place because I couldn't get in

touch with her. I needed to explain to her about Liam. Was going to tell her everything. I got there, and her front door was standing wide open, her phone in pieces on the floor. She's gone, man."

"Shit," he hissed. "Did you call the cops?"

"First thing…gave them Veronica's address. I know she's involved, one way or another."

"Where are you?"

"On my way over there."

"Goddamn it, Zee. You can't go running in like some kind of white knight. If what you said about Alexis' sister pans out, that guy is dangerous."

My laughter was sharp. "We already know that piece of shit is dangerous. He proved it the first night in that alley. Whatever happens, make sure Liam is taken care of."

"Don't talk like that, Zee. Just…step back. Take a breather and figure out the right way to handle this before you go in there with guns blazing." Anthony sucked in a breath when he realized what he said.

"I appreciate everything, Anthony. You've had my back on this the whole time. Took care of the situation and, in turn took care of Liam. You don't know what that means to me."

Without a parting word, I ended the call and tossed my phone to my lap, clenching the steering wheel in fists as I swerved and careened through traffic.

Panic and rage ricocheted through the cabin of my car. Every pass growing stronger. That energy a fucking blaze of blinding light.

Alexis.

She was *mine.*

And I'd gladly die before I let anyone hurt her.

Just like I would've done that night.

I got it. What my spirit had already recognized in her. That goodness that was meant to be a part of this world.

A huge SUV blared its horn when I swerved in front of it to take a sharp left turn. But I couldn't stop, wouldn't slow.

My phone pinged with a text message just as I was turning

onto the last street before I got to Veronica's.

It popped up on the touchscreen.

New text message from Unknown.

I pressed the button for the text to voice. The canned voice rang through the speakers.

You want to see Alexis again, bring the kid and $20,000.

An address came in behind it.

What the fuck?

This dude was insane. No question it was him, Veronica his goddamned pawn. I couldn't help but wonder if she had been all along.

Quickly, I punched the address into the navigation and made a second call to 9-1-1, praying they would listen and not think I was leading them on some kind of wild goose chase. I probably sounded like a lunatic.

God knew I felt like a madman.

Took me all of three minutes to come to the address. The same damned street I'd been walking when I'd found Alexis.

My heart roared so loud I could hear it in my ears when I fumbled out of my car.

In front of me was a deserted building, two stories high that looked like it used to be some kind of retail store. The bottom floor was a wall of windows that were cracked and splintered and littered with the evidence of bullet holes. Graffiti marked its exterior walls in despair and hate.

A tremor of violence shivered all the way to my bones. I edged forward. Anxiety clamped down on every cell in my body, the fear I felt fuel for the desperation to get this girl back, safe where she belonged.

I peered toward the second floor windows, wondering just where the fucker was. If he was watching. Waiting for me.

There was no doubt in my mind this bastard had me walking straight into a trap.

But if money was his end game, wiping me out would be about the fucking dumbest mistake the asshole could make. Problem was, I didn't know just what I was dealing with, had no clue the lengths he would go.

Daylight slowly slipped away, casting the heavens in pinks and grays that glittered through the air and tumbled across the ground. It darkened against the cracked, fractured windows. Darkness spilled inside its walls like the pour of a river, filling it up with the intent to desolate and drown.

I edged closer, my boots crunching on a piece of broken glass on the sidewalk. It rang out like a warning.

Caution slowed my steps, and I did my best to bide my time, to be rational, to find reason, a solution while I silently pled with the cops to show.

A muted whimper echoed from deep within the walls.

My chest tightened to a fist.

Alexis.

There was absolutely nothing I could do. No reason to be found. No thought of consequences or repercussions when my entire being shot into action.

There was only one outcome I could see.

Alexis safe.

Alexis home.

I yanked at the main door.

Locked.

Frantic, I moved, searching, sucking in a deep breath when I reared back, lifted my leg, and shoved the sole of my boot against a splintered pane of glass.

It dented, the fractures multiplying into a million tiny squares. Drawing my leg back, I rammed my boot back into the same spot with all the force I could find.

With my desperation.

With this love.

Fuck.

I shook my head, trying to purge the thoughts that were coming at me just as furious as the fear. The window gave, finally breaking.

Pieces shattered from their hold and pinged across the floor.

Raging, I stepped through, eyes wild as they narrowed, pinpoints as I peered into the depths of the rundown store.

Garbage littered the floor, more graffiti inside, light fixtures destroyed and dangling from the ceiling where they'd been ripped from their holdings.

But it was the needles discarded on the floor like tokens of their victims that kicked me in the gut. The abhorrent reality of it stung my spirit.

Memories of Mark flashed through my mind.

His smile.

His talent.

The loss. The loss. The loss.

I reeled with the impact of it, this place nothing but a shrine to the casualties of the souls that had been swallowed by addiction. I blinked against the tragedy of it, turning my ear deeper to the foul dungeon's depths.

Quiet echoed back, dense and malicious.

The sound of evil.

Doubted it made much difference at all that I kept my footsteps quieted and contained.

Asshole already knew I was coming.

Still, I stole forward cautiously, slowing even further when I edged around the display case near the back.

I pressed my back up against the wall and inched closer to the archway that led to another room in the back. My chest heaved with the strain of my breaths, muscles tight with adrenaline.

I gulped down a stealing breath and rounded the corner.

Then I froze.

Fury licked at my insides. Flaming. Scorching. Inciting a war.

That foul piece of shit was leaning casually against a pillar in the middle of the room. Like he was the king and this vile, run-down building was his kingdom.

Maybe I should've expected it. But I couldn't stop the horrified shock when I found Veronica hidden deep in the shadows, this deep, gutting pain that she was actually there and involved this way.

She was a raging silhouette of agitation. Arms crossed over her chest, hugging herself as she stalked one direction and then spun to head the other.

An illicit storm. Out of her mind.

Gone.

There was no other explanation.

It was Mark who'd told me it was the needle that made you do wicked things.

Yet, none of it compared to the terror that ravaged my senses when my frantic gaze caught movement to the side of the pillar.

Alexis and Avril.

Both were huddled on the ground, bound at the wrists and ankles. Alexis's head was twisted as far as it could be, like even then, she was struggling to find me in the darkness.

Lighting the way.

The space between us leapt, fierce and hot. Desperate and mad. Those blue eyes a storm of terror.

Craig tossed a lighter into the air and caught it in his hand, like he was just standing there passing time. A sneer curved one side of his mouth. "I don't see the kid."

Protectiveness rushed through me, this crashing wave that stole my breath. "You're obviously more of a fool than I thought you were if you're actually stupid enough to think I'd bring him down here."

Maybe I should've acted like I was caving. But I was putting an end to Liam being used as a tool for greed.

Veronica increased her pacing, fidgeting when she suddenly

took a step in our direction. "Zee, just give him the money and bring Liam back. Where he belongs."

I glared at her. "Where he belongs? In this mess? I can't fucking believe you'd subject him to this, Veronica. All these years, I wanted to think better of you, thinking there might be a spec of good in your black soul. But I'm done doing your bidding with the hopes it might give Liam a better life. What Liam needs is to be with me. Where I can take care of him. Protect him."

My attention moved to Alexis and Avril on the ground. "And this…you're an accessory to this?"

She might have been a bitch. I'd never thought her a monster.

Craig kept tossing that lighter. So damned casual. But there was nothin' casual about his words. "You see…now that's where there's gonna be a problem. I've grown partial to that nice, fat check you like to drop in Veronica's account every month to take care of that rotten kid."

Rotten kid?

Aggression curled my fists, body rocking with the need to take the bastard out.

I forced myself to stay rooted.

Buying that time.

Praying the cops had taken my call as seriously as it was.

Craig tsked, and I wanted to fucking vomit when his corrupt gaze glided to Alexis. "And then we had sweet, unsuspecting Alexis running this way every time her sister made even a peep." He glanced between me and her, wearing that sneer like pride. "Seems the two of you have made quite the contribution."

"Pretty sure you already know that game's up."

He cocked his head. "You sure about that?"

"Not giving either of you another dime. Now, I suggest you give me Alexis and Avril and we'll be on our way. Give you a little headway to clear out before the cops show."

I was playing with fire. I knew it.

Making demands. Tossing in the word about the cops was a

low, dark threat I was only praying he'd heed.

The fact he even had Alexis there showed how desperate he was. If he were smart, he'd give it up, let both of them go.

But that was the thing about those living on the outside of the law. They were always running a step ahead of it, dodging it at every turn, thinking they were above it.

Craig suddenly reached down and grabbed Alexis by the hair. She screamed out in pain when he jerked her up, and my insides curled into rage, the asshole forcing her to stand when her ankles were bound.

The only thing I wanted was to lunge at him. Destroy him. But I was frozen, a chill slicking down my spine like ice, petrifying everything when he reached behind him.

A flash of metal struck through the gloom.

Anger jerked my muscles, twisting them in taut, rigid bows that ached to be released as I stood there.

"Craig," Veronica whispered on a plea. "This wasn't part of the plan. What do you think you're doing? You told me we were here to get Liam back. That's it. The girls for my son. That was what you promised. You promised."

Her words turned frantic at the end.

Fisting his hand tighter in Alexis's hair, he swiveled a fraction to look at Veronica, gun waving in the air. "Shut the fuck up, Veronica. You know better than to open your mouth."

Alexis whimpered.

Fear and pain.

Fear and pain.

My heart shredded into a million fiery pieces while I stood there, trying to calculate how to set her free. How not to set this guy off when he was so clearly gonna blow.

Craig turned back to stare me down, aiming the barrel of the gun at Alexis's head. "These girls…all of them…a fucking dime a dozen. Just like her sister. You think anyone's gonna even notice if she goes missin'?"

My guts curled with nausea. Terror for Alexis. For Avril. Sickness at the realization this was no new thing he was talking about.

Avril, just like the girl I'd found with her in Veronica's apartment, weren't anything but dispensable. Disposable. Puppets he left mangled before he discarded them like trash.

"Craig," Veronica rasped, word rippling with her stunned fear. Like she'd had no idea just what this guy was made of.

That he was vile and sick.

Cold laughter rocked from the well of my chest, my feet pinned to the ground to keep me from rushing forward while I did my best to shift his attention to me. "Are you really dumb enough to think someone wouldn't notice if I went missing?"

Fight me, asshole. Fight me. Let her go.

I twitched in restraint.

And Alexis…that sweet, good girl, I could see her pleading with me, her thoughts in turmoil.

Help us.

Run.

Go.

Please.

"That's funny. No one seemed to be all that concerned when they found your brother face down in a pile of his own puke, did they?"

Shocked horror kicked me in the gut, and I barely rasped out, "What did you say?"

He grinned, still holding on to Alexis like she didn't mean anything. "Come now, Zee. Are you really that stupid? Who do you think it was milking the info out of him?" He shrugged like what he was saying was inconsequential. Like he weren't tearing me into a million pieces. "Told Jennings keeping him around wasn't worth the risk. All these years, and not even you were smart enough to make the connection."

That familiarity came crashing in. Vivid. The realization of where I'd seen him before.

The last night I'd seen Mark alive.

A roar tore up my throat, and I started to lunge for the bastard, rage clouding my eyes.

I froze when he jerked Alexis' head, and she cried out, that cry downshifting into an agonized whimper when he cocked the gun against her head. "How about we test this whole theory out on her? Then we can have a little conversation about the boy."

Everything slowed in the same second every thread of sanity tying me to the ground snapped.

I charged.

His eyes grew wide right before I rammed my shoulder into his stomach, arms around his waist. Our footing broke, and the two of us flew through the air.

Alexis' scream was nothing but a resonance of the gunshot that rang in the air.

We hit the floor with a thud, and I scrambled to get on top, pinning him down while he struggled to break free. "Motherfucker."

My fist rammed into his face. Cocking back, I did it again. And again.

Craig fought like the bastard he was.

Nothing to lose.

I had no idea what was more dangerous.

That or the fact that I stood to lose everything.

He managed to toss me off, and he scrambled to roll me over and get on top of me and take control.

My knee came up in the same second and nailed him in the ribs.

A moan ripped from his bloody mouth, and in a second flat, I had the prick pinned on his back, his arms flailing and grappling.

He took hold of something. A split second later, the gun was in my face. A sharp gust of surprise jetted from my lungs, and I went for his wrist, struggling to shake it loose.

From out of nowhere, a blow hit me from the side.

Full body.

Veronica.

That was at the very same second another gunshot pierced the air. Fear clawed through my body, but I wrangled the gun free, slammed the butt of it across his face.

Gasping, I flung myself off of him and climbed to my hands and knees, crawling to where she was whimpering, hands pressed to her stomach as blood spilled out.

I gathered her in my arms. "Oh God."

She gurgled. "I'm so sorry. I didn't mean for this to happen. I loved you. I did."

I blinked as I choked over a sob that climbed my throat.

I could barely make out her last words.

"Take care of him."

forty-eight

ALEXIS

Disoriented, my eyes fluttered open to a faint beeping that echoed in the room. Everything was a dull, aching haze before it quickened into focus. Panic welled as horror rushed forward.

"Alexis…lie back…don't try to get up."

I settled back down, blinking toward the ceiling as I tried to make sense of how I'd gotten there.

That man at my door, that woman in the car.

Avril. Me. Bound.

Darkness. Gunshots.

Zee.

Zee.

Zee.

I gasped around the intensity of it as a fresh surge of terror and anxiety washed over me.

"Avril…Zee." The plea barely scraped up my raw throat.

Chelsey smiled, running her fingers through my hair. "Safe. Avril is on another floor. She had a broken collarbone and some bruises. Physically, she's going to be fine. It's all the emotional stuff that remains unseen."

"Zee?"

She bit her bottom lip, her expression ridged in both sympathy and understanding. "He's been pacing outside your door for the last six hours. I wouldn't let him in until I talked to you first."

A strained breath blew through my dry lips. It was relief and confusion and uncertainty.

This giving boy who again would have traded his life for mine. For my sister's. The same man who'd drawn me so close and had still kept me a world away. Outside of the things that were most important.

"Are you up to seeing him? I think if I don't go out there soon and give him an update, he's going to bust down the door."

"That sounds about like him."

Her mouth twisted, her eyes searching. "He saved you both."

My nod was jerky. "Yeah…I don't know if Avril or I would have made it out of there without him."

I also wasn't sure if we'd have been in that situation in the first place if it weren't for him. If it was about Avril or about him or simply about greed.

I wasn't sure of anything except that I was more grateful for what he'd done than I'd ever been for anything in all my life. It was a feeling that was all-consuming. All-powerful.

Almost as intense as the sadness that had seeped like poison into my veins. That feeling of standing there, looking at the man I loved, and wondering if I knew him at all.

What of us had been real? Or had everything been fake?

"Are you ready to talk to him?"

I swallowed around the lump that tasted like grief and shards of glass. "Yeah…you can let him in."

"Okay." She edged forward and placed a kiss on my forehead. "I'm so glad you're okay. I always, always worry about you, Alexis. But this time…" Grief clogged her words. "This time I was terrified I was going to lose you. I don't know where that would leave me."

Fighting the moisture in my eyes, I blinked up at her. "It's okay…it's over now."

With trembling lips, she nodded before she straightened and headed for the door. It swung open and started to close behind her when a hand caught it.

And that energy. It swelled and rippled and taunted. Zee stood at the door with so much torment on his face. Grief. Stricken. Broken.

And somehow whole.

My savior.

"Hey." It rumbled across the room.

"Hi," I whispered.

My eyes wandered, taking him in, the memories of that dark dungeon sending a shiver of fear through me. "Are you hurt?"

He shook his head, voice so hard. "No."

Tears stung my eyes and burned with guilt. "I'm so glad."

He roughed a hand down his face. The shooting star trembled and shook. "Fuck…Alexis. You were worried about me? He took you. I can't—" He turned around, setting his hands on his hips.

I blinked through the moisture in my eyes. "It was my fault. I'm always so reckless. The doorbell rang, and I…I didn't even hesitate to open the door because I thought it was you."

I guessed maybe that revealed to him exactly how I felt about him. That I would always run toward him and never from him, even though I felt wounded that he'd keep something so significant from me.

A child.

Questions swirled, but I kept them tamed as I watched the distressed grimace pinch his face.

"Your fault?" he murmured with pain, finally turning back to me. "You've been doing what you've thought was right all along, Alexis. Fighting for your sister. While I've been nothing but a fool, trying to keep something hidden, thinking it would protect a little boy who I'd gladly die for. They had been playing me the whole time."

I wanted to ask him a million questions about the boy. For an explanation. For a reason. For anything that would make that secrecy okay.

Instead, a stutter of words poured out with my confusion. "That woman? Veronica. She knew Craig…and…and my sister? I don't…I don't understand."

I sucked in a quivering breath. "When Craig came, Veronica…she was in the car. They had my sister."

Zee sank into a chair and furiously scrubbed at his face. As if he were trying to break through the veil. One made up of silence and secrets.

"I had no clue they were connected, Alexis. I promise you. There was something about that asshole that night when I first found you…something that felt familiar. But I'd chalked it up to the adrenaline. Thought it was just an amplification of the aggression I felt, thinking I recognized the scumbag from before."

"And you did know him?" I urged through my bewilderment.

His head barely shook, as if he wanted to ward off the memories. "There was this birthday party for my brother. Veronica…"

This time when he said her name, he cringed and then swallowed, seemingly having to force himself to continue with the explanation. "My brother and Veronica…they were together for a while."

Part of me wanted to weep with relief, because if it was Mark who'd been with Veronica, then my hurt over his secrecy had been nothing but presumption and speculation. But there was something about Zee's demeanor that held the solace at bay.

Hurt radiated from him, and his voice drew quiet and strained. "That night was the last time I saw him."

He blinked, as if he were trying to see into a distant memory. "Craig was there talking to Veronica. They were hidden deep in the backyard where it was hard to see them. Veronica had never exactly come across as chaste, so I think

Mark and I both had figured they'd had some kind of past or were right in the middle of one. Guess all along I should have realized it went much deeper than that."

"They were together…Veronica and Mark…when he died?"

Zee flinched at the question. "Not sure I would call it that."

A disorder of facts spun through my mind, the past and the present. They were chaos, a jumble of details that twisted and turned before they'd all somehow intersected yesterday in what could have been my greatest tragedy.

I could have lost Avril. I could have lost Zee.

Grief constricted my already bruised chest as I tried to fumble through the details. "What happened…after? I heard the gunshot right before I hit my head and everything went black."

Hesitating, he glanced to the wall, caution in his gaze when he finally looked back at me. Those bronze eyes flamed with hatred.

"He had that gun at your head." Every muscle in his body tightened when he said it, the words growing hard. "Maybe I should've waited. Let it play out. But I couldn't take that chance, Alexis. I fucking couldn't risk him hurting you. So, I lunged for him. I wanted to die when I heard the gun pop off, not knowing if you were in its path, desperate to get to you but knowing I had to put a stop to it all if you and Avril were ever really gonna be safe."

His massive throat bobbed when he swallowed. "We were rolling around on the ground. Throwing blows. Grappling for the gun."

His head shook. "Then Veronica—" The word broke off and he roughed a hand through his hair.

"Fuck," he cursed, ramming the heel of his hand in his eye, choking around grief.

It trembled through me, and he was talking toward the floor as he spat the words. "She dove at us. I don't fucking know which of us she was trying to protect…me or that asshole."

He looked up, moisture in his eyes. "She took the bullet that was meant for me." Horror billowed from him. "She's gone."

And I didn't understand this feeling. This constricting, strangling feeling. I wanted to weep.

For her.

For him.

For that little boy.

I didn't know.

All I knew was it hurt and gutted and made me question my sanity.

"Zee…I'm…so sorry." The words clogged and hung onto my throat, as if they didn't know if they really wanted to be released.

How could I feel sympathy for the woman who had done this to me? To Avril? But I did.

He choked around a sob. "I just…I don't fucking know how I'm going to tell him."

"The little boy?" Even though they were barely a breath, the words knocked through both of us with the force of a sledgehammer. Brutal. "Is that what you were hiding from me? That you have a family? Tell me who she really was and what she meant to you. I just…I don't understand."

I could feel the tremble of my chin. "And I want to."

He gripped the back of his neck in both hands, before he suddenly hauled his chair up close to the side of my bed, the legs screeching on the floor and his intensity invading the space.

It stole my breath. The proximity and the severity.

Agony lashed across his face, and he gripped my hand in both of his, his voice rough. "I'm ready to give you my truth."

forty-nine

ZEE
TWENTY YEARS OLD

"Just wanted to tell you goodbye. Pretty sure they're coming for me. Don't think I'm gonna be seeing you again. But I guess it doesn't matter all that much when it was you who stabbed me in the back."

"Who?" Zee demanded.

A smoky dimness cloaked the night sky. City lights glowed against the fog that sagged so low and thick Zee could almost reach out and touch it.

It cast his entire world in an ominous haze, everything he'd ever known vapors and mist.

"Doesn't matter."

"It doesn't matter?" Zee turned frantic, begging through the phone. "I'm sorry, Mark. I'm so goddamned sorry."

"You're sorry? You were my best friend. My brother. I *trusted* you. Would have trusted you with my life. And I told you I was fuckin' sorry for answering that phone…but you've gotta know what it looked like when I walked in on you two."

Zee blinked hard, trying to see through the torment. "It was a mistake."

But simply labeling it a mistake felt like committing treason. Another dose added to the mounting disloyalty.

Mark's words trembled with anger. "A mistake? You fucked my girlfriend. Didn't think it was possible for you to commit something like that."

Zee's hand fisted in his hair, and he began to pace. With each desperate step, loneliness closed in. His chest felt too tight and too empty, like he could feel the connection that had always bound them together loosen.

Because he couldn't ever take back what he'd done.

"She said…she said you'd broken up with her. That you *hit* her."

"And you believed her." It wasn't a question, just a sinking acceptance that severed a little more of who Zee and Mark once were. "You really think I'd hit her? I loved her."

Sickness clawed at Zee's being, sinking in like fangs and dripping venom into his soul.

He bent in two, retching on the ground.

What did I do?

What did I do?

The world spun faster.

Dizzying.

Ruining.

Toppling.

"I didn't…I'd never—"

Zee could feel the world splintering, his foundation crumbling beneath his feet.

Opening to reveal his wrong.

It tossed him headfirst into a bottomless chasm.

Endless.

Purgatory.

Zee started to ramble, desperate for a solution. For the two of them to find solid ground. That place where they belonged. Where Mark was his hero and he was Mark's rock.

"I'm sorry, man. I'll do anything. Anything. Come back to LA. We'll work it out. Figure out how to get you out of this trouble. Just…tell me you forgive me. Tell me you're okay…that this won't cause you to slip. You're scaring me, man. You're scaring me."

Mark's laughter was hollow. "What's the point of staying clean…the point in working hard for what is right…when it's just taken away from you anyway?"

Zee gulped around the agony. "Mark—"

"I have to go."

He ended the call and Zee choked over a strike of fear that hit him like a bolt of lightning.

Without giving it a second thought, he dialed Baz. It went straight to voice mail.

Searching for an answer, for courage, Zee turned his face to the heavens. It glowed like he was at the brink of day without the promise of a sunrise.

The stars were obscured.

Hidden.

Stars he knew shined and glimmered so damned bright when you stepped out of the limelight and depravity of this sordid city. Somehow, he'd always thought those twinkling stars the guardians of the wishes he'd cast upon their fallen as a child.

As if they held them protectively where they forever danced until the day those wishes were released and that dream became a reality.

In that moment, Zee swore he heard a silent curse uttered that left them permanently dimmed.

As a kid, Zee had breathed a million of those wishes.

Countless.

Infinite.

Now he could feel them falling all around him. Burning and bleeding out.

Disintegrating into nothing.

"He's gone, Zee. He's gone. I'm so damned sorry. He's gone."

Denial screamed in Zee's head while grief clutched him like a vice. Squeezing him in two.

He knew. He knew. He knew.

"No," Zee begged.

On the other end of the line, Baz stumbled over deep, guttural cries, floored by grief.

It was palpable. Too much. Too much.

Zee choked over the emotion.

What did I do? What did I do?

"No," he whimpered again. His spirit thrashed, crashed and collided with his heart that wept. "No."

"I found him, Zee. I fucking found him. Face down on the tour bus. I should have known. I should have known. He'd been clean. He'd been clean, but he was acting sketchy. All itchy and wired. Should have known he was gettin' ready to slip."

Zee tore at his hair as the words tumbled out. "Someone…someone was after him."

Another sob ripped through the line. "No, Zee. No. He OD'ed. There was a bag…I was there. I found him. I found him. I tried. I fucking tried to breathe life back into him. I promise. I tried so fucking hard. He was already gone. Oh…God—"

Baz broke on the confession.

Sobs tore through the air.

Agony.

Torment.

It was my fault.

My fault.

I did this.

Zee dropped to his knees.

Because he no longer knew how to stand.

Wind whipped through the air like a heated tornado that spun and churned and destroyed. It lashed and beat, catching up the cries that echoed at Mark's graveside.

The coffin was lowered into the ground.

Zee's mother moaned. The deepest kind of grief.

Zee clenched his fists and ground his teeth against the agony that shredded his insides.

Grief and guilt and devastation.

His mother buried her face in his father's chest, and Zee stood there. Alone. Drowning in a hollowness unlike anything he'd ever experienced. Excruciating. Violent. Piercing.

He watched as his mother stepped forward and tossed a handful of dirt onto the gleaming black wood. The tiny particles scattered across the top like a booming proclamation.

The final declaration that Zee had nothing left.

His mother's knees buckled, and his father led her away, while Zee stood there with his throat thick and his eyes stinging.

Baz stepped up and squeezed his shoulder. "He loved you, Zee. Know this has to be killing you…but if you know one thing, I want you to know that."

Zee mashed his eyes shut, desperate to confess it all. To admit to Baz what he'd done. To tell him Mark had begged him for help, told him he was afraid, and in his petulant anger, he'd turned him away.

Instead, he slowly turned when Baz's spine stiffened, hackles almost visible as he lifted his shoulders and cocked his head.

Veronica strode through the grass, a clingy black dress displaying her body and black sunglasses hiding her eyes.

Zee fought the overwhelming urge to vomit.

Baz pointed at her. "I dare you to take another step closer."

Her chin trembled as she came to a stop, confusion in the way she released a surprised breath. "I came to pay my respects. He was my boyfriend. I loved him."

Baz scoffed. "He's dead because of you. You were the one who dragged him back into that mess when he tried to get clean."

"No."

Ash and Lyrik took to either of his sides, making a wall, like it was their last chance to protect Mark from her. Like maybe they wished they had taken that stance all along.

"Go. None of us ever want to see you again. You come around? Promise you, I'll make sure you regret it."

Bitterness and anger pushed through Zee's being. He hated. He fucking hated.

He strode up the stone steps to the building that had intimidated him when he'd first walked through its doors when he was sixteen years old. The culmination of his every goal.

Now his heavy footsteps echoed through the vacant halls. He knocked at the Dean's door and opened it when he heard a gruff, "Come in."

Zee had little left to give.

But this. This he could offer.

Zee cast his dreams at the feet of the Dean and left them there.

For his brother.

For his honor.

For his legacy.

The next day, Zee rang the doorbell to the Sunder house in the Hills. Two months before, the guys had purchased it. They'd crawled their way out of dives and into theaters and stadiums. This place had become like a testimony.

Not to the wealth and the number of dollars in their bank

accounts. But as a declaration of their success. The fact they'd made it even after all the bullshit they'd been through. The adversity and affliction. The tragedy and addiction.

Now it stood like a sinister reminder that Mark had not.

You did this.

You did this.

You did this.

Emotion raced Zee's throat, this tingly, burning feeling he beat down into the blackened pit of his soul. He shifted his feet, anxious, waiting, a heavy backpack on his shoulder.

Inside the bag were his only remaining belongings.

The tour had been sidelined. The guys came back for the funeral and to figure out what direction they were gonna go.

Lost.

One side of the ornate doors swung open. Baz stood in the middle of it. Stricken by grief.

"Zee," he murmured in surprise.

"I'm in."

The doorbell rang incessantly. Over and over. Devastation slowed his feet, his mind foggy from wasting the day away skating the fringes of sleep in his bed.

He'd have to get it together soon. For the guys. He had to take care of them. Protect this band. Make sure they made it.

Mark had told him the band staying together was the absolute most important thing to him.

Zee made a silent promise he would never let his brother's dream go.

He snagged a shirt from the floor and threw it over his head. He jogged downstairs and into the stilled vacancy of the mansion in the Hills that had become his home.

"Coming," he yelled, hustling when the bell rang two times in a row.

He jerked open the door and then stumbled back. The anger that struck him was the most intense kind.

Brutal and violent and savage.

But hate always was.

Violent.

Veronica stood in the doorway, wearing frayed, ripped jeans and a super tight red tee.

"What the fuck are you doing here? You were told when you showed up at the funeral if we ever saw your face again, you would regret it. Did you think it was a joke?"

Nervously, she shifted on her feet, peering over his shoulder into the rambling foyer of the house. "The rest of the guys are gone?"

He pressed his hand to the wall, leaning toward her face and spitting the words. "I take it by the fact you're actually standing there, you already know the answer to that."

On a hard swallow, she nodded. "Yeah. I heard they were gone."

She reached out and touched his shoulder. "I need to talk to you."

Zee snagged her by the wrist and jerked her away. "Don't fucking touch me. You did this. You did this. He's gone because of you."

She blinked at him. "I wasn't alone in this."

Hatred burned, and Zee stepped back, trying to catch his breath, to keep himself from coming unglued. "You came to me…took advantage of the moment. Of the fact Julie left me. You *lied* to me."

"I was lonely," she shot back on a wounded cry.

"You were lonely? That's your fucking excuse?"

She wiped her cheek with the back of her hand, her shoulders heaving. "Please…I need to talk to you."

The anger he felt butted against the guilt. The fact that ultimately he'd been responsible.

He widened the door. "Five minutes then you're gone. Things aren't gonna be pretty if the guys catch wind of you coming around here."

Dropping her head, she angled past him, heels clicking on the marble floors as she stepped inside. She stopped just at the end of the foyer, her arms crossed over her chest as she looked out over the expansive living area and to the wall of windows that overlooked the glittering pool and the city sprawled out below.

Seeing her there made Zee's skin crawl. She shouldn't be. It was a disrespect to Mark.

"What do you want, Veronica? Tell me and then get the hell out."

She looked to her feet, before she shifted enough to peer back at him. "I need money."

Rage boiled through his blood, and it took everything he had to remain rooted. To keep from rushing her and tossing her out. "You need money?" It dropped like an accusation and disbelief.

She hugged her arms tighter. "I…just three hundred dollars and I'll go. You won't ever have to see me again."

A sinking awareness washed over him, and his mouth went dry as he forced out the words. "For what?"

More tears streaked free. "I'm pregnant."

Panic and grief came so close to dropping him to his knees. It was the hate and fear that kept him standing. "What are you saying?"

Her voice turned frantic. "I'm saying I'm pregnant and my boyfriend is dead and I *can't* do this. That's what I'm saying."

Terror bottled in his throat, the words barely a breath. "It's Mark's?"

The nod of her head was spastic. "Please, you don't know what it's like having to stand here and ask you for help. I know you hate me…but please…I just need you to help me out this once."

"No." It flew from his mouth. A desperate demand. "I won't let you take my brother's kid from me, too."

Disbelief twisted through her features. "You think this is about you?"

"I think this is about my brother. About the fact that baby is the last thing we have of him."

Her head shook. "I don't…I don't want to do this alone. I can't, Zee. I'm not equipped."

He rushed forward and gripped her by the forearms. "I'll do…anything. Tell me what you need. Just…let me take care of you."

"I don't want to be a single mom."

"You don't have to be."

"What are you saying?"

"I'm saying, I'll be whatever you need me to be."

She looked around the house. "They'll never go for it. They hate me."

"They should. If they knew, they'd hate me, too."

Doubt filled her expression. "So, we don't tell them?"

"No. We don't tell them."

Maybe it was to protect the baby. Maybe it was to protect himself. Zee didn't know. He only knew offering this fucked-up solution was the only thing he could do.

The only thing that felt right in the midst of everything that had gone all wrong.

Veronica reached up and touched his cheek. "If we do this, you belong to me."

"No drugs, Veronica. You take care of Mark's child…take care of yourself…and I promise, I'm yours."

Night pressed all around. Heart pounding in his throat, he jumped out of the taxi and raced through the hospital doors.

The last seven hours had been agonizing. Getting the text. The lie telling his crew he needed to cut his trip short because his mother needed him. The flight across country that felt like it'd taken a lifetime. The worry and questions and anxiety that he had made the wrong decision.

His entire body vibrated as he took the elevator, his gaze frantic as he stepped off it and explained who he was at the nurses' station and showed his ID.

He was a mess when he came to the door. Sucking in a

steeling breath, he dropped his head, closed his eyes, and whispered a silent prayer.

I'm doing this for you, Mark. I'll regret what I did to you every fucking day of my life. But I will do this to honor you.

Then Zee pushed open the door. Veronica was asleep. Beside her was one of those hospital bassinets.

Zee kept his footsteps light as he edged forward, his pulse a stampede, so fast he swore he could hear it ricocheting around the room. He lost his breath when he looked down to find the child nestled inside.

Dark, wide eyes blinked up through the muted light, a single arm breaking free as the baby flailed against the confines of the blanket he was wrapped in, the tiniest, sweetest sounds grunting from his mouth.

A swell of emotion crashed over Zee.

Grief and hope.

Grief and hope.

He felt the world freeze when he leaned down and carefully picked up the baby boy. For the first time since he'd lost his brother, Zee felt like he could fully breathe.

He held the child against his chest and silently carried him over to the chair in the corner. He sat down and cradled him in the safety of his arms.

Sitting there, Zee had no questions that remained.

He would do anything—give up anything—for even a second to have this part of his brother.

Zee lifted him up, pressed a kiss to his forehead, and breathed him in.

Zee had loved before.

But never had he loved like this.

Not the way he loved Liam Kennedy.

Zee jerked his head up when the door cracked open. Anthony stuck his head inside before he came the rest of the way inside. Worry crested his brow. "Are you sure you want to do this?"

Zee swallowed around the emotion. "I've never been so sure of anything in all my life."

Through the darkness of the bedroom, Zee lay on his back staring into the shadows that danced and played across the ceiling. Searching. Trying to focus.

Straining to hear it.

Desperate to *feel* it.

The missing strains of music that had once twisted through him like magic and poured from his fingertips. Since the day he'd lost his brother, they'd been silenced.

It seemed insane he spent his life in recording studios and on stages, playing other people's music. The songs they'd written. While that voice had dried up inside him.

It left a hollow, vacant space that moaned. Loudest in the quiet, lonely hours like this.

A hand fumbled for him in the night. He tried not to cringe, tried to shove off the nausea that gathered like a swilling tide and soaked him through.

Veronica shifted and climbed over him.

"I missed you so much," she murmured, her hair falling all around her. "Three months is too long, Zee. I can't stand being here by myself like this."

He stared at her, wondering how he'd allowed his life to spin out of control.

His words were quiet and raw. "Yeah. The last leg of this tour was long."

Truth of the matter? It hadn't been Veronica he'd been missing. It was the two-year-old little boy asleep in the next room. The one thing that brought him back there, time and time again.

"Did you miss me?" It sounded like a plea.

Agitation tightened his muscles, and Zee's tongue darted out to wet his lips as he struggled to form the lie.

"What's wrong?" she whispered through his hesitation.

Sickness crawled from his stomach and up his throat, the words dry and pained as he forced them from his tongue. "I can't do this anymore, Veronica."

She jerked back an inch. "What can't you do?"

"This…us. Every time I touch you…I—"

He searched for words that wouldn't spear her. Hurt her. He came up short. Because there was no chance this situation wasn't damaging them both.

"Every time I touch you, I feel another piece of myself die."

Like she'd been struck, she fumbled back. "What?"

Zee sat up, turning his back to her as he swung his legs over the side of the bed and slumped over. He scrubbed both hands over the weariness on his face. "You've got to feel this, Veronica. What's not there. What's not ever gonna be."

Her hazardous words slammed him from behind. "I love you, Zee. I'm in love with you."

Zee rammed his eyes closed against her confession. Like it could guard him or maybe…maybe make him feel an ounce of it. But the only thing he saw behind his lids was regret. "I can't love you, Veronica. I can't. I'm sorry."

She flew off the bed, moving in front of him. "What are you saying?"

"I'm saying we've got to end this madness. I can't keep sneaking into your bed and pretending like it's real."

Her head shook and her bottom lip trembled. "I'll take him, Zee. I'll take him away from here and you'll never see him again."

Zee shot to his feet. "You can't fuck with him like that, Veronica. He's your son. He loves me. He needs me."

"What if I need you, too?"

"You don't."

"I do. You leave me….and…and you'll never see him again. I told you, you belong to me. You belong to me. You promised you'd take care of me."

Zee took her by the outside of her upper arms and dragged her up close to his face. "That's the way it's gonna be? I don't do your bidding and you hurt both me and him?"

Veronica lifted her chin. "You promised." Spite filled her eyes. "And I promise, you will always belong to me."

fifty
ALEXIS

The tears were hot. Suffocating. They wouldn't stop while Zee sat there and confessed his truth.

Agony. Grief. Regret.

They poured from every word.

"Do you know for sure he's Mark's?" The words cracked on my tongue.

He looked to where he had his fingers threaded. Pieces of his light brown hair flopped forward as if it might shield me from some of his pain.

"Anthony demanded some sort of paternity test be done when I first went to him for help, but I refused. I told him it didn't matter. I didn't want to know. Liam calls me daddy, but I know, Alexis. I knew from the first time I held him that he belonged to my brother. But that doesn't mean I don't consider him my kid."

"Oh God, Zee," I whispered, wishing I could hold some of his pain.

Anguish burned through his rasped words. "And

now…knowing she'd been with that vile piece of shit during that time, and now she's gone because of him? What the fuck am I gonna do?"

He slumped over, gripping the back of his head as he lost himself to sorrow, a gut-wrenching sob so deep it echoed from the walls. "How am I gonna tell Liam? How is he ever going to be okay after this?"

"Zee," I pleaded, wanting to tell him we'd figure it out.

Together.

But my head snapped up with light tapping that sounded against the door. It cracked open to reveal the same man who had been outside the police station and at the hospital the day Colton was born.

The expression on his face was grim. "I'm sorry to interrupt."

"Anthony." Zee looked back at him, quickly running a hand over the moisture streaking his face. "It's okay."

"The investigator is here, along with a social worker from the state. They need to talk to you."

Zee's spine stiffened. Slowly, he stood and gathered himself. "Okay."

He started for the door before he hesitated to peer back at me. I'd always thought this powerful man held a vibe of vulnerability about him. Something so intrinsically beautiful and brilliant, yet somehow soft.

But I didn't think I'd ever seen him so clearly than right then.

The protectiveness, the loyalty, and the devotion and from where it all stemmed.

His jaw trembled before it clenched in restraint, those bronze eyes begging me to see. "I'm so sorry."

Then he turned and followed Anthony out the door.

Terror gripped me.

Because I was sure I'd never heard a more distinct goodbye.

fifty-one

ZEE

The entire room spun.

Dizzying.

Gutting.

Too much.

I dropped my head between my knees and attempted to find the breath the news had knocked from my lungs.

Mark. Mark. Mark. My brother's face spun through my mind like a whirlwind while every silent promise I'd made him battled with the reality.

Confusing and disorienting.

Anthony stood over me. "Are you okay?"

Helplessly, I looked up at him, wishing I could go back and refuse the test the social worker had demanded two days ago when I'd told her the entire story. "I don't think I am."

Anthony knelt down in front of me. A friend. A father figure in this fucked-up situation when I couldn't seek my own. I could never admit to my parents what I'd done or the consequences or repercussions of it.

"You've always been his father, Zee. Always. From day one. Nothing has changed except for the fact you really are."

I swallowed around what felt like razors lining my throat. "Then why does it feel like I lost a piece of my brother?"

Anthony's words tightened with emphasis. "Because that's what you've done all these years, Zee. You've clung to the idea that there might be something left of Mark when you didn't want to let him go. You accepted Veronica's claim that he was Mark's because that's what you wanted him to be, thinking it would carry on your brother's legacy. That a tangible piece of him would remain in this world."

Grief thickened my words. "But I felt it…" I touched my chest. "Right here…when I held Liam. Every single time I've ever held him, I felt it right here."

"What did you feel?"

I struggled for a definition of that undefinable feeling, blinking through the emotions as I allowed myself to experience them one more time. "Belonging. Peace. Like I was holding something sacred. A treasure that had been entrusted to me."

Anthony set his hands on each of my shoulders. "That's what being a father feels like, Zee. That's love. Pure and unadulterated. Unconditional. What you feel for Liam doesn't have anything to do with your brother. You feel that because he's your son."

I gasped around the reality.

Liam is my son.

Liam is my son.

"How's it possible to feel so heartbroken, so utterly destroyed, and feel like I gained the world at the same time?" I choked over the question.

Anthony squeezed my shoulders tighter. "Because you've never truly mourned the loss of Mark, Zee. You've been frantically clinging to everything left of him, trying to keep it alive when it was already gone. You've been trying to fill his shoes when he never asked you to. All these years, you've been representing someone else, and never, in all that time, have you stood for yourself. You let yourself be used and manipulated by Veronica, accepting that abuse because you thought you were honoring your brother."

"I didn't know what else to do," I said quietly.

He inhaled a deep breath as he rose. "But now you do, Zee. You mourn and you let yourself hurt, because you lost your brother. You grieve and you don't feel guilty about it. You deserve to miss him, no matter the mistakes the two of you made. Because you can't change the past or what either of you did. But what you can do is finally say goodbye. Then you get it together and decide what it is you stand for."

With my palm, I swiped the evidence of the grief from my face, and I pushed to my feet. "I stand for Liam."

I pulled up to the curb at Sebastian and Shea's Los Angeles pad, an older, rambling, ranch-style house situated on an acre of land with a huge backyard.

They say you know who your true friends are by their actions during the hard times. The way they treat you when you're at your lowest.

I'd spent years terrified of what the guys would think when they found out what I'd done. When they knew I'd betrayed my brother, and then turned around and kept a secret I had no right to keep, thinking it was the right way.

The only way.

I should have known better.

I should have known better all along. Because I knew it when I climbed out of my car and into the blazing afternoon sun and saw Sebastian anxiously awaiting my arrival.

My footsteps were slow and heavy as I walked toward him, not because I was worried about his judgment, but because I had no idea how I was gonna handle seeing Liam for the first time after finding out he was mine.

That he truly belonged to me.

Baz nervously tapped a fist into his opposite palm while he watched me approach. The second I got close enough, he hauled me up for a tight hug, his fists winding in my shirt at my back.

His words were gruff where he promised them at my ear, "I don't even fucking know what to say, Zee. Sorry doesn't seem right, but after everything that went down over the last couple of days, I am. I know you've got to be hurtin'. Just know, whatever you need, we're here. Me. The guys. The girls. Our families are yours. Same way as they've always been."

I clutched him. "Thank you, brother. You don't know what that means to me."

Twice, he clapped my back in encouragement. "Always."

He stepped back, and I stood there, trying to gather myself before I forced myself to head for the front door.

Clicking the latch, I gave it a little nudge. The door swung open wide, my heart in my throat when I stepped inside. My eyes went directly to where he was on his belly on the living room floor, playing a game with Kallie and Brendon, his face upturned toward the ceiling.

And he was laughing.

Laughing this free laugh that pummeled me. Life and grief and gratefulness.

Fingertips brushed my arm, and I glanced to the side. Shea gave me a tender smile, pure understanding, lacking any doubt or blame.

And I couldn't hesitate anymore. I was moving across the floor, sweeping Liam into my arms, and hugging him against my chest.

"Daddy!" he cried through a laugh, winding his thin arms around my neck. "You wanna play with us? We're having so much fun."

I buried my face in his shoulder, clinging to him—for dear life. And I wasn't ever going to let him go.

I pulled the blanket up higher over his shoulders, my breaths shallow as I looked down at where Liam slept in my bed in my loft. I ran my fingers through the soft locks of his light brown hair, listening to the choppy rise and fall of his breaths as he succumbed to sleep.

My son.

Night poured in through the windows, the stars hidden and secluded.

Muted.

Like his grief.

Telling him about his mother was the single most difficult thing I'd ever had to do. He'd withdrawn inside himself, his sobs restrained and jerky, his face buried in my shirt as I rocked him for hours in the silence that had only been broken by my promises.

That I loved him.

That I would never leave him again.

That it was just him and me.

When he'd finally drifted off, I'd carried him upstairs, knowing I wanted to be right there for him in case he woke in the middle of the night.

I stared down at the innocence of his precious face and made a thousand new silent vows.

I will protect you. I will live for you. I will die for you.

The truth was, they'd always been there before. But I got them now.

I finally understood what sacrifice really meant.

Birds chirped where they rustled through the trees, the air

calm and the sky blue.

Which seemed damned ridiculous considering the storm that billowed and blew within me. It was an ache that pounded through my body and stabbed at my spirit.

Standing on her porch, I struggled for a breath. For resolve. To remember why I was doing what I was doing.

I'd always known giving into the need I had for this girl was going to destroy me.

That it was reckless.

Just asking for trouble.

I guess I'd expected repercussions.

A fallout.

I'd just never truly bargained on everything crumbling. For Liam's world to shatter.

It was time I built him a new foundation.

Pulling in a steadying breath, I knocked softly at her door, my hands twisting into apprehensive fists when I heard the movement on the other side. I could almost picture her inside, moving barefoot across the floor, hoisting up on her toes to look through the peephole.

I didn't want to imagine the things she might be thinking when she discovered it was me.

Metal ground against metal as the lock was twisted, and the door creaked open a fraction.

I'd thought I was prepared. That I'd told myself enough lies that I could handle seeing Alexis standing in her doorway, wearing that same pink outfit she'd been wearing the first time I'd come over, white hair piled in a wild twist high on the top of her head.

But it was her eyes that nearly knocked me to my knees. A collision of sea and sky. A squall of torment and relief.

"Zee," she whispered desperately.

She'd tried to call me several times over the last couple of days, and I'd been nothing but a coward, texting her back lame excuse after lame excuse that I was taking care of some things that needed to be handled, and I would get in touch with her soon.

Two days had passed since I'd told Liam the news. I'd spent every second with him, trying to get him to open up, letting him know it was okay to cry and be mad and scared. That it was okay for him to ask questions.

This morning when he'd asked when he would get to go play with Kallie and Brendon again, I'd called Shea and asked if it was okay if I dropped him off for an hour or two.

Because this…

This needed to be done.

"You should come inside," she murmured as she stepped back so she could open the door wider.

My chin trembled. "Awful brave."

Heartache shivered across her features as I took her back to that moment a month ago when I'd shown up. When I realized I couldn't stay away. To the moment when it'd felt like we were embarking on something magical.

Because with Alexis?

That was what it was.

Magic.

But only fools believed in magic.

I could feel her nerves rippling through the room as I stepped inside her house. Energy flamed in the space between us. Coming alive the way it always did. Stretching out its fingers, begging me to erase the distance.

My spirit recognized her.

Recognized us.

I got the feeling that was a flame that would never die.

"Would you like some tea?" Her wary voice hit me.

Pulling in a breath, I slowly turned around to face her. "No, Alexis. I'm sorry, but I won't be staying that long."

Her eyes pinched closed. Like it might hide the brutal anguish that filled them. But I was pretty sure I saw this girl better than I'd ever seen anyone in my life.

Slowly, she blinked them open. "What are you saying?"

Regret ticked my jaw, and I forced out the words. "I'm saying what I've been saying all along. What I told you again and again. That in the end, I would fuck everything up. That since the moment I met you, I was doing things I couldn't do. Disregarding the things I needed to protect most. Just like I told you I would."

She held her arms protectively against her chest. "You blame me for what happened? For what happened to Liam's mom?"

I couldn't stop myself. I surged forward and gripped her unforgettable face in my hands. "No." My tone was harsh, demanding that she understand. "Never. But it's time I finally do what's right."

I released her like the contact burned and forced myself to put some distance between us, turning away so I didn't have to look at her face when I made the admission. "Liam is mine."

"He's…your son?"

My head nodded as I struggled with a way to form an explanation. To catch her up in the same moment I was trying to break us apart. "Craig made a statement to the police. Veronica already knew she was pregnant when Mark died…knew it wasn't his. Knew it was mine."

Bitterness twisted my guts. "She knew the whole fucking time. The guy I told you about, Martin Jennings, who we found out had been responsible for Mark's death?"

She nodded for me to continue.

"You were right in thinking they were looking for something bigger to pin on Craig. He was one of Martin Jennings' parasites, running around doing his dirty work while that bastard Jennings pretended his hands were clean. Turns out Jennings had been using Craig to draw Mark deeper into the life. Trying to gauge just what Mark knew about the fucked-up attack on Shea and what he was planning on doing to her."

I pressed a fist to my mouth, fighting the bitterness, the true reason for this entire mess.

Greed.

Martin's greed.

Craig's greed.

Veronica's greed.

But lust for money was the world's favorite sin.

"Zee." Alexis' voice wrapped around me.

Compassion and warmth.

A comfort I couldn't accept.

I started pacing. "Once Mark was gone, that left Craig and Veronica to figure out how to hook me in and swindle the most money out of me once Mark was out of the picture. They viewed me as an opportunity that they took full advantage of."

I swung around to fully look at her. "I was a fool, Alexis. Such a goddamned fool, and I wasted so much time, terrified of losing Liam. Terrified of losing what I thought was my last physical connection to my brother, so I continued to play Veronica's twisted games. Instead, what I lost was six years of truly knowing *my* son. Tiptoeing around Veronica's rules. Barely seeing him. Missing him night and day."

And this girl…this girl looked at me with all that grace and belief.

She pressed her hands over her heart. The girl so goddamned sweet.

"You told me once if you could do anything for yourself, you'd set yourself free. Don't you see it, Zee? Now you get to be. You don't have to hide from me anymore. You don't have to hide from living your *life*."

She took a pleading step forward.

Filling my senses with her light.

I wanted to step away, but I could feel myself leaning her direction, needing to fill myself with her memory.

Her tone turned soft, so caring and sweet. "I know you have a past, Zee. I've known it all along, even though I didn't know the details. And now that I do, I love you even more. I love you. God…I love you so much."

I choked over the breath I sucked into my failing lungs.

Struck.

Gutted.

Everything was on fire, this blaze that singed me from the inside out. She'd never said it aloud before. But I'd known, hadn't I?

There'd been no missing it swimming in the warmth of her gaze. No missing it in the bliss of her touch.

It took about all I had to edge back and say the words that were thick with regret. "I have a little boy who's terrified right now, Alexis. A boy who just lost his mother. A boy who witnessed God knows what. He's my responsibility. My heart. My life. And right now, I need to focus on him. I need to make sure he heals and knows he's safe and that he's always gonna have me right there to protect him."

Hurt lashed across her face, and she pressed her palms right over her heart. "Why can't you do that with me?"

I reached out, my hand trembling when I set it on one side of her face. My thumb brushed the single tear that slipped from her eye. "Because I don't deserve him, Alexis, but I'm gonna do my best by giving him every part of me."

Before I could get lost in the depths of those stormy eyes, I ripped myself away, forcing myself just to move. To get the hell out of there before my resistance failed the exact same way it seemed to do every time I was in her space.

I bolted out her door and down the two porch steps. I squinted against the glaring sunlight that blazed hot. Just as hot as my insides.

God. I felt like I was burning up.

I fisted my hand, the one with the star tattoo, that forever reminder of what I'd done. Swore I could feel another piece of myself disintegrating as I rushed down her walk and toward my car parked at the curb.

"Zee." It was a frantic plea. A chill blasted across my skin when I felt her presence come closer. Grow denser.

Delicate arms wrapped around me. Refusing to let me go. "Please…don't go. We can figure it out. I promise, I'll be good to him. So good to him. I don't care that he's not mine. I'll love him simply because he's yours."

Agony constricted my heart, mashing it in its fiery hold. I gasped around it, my hand on the two of hers locked around my waist. I unwound them and twisted around to look at her.

She stood there beneath the sun. All lit up. Hair on fire and face aglow.

An angel.

The brightest light in the midst of my darkness.

Starshine.

I gripped her by both sides of the neck, my thumbs running the curve of her jaw, my insides knotted. "If I could go back, Alexis, if I could go back and make everything right, it'd be you. It'd be you and Liam and me. But I've already fucked up too much, and I refuse to make that mistake with you, and I refuse to make another with him. I've got to figure out my life, and I've got to do it right, and I can't keep dragging you into my mess when I don't have a clue what the fuck I'm doing."

I jerked back and inched away, another piece of me dying when I watched the pain I'd inflicted whip across her features. I finally turned and jogged around the front of my car, freezing for a moment as I opened the door when I heard the guttural sob that tore from her throat.

For a flash, I squeezed my eyes shut, wishing on a star, on a wish, for something better. For a way to make it right. For her. For Liam. For me.

As a kid, I had breathed a million of those wishes.

Countless.

Infinite.

But nothing had changed the silent curse that had been uttered the day I betrayed my brother. One that had left them permanently dimmed.

Where they forever burned and bled out.

Disintegrating into nothing.

fifty-two

ALEXIS

A swath of sunlight streamed in through the bay window.

Silence seemed to ride in on it. Hovering in the air.

Too profound.

Too dense.

I was sure I'd never felt so alone.

I hugged my favorite book to my chest, my old copy of *Little Women* tattered at the edges, the pages worn from the swipe of my fingers as I'd devoured its words time and again.

Today, I just held it, embraced it like an old friend. A companion in the desolation.

Two weeks had passed since Zee had come here and nailed the final stakes into my heart.

Since then, I'd tried desperately to be strong. To remember the beauty waiting all around.

To find my solace in the fact that because of him, Avril was safe. She was now in rehab, trying to turn her life around, promising to be strong.

God, I was so grateful to Zee for what he had done. The

ultimate sacrifice he'd been willing to make for her.

For me.

He'd set her free.

It just killed me that in the end he hadn't had the strength to *finish* the fight for me.

To finish the fight for us.

Zee had lived a life of surrender.

His days atonement.

And even though his freedom was right there, waiting for him to reach out and take it, he was still prisoner to the shackles of regret. Still chained to the idea that he had something to repay rather than embracing what he'd been given as a gift.

A son.

Was there anything more precious than that?

But I understood.

I did.

But that didn't mean it didn't cut and slash and sting.

He'd warned me he didn't have anything to offer beyond the temporary.

It hadn't mattered.

I'd dived in.

Heart first.

The way I always did.

Giving him all of me and praying he would love me the way I longed for him to love me.

The way I loved him.

Maybe it'd been inevitable—the falling part—because falling for Zachary Kennedy had been the easiest thing I'd ever done.

Letting him go was the hardest.

"Fall with me," I whispered. He leaned down, lips just brushing mine, and Zachary Kennedy murmured his truth. "I already jumped."

My heart clenched in pain, and I tucked my knees closer to my chest.

Because with Zachary Kennedy, I'd had no choice but to fall.

There'd been nothing I could do but follow the call of my heart.

fifty-three

ZEE

"There you go, Daddy."

My heart snagged somewhere in my throat when I looked down at my little boy. Obviously, the kid had no clue what it did to me, hearing him saying it after everything.

He held his dinner plate up to me where I was at the sink washing dishes, a grin splitting his precious face. Through all of dinner, he'd been laughing with Kallie and Brendon, fitting right in, like he'd belonged there all along.

Like he'd been there all along.

The way he should have been.

Shea had insisted everyone come over for dinner tonight.

It wasn't that I'd hesitated to accept the offer. Still, I couldn't escape this uneasiness at being together with the entire group for the first time since everyone had found out, which was why I was basically hiding out in the kitchen. Keeping distance.

Turned out it was impossible to just wipe away the worry I'd carried around for the last seven years. Now every single one of them knew the hand I'd had in Mark's death.

My neglect.

My betrayal.

It left me wondering just what each of the guys was really thinking when they glanced my way.

"Thank you, buddy," I murmured to him, taking his plate and hooking my index finger under his chin.

He grinned a little wider, the happiness held in his expression constricting my chest into a frenzy.

Devotion and love.

"Can I go play now? I ate my dinner all gone."

"Of course you can."

It was crazy having him in my life, every day and every moment. Having him as a member of this mixed up, muddled family was something I'd never really allowed myself to long for. I'd always figured it was impossible, even though flickers of that yearning would rise up, and I'd wish things were different.

Those stars had finally aligned.

Still, I knew deep within something was out of order. The way I missed and longed and ached as I remained wide awake night after night, staring at the ceiling as I suffered through the loss of the girl.

Alexis.

That beam of shining light I hadn't expected.

Liam bounded out of the room, shouting for Brendon to come and find him while I turned back to rinsing the plates in the sink.

"You're doing great with him."

I sucked in a breath when I heard the words, soft with a Southern drawl. I shifted to look over my shoulder at Shea, who was leaning against the edge of the archway with her arms crossed over her chest.

"I'm trying," I told her.

"Raisin' kids is the single best and most difficult thing we ever get to do," she mused.

"Yeah," I agreed as I returned to rinsing the dishes, doing

my best to ignore the weight of her stare. A strained silence filled the kitchen.

"You know I'm no stranger to keeping secrets," she finally said.

Carefully, I glanced back at her when she took a step forward. I gave her a nod. "You did it because you thought you had to."

"Exactly." She rested her forearms on the island. "And all of us, we understand that's what you were trying to do to. That you were protecting what meant the most to you. Not sure if you were going about it the right way, but doing it anyway because it was the only choice you had."

Emotion flared in my stomach. Gratefulness and regret. It only amplified when I felt the movement at the archway. Baz walked through, followed by Lyrik and Tamar, Ash and Willow, then Austin and Edie.

I turned to face them, my gaze bouncing to each face of this family.

Some bound by blood. Some by marriage. Others simply by the bonds that had been forged.

Baz roughed a hand through his hair. "We want you to know we get it. Need you to know there isn't a chance we blame you for Mark's death. Shit happened, and you and Mark both made some terrible mistakes, but that will never, ever make you any less."

My heart rate kicked a fraction as something fervent filled the air.

Lyrik stepped forward. "Want you to know how much I respect you, Zee. What you've been doing for Liam all these years, thinking he wasn't your own and standing up and taking care of him anyway? That's what a real man does."

Anxiously, I rubbed a hand over my mouth. "Thank you," I murmured.

Ash slung his arm around Willow, who was holding their newborn. "I gave you shit for years, Zee, taunting you for the fact you never took girls home, thinking you were shy or weird or some shit like that, the whole time having no clue the sacrifices you were making."

He looked at Willow then back to me. "Come to find out, you had it right all along. You were living for what was most important to you. But I want you to know my goading was only because I wanted you to *live.* To truly experience life. For you to step out front when you were always content to remain in the shadows. Most of all, I need you to know, I will always have your back. Me and Willow? We'll be there for you, whatever you need."

My chest tightened, floored by the support.

Austin eased up to Baz's side. "We've got your back, Zee. No matter what."

My tongue felt heavy, and I was unable to form words, struck with the magnitude of what this was. Them coming forward and taking a stand.

For me.

For Liam.

Willow stepped forward, her expression tender. "You've probably already figured it out, but just in case you were wondering, all of us…"

She gestured around the room with her free hand. "We wanted to say it aloud so there would never be any doubt. We love you, Zee, and we love Liam. Nothing can change that. No one blames you. No one judges you. And we want you to know we will *all* be here for you, whatever you need. You are not alone."

Relief crashed over me. Pulling me under and making it difficult to breathe. It splintered the last chains that had continued to condemn me, the ones that locked me in shame and regret and disgrace.

I reached out, holding on to the counter for support, just fucking trying to keep it together.

I looked to the floor for a few beats before I gathered myself enough to face them, voice gruff. "You can't know what that means. The fact all of you are willing to stand there after what I did."

I struggled for the words, for the right emotion when

everything felt so fucking conflicted. "It's hard…all of a sudden having him living with me. Not because I don't want him, but because I don't have a fucking clue what I'm doing."

Lyrik rubbed his jaw. "There's no shame in that, Zee."

My pleading gaze bounced around at each of them. "I need you. I need your advice, and I need your support, because I don't know how to do this alone."

Edie released a breath. "Of course, Zee. That is what family is for."

"And what about Alexis?" Shea's question hit me from out of nowhere. Pointed. An arrow that staked me right in the goddamned heart.

"What about her?" Didn't mean for it to come across so bitter. But I was pissed. I blinked as I realized it, that feeling that grappled to take hold. The anger over the situation. Anger at myself for always fucking it up.

Shea's eyebrows disappeared behind her bangs. "What about her? We all know full well you would have died for her that day, Zee. And now you're going to stand here and pretend she doesn't mean something to you?"

"Of course she means something to me." My head shook. "But I…I have Liam. He's my responsibility. My first concern."

"And Alexis didn't want to take on that kind of responsibility?" Confusion spun through Willow's question, like she already didn't believe it when she asked it.

My heart thundered in its confines, throbbing and fighting against the boundaries that always seemed to rule my life. "Not that…I just…I need to focus on him. He's been through so much and—"

"And you don't love her, so you don't want the distraction?" Shea prodded.

Love her.

All along, I'd refused to entertain the notion, pretending that feeling wasn't there when it kept nudging and pricking at my consciousness.

"I didn't say that," I rasped out, feeling overwhelmed.

Shea straightened with the demand that flew from her mouth. "What did she say when you told her about him, Zee? Because what I'm hearing is you love her but you think you can't be with her because of Liam."

Shame and regret. I kept trying to break from their ties. But there they were, pressing up and taking hold. I hesitated.

"What did she say?" Shea insisted, somehow soft, but the demand hard enough to pull the admission from my tongue.

"She said she'd love him simply because he was mine."

Tamar groaned toward the ceiling then looked at Shea. "Do you want me to smack him or do you want to do the honor?"

"Oh, I'm pretty sure Zee is already over there beating himself up. I really don't think it's necessary. Isn't that right, Zee? Tell me you aren't over there wishing she was here."

A frustrated breath heaved from my lungs. "Of course I wish she was here."

Shea's brow twisted in emphasis. "And how is this any different from what you've been doing all along? Living for Liam *doesn't* mean you don't get to live for yourself, too."

Baz edged forward. "You played for her, Zee. The piano, man. You and I both know that means something."

Somehow, the guy just always got me, targeting in for an easy read. "You think we didn't notice you stopped playin' *your* music when you stepped into your brother's place? She touched something inside you. That's something you can't ignore."

His words gutted me. The girl was music. Harmony. And the second I'd cut her from my life, the songs had gone quiet. Ever since, I'd been taunted by the silence.

I looked up at him. "It meant everything. But God, the girl has to hate me. The way I handled it was…shitty. She was begging me to give her a chance and I refused to."

Fuck. What did I do?

Ash cracked a grin. "Well, you kinda lost practice with the ladies. What else could she expect?"

"Better than that," I mumbled.

"Then I guess we'd better show her *better than that*," Shea said.

A smirk stretched across Tamar's red lips. "I'm thinking I like this idea. Looks like we have some work to do."

fifty-four

ALEXIS

I jumped when the doorbell rang. I shook off the flickers of fear that threatened to take residence in my spirit. It would be so easy to succumb to it, to the memories of the trauma of that day.

But I…

I wanted to live.

Every day. Every moment.

I didn't want to be afraid.

Too much time was wasted on regret.

"Coming," I called as I crossed the floor. I hoisted up onto my toes to peer out the peephole.

A shocked gasp blew from my lungs, and I stumbled back, blinking as I tried to process what anxiously waited for me on the other side. Wondering if I was hallucinating.

My heart rate kicked when it rang again.

Quickly, I worked through the lock, both eager and wary as I opened the door. "What's going on?"

A hand came out to push against my door.

"Alexis, just the girl we wanted to see," Shea said as she walked in as if she'd been there a million times. Kallie's hand was wound in hers, the little girl bouncing in excitement as they stepped inside.

I stepped back. Confused and stunned and fighting the thrill that began to whip through my spirit.

Tamar strode in behind her, wearing a pair of super high red heels and the tightest black leather pants I'd ever seen. She shot me a playful wink as she passed, a garment bag slung over a shoulder and her baby girl hitched to her opposite hip.

"What…?" I couldn't find the words to even finish the question.

Edie angled by carrying Sadie, her face almost full of an apology as she dipped her head, though she was wearing the hint of a smile at the corner of her mouth.

"Hi," she whispered.

Willow touched my arm as she entered, sympathy in her expression and compassion in her eyes. "We're sorry for just barging in…we wouldn't do it under normal circumstances."

Normal circumstances? If it weren't for the mischief and excitement playing in their eyes, I would have already sunken to my knees in dread, thinking something terrible had to have happened for them to knock on my door.

Instead, I was latching onto their vibe, teeth hooking into my bottom lip as my heart beat faster and faster.

"Someone tell me what's going on," I finally managed.

Jumping in place, Kallie flapped her arms. "You have to get ready. We're going to make you so, so pretty!"

Amused, Shea grinned at her daughter. "I think she's already so pretty."

She turned back to me, eyeing me as if she were gauging my reaction. "We're just going to put her in an extra special dress, aren't we?"

My gaze frantically jumped over the women standing in my living room.

Women who I'd considered friends. Women I'd hazarded daydreaming could one day be family. Women I'd thought I'd never see again.

Now they were staring back at me in both sympathy and anticipation.

My fingers trembled, and I wrung them together. "Someone please tell me what's happening."

Shea nudged Kallie, and Kallie grinned at her before she bounced forward, drawing attention to the card in her hand.

"This is for you," she whispered as if it were a secret.

My chest squeezed, so tightly I rasped in a breath.

"Thank you," I said quietly as I warily accepted it, my hands shaking as I read my name scrawled in masculine script across the envelope.

I swallowed around the lump that grew prominent at the base of my throat.

My heart throbbing and my breaths shallow.

Fingers fumbling, I turned it over and broke the seal, pulling out the flat card inside.

I scanned what was printed on the front.

My pulse jumped into a frantic thunder, an overpowering drum I could feel beating in my ears and strumming through my veins.

It was a print of a constellation.

Lyra.

The Harp.

Beauty and music.

Stamped below it was the name of a music hall downtown and the time indicated 9:00 pm.

Love bounded around me. Memories of the boy and his beauty as he'd sat at the piano. This man who'd captured me with every brilliant part of his mind and the sacrifice in his soul.

"Zee," I whispered. A question. A statement.

Taking a step forward, Shea gave one slow nod. "He would be honored if you would attend his first piano concert in seven years."

I gasped around the magnitude of it, struck by relief and belief.

But that self-preservation I could rarely find was right there, whispering the pain he'd left behind.

"I don't…" The words trembled free. Reservations and doubt.

Shea blinked knowingly. "Most of us rarely do, Alexis. We don't know and we can never be sure. We only have the chances we're given."

"I think you should at least go and listen. You might like what he has to say," Willow urged, words laden with encouragement.

"I—" I gulped, a shiver racing through my being, the feeling at odds with the hope that spiked in my spirit.

Tamar smiled at me, soft for a girl who seemed so utterly hard. "Love's a gamble, Alexis. The question is, are you willing to take the risk?"

No fear. Just life.

I bit down on my bottom lip that quivered, fighting the well of moisture that threatened my eyes. A smile pulled to my mouth. "Let's see that dress."

fifty-five

ALEXIS

Two hours later, I was in the back of a limo with all the women of Sunder. We inched down a busy, narrow street in historic downtown Los Angeles as I fidgeted with the plunging neckline of my dress.

My hair was coiled in a soft twist, wavy pieces falling down around my face, and the heels I wore were higher than anything I'd ever chanced stepping out in before.

And this dress…

This dress…

It was gorgeous and outrageous, lined in tiny blue sequins that somehow didn't come across as tacky but instead sexy and elegant.

I felt beautiful…and terrified. I had no idea what was waiting for me at the end of the night. The only thing I knew was the girls were right. I *had* to take this chance. Life was meant to be lived, and I always, always wanted to live mine to the fullest.

By saving me, Zee had ensured I had those chances to take,

so I was taking one more on him.

City lights flashed from a dazzling array of blinking signs boasting the best night life.

Nervous anticipation clawed beneath the surface of my skin as the limo slowed and came to a stop in front of the old movie palace that hailed from the thirties.

An old-style vertical sign hung from its ornate exterior, the box office tucked beneath the marquee that danced with large twinkling bulbs.

A thrill tumbled through my body, and I sucked in a breath as I peered out the window.

I gasp out a small, surprised laugh when the back door swung open, and Ash suddenly ducked his head inside, extending a hand my direction.

"Madam," he exaggerated with a bow. He was wearing a pair of snug black dress slacks and a white button-up with the sleeves rolled up his forearms, the outfit paired with suspenders.

A giggle slipped free as I looked around at all the women staring back at me with smiles on their faces before I accepted his hand and allowed him to help me down onto the sidewalk. A cool breeze kissed my skin, and a shiver of chills lifted as I stared at the theatre.

"Have fun!" a chorus of voices called before the limo door slammed shut behind me. I jerked to look over my shoulder as it began to slowly pull from the curb.

"Aren't they coming?"

Ash shot me a smirk as he extended me an elbow. "Nah, darlin'. I think this might be an exclusive kind of viewing."

Oh God.

My heart sped as awareness took hold.

This was for me.

For us.

My knees were shaking as Ash led me toward the single door that was propped open. The box office windows were closed and the silence was thick and profound as we stepped into the lobby.

Maybe I should have realized something was up when none of the women had changed when they'd gotten me ready. I'd been too wrapped up in what was about to happen. This moment significant.

Critical.

Another beginning or a permanent end.

I sucked in an awed breath at the opulence when we stepped inside.

The lobby was at least six stories high and crystal chandeliers hung from their heights. Pillars rose on all sides and murals lined the walls, the carvings ornate and elaborate. A grand staircase ascending to the balconies rested in the middle, and the stairs were covered in the same red-and-gold tapestry as the floors.

"Oh my God," I whispered.

Ash patted my hand. "No need to be nervous, darlin'."

"How could I not be?"

He guided us to the side of the stairs and toward the main entry to the auditorium floor.

"Think it's safe to say our boy is about as nervous as they come, so you're in good company."

The auditorium was just as lavish as the lobby. The walls were a stunning display of architecture and art, lined with coved balcony seats that jutted out in welcome of the performance, and the rows of seats taking up the floor were covered in plush maroon velvet and edged in gold.

But none of that held my attention.

The only thing I could see was the Grand piano that sat in the middle of the stage. It was bathed in the warm wash of spotlights perfectly angled to capture the bench where the pianist would sit.

I struggled for a breath when we made it halfway down the middle aisle.

"You okay?" Ash asked.

I forced myself to nod.

"Where would you like to sit?" He waved a hand out over the empty seats. "House is yours."

"Right here is good." I couldn't bring myself to get any closer.

Not without being completely consumed by this brilliant boy.

Ash's mouth tweaked in a knowing smile before he released me, murmuring, "Enjoy the show," with another bow.

Anxiously, I eased into a seat.

Movement caught my eye to the right of the stage. I leaned forward, captured by an expectation unlike anything I'd ever experienced.

Zee.

Zee.

The bold, gorgeous man slowly made his way out onto the stage.

Confident. Owning the space as if he'd never stepped away.

I swore, he was the most intriguing man I'd ever seen.

He wore an outfit identical to Ash's, his pants fitted, sleeves rolled up those arms and exposing the ink etched into his skin. His head was tilted down, his face hidden beneath the shadow drawn by the lock of hair guarding his expression.

But I could feel it. The emotion that rippled through the auditorium like a shockwave.

Annihilating everything in its path.

I sucked in a ragged breath. The air thinned.

Tears gathered in my eyes as I watched him take a seat at the place where he'd always belonged.

Clearing his throat, he looked out into the darkness.

Without a doubt, I was cast in shadows. Hidden.

But it didn't matter.

That bronze gaze found me. Penetrating and piercing.

My stomach tightened as I felt everything gather to a pinpoint.

Waiting on a moment.

For *this* moment.

He settled his fingers on the keys.

A shudder captured his body and his tongue darted out to wet his lips.

Shivers flushed across my skin when his powerful voice struck the air.

"When I was a little boy, I made a million wishes that one day I'd get to sit right here. On a stage just like this. I couldn't imagine anything better than people piling in to hear me play, thinking I might have the chance to affect them the same way the music affected me."

My body shifted forward, drawn to him through the hazy distance.

"And I'd had that dream right in the palm of my hands. Already becoming a reality. But I fucked it all away." The words grated from his mouth. "The day my brother died, a piece of me died, too. And that music, Alexis? That music that had been there since the day I was born was silenced. I couldn't hear it. Couldn't feel it anymore. It left this vacancy inside me that I'd accepted as a reminder of what I'd done. Welcomed it as a punishment for what I'd cost my brother. That silent echo the price for what I owed him."

His thick throat bobbed heavily as he swallowed. "For seven years, I tried to fill his shoes. Did everything in my power to make it up to him when I knew nothin' I did would ever be enough. But I was committed to seeing it through anyway. I never expected anything to change. Not ever. I'd been happy to live out this life sentence if it meant protecting a little boy who'd become the entire meaning of my life."

His jaw clenched, and he pulled in a deep breath as I battled to draw one of my own.

"Then there was this girl…this brilliant girl who'd needed me in one of the darkest moments of her life." His voice deepened in sincerity. "I'd thought it was chance, finding her that way, rushing in to save her and having no clue what it was I was saving her from."

His fingers pressed down, playing a single chord.

It resonated through my being, the beat of my heart turning erratic.

"I was terrified when I realized when I was with her I could feel it again. Music. Strains of a song that had been silenced for so many years."

My insides clenched.

Oh God. This boy. This brilliant boy.

"It didn't take me long to realize it was her song," he continued, voice rough. "That *she* was the music. That she was the harmony behind it that stirred my spirit and itched my fingers to play."

His mouth tweaked at the corner, a broken bow of sadness and a crest of hope. "I was terrified of her because she represented everything I couldn't have. Because she made me want the things that had been missing. Because she filled the spaces that had been empty and filled me with song."

My hands went to my thundering heart, as if it might stand the chance of keeping it from beating from its confines.

Regret poured from his mouth. "I hurt her because I was a coward, thinking again I didn't deserve something so right. Something so good. Thinking maybe I was being selfish if I asked her to stay."

His head slowly shook as he played another echoing chord. "But I realized I don't want that silence in my life. I want the beauty. I want the music. God, Alexis, I want to live. And I know every time I turn around, I fuck things up. Make the wrong decision. But I know sitting here tonight, I'm finally making the right one. I should have said these things all along, and I hope maybe there's a chance you'll hear them tonight. I hope maybe…maybe you'll *listen*."

Emotion rushed me. Wave after wave, joy and pain as I watched Zee turn to the piano. His eyes dropped closed and his expression hardened.

A mesmerizing intensity. Deep and real.

It lifted and rose as his fingers began to move across the keys.

The sound strummed through my body like a caress.

His masterful fingers weaved that same web of beauty, the same maze of sorrow, that had staggered me the first day I'd come to his loft.

The impact of it slammed me. The energy pulsed and

lapped, incited by the talented stroke of his hands as they danced across the keys.

That day back at his loft, I'd wanted to beg him to sing the lyrics. To let me hear what this sad, mesmerizing song meant. I'd wanted to know. To understand.

And now he was offering it to me.

His voice was both smooth and rough. It skated my skin like desire. Like relief.

Live my life in silence
A razor-sharp edge
Easy destruction my surrender
Fractured honor my sacrifice
I cast my dreams upon the stars
Then turned and left them there

I choked over a tiny sob as he allowed me into a place he'd never allowed me before.

As he let me glimpse inside.

Let me into that place where he kept his secrets and his pain.

His voice lifted and the song took a turn, rising into the chorus that penetrated the air.

Written in the skies
Bleeding stars and broken hearts
Scattered wishes and shattered dreams

That's exactly what I felt.

Shattered.

Consumed by this broken heart I could feel him healing with each of his words.

His voice drove deep again, slowing as he hit the second verse.

Never knew you were strewn
Right there with them

Burning bright and healing life
Starshine in my eyes
Now I'm blinded

Starshine.

I blinked around the tears that filled my eyes, unable to hold them back as this beautiful man's powerful voice reverberated through the auditorium.

Written in the skies
Bleeding stars and broken hearts
Scattered wishes and shattered dreams

Questions and uncertainty threaded into the passion of his song as he again slowed, the sound coming from the piano growing quiet as his voice tilted into a raspy plea.

You say there's nothing to fear
But it's not that easy
When fear's the only thing you've got
Take a chance, take a chance
And it's killing me the only chance I want
Is the one I don't know how to take

For a moment the song completely blinked out, and a bated silence held fast to the atmosphere.

My breath was hitched in my lungs.

Desperate in this anticipation that threaded through my spirit.

Then he drove back into the song as a medley of voices suddenly joined him.

But now I'm blinded
Starshine in my eyes
Bleeding Stars and mended hearts

One by one, they walked out onto the stage. Baz, Austin,

Lyrik, and Ash, all dressed alike. Tamar, Edie, Shea, and Willow, who had changed into gowns.

Each of them were singing as they crossed the stage to stand at Zee's side.

A part of him.

His support.

His family.

I could do nothing but rise to my feet.

Overwhelmed.

Overcome by this beauty.

And my heart, it beat wildly with his song, a confession that stitched together to become a part of me.

And it's you
Starshine in my eyes
Bleeding stars and mended hearts
They're falling for you

They all sang, some in tenor, baritone, and bass. Shea's sweet voice lifted above them for a few moments in a perfect harmony.

Catch me when I fall
Are you gonna catch me when I fall

Then they all slowed and quieted, the piano barely a trickle of sound as Zee once again began to sing alone. His mouth was right at the mic, and his vulnerable, perfect heart was on display.

Starshine in my eyes
And I'm falling for you
This mended heart
It's falling for you
Catch me when I fall.
Starshine
Are you gonna catch me when I fall

He heaved out a breath, his eyes closed for a moment before he opened them and peered directly at me. "I know my life is complicated, Alexis. That I have a kid who's been through more than any kid ever should. That he's gonna need me every second of every day. But the truth of the matter is, I need you, too. Need your light. Your music. Your song. Take a chance on me, Alexis. No fear. Just life."

And there was no hesitation.

No question.

I was running down the aisle.

Toward this brilliant, unforgettable man.

No fear. Just life.

fifty-six

ZEE

That space between us had come alive. The way it always did when she was near. Though this time—this time it throbbed with devotion. With something that sang with permanence and loyalty. The kind of hope I'd been too terrified to allow myself to feel.

I stood from my seat at the piano with my family standing around me.

There with their unwavering support.

My head spun.

My heart a goddamned riot when I saw Alexis running down the aisle.

Coming for me.

I moved to the end of the stage and jumped off just as she reached the end.

I swept her up and she wrapped her arms around my neck.

God, how could anything feel so good?

So perfect.

Overcome, I swung her round and round while I held her

against me.

That sweetness filled my senses like a drug.

Good and pure.

Slowly, I let her slide down my body. I cupped the side of her face, and my thumb brushed beneath the hollow of her eye.

My heart forever in her hands. "Starshine."

I stared down at her through the pale light that drifted in through the windows that overlooked the city. Right after the concert, I'd brought her here.

Needing her alone.

To feel her.

Touch her.

Make her all the promises only my body could say.

My strokes were slow and unhurried as I filled her.

Devout as I worshiped her in the shadows of my loft.

My hand was on her face and the other was twisted in her hair.

Her mouth parted as she clung to me.

We both came.

Silently.

Reverently.

For a few moments we both lay there gasping.

Our minds catching up to the moment our hearts had been racing for all along.

Slowly, I edged back, my thumb brushing the angle of her cheek. "I love you, Alexis Kensington."

It was the first time I'd told her, and I was sure I'd never spoken a greater truth.

Love shined back at me, those deep blue eyes filled with faith. With the undying belief that had restored what had been lacking in me.

Fingertips fluttered up to caress my face. A whisper. A promise. "And I will always love you, Zachary Kennedy. Thank you for taking a chance on me. For trusting me to be around him."

Shifting us both to our sides, I ran the pad of my thumb across her bottom lip. "It was never that I didn't trust you, Alexis. It's that I had to find a way to trust to myself. I had to finally come to the place where I was able to accept that I have something good to give, too. I'd been living in my own exile for so long, I'd thought it'd be some kind of sin for me to break out of it. But you…you showed me that life is for living."

She lightly scratched her fingertips over the beard on my jaw. "And now you're ready to live."

"I'm so ready to live."

Her voice softened in wonder and encouragement, that potent gaze searching my face. "What's it like, having him with you now? How does it feel to be a dad?"

An affectionate sigh rippled into the dimness. "Realized I always knew something was missing, and I just didn't know what it was. It feels like I finally found it—both Liam and you."

She blinked, her tone deep with significance. "We can take it as slow as you need us to, Zee. I promise I won't barge into his life."

Liam had been all too happy when I'd asked him if it was okay if he spent the night at Baz and Shea's tonight. I'd needed this time with Alexis. Time for us to talk. To lay it all out.

I was ready. No more questions.

I dipped down and brushed my lips over hers. "Not sure I know how to take things slow with you."

She giggled. It traveled through me like a song. A song that rang with joy. With peace. "We aren't very good with slow, are we?"

"Nah. Think it was our hearts that knew all along, pushing us toward where we belonged."

Her teeth clamped down on her bottom lip. "I think I knew

the first time I saw you."

I nuzzled her neck, letting myself grin through the happiness of it. The joy of finally believing.

Sobering, I pulled back, fidgeting with a lock of her hair. "I just…I have to have stability for him, Alexis. And if you want to be a part of his life, I have to know that you're all in. Things are gonna be rough for a while with him. He's doing well, dealing with the loss of his mom, but I know there are going to be difficult times ahead. And God…I don't ever want you to question where I want you to be, because the only place I want you is with us."

"What are you saying, Zee?"

It was almost a chuckle that slipped free. "Guess I'm giving you one last chance to run before I keep you forever."

Moisture shimmered in her eyes. "The only running I'm going to be doing is to you."

Relief took me whole.

Complete.

"I love you, Lex."

She edged forward a fraction so her mouth could meet mine.

Fire.

Flames.

Freedom.

She took my hand with the star and pressed it to her lips, her voice a whisper against the skin. "You were everything I'd ever wished for. Before I even knew what that meant."

fifty-seven

ALEXIS

Anxiety thrummed a steady beat through my being. Sweat gathered at the nape of my neck, and I sucked in a breath, trying to get myself together, to keep from fidgeting while I waited outside the massive doors of Zee's loft.

With shaky hands, I straightened my skirt for what had to be the hundredth time.

I was certain I'd never been so nervous in all my life.

I was also certain I had never stood on the precipice of something so important.

There are moments in our lives when we know things are about to change.

But this change?

This might be the most significant of all my life.

My pulse raced, my spirit heavy with anticipation.

Hope and fear.

Hope and fear.

They wound and wound, stirring my conviction.

I'd never been one to tiptoe.

I'd always rushed into every situation.

Eager to find what it might offer.

But this time I did it with complete regard. With full consideration that had taken little thought or deliberation.

Because my heart had already screamed its decision

The lock screeched, and my heart kicked into overdrive when the door swung open.

Zee stood there, that beautiful, intoxicating man who had become my world.

This man who was inviting me deeper into his.

The stand for something more important than I'd ever stood for in all my life.

A shiver tickled across my skin when he slanted me the best kind of smile. One harnessed in affection and his own nerves.

"Hey," he said quietly as he widened the door.

"Hi," I breathed, softly smiling over at him as I stepped inside before I let my gaze travel into the living area.

Sunlight poured in through the windows, like a spotlight cast on the tiny figure on the rug.

Instantly my attention was there.

Locked on the child as everything froze. My breath and my spirit and my heart.

That moment sacred. Forever etched in my mind.

He was sitting with his legs crisscrossed, leaning over a pile of Legos he focused on constructing.

My feet cautiously carried me across the floor.

While every other part of me suddenly went wild. Reaching and stretching and amplifying. Hope stretched out ahead of me like the brightest beacon.

Calling me home.

His head jerked up when he heard me approach.

The little boy with light brown hair and eyes the color of bronze. He grinned the widest smile. Vulnerable and sweet.

"Hi. My daddy said you were gonna come over and play with us. You wanna? I'm building a castle because when I grow up, I'm gonna be a knight."

I dropped to my knees in front of him.

Heart first.

"I'd love to play."

"What's your favorite color?" he asked, looking back into his pile so he could dig it out for me.

I glanced over at Zee, who stood staring down at us.

That energy alive.

Lapping and churning with an overpowering peace.

And sitting there I finally knew exactly what it was I'd been wishing for.

epilogue

ZEE

Warm laughter echoed from the walls. I sank back into the comfy couch as I let my gaze wander Shea and Sebastian's living room at their place out on Tybee Island.

Baz, Austin, Ash, and their families had mostly settled here in the Savannah area, considering this was where they wanted to raise their families.

Lyrik and Tamar still spent most of their time in Los Angeles where they could be closer to Brendon.

Of course, that was where Alexis and I planned on laying down roots, too, so she could keep close to her sisters.

Avril was six months clean, living in a halfway house of sorts as she learned to get back on her feet. Fighting everyday but knowing living would always be worth the fight.

I'd always feared if Sunder wasn't continually making music, touring, and fighting to be on top, we'd lose sight of the dreams. But those bonds hadn't loosened and had only seemed to strengthen as the demands of the rock star life were shifted. Even though our permanent homes were on opposite sides of the country, that didn't mean we all didn't get together as much as we could.

Which was why we were all here to celebrate the holiday.

The lights were cast low and Shea had candles set about out of reach of small hands.

A spray of what had to be a million white twinkle lights sparkled from the tall Christmas tree set up against the panes of glass that overlooked the sea, and the rolling waves crashing on the beach just beyond the darkened windows only added to the contentment that stretched its fingers out like welcome.

Sunder was scattered about the massive room. Shea and Edie were chatting in the kitchen, Baz and Austin not far where they rested on stools at the island.

Lyrik and Tamar had curled up together on another couch, and Ash and Willow were murmuring to each other where they shared a lounger next to the fire.

The flames lapped and danced, reflecting on the glass and sending a warm glow across the entire room.

What made it best?

All the kids were in the middle of the floor playing with the gifts they'd ripped open.

My chest pressed full, unable to reconcile the satisfaction I felt. The easiness I'd never really realized had been missing until it was there. This peace that soothed the wounds that I'd thought would forever remain raw.

That peace only amplified when I let my eyes settle on the two who were in the middle of it all.

Liam was right at Alexis' side, which was where he always seemed to want to be, laughing hysterically as she poked him in the belly. He grabbed that spot, crying out "no" when it was clear he was begging her to continue.

Yeah.

Things had been rough. But they were getting better. Every day. Knew Veronica would always be a loss for Liam, and I'd never discount the fact my son had lost his mother. I could only be grateful for what Alexis and I could give him.

Safety and security and stability.

A big house with an even bigger yard.

Our time.

Our love.

And God, was there a ton of it. So much love it should have been impossible. But it was real. Just as real as the love that bounded against these floors and echoed against these walls.

"All right, tea and cocoa is ready." Shea set a tray of hot teas on the huge, square coffee table that'd been moved out of the way so the kids could all get near the base of the tree, and Baz followed her in with a tray of hot cocoas for the kids.

"Yay." It was a chorus of cheers from the kids. Apparently, a cup of hot cocoa on Christmas Eve was a big deal.

A tradition in the making.

Ash stood and helped pass out the saucers and cups.

"I do believe this calls for a toast," he said with one of those smirks.

Lyrik shook his head. "Of course it does."

Ash chuckled, but his expression turned serious. "We've all been through some really rough times. Tragedies and more disappointments than any of us could count."

His gaze bounced around the room. "But I think it's safe to say that our luck has won out."

He shook his head. "Never thought I'd find love the way I did"—he gestured with his cup to all of us around the room—"and I'm betting none of you did, either. Sunder is still making magic, but we're doing it on our terms because every single one of us knows what's most important."

He blinked, his throat heavy. "Family."

Everyone lifted their cups. "To family."

Warmth covered me, and I shifted to look at where Alexis was gazing down at my son.

So damned tenderly it twisted through me like a hurricane.

Maybe she felt my eyes on her, because she turned to look at me.

Faith and goodness and belief.

This girl.

I couldn't have asked for anyone better, and I'd never thought I'd have a match. But this girl, she was my heart.

My spirit.

My soul.

That space between us came alive. A stir of energy and need. Didn't matter that I had her. I couldn't ever get enough.

As if she were drawn, she slowly pushed to her feet, swaying over to me wearing a sweater that hugged her in all the right ways, those eyes alive and that smile sweet.

I stretched my hand out for her, pulling her to me just as anxiously as she was crawling onto my lap. I wrapped an arm around her, my nose at her temple. "Merry Christmas, baby."

She looked up at me. "This is the best Christmas I've ever had. Thank you so much for letting me share it with you."

I hugged her a little closer. "And where else would you be?"

"I don't ever want to be anywhere else."

"Now I'm thinking I like the sound of that."

Her teeth clamped down on her bottom lip, and that redness rushed to her face. "Yeah?"

"Yeah, I really like the sound of that."

I turned to look at where Liam was giggling at some goofy face Brendon was making, my voice soft. "Hey, Liam."

His head popped up, grin set in place. "What is it, Daddy?"

"You remember that special present we have?"

His entire being lit up, and he scrambled to his feet. "Yes! I've got it, I've got it."

He rushed to where it was hidden on the back side of the tree, weaving through everyone as he came our direction.

Swore I could feel Alexis' heart rate amp, rising as this steady beat began to drum between us.

A connection unfathomable.

A bond unshakeable.

Liam was bouncing like he just might pee his pants with the amount of excitement he had over the secret he'd kept for the last week which was hidden behind his back.

Figured that was about as much time as I could expect of him, the boy the perfect accessory with his little winks and attempts at throwing her off track.

I shifted Alexis off my lap and to the couch then slid off and twisted around to face her.

Just as I dropped to my knee.

Liam was right at my side.

A soft gasp left that pouty mouth, her throat wobbling as she looked between Liam and me.

Hopefully.

Because that was what she was.

Hope.

Goodness.

An angel.

Starshine.

"Liam has something special he wants to give you, don't you, Liam?"

He nodded emphatically, quick to pull the gift out from behind his back and shove it her direction.

There was no missing the collective breath sucked in by my crew. The guys and the girls and the kids.

Truth was, I wouldn't want this taking place any other way.

I'd hidden what was important away for too long.

Not ever again.

Alexis pressed shaky fingers to her chest, that gaze sliding to me before she turned all her attention on Liam, who still held the tiny box wrapped in gold paper out in the palms of both hands.

She reached out, trembling, struggling for breath while I did my best to choke down the emotion that spilled from my spirit, gathering fast and pressing out.

"I wrapped it," Liam whispered quietly, like he was seeking her approval. The little man needed constant reassurance, which we continually gave to him.

"You did a great job," she said, though the words were merely a rasp. She inhaled as she carefully unwrapped it.

The black velvet box barely peeked out when Liam started jumping and clapping. "Me and Daddy want you to marry us. You wanna marry us?"

She looked over at me, eyes glittering with moisture. My words were soft. "Yeah, Alexis, you want to marry us?"

She slipped off the couch and onto her knees. "Nothing would make me happier than to marry you."

Liam whooped, spinning around and shouting at the rest of the family, "She said yes! I'm gettin' married."

She smiled at my son who had become hers. "Of course we're getting married," she told him, her fingers a gentle caress beneath his chin.

He beamed at her while she watched him with outright adoration.

Her love for him was enough to knock me from my feet every time I saw them together.

Everyone cheered. Honestly, they were probably already expecting this, considering I really wasn't all that hard to read. Not since I let all the bullshit secrets go.

Alexis clutched my hand, like she needed the support. Like she was overcome.

But that was the thing.

I'd never been known as a fighter.

But I knew the first night I met her, I'd never regret fighting for her.

Maybe for all those years I'd forgotten what I was living for.

But no more.

Alexis had taught me what it was like to be free. She taught me to trust in faith and love.

Because of her?

I remembered what it was like to Stand.

I slipped the ring on her finger and brought it to my lips. "Forever."

Alexis nodded through the tears that streamed down her face. With a soggy smile, she angled her head to the piano sitting on the opposite wall. "Play with me, little drummer boy? It was always a wish, you know."

Love pressed and pulsed, and I looked around at the happiness on my family's faces.

Bleeding Stars.

Who'd have known they'd been raining wishes on all of us all along.

the end

Thank you for reading *stand*! Did you love getting to know Zee and Alexis? Please consider leaving a review!

I invite you to sign up for mobile updates to receive short, but sweet updates on all my latest releases.
Text "aljackson" to 24587
(US Only)
or
Sign up for my newsletter
http://smarturl.it/NewsFromALJackson

Watch for A.L. Jackson's brand new series, FIGHT FOR ME, coming Fall 2017

MORE FROM A.L. JACKSON

Bleeding Stars

A Stone in the Sea
Drowning to Breathe
Where Lightning Strikes
Wait
Stay

The Regret Series
Lost to You
Take This Regret
If Forever Comes

The Closer to You Series
Come to Me Quietly
Come to Me Softly
Come to Me Recklessly

Stand-Alone Novels
Pulled
When We Collide

Coming Soon from A.L. Jackson
SHOW ME THE WAY
The first sexy, heart-warming romance in the new Fight For Me series, coming mid-2017

HOLLYWOOD CHRONICLES
A collaboration with USA Today Bestselling Author, Rebecca Shea

ABOUT THE AUTHOR

A.L. Jackson is the New York Times & USA Today Bestselling author of contemporary romance. She writes emotional, sexy, heart-filled stories about boys who usually like to be a little bit bad.

Her bestselling series include THE REGRET SERIES, CLOSER TO YOU, as well as the newest BLEEDING STARS novels.

Watch for SHOW ME THE WAY, the first sexy, heart-warming romance in the new Fight For Me series, coming mid-2017

If she's not writing, you can find her hanging out by the pool with her family, sipping cocktails with her friends, or of course with her nose buried in a book.

Be sure not to miss new releases and sales from A.L. Jackson - Sign up to receive her newsletter http://smarturl.it/NewsFromALJackson or text "aljackson" to 24587 to receive short but sweet updates on all the important news.

Connect with A.L. Jackson online:

Page http://smarturl.it/ALJacksonPage
Newsletter http://smarturl.it/NewsFromALJackson
Angels http://smarturl.it/AmysAngelsRock
Amazon http://smarturl.it/ALJacksonAmzn
Book Bub http://smarturl.it/ALJacksonBookbub
Text "aljackson" to 24587 to receive short but sweet updates on all the important news.